WARRING TIDES

MK AHEARN

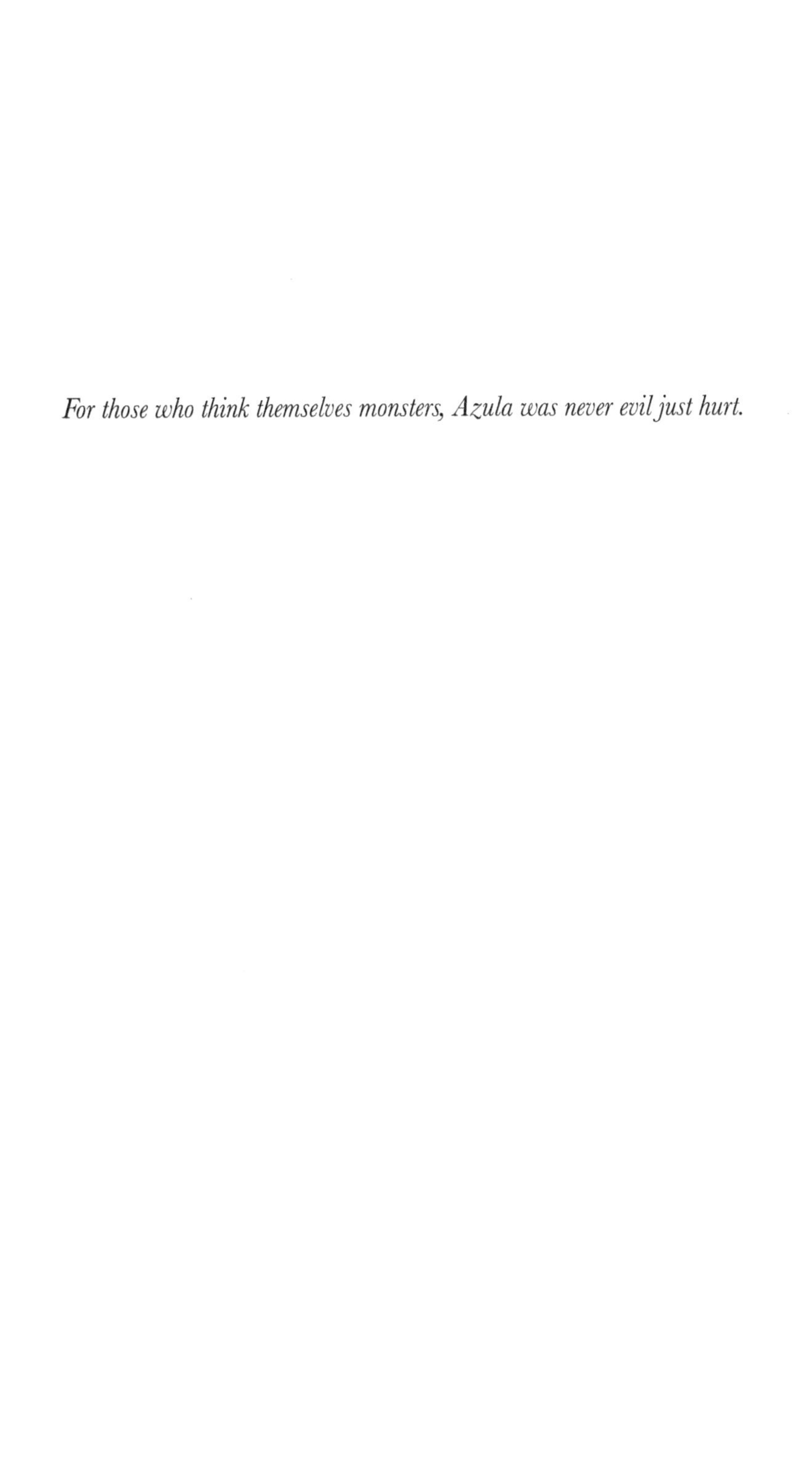

For those who think themselves monsters, Azula was never evil just hurt.

TRIGGER WARNINGS

This book contains swearing, sexually explicit scenes, violence, assault, and death of parents. Please keep this in mind when reading this story.

ZETRON
GRALAR
THE MARKET

MORYA
LUHEO

MORWEN

ALUA
SERPENT'S COVE

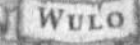

WULO

RADEN
THE WATERFALL
DRAGON TERRITORY

ABELON

PRONUNCIATION GUIDE

GODDESSES
Mavalu: Mah-vah-loo
Aeris: Air-us
Odaesia: Oh-day- juh
Isleen: Is-leen

KINGDOMS
Luheo: Loo-he-oh
Abelon: Ab-ah-lon
Morwen: More-win
Zetron: Zeh-tron

CAPITAL CITIES
Morya: More-yah
Alua: Ah-loo-ah
Gralar: Grah-lar
Raden: Rah-den

DRAGONS AND SERPENTS
Imry: Im-ree
Veros: Vah-roh-s
Nondaar: None-dah-r
Elios: Eel-ee-oh-s
Talay: Tay-lay

CHAPTER 1
NYLA

It took three days...

It took three days before I broke, a shell of myself, discarded in the cold cell that had become my home. I wrapped my arms around my legs, holding them tight and praying to the goddess Mavulu that the pain would soon be over. My back ached like nothing I had ever experienced.

It took everything in me to stay conscious. My stomach turned, and I found myself holding back the contents for the tenth time that day. The pain only grew worse with time.

How did Bellamy ever endure the torture? The countless burns and lessons taught?

I felt like I was withering away, no end in sight. My body was stuck in limbo, all too aware of the excruciating pain of living and not ready to give up yet.

Footsteps echoed down the hall outside my cell door. There was a small, barred window on the door, but I didn't have the strength to move and look out it. Based on the length of time I had spent sitting alone in the cell, it had to be another guard bringing me food, a meal that would only upset my stomach further. A lump formed in my gut, and I groaned in agony at the nausea washing over me again.

The handle on the door turned after I heard the familiar click of the lock, and my heart raced as I watched the door crack open. If it wasn't a meal, then I knew what I was in store for: another round of torture, trying to force the words they wanted to hear from me.

I slid back instinctively, and my back hit the wall. I moaned, the pain taking over my entire body. I took a deep breath, trying to halt the tears threatening to spill over.

"Nyla?" a deep, recognizable voice said.

I looked up to find Cyrus staring down at me. My heart stopped and my breath caught. His hands were empty, no meal in sight. I knew I had been wrong.

Why did Bellamy leave me behind? He could've took me with him, took more time to convince me to go. I would've eventually broken for him. I knew, deep down, if my brother had pushed harder, I would've went with him, but he left without a single effort to bring me.

He left with Koraine, and now, the pair was long gone. The wedding was cancelled. They were considered traitors throughout Abelon, a price on their heads.

I'd heard the guards discussing it in the hall. I didn't believe it at first. Bellamy was to be king; how could he be a traitor to the crown? I needed answers, needed to understand why he would leave me behind.

The next time the guards came for me and threw me in front of my father, I begged for answers. I asked him where Bellamy had gone, why he'd left. I asked about Koraine and the wedding. Words spilled out of my mouth like I couldn't stop them.

Instead of answering the questions, I was met with pain. Whips of flames licked at my back, tearing through my clothes and marring my skin. The burns turned into blisters and wounds, ones I had no way to heal.

"How did Bellamy escape Abelon? Did you help? Did you assist in planning his treachery?"

The king shouted the questions over and over, yet I always gave the same answers. I knew nothing of the prince fleeing. I'd only seen Bellamy briefly before his escape.

I'd worked up the courage to ask about my mother only once, and he'd immediately turned cold. His dark black eyes stared down on me, and my shoulders sunk, my breathing labored as I tried to remain awake after the torture.

"How could you ever believe I would kill her?" he demanded.

Tears dripped down my cheeks as I recalled the conversation. It had broken me to ask it. I was torn between believing my brother and father. Nothing inside me wanted to believe he would have her killed. It didn't make sense. She loved Abelon, and the people would've done anything for her. With her gone, many citizens despised my father. It only hurt his rule losing her.

"Let's go," Cyrus barked, holding out a hand to help me.

"I can do it myself," I spat.

I no longer trusted anyone beside myself. A few of the lashings I'd received had been done by Cyrus himself, acting on order of my father.

It was my father's way of getting whatever he wanted, and currently, that was information. I knew it would continue until he was satisfied. Bellamy had made him look a fool. The heir to the throne committed treason and fled with Abelon's enemy. The information alone could destroy the king's claim to the throne.

The nobles were always searching for a reason to reach for more power and without a suitable heir, my father was left vulnerable and weak. He knew it and was already doing everything in his power to turn the tides.

I pushed myself up against the wall, my back screaming at me with every movement. My brows pulled together, and I tried not to let the pain show on my face.

I was strong, and I wouldn't be so easily destroyed.

I slowly followed Cyrus out of the cell and through the halls of the palace. I didn't need someone to lead the way through my own home. I was a princess; I would cling to any respect I had left for the title I bore.

Cyrus sneered at me when I paused to catch my breath for a moment. I knew if I pushed too fast, the burns would force me to stop completely. I tried to continue again as fast as I could, but it wasn't fast enough for him.

My feet felt heavy with each step I took down the never-ending halls. I recognized the path we took without Cyrus telling me. Soon, we'd find ourselves in the throne room, facing my father once more. I tried to prepare myself for another round of torture, another set of flaming lashes for information I didn't have. I swallowed hard, my throat burning from the number of times I had been sick the hours before.

I wasn't certain if my back could handle any more wounds. If they continued at this rate, I would be dead before the week's end.

The door to the throne room opened before me, and I

realized I had become lost to my thoughts. I spotted the large columns of flames behind my father before I saw him seated, watching me. He wore his crown and red finery that matched the heat of the flames.

A bead of sweat fell down my face, my nerves rising and the heat of the room already getting to me.

My feet slowed, walking down the center of the room.

"Move," Cyrus said, jabbing me in the side with his elbow. He paused to stay in the back of the room but forced me to continue forward.

I approached the base of the dais, raising my gaze to the throne and my father. His stern face revealed nothing.

Every time I had to face him, I felt the resentment grow for my brother. An ocean had been placed between us, and I no longer had any excuses to make for him. Even though I had resisted leaving, I knew deep down, he could've tried harder and found a way.

He knew what the consequences of leaving and not taking me would be. Someone would need to bear the punishment, and my father had wasted no time picking me.

I bowed my head, trying to save myself from any unnecessary pain or fight. Everything inside me burned. My anger was building, and I could feel shreds of who I was before slipping away.

I had dreams of seeing the world, and now, I only wished to see it burn for what it had done to me.

"Do you know where Bellamy and his bride are fleeing to?" the king asked, and I raised my head, finding his intense stare.

"No," I answered weakly. My throat felt like I was swallowing glass with each word.

"My scouts spotted them close to Morwen. Your brother has sought refuge with the enemy," my father explained.

I frowned, not able to comprehend the words he had just thrown at me. Since childhood, Bellamy had hated Morwenians. He had only recently found it in his heart to let Koraine in. How could he betray us all and turn to them?

He left me behind and went to our enemy. Everything my father accused him of started to feel more within reach. The lies about my mother's death, the betrayal, leaving me behind—could it all have been orchestrated by Koraine?

I had come to love Koraine the way one would a sister, yet I found myself replaying every moment I spent with her in my head.

"You will find him and bring him home," the king started.

"What?" I asked, snapped back into reality.

"You heard me, child," the king said. "Prove to me you aren't useless."

The word made my blood boil. I was the child he had cast aside because I wasn't his heir. My mother had never seen me that way. She had always seen my talents and desire to be something more than just a princess locked away. The thought of her pained my heart.

"You will find that worthless brother of yours, and you will bring him back here," the king demanded.

"And if I refuse?" I asked. Why would I want to bring Bellamy back? He betrayed us all. He was the last person I wished to spend my days hunting.

"Then you will die here," the king said. "And the moment I find the prince myself, he will face the same fate."

I knew he wasn't lying; I could see the rage in his eyes.

He was prepared to sacrifice his children just to fix the problem. I had wished for death multiple times over the last few days, but somehow, when faced with it, I wasn't ready.

"I am preparing for war, and when it does come, I will unleash flames across the four kingdoms. I am done vying for power and land. If we must live amid the flames and ash, then I will burn the world and watch it join us. If you return home with the prince, I will know you are worthy of being saved from what is coming."

I was more than just a weak princess, more than just a pawn in this play for power. I would drag Bellamy home and prove my worth. I would demand the prince face his punishment for betraying our kingdom. I would force him to pay for leaving me behind. I wished to see him face the consequence of leaving, but I did not wish to see him perish with the rest of the kingdoms.

Every last bit of my humanity was slipping away.

My father frowned, recognizing the sheer determination and fury in my gaze.

"I will find him, and I will bring him home," I said.

My hair clung to my face in long, straggly black strands. My clothing was torn in most places from burns. I turned away from my father without being dismissed and walked out of the throne room, anger alone driving my pace.

Bellamy knew leaving would incite a power struggle. He knew the consequences, and yet, he left, without a single regard for anyone but himself. He'd left me behind. I was the one person who had been there for him all his life, and he discarded me the first chance he got.

I felt like a battle was tearing through me. He was my brother and always would be, but his betrayal cut straight through my heart. The only way to survive the pain and fight through it was to make myself numb to the world.

I let the pain turn into strength. I forged myself into a monster who would crawl back from the pit she'd been tossed into. My agony became fury, and I weaponized it.

If Bellamy wanted a war, then I would bring it to the doorstep of Morwen.

CHAPTER 2

KORAINE

Exhaustion threatened to make my knees buckle as I stood before my father. It was the first I had seen him in months. He somehow looked more aged than when I last saw him, like stress had chipped away at him as time passed. I wanted to scream at him and hug him all in the same heartbeat.

My family had stayed in Morwen when I left for Abelon. I'd endured months alone without them. Even when my father's betrayal had led me to the fire kingdom, I still couldn't help the hope forming in my chest.

I felt Bellamy move protectively beside me.

My father's eyes narrowed on the prince, disgust plastered across his face. His disproval made my stomach sink. Bellamy had sacrificed everything to bring me home, had given up his right to the throne and defied his own father, and still, he was treated like a criminal.

"We will hand him over and be done with it," my father sneered, his gaze on Bellamy. He couldn't even look me in the eyes. I could feel the way he avoided my stare.

"No," I protested.

He looked to the king for approval, ignoring his own daughter. Already, I felt that small spark of hope fading by the second. The man I thought would embrace me on my return couldn't even bear my presence anymore. Did it disappoint him that much to see his only daughter side by side with the prince of his enemy? Could he not put aside his own biases for a moment to hear me out?

Had I not proven myself enough to be heard?

I had survived and made it home, with information on the fire kingdom, our sworn enemy. Without the help of my kingdom, I was powerless to face the King of Abelon on my own. His reign needed to come to an end. With Bellamy on the throne, there would be a chance for peace between our kingdoms. Our marriage would unite our people.

Abelon would no longer need to suffer living on desolate lands. We would share resources and trade. Morwen would provide fish and crops, and in return, Abelon had coal to supply our kingdom of water.

It was a deal no kingdom could resist.

It was also a deal the king and my father couldn't grasp, a distant dream of two escaped fugitives with a bounty on their head by the same kingdom. In my heart, I knew it would take more to convince them than just showing up, but I had been blinded by the idea of returning to the family I once knew.

"You can't expect us to let him stay here," my father replied, and I didn't miss the way he glared at Bellamy as he said it.

"I can and I do," I countered, placing my hands on my hips. I wouldn't back down.

If my father wanted to be the stoic general, then I would be the hardened warrior I had been forced to become. I wasn't one of his men who would back down or blindly follow his command.

"Bellamy saved me and brought me home. He looked after me when no one else was there for me," I said, watching as my words hit him like physical strikes. He flinched at the insinuation. "I expect him to be received with the respect he deserves. You forced me to leave Morwen and negotiate for peace. I did what was asked of me. I married the prince and I return home, only to be thrown in a dungeon for days. I survived what you all thought to be a death sentence. I deserve to be treated with respect, and I deserve to be heard out."

I took a step away from Bellamy and toward my father, the king watching and waiting. I could feel my strength returning with each word I spoke. I fully believed in everything I said, in myself.

My father glanced to the king again for direction. The older man stepped toward me, no longer passively watching. His tan skin matched my father's, and he had the same dark hair as his daughter. With how close I stood to him, I could see the grey creeping into the hairline. His crown sat perfectly on top his head, helping to hide the signs of aging.

"We turn him over," the king said without a second thought. "Seize him," he demanded.

Warriors rushed forward, and I moved protectively back toward Bellamy.

"Move out of their way, Koraine," my father demanded.

"No." I stood my ground. If they wanted to drag him away, they'd need to take me as well.

"Koraine, you're making this harder than it needs to be," my father scolded like I was a child. I saw the orb of water forming in his hand and called on my own ability.

I felt the comfort of the water as it formed in my palm. I let the swirl of water twirl up, catching my father's eye as he frowned.

"Would you truly fight your own family?" he asked, and I swore I heard sadness in the question.

"I'm fighting *for* my family," I said firmly.

He stepped forward, signaling the other warriors to do the same. I felt them closing in around us, and I split the water between both hands, raising them instinctively. I was prepared to fight my way through. Even if we made it through these warriors, there were still more throughout the palace.

The king watched, amused. I heard a snort from behind the king, Princess Asuna watching with a smug look on her face and arms crossed.

One of the warriors raised a hand, ready to attack on my father's command. I tensed, knowing I would need to block his water; Bellamy was in no condition to fight after the abuse he'd been subjected to.

His body was covered in bruises, and even as he readied himself, he moved slower than usual.

The warrior pushed a hand out, letting a whip of water fly toward us. I held my hands up, shaping the water into a shield to block the attack.

Before it could reach us, the doors to the throne room flew open, and the warrior pulled the water back as every-one's gazes shifted to the entrance.

"Caspian!" I shouted, spotting my brothers. Relief

washed over me, knowing they would come to my aid. My father may have been persuaded by the king, but Caspian and Emmett always had my back.

Caspian gave me a quick smile, his dark hair pulled out of his face into a bun.

Then my eyes met Emmett's, and I felt my shoulders sink inward. His disapproving stare was enough to make me doubt myself. I hadn't seen him before leaving for Abelon, and I could tell my father had filled his head with lies. He had always been a loyal warrior. If his general gave him an order or information, he would stand by it to the end.

Emmett was the spitting image of my father. I could already see matching stress lines forming on his forehead, his short, dark hair showing signs of grey. He was only a few years older than me, but he looked like he could be far older.

I shook my head slowly, realizing I would never break through to him.

Both my brothers appeared tense, and a pit formed in my stomach when I realized all but one of my family members were here.

My only hope would be Caspian. My mother must be resting somewhere else in the palace, or at home maintaining the property. If she knew I was back, she would have come. My father likely kept the information from her. Something was off—I needed to know what, but there were more pressing matters to confront before then.

"Koraine, step aside," Emmett demanded, falling immediately into line beside my father. He was clever and read the room faster than Caspian had.

My muscles trembled with anger; I wished my family

would understand. Their ignorance would be their downfall. I gave Caspian a pleading look, hoping he'd come to his senses.

Hesitantly, he glanced from me to my father and brother.

"Koraine, please," he started, and I realized he too would disappoint me.

I called on my water again, preparing to give this battle my all. I would protect Bellamy, and we would find a way out of this palace, then far from this kingdom and the fire kingdom that hunted us.

A hand on my shoulder snapped me out of my focus, and I found Bellamy beside me, an exhausted and worried look on his face. He let out a sigh.

"Koraine, listen to them," he pleaded with me.

"No," I started, my heart aching. My voice felt distant; I couldn't believe the words coming from his mouth. Was he really giving up after coming all this way?

"I will not have you fight your own people for me," Bellamy went on. "That is not why we came here. We came for peace. I will not fight the water kingdom. If you want to hand me over to protect your people, then that is what I will do," Bellamy finished, meeting my father's gaze.

"No, you can't," I said, my voice rising.

Caspian moved in quickly, before I could even react. His strong arms wrapped around me, pulling me away from the prince. I struggled against his grasp, kicking and squirming, trying to break free, but it was no use. Caspian was much larger and stronger than me; with my arms restrained, my water was almost useless.

"Please," I cried, tears beginning to cloud my vision. "They'll kill him."

"They'll kill you," Caspian said, his voice low and devastated.

I watched in horror as the guards seized Bellamy, knocking him to the ground.

"Stop!" I sobbed. "Stop hurting him! He's going willingly," I begged.

"He brought our enemy to our lands and threatened our safety," my father spat. "You will never be accepted here," he added, staring down at Bellamy.

"Caspian, please help him," I begged, thrashing in his arms.

His grasp around me tightened as he pulled me back toward the far wall of the throne room. I caught Asuna's eye, and she scowled at me. We had done nothing wrong, yet we were being treated as traitors.

"Bellamy!" I cried out. My heart was racing, and I could feel the fight leaving my body as the guards took hold of his arms and dragged him away. He turned his head to look at me once more and then let it hang.

Everything inside me shattered down to my very soul. The man I loved was being dragged away, sentenced to death. I tried one last attempt at breaking free. Wiggling, I swore I felt Caspian loosen his grasp for only a second.

This one chance wouldn't slip past me.

I threw myself forward, escaping his arms and running toward the warriors hauling the prince away.

"Bellamy," I called after him. It was too late for the warriors to react to me rushing forward. I didn't try to fight them; I knew it wouldn't work. I was smarter than that.

Instead, I let the room believe I had been defeated. They should've known better than to underestimate me after everything I had survived.

I threw my arms around Bellamy's neck, nuzzling in to him. In a tone low enough I almost couldn't hear myself, I whispered into his ear.

"Tonight, I'll come for you," I assured him.

I pulled away, expecting to see his disapproval at my plan, but instead, I found something else in his rich, dark eyes.

Pride.

"I love you, my moon," he said before the warriors adjusted their grip and pulled him away from me.

I was left on my knees as they dragged him out of the room, the door slamming shut behind them.

"I love you too," I whispered.

My white hair fell over my shoulders as my head dropped. I refused to meet the gaze of anyone else in the room. Footsteps echoed across the tiled floor, and slowly, the room emptied. Caspian placed a gentle hand on my shoulder, giving it a squeeze. I knew he'd done me a favor, and for that, I was grateful.

His footsteps were the last I heard leaving the room, and when I knew I was finally alone, I stood. Slowly lifting my head, I glanced around the throne room.

My anger grew, and I drew water from a fountain nearby the throne itself. The water swirled around me, building in power as I poured my energy into it. The more I pulled, the stronger the miniature vortex I formed around myself. Rage filled my bleeding heart, and I knew not a single thing could ever stop the sun and moon from rising.

I'd found Caspian waiting for me a short way down the hall from the throne room, and he'd led to me to the room I spent the rest of the day in. I'd barely spoken a word to him, unable to bring myself to hear the reason he too had betrayed me. His small favor was not enough to mend the heartbreak I felt each time I looked at my brother.

I paced back and forth in the room, waiting for night to fall. The sun set slowly over the water kingdom, the sky alight in orange and pink. Out the single window, I had a view of the Vitrum Sea, spotted with foreign ships and red flags. The princess had brought a small army along with her, enough to siege the city but not enough to win over the kingdom.

The room was small, but better than the one Morwen had afforded me on the ship they'd stuck me on when they forced me off to Abelon. I refused to settle in to it, knowing I would be leaving shortly.

After a few hours of pacing and finding trinkets in the room to fiddle with, the moon finally illuminated the night sky. Glancing out the window, I felt a call to it. The way it cast a reflection over the sea and lulled the waves, I knew deep down, I was most at home under its protection.

In the stealth of night, I would do my worst.

I would free the Prince of Abelon, and we would flee. There had to be another way to save the kingdoms from the approaching war. I had to believe deep down it was not inevitable. With the help of the earth or air kingdom, we could stand a chance. Bellamy and I just had to make it to one and convince them of what we knew.

It was easier said than done, I knew, but I wasn't ready to give up.

A silver movement, out of the corner of my eye, caught my attention. Landing on the window's ledge, a silver creature slowed it's wings enough for me to catch a glimpse of it.

It's wings were outlined with a dark blue and black, and its head had a marking right in the center. I moved closer and saw the crescent moon that marked the lunar moth.

I tried to take a step closer and the beautiful creature flew off, like it was heading straight toward the moon.

I turned my focus back to the room.

I fashioned a sheet I found into a cloak, the pale blue material ripping easily as I tore it to the proper size. I found a stray ribbon, tying it like a necklace around my neck to hold the sheet in place. I pulled it up over my head and tucked my white locks of hair under it. It wasn't perfect, but it would have to do.

My hair stood out amongst the other women wandering the palace, and I knew it would give me away, even to someone who spotted me from afar.

I walked over to the door and turned the knob carefully.

There was no way to know if any warriors stood guard in the hall. I had been too occupied by my thoughts when walking to the room to notice.

I poked my head out but spotted no one. The empty hall was dark, the only was from the moon pouring in through a window at one end.

Slipping through the door, I shut it behind me, careful to be quiet. I didn't want anyone passing through the hall to notice I had left. The fewer souls who noticed my absence, the better. I was working with limited time, and I needed to give us the best chance at escape.

Each step I took was meticulous, unsure if the sound of my footsteps would carry. I made my way down the hall in the opposite direction of the window.

I continued my journey down the hall; only a few minutes had passed, but I had yet to see anyone, which had me on edge. I needed to find my way back to the cells where they held us the days prior—there was a high chance that's where they were keeping Bellamy again.

I walked back to the throne room, having memorized the way earlier. From the throne room, I figured I had a good chance of finding my way back to the dungeon. I knew it was only two floors beneath me, recalling the warriors who dragged me up the stairs earlier.

I let my feet and memory guide me. Everything had happened so fast only hours before; there wasn't a second I thought I would ever intentionally go back to that cage.

A hunch told me to continue down a hall leading off to the right of the throne room. I had been blindfolded, relying on sheer memory now. I couldn't depend on any of the decor hanging on the walls or the recognizable statues and fountains all over the palace.

There was a door at the very end of the hall, and I hurried to open it. The moment I did, I heard voices carrying up the steps behind the door, none of which I recognized.

I softly closed it, hoping the Warriors did not hear me.

I glanced frantically around the hall, looking for somewhere to hide. Their steps pounded up the stairs, louder and louder, and I knew I was almost out of time.

A door a few steps away stood out, my only option left lest I be caught. I hurried over to it, light on my feet. Opening the door, I slid inside and closed it behind me as another nearby door opened. I prayed to the goddesses the warriors didn't hear the faint click of the lock.

Soft whispers carried through the air but didn't pierce the thick wood of the door. I tried pressing my ear to the structure, but it was no use, the muffled voices unable to be made out.

A few minutes passed before I felt safe enough to open the door. I hurried over to the door, yanking it open to find the hall was clear. There were winding wooden steps in front of me, and I recalled taking similar steps earlier in the day.

My feet flew down the steps, and I could feel my heart racing the faster I moved. I needed to hurry and find Bellamy; I could feel my time dwindling. Each second I took was a second too long. If we didn't leave Morwen now, we would miss our chance.

The king was smart; he wouldn't hold Bellamy in the dungeons longer than needed. The moment he could, he'd hand him over to Nyla.

My mouth felt dry thinking of the princess who had befriended me. Only days prior, we had been giggling, talking about my wedding. Now, she was threatening to burn my home, the people I loved.

How could she betray us?

Bellamy had given her the chance to join us, and she turned him down.

I reached the bottom of the steps, stumbling a bit, not

realizing it was the last step. Steadying myself, I started forward. It was dark, and this floor of the palace felt colder. The ground was solid stone, and the walls felt similar as I ran my hand along one.

I paused for only a moment to let my eyes adjust and confirm I was heading in the correct direction. Before I could take another step, I swore I heard a quiet breath behind me.

I went to turn but was stopped by a strong arm wrapping around my waist and a hand covering my mouth. I kicked and thrashed, but it was no use. They dragged me back into their arms, waiting for me to stop fighting. My heart sunk.

I'd been caught.

CHAPTER 3

KORAINE

"Stop struggling," Caspian's low voice whispered against my ear.

My body went rigid. My brother had a tight grasp on me in the shadows of the dungeon hall. If I could convince him to let me go, this wouldn't be a completely failed effort. He was the most likely to listen to me.

His hand still covered my mouth, and I could feel his heart pounding against my back. He was breathing heavy, and I knew I was running out of time. I needed to win his support, fast.

I bit down on the skin pressed to my lips.

His hand flew from my mouth as he let go of my waist. I spun around to face him, crossing my arms.

"You need to let me go," I started. "I will fight you if I have to, but I don't want it to come to that."

My younger brother stared down at me, his face revealing nothing. My fists clenched, arms still crossed while I narrowed my eyes on him. I could feel myself slowly inching toward my ability. Water was a comfort, and I needed its strength if Caspian refused.

"Go back," I demanded. "Pretend you never saw me. Father doesn't have to know. No one will know you aided me, because they won't catch Bellamy and me. We will be gone before sunrise."

My patience was wearing thin, and I was tempted to call on my water and force him back, Not a single force could keep me from the prince. I didn't care that it had been mere months; no one had seen me the way Bellamy did. It was as if I had known him all my life. He believed in me in a way my father never had.

"Caspian," I growled, watching him, unmoving.

"Okay," he said, but I barely registered the word over the sound of blood rushing through my ears. My anxiety and patience had taken over completely.

"This will be my last warning," I began.

"I said okay," Caspian interrupted.

"What?" I stuttered.

"I won't stop you, but I am not going back either."

I opened my mouth, but he held up a hand to stop me. He moved forward, brushing by me in the direction I'd come from. I turned to follow, my head spinning with thoughts. Why wasn't Caspian stopping me? I had fully expected a fight, but instead, he was leading me right in the direction of Bellamy.

"I already scoped out the rest of the way to the dungeon," Caspian said in a low tone. "There are not any guards on the way, but there is one posted in the dungeon itself. But I imagine you have a plan," he finished.

"A plan?" I questioned.

I should've had a plan, but I had been distracted with the thought of escape and praying Bellamy was alright. I never stopped to think through my plan to break him free.

"You don't have a plan?" Caspian asked, suddenly halting.

He turned to look at me, and my cheeks reddened at the expectant look on his face.

"No," I answered sheepishly.

"Koraine!" Caspian shouted, startling me.

"Keep your voice down," I hushed. "I don't need a plan. My plan is to free Bellamy and flee from Morwen. I will figure the rest out as I go, but I do not have time to sit around and plan. His sister is about to burn down Alua, and our king wants to hand him over to his maniac father, who will kill him. I will not waste another second," I insisted.

I stalked off, not caring if Caspian followed. His footsteps echoed behind me, picking up his pace.

"Stop," he said, catching up to me. I ignored him and kept walking.

"Koraine, seriously. Stop and think about this for a moment. There's a guard you need to get through," he added.

"Why are you even helping me?" I asked. There wasn't a single second I imagined this rescue being attempted with Caspian's help.

He had taken my father's side in the throne room. Bellamy was dragged off, and he held me back, only allowing me freedom when he knew the prince was secure. My stomach dropped thinking about it, and a new anger took seed.

"Because I want to help," he started. "I wasn't there to

help when they sent you to Abelon. I won't let you face this alone now."

"No one was there for me, and I handled myself just fine. I do not need help," I muttered.

I sensed his muscles go rigid and knew I had struck a nerve.

"Koraine, that's not fair. I didn't know," he said. "Please, let me help you with this. I'm your brother. I should be looking after you, not letting you face an entire kingdom on your own."

"It's going to take a lot more than just you and me to stop Abelon," I admitted. Slowly, I was coming around to the idea of accepting his help.

I knew I stood a better chance of making it through with his assistance. I'd figure out how I felt after; it would be ignorant not to take the help.

"Then we will find more help, but right now, we need a plan to rescue that prince of yours," he said softly.

I nodded, still heading in the direction of the dungeons. We had only a few more halls before I estimated we would reach the door.

"If one of us handles distracting the guard, the other can work on opening the cell," I suggested.

"Which one of us is taking the guard?" Caspian asked with a smirk.

"He's all yours," I offered.

I watched the grin spread and felt my own lips curling up into a smile. It felt normal being home again, finding trouble with my brother. Yet, this trouble held the fate of all four kingdoms in its hands.

I spotted the door the moment we rounded the last

corner. The sound of prisoners' moans and clanks against the barred doors carried through the air. My stomach turned at the thought of Bellamy spending another second locked up.

They'd beaten him and left him covered in bruises. Had they done worse since we'd been separated?

I tried to push the intrusive thoughts aside to focus. It would do me no good to be this distracted. Without focus, I would ruin our advantage. The guard had no idea we were just outside the door, and there were two of us compared to one of them.

I decided to hit them with as much surprise as possible. Calling on my water, I manipulated a stream and slammed it into the door as hard as I could. It burst open, surprising the guard, the stream slamming into him. He stumbled backward before regaining his composure.

Caspian didn't give the warrior long to recover, throwing another attack at him.

"Go," he said to me, continuing his assault.

I sprinted past the guard while he was distracted, searching each of the cells as I went. Prisoners sat in misery behind bars, but I ignored them. I couldn't let them distract me. There was only one person who mattered.

It took a total of five cells before I found the one I was looking for. He was almost last in the row, and when I arrived, I recognized Bellamy's tattered clothing. His back was to me, and he was seated, leaning against the stone wall.

"Bellamy," I said, my voice breaking.

He was hunched over, his entire body defeated.

"Bellamy," I called a bit louder, and he stirred.

The prince shifted, moaning in pain. His face was

covered in scratches and bruises, and one of his eyes was swollen.

"What did they do to you?" I asked, my heart breaking.

I could see the defeat written on his face. My heart bled for him. I wanted to rush to his side, but the bars between us kept me out.

I pulled on the bars hoping they'd budge, but it was no use. Only the key the guard held would open the cell.

"Koraine?" Bellamy rasped, squinting his one good eye. "How?" was all he could manage.

"I've come to take you far from Morwen," I assured him. "I won't let them hand you over tomorrow."

A blast of water narrowly missed my head, splashing against the wall beside me. I turned quickly to gauge how Caspian was holding up.

He was locked in battle with the warrior. Worry washed over me, hoping no others would hear. If more came, I wasn't convinced we'd be able to break Bellamy free.

I needed to work faster.

If I could break the lock—

An idea formed in my head.

"Bellamy," I said, beckoning him toward the cell door.

He used the wall to push himself up, leaning on it as he hobbled toward me. I noticed the limp he had in each step he took and heard the slight wince.

I tried to push it out of my brain and focus on the goal in front of me.

Bellamy stood inches from the bars. I knew water alone wasn't enough to break the lock, but with heat, it could work.

"I need you to heat the lock with your fire," I explained.

Bellamy stared at me for a moment, and I prepared to repeat myself, convinced he hadn't heard me. He had barely reacted.

"I need—"

"Why are you here?" he asked.

"Bellamy, we don't have time for this," I argued.

The warrior behind me groaned in pain, and I turned to find Caspian and him engaged in hand-to-hand combat.

Caspian took a painful blow to his knee, dropping to the ground.

I quickly called on my water and sent it flying toward the warrior before he could deliver a final blow on my brother. Caspian gave me a quick smile before launching back to his feet and keeping the guard distracted.

"Bellamy, please," I insisted.

"Koraine, you should have stayed with your family. You should have let them trade me. She will burn your home to the ground," he said, his eyes distant with what I realized was fear.

"But I didn't," I said sternly. "I'm here instead. Now, let me save you," I huffed, and Bellamy let out a soft laugh.

"Stubborn as always, my moon," he said.

At least they hadn't stolen his spirit.

"Heat this lock," I said.

He sighed as flames burst to life in his hands. They were small, but they were enough. He held them to the lock, the metal turning a bright red with the flames against it.

"Now stop," I instructed after a minute.

I let an orb of water form in my hands and manipulated the water to cover the lock. Bellamy watched with intense concentration as ice formed over the lock, my ability freezing the water. I cooled the metal as quickly as I could.

I melted the ice, letting the water drip off the metal to find a few cracks in its integrity.

It was working.

I pulled on the bars, hoping we'd be lucky, but the lock didn't budge.

"Again," I instructed.

Bellamy set to work heating the metal, and I followed with cooling it down. We worked as a team, moving with haste as the warrior and Caspian remained locked in combat. Only minutes had fully passed since we entered the dungeon, but it felt like hours. Any moment, I knew, our time could run out.

We repeated the pattern two more times before I heard Caspian cry out. He was gripping his arm, holding it close to his body, and I saw the pain written on his face. He bit his lip and raised his good hand, letting go of the other arm.

He backed away from the warrior, manipulating a shield of water to protect himself with his raised hand.

I needed to help him, but I was so close to freeing Bellamy.

If the lock didn't break soon, I would have to abandon the prince.

Bellamy finished heating the lock once more, and I poured all my energy into cooling the metal fast. The quicker it cooled, the better. I poured my energy into the ice forming around the lock then let it melt. The bars made a loud clang when I pulled on them, tugging and pushing as hard as I could. Bellamy step forward, helping me.

The metal cracked again, this time giving way. The cell

door flung toward me, and before I knew what was happening, Bellamy fell forward, wrapping his arms around me. I felt his chin rest on my head and savored the moment.

I pulled back, immediately looking to Caspian. He caught my gaze and let a large lash of water fly toward the warrior. The blow landed, and the warrior stumbled. I threw my own stream of water toward the warrior before he regained his balance. His head clashed against the stone wall, knocking him unconscious.

"You couldn't have done that ten minutes ago?" Caspian asked pointedly.

"I was busy," I retorted.

I walked over to join Caspian at the exit to the dungeon and shoved his arm softly.

"I missed you too," I whispered. If there was a single person I was thankful to see again, it was Caspian. He was the person in my family who always understood me. Deep down, I was relieved to have him back. I knew after a while, he'd come to like Bellamy. The pair was more alike than either thought.

"We need to go before they discover the body," I said, hating to head straight back into danger. The longer we spent in the palace, the more at risk we were of being discovered.

"How are we going to escape this kingdom?" Caspian asked.

I looked to Bellamy, taking in all his wounds and bruises. I knew he wouldn't make it far on foot. If we could fly him, we might be able to transport him out of Morwen, but the palace would notice any dragon approaching and take it as a sign of Abelon attacking.

"We aren't fleeing yet," Bellamy said.

"What?" Caspian shouted.

"Keep your voice down," I scolded. "We have no idea when the next warrior might walk down here."

"I need to talk to my sister," Bellamy said.

I glanced over to his face, his eyes dark with sadness and his brows followed. If he could reason with Nyla, there was a chance she wouldn't attack Morwen. I knew exactly why he wanted to go out there. Bellamy had left his sister behind. It was a hard decision, but one that had to be made. She wouldn't budge, couldn't wrap her mind around the idea of their own father killing their mother.

I nodded slowly.

"You can't be serious?" Caspian asked, looking at me.

"If I could just talk to her, reason with her, we may be able to save your people from death and destruction," Bellamy explained.

"Do you really believe she will listen to reason? She's an Abelonian," Caspian accused.

"She's my sister," Bellamy answered. "I have to believe."

"If Bellamy believes there is a chance we can stop the siege, we should take it," I insisted.

I shifted to stand beside Bellamy, and my brother huffed, crossing his arms and narrowing his eyes on both of us.

"What happened to you over there?" Caspian asked. "You aren't the same naïve girl who left Morwen."

I shuddered at the thought of the weak and helpless girl who left the same city not long before. The fire kingdom had hardened me, turned into something I never would've recognized only a few years before.

"She survived," Bellamy answered.

It felt odd hearing him say it, but the reality was, I had fought to keep my life and fought to become a warrior. I was forced to become this, something I never asked for.

Caspian just nodded. He didn't push any further or ask any more prying questions. Instead, he turned to leave the dungeon, prompting us to follow.

We had minimal time to make it out of the palace and to the ships before another warrior came to the dungeon or sunrise approached and they came to retrieve the prince.

"Are you sure about this?" I whispered to Bellamy.

He grabbed my hand, and I could feel the cuts on his knuckles from fighting back .

"I know my sister. She will at least hear us out," Bellamy said.

That didn't give me much hope, but I had to place my trust in the prince.

CHAPTER 4
BELLAMY

Koraine helped me on to the sea serpent, her brother's own creature beside Talay.

I caught his eye while I sized up the beast. It was longer than Koraine's own, a deeper shade of blue.

"Elios," Caspian said. His tone was short and to the point. I knew he was only tolerating me for the sake of his sister.

The beast was stunning, its scales catching the sunlight and blending with the hues of the waves. I was mesmerized watching it. Even with the time spent near Koraine's serpent, I still was left in awe seeing another.

I focused back on Koraine, wrapping my arms around her before the serpent began to move.

The ships were not far ahead of us, and I could see the flames lit on the deck, even from the docks. Talay sped off, Elios following closely beside the sea serpent. The beasts kept their heads and a portion of their upper bodies above the waves while they carried us, and I knew it was for my own benefit. Koraine and Caspian could easily dive under with their own abilities to control water, but I could not.

"Thank you," I whispered to Koraine, and she turned her head, barely able to look at me.

"For what?" she asked.

"I appreciate this," I said. "I'm still not super comfortable around water."

She nodded slowly, and I saw the beginning of a smile.

"I'd do anything for you," she finally said. Her voice sounded distant, like her mind was somewhere else.

These past few days, I imagined the future that would come if my father brought the force of his armies to these shores. He was intent on bringing destruction to the world, sinking the kingdoms into chaos.

The serpents approached the ships, and I knew exactly which belonged to my sister. Not many would notice the difference, but this ship was the only one flying the royal flag instead of the fire kingdom sigil. There was a slight difference between the flame on this flag and the others, and I instantly recognized it. It was subtle enough that most of our enemies never caught on. It signified where the commanding officer was stationed when Abelonian armies set sail.

The serpents extended out of the water enough for us to climb onto the ship. I stood on the deck, my knees wobbly, though I wasn't sure if it was nerves or new injuries.

Guards instantly surrounded us. I knew I'd walked Koraine and Caspian into danger. There was no avoiding it. If I wanted to reach my sister, I had to take that risk.

"Where is Nyla?" I snarled at the guards, trying to keep my voice as level and low as possible.

"We don't answer to you," one guard spat. "Traitor"

Again, I asked, "Where is the princess?"

I narrowed my eyes, staring at the guard in the center. I recognized him, his ranking higher than most of the other guards surrounding him. I couldn't recall his name out of the many guards in my father's army, but I knew if anyone would concede to my request, it would have to be him.

I felt Koraine beside me, her guard up and ready to fight her way out if needed. Caspian stood beside her; I didn't dare look at him, but I knew he would be ready.

Not a single guard budged. Several seconds passed as my heart pounded out of my chest; I felt like I could hear it ringing in my ears. The silence that filled the space between us was loud.

"Move," a voice behind the guards commanded, and they shuffled to form a path, quickly falling into place.

There Nyla stood, her dragon behind her in the sky.

Her eyes connected with mine and I could see she was not the same woman we left in Abelon. She wore a long, maroon gown and breastplate fitted for a queen, made of iron. It felt out of place on her. She was never meant to be a fighter. It was always meant to be me, the one who looked after us after my mom was gone, the one who would bear the burden of the fire kingdom on my back.

"Princess," I addressed.

"Traitor," she answered.

I felt like someone stabbed me in the gut the moment it left her mouth. She couldn't truly believe the lies my father had spewed.

Nyla had known how my father was, had known about

all his punishments. How could she side with the man who had tortured me, burnt down cities, killed our mother?

That had to be it.

She didn't believe he had killed our mother. I tried to beg her to leave Abelon with us, but it was too much. The knowledge seemed impossible. How could our own father kill our mother?

"I'm not the traitor," I said with an even tone.

I watched her eyes shift to Koraine. "Traitor," she growled again.

Flames appeared in both of Nyla's hands, covering her fist.

I shifted my weight instinctively toward Koraine to protect her. What happened in those few days since I last saw my sister?

Something was different. *She* was different. There was a new darkness there. Had my father sunk his talons in that deeply in the time I was gone?

"Why have you come?" I asked. I could feel Koraine's unease as she brushed her fingers against my hand, showing silent support.

"I've come to bring you home," Nyla stated, narrowing her eyes.

"I'm not going with you," I said firmly.

I held my breath as I watched her nostrils flare in response. With a small flick of her fingers, Koraine tugged at the sea beside me, and I spotted the water rising to join her.

"There's no need for that," Nyla said, narrowing her eyes on Koraine. "I thought we were to be sisters, after all."

The way she said sisters felt like poison seeping through the air.

If Nyla wanted to burn Morwen, she'd have to get through us first, and I wasn't going to stand by and let that happen. This kingdom had been through far too many horrors.

"You don't understand. If you would just believe me when I tell you he killed our mother—" I started.

Since we were children, Nyla always had a stubborn side. Once she set her mind to something, there was no convincing her otherwise.

"Lies," she snarled.

"You don't understand, Nyla. He doesn't want to protect us. He killed her just for power," I tried. Each attempt felt more urgent, like my sister was slipping away. I was reaching out, but her hand was just out of my grasp to pull her back.

"No, you don't understand, Bellamy. He doesn't just want more power or land. He wants to watch the world burn to the ground, the sky rain ashes. He wants to rule over a world built on flames, with all bowing to his rule."

"No," I whispered, and everyone tensed. Even the Abelonian guards gave the princess worried glances.

"He won't stop until he has what he wants. Return home, make things right with him. I don't wish to see you burned with the rest of the kingdoms," Nyla said, pleading with me now.

Somewhere deep down, I knew she truly believed my father would spare my life if I returned home. I knew better. He would kill me the first chance he got. An accident or war would find a way to drag me to death's door.

"I won't go back there," I stated. I could barely meet her gaze, ashamed of what I had done. I had turned her into this vengeful warrior.

I was the reason she was here, and because of me, innocent people would face the wrath of fire. I swallowed hard
before continuing. "Come with us Nyla," I pleaded.

"I cannot," she said firmly. "I will not betray my king,
the people I rule, and the one I am to marry."

My heart stopped. The one she was to marry?

What had my father done?

Horror was written on my face, and I watched Nyla cock
her head, reading my reaction.

"The king has announced my betrothal to Cyrus," she
said firmly, but I didn't miss the way her nostrils flared.

"But that's not who you are," Koraine said, her brows
knotting.

My heart felt heavier in my chest.

"Do you think the king cares? Do you think he stopped
for one second to consider what I wanted? Do you think that
crossed his mind when he gave me these?" she asked,
turning to show us her back.

Her shoulder blades were streaked in the same burn
marks as my arms.

"No," I whispered, my heart completely shattering.

"This is what happens when you disobey him. This is
the price paid," she said, turning back to us.

"Nyla, you have to see how insane this is," I pleaded.
"Join us. Help us remove him from power."

"Do you think it ends with him? What of Cyrus or the
other noble families? They'll never accept your rule now
that you are a traitor to our people. You fled when we
needed you most," she accused, nodding in my direction. "I
will bring you home. I will ascend the throne as father's heir,
and once I am in power, you will be free to live how you

please in Abelon, and I will be able to live whatever life I choose as queen."

"They'll execute him and you know it," Koraine shouted, her eyes narrowing on the princess.

"Koraine—" I started.

"No!" she snapped. "Do not, even for a second, think about agreeing to this." A small stream of water rose out of the sea, matching her anger.

"Koraine, if I go, she will leave Morwen alone. You've never seen her power. Don't for a second underestimate her and think she won't truly burn this city to the ground," I warned.

"She hasn't seen my full power either," she said as another stream rose on her other side, the pillars of water towering over me.

"I'd hoped it wouldn't come to this," Nyla sighed. "Do you really think you don't have weakness to you, brother?" Nyla nodded toward Koraine. "I may not know your power, but I do not need to."

I wanted to move in front of Koraine, but I'd only tempt my sister. The sweet-natured woman was nowhere to be found. The scars still fresh on her back marked the change.

"I don't mean her," Nyla said, rolling her eyes. "You may treat me as naive and incapable, but I've watched you throughout the years. I always prepared myself for the worst, for when father turned his lessons on me, or when you finally couldn't take them anymore and—"

She didn't finish the sentence. There was hope a small part of Nyla still existed. The thought of my demise pained her.

"I knew I'd need my own allies within the palace walls.

Who would look after me if you couldn't? Who would I turn to after you married Koraine and were busy preparing to be king?"

Her lips curled into a wicked smile. My stomach turned, and I felt the palms of my hands turn slick with sweat. I heard a scuffling sound behind the guards—they were dragging someone. The moment the prisoner came into view, my heart sunk.

Ervin was held between a pair of guards dragging him, struggling to free himself from their grasp.

"No," I gasped. Out of everything and everyone I held dear, I never imagined Nyla would drag Ervin into this. He was more of a father to me than anyone had ever been.

Her palm filled with flame, extended close to his face. Hair from his beard singed, the fire flickering dangerously close. She pulled back as I flinched, smiling maniacally in my direction. Something deep had broken in my sister.

A part of her had closed off. Everything she had been, she'd tucked so far inside, away from my father's grasp, that she lost sight of herself. Revenge for abandoning her clouded her thoughts, and all she knew now was the hate my father filled her with.

She needed someone to blame for her pain, and she'd picked me.

I couldn't blame her.

I blamed myself.

Guilt ate at my soul and tore me apart. If I had been there to protect her, to take the lashes of flames, she wouldn't be here.

Koraine shifted uncomfortably beside me, waiting for

my decision. We could abandon everything, leave the ship behind, but that meant abandoning Ervin and letting Morwen suffer.

I wouldn't run again.

"I'll come home," I said finally. "But let Ervin go."

"No!" Ervin shouted, but Nyla brought the flames closer to his face again. He closed his mouth and watched with hesitation.

"It's my choice," I said.

"Bellamy—" Koraine whispered.

I squeezed her hand.

"Trust me," I said, finding her vibrant blue eyes.

I needed her to understand. I wouldn't let anyone suffer again at the hands of my father.

Something shifted in her gaze—understanding.

I stepped forward.

"Let him go," I demanded.

Another step, and I was closing the distance between my sister and me. Ervin found my stare, and I tried my best to convey the message.

One more step, and I'd be close enough, Koraine and Caspian just out of reach.

The ship erupted into chaos. I lashed out with my flames, sending a quick, swiping arc in front of me. Nyla deflected, but a few guards weren't fast enough. She let go of Ervin to contain the flames flying in her direction, and the old man hurried over to our group.

Many winced in pain when the flames hit. I hadn't mean to kill, only to cause enough of a distraction to escape. It was clear Nyla was too far gone to reason with. The moment she brought Ervin to the deck, I knew it was over. We would have to retreat, and I would have to let her go again.

The commanding princess before me was not the sister I once recognized.

"Go," I shouted at the group.

We dove off the ship and into the water. I trusted Koraine with my life; this was the second time I had jumped into the sea without a second thought for her.

I knew she wouldn't let anything happen to me in the water. Immediately, a bubble formed around me, pushing the water away and creating an air pocket under the waves. Koraine appeared in front of me, taking my hand. We were inside the same bubble, Caspian close beside us in his own with Ervin.

Serpents appeared only feet away from us, their large bodies pushing through the current.

Koraine reached out, grabbing Talay's head as Caspian grabbed Elios.

The serpents swam us away from the ships. Without us coming to the surface, Abelon had no way of knowing where we were.

My stomach felt heavy thinking about my sister. My father had tortured her into submission. She fought and lost. Guilt washed over me, and I could barely hold back the bile rising in my throat. I'd left her to him. I knew what his lessons were like, knew he would blame her for leaving. Why hadn't I tried harder?

The serpents moved faster than I could comprehend. In was the same way dragons commanded the sky, the serpents manipulated the sea.

We made it unharmed to a cove, the serpents finally breaking through the surface of the water. Koraine climbed out, standing on the rocky shore. She extended a hand, helping me out of the waves. I found Caspian was already out, staring me down, having pulled Ervin from the water.

"So much for listening to reason," he snarled.

"Caspian…" Koraine warned.

The cove had access straight to the palace via a tunnel that led there. We ran the length of it, never stopping, knowing that the siege could come at any moment. The moment we left the tunnel, I heard it in the distance: the sound of alarm bells ringing. My heart raced; we were too late. Without our warning, they would have no idea the attack was coming. They still thought I was safely in my cell, waiting for them to trade me.

We hurried through the halls, Ervin keeping a surprisingly quick pace, though I kept glancing back to check on him.

"I'm old, not fragile," he chuckled.

I tried to smile, but it barely reached my eyes, though the anxiety of the bells ringing prevented it from going further.

We found ourselves at a staircase leading up to the throne room. If the King was stationed anywhere central to give orders, it'd be there.

Koraine climbed the steps in front of me, flashes of white hair swaying inches away. I wanted to reach out and take her hand but held back.

By the time we reached the top of the stairs, my lungs screamed for air. We had barely stopped moving since the ship.

It was only a short walk to the throne room, and

Caspian held the door open for us to all enter. Immediately, I felt all eyes fall on us, disdain filling the air, intoxicating me.

The King rose from his throne, his disapproving stare bearing into my soul.

CHAPTER 5
NYLA

THE MOMENT my brother dove off the ship, I knew I'd suffered a setback. My one piece of leverage over Bellamy was now in my brother's company. I needed a new plan, fast.

If Bellamy wouldn't come willingly, my only option would be to drag him back home. If I returned to Abelon without the prince, my father would have both our heads. I knew there was truth behind his ruthlessness; I'd experienced it myself.

The burn marks on my back still ached with phantom pain, reminding me of everything I had suffered. The torture I had endured because of my brother's foolish actions was still a fresh wound.

Anger built within me.

My hands were covered in flames, uncontrollable and untamable.

"Find them," I commanded.

My dragon landed on the ship, sensing my distress. I knew if anyone could find them, it would be her.

"Go," I said gently.

She didn't need further command. She took off into the sky, flying circles, surveying the sea, looking for them. I knew the chances of us finding them under the water were minimal, but I would leave no stone unturned to capture my brother.

If he wouldn't come easily, then we do it the hard way.

"We sail for shore now," I commanded of the nearby guards. "Alert the other ships."

"But princess, we gave them till morning," a guard noted.

Sheer fury ran through me. I'd already been humiliated by my brother, I would not be questioned by my guards.

I held a hand, lit with flames, close to his face. The guard tensed and shut his mouth.

"Do I sound like I want to be questioned?" I asked. "We know they don't have the prince to trade. We attack now," I growled.

"Yes, my princess," the guard choked out.

The guards lit the signals, were torches at the head of each ship. The other ships followed suit, preparing to make our way to shore. I knew Morwen would not be ready for us, but I didn't care. If they could not turn over my brother, I would find him myself.

The ship lurched forward, and we made quick time. Our surprise movement meant we met no resistance from water manipulators.

I heard the alarm bells ring the closer we got to shore, but it was too late. We would make our way onto land, whether the Morwenians wanted us to or not.

The moment my ship anchored, I found the nearest small row boat.

The water close to the docks was too rocky to bring our ships fully to shore.

I signaled the guards with me to follow. Our ship had a total of five small boats, and the other ships had similar. I helped row the moment the boat was lowered into the water, quickly swallowing the remaining length between the ship and shore.

I hopped out of the boat as soon as we were only inches from shore. I landed on a short dock, hurrying up the length of it. A few warriors had already found their way down to the docks to greet us with resistance.

A stream of water flew my direction, but I deflected them with my own flames. There would be no stopping me.

I'd taken lessons here and there from Bellamy and other guards on how to defend myself. It was the clever thing to do when our kingdom was everyone's enemy. I'd spent time practicing on my own. building my strength. Most assumed I was the helpless princess, and I liked it that way. I never wanted my father to suspect I could fight back.

It had done me no good when it came to it, though. All my preparation still lead to suffering.

The training came in use needing it to fight off warriors, many of whom had novice skills. I may not be able to fight my own father, the king of the fire kingdom, but I could handle these warriors myself.

I threw balls of fire in multiple directions, trying to break through the growing wall of guards. My men joined me, engaging in their own battles. Fire rained over our heads as our ships catapulted balls of flame to the shore.

My lips curled into a cruel smile, only then remembering that the men we left behind could still be of use.

This was my first battle, and there was still much for me to learn.

I watched the flames strike buildings close to the docks. Their structures caught fire, filling the air with ash and embers.

Nearby, Morwenians fled their homes, letting out screams of horror when they caught sight of the raining fire.

One of my attacks connected with a warrior before he could deflect it. I took the opportunity and rushed forward. It was the first opening in the wall of men decorated in blue uniforms.

I wasn't familiar with the city of Alua, but it wasn't hard to spot the palace, its tall, silver gates making it stand out.

Two guards followed me through the opening of men and remained by my side. We rushed through the streets, met with little resistance.

I knew my brother would hide behind the tall walls of the palace.

I remained hopeful the King of Morwen would be willing to hand him over. If Bellamy was foolish enough to return to the palace, I doubted he would find many allies.

The city wasn't as large as Raden, and it took us little time to make our way to the palace gates.

Warriors shouted different commands, my guards and I hidden in the shadows. We stood with our backs to the wall directly across from the tall gates. Without the light of day, the warriors could not see us.

"They have to open those gates if they want to send more men down to the docks," one of my guards said.

My heart sped up, and I felt frozen in place. I'd made it this far; there was no turning back. I needed to step up, and I needed to take command.

"The moment those gates open, we go," I whispered the order.

The guards both nodded their agreement. They looked at me with respect, and my chest filled with pride.

My father had doubted my abilities and underestimated me. I would prove I could handle this mission. I would show him I was more than the helpless princess.

Two more guards found their way to us as we waited patiently.

"Our men are holding them at the docks. They will need to send more men soon or risk all of us breaking through their defense."

I felt a weight lift from my shoulders. The plan was falling into place, and soon, I would find myself within the palace. It wouldn't take long to find Bellamy once I convinced these people to turn on him. They already agreed once, sending a messenger to tell me that at dawn, they'd trade him for their safety.

Koraine had ruined that for them. She couldn't help herself from trying to save my brother from his inevitable fate. Everything always led back to her. My heart felt torn, part of it still aching from the friendship I had formed with her. None of it had been a lie to me. She had stolen my brother, the only family I felt I had left, and turned him against our kingdom. The other half of my heart bled with anger. She had betrayed me.

If Bellamy couldn't realize what Koraine was doing to him, I would have to show him.

My father would spare our lives when we returned, and I would make it right. My brother had become a traitor, but there was still hope to fix it. Even in my anger toward him for the pain and suffering I had gone through, I still wanted to right the wrong.

The gates opened, and I saw the warriors waiting behind them. The moment the gap was big enough, they rushed through it. My four men and I pressed our backs tightly to the wall to remain hidden. The warriors rushed toward the docks, choosing a different path to lead them there.

I let out a sigh, my heart racing.

Every second that ticked by, I felt more unsettled. I needed to find my brother, fast.

The men I brought with me were not a full army, and they would not be able to stand the full strength of Morwen's for long.

"Go," I ordered.

Two guards stepped in front of me, leading the way, and the remaining two followed behind me. I was surrounded and protected by my men. I hated to admit it, but I needed the protection. Entering the palace would be no easy feat .

The five of us slipped through the gates before they shut and before Morwen realized their enemy was within their walls.

Warriors rushed forward, but we were faster. Flames were thrown up as a wall of defense around us, and I sat untouchable in the center of them.

The attacks of water did no good, the guards intercepting each. Abelon's army was the best there was. These warriors didn't stand a chance without more men. I counted only eight warriors guarding the gates, many of them deployed to the docks to aid in the battle.

I threw up a shield of flame, an attack of water barreling toward us from above. I scanned the palace and spotted another warrior on a balcony, joining the fight.

We need to move inside; we were open targets in the courtyard.

"Let's move," I commanded.

KORAINE

"WHAT HAVE YOU DONE?" my father asked, horrified.

"We aren't turning him over," I said adamantly.

"You ruined any chance of that," Emmett hissed.

My oldest brother glared at Caspian and me, disdain written all over his face.

"It never would have ended. Abelon would've come back. Even if we gave them the Prince, it wouldn't have been enough. Princess Nyla said it herself—the king wants to watch the rest of the kingdoms burn," I said, trying to reason with them.

"It's true; I heard the threat myself," Caspian added.

"You lost all respect and trust when you aided her," Emmett snarled.

The King of Morwen watched me, his brows furrowed and his wrinkled fingers stroking his beard. "They are already at our docks. I do not have enough warriors ready and stationed here for a siege like this. It will take hours before we are able to push them back. I do not want my daughter a victim of this carelessness. The strategic move was handing the prince over to protect Morwen's peace," the king stated. "Even if they came back, we could've prepared. The fire kingdom has always been a looming threat."

He had a point, and my cheeks reddened, realizing my haste and selfish actions. I'd risked the entire water kingdom for Bellamy. For love. I no longer belonged to Morwen. I was not the same as them.

Princess Asuna stood tall beside her father, a scowl on her face, her arms crossed tightly. Before she addressed us, she unfolded her arms and patted down her light blue skirt hanging to her ankles.

"I am to be married. I'm expected to travel to the Earth kingdom. No man will want to marry me if my father is caught in the middle of a war. And now, with the fire kingdom attacking, you have made me a target. The princess will come for me the same as she is coming for you."

She narrowed her eyes. "You will all pay for this," she snarled.

Water floated in her palm, and my body tensed, remembering the way she made ice dance up Bellamy's body. We found ourselves in the same position as before: enemies to both thrones, preparing for the worst.

"What if we take you with us?" Ervin spoke up. The old man had been quiet and watchful until that moment.

Bellamy chimed in, "We will take you safely to the earth kingdom. We will all flee this city while the warriors send my father's army home. I promise, I will protect you with my life and get you to your betrothed."

I was hesitant to join the conversation. I knew it was our

best chance, but I didn't want to be responsible for the princess. She had a hand in sending me to Abelon, she tortured Bellamy, And now, she was prepared to torture us again. Why would I care if the fire kingdom came for her?

"I will never—" she started.

"If you escort my daughter to the Earth Kingdom unharmed, I will pardon you."

The room fell silent.

"Father—" Asena began to argue.

"You will go with them. It is our best chance of keeping you safe. I know what the prince and now the general's daughter are capable of; both are better suited to protect you than the warriors here. Caspian will travel with them, and I trust he will serve the crown proudly as the loyal warrior I know he wishes to be," the king said, his eyes falling on my brother.

Caspian shifted uncomfortably under the weight of the king's glare. Beside him, Emmett turned his head, and I saw the annoyance in his eyes. Caspian had never wanted to be the loyal warrior; it was always Emmett. The king had just handed my brother the most important task, and I knew that stung.

My father placed a hand on Emmett's shoulder and squeezed. It was subtle, but I saw it.

Caspian swallowed before answering. "I would be honored," he said, his voice deepened. I had to hold back a laugh at the absurdity of it.

Caspian was no warrior, but I would trust no one else to travel with us across the sea.

"You are going to trust them with my safety? The same

traitors we were about to turn over to the fire kingdom?" the princess noted to her father.

She had a point. I felt like I was missing an approaching catch. The king had trusted us too easily, and my stomach was unprepared for whatever came next.

"No, I do not trust them, but I am no fool. I know when my back is to the wall and I need to retreat and make the unlikely decision," he said. He turned to face my father. "General Neroe, you are my loyal advisor and one of the best generals in this kingdom. What would you advise me to do in this position?"

My father nodded slowly, and I saw him look over each of us. A knot formed in my stomach, and I prayed my father would give us the opportunity to make it out of here with our lives.

He turned to the king, his good hand holding his other arm that I knew still ached. It was his one tell. When he was stressed, he would massage at the old war injury.

" I trained Caspian myself. He is more than capable. The prince of the fire kingdom has a reputation that proceeds him. There is no other fire manipulator more powerful than him, other than his own father. And my daughter—" He paused, glancing back at me, and I couldn't read his expression.

"My daughter is no longer the feeble woman she was when she left these shores. You would be a fool not to send them to the earth kingdom. This city is not safe, and until it is, your heir should not be within these walls. If you wish to protect your alliance with the earth kingdom, my advice would be to let them escort her."

Asena did not argue, but her eyes widened. I tried hard

to keep my face neutral, but it was hard to hide the shock from my face.

"It is decided," the king commanded. "You will leave now, and you will take my daughter with you. You will find a ship in the small cove at the end of the west tunnel. You may take that. I trust you know how to captain a ship, Caspian?" the king asked.

"I do, Your Majesty."

A warrior came rushing through the door. "They are through the gates! The fire kingdom is in the palace!" he shouted.

The room descended into chaos, warriors rushing into position and the king hurrying us to leave. I did not get to say thank you or goodbye to my father before we were ushered through a side door.

The princess begrudgingly followed us. I heard shouts ringing throughout the palace while we made our way through the halls. It would not be a far journey, and there were many tunnels leading from the palace to the various coves along the coast.

My heart pounded in my chest, and I felt my mouth go dry, trying to calm my nerves.

We'd barely made it with our lives, which was becoming a recurring theme the past few days. I was eager to get to the ship.

A few days at sea would give us time to regroup and come up with a plan. If we were heading into the earth kingdom, it would be our first stop to convincing the kingdoms to ally with us.

We rounded a corner and were met with warriors hurrying toward us.

"Fire kingdom," one breathed, hurrying past.

I hear the piercing yell of a warrior out of our sight down another nearby corridor.

"Nyla?" I asked, and Bellamy nodded.

"There is no doubt in my mind that she would find her way into this palace," he stated.

"The tunnel is that way," Caspian noted.

"Do I have to do everything myself? Follow me," Asena huffed out.

"Where are we going?" Caspian questioned as we moved.

"Trust me," she said, rolling her eyes.

"After everything back there, I don't think so," Caspian whispered.

"Fine." The princess froze. "Then you can stay here and deal with the other princess currently burning down this palace."

My stomach turned at the idea. I'd seen Nyla on the ship; she was no longer the innocent princess. There had been fury and pain in those eyes, the burns on her back fueling her.

"I didn't think so," Asena answered after seeing our faces pale at the idea. "There's an older tunnel that leads to the same cove. The warriors just don't like to use it."

"Why?" I asked, but she ignored me, hurrying off.

CHAPTER 7
NYLA

THE INSIDE of the palace was constructed far differently than the fire kingdom's. The colors were an eye sore, everything completely covered in blues and silvers. I was accustomed to the red, gold, and black of my home.

Nothing could stop me once I entered the palace. Multiple warriors tried and failed, but I was on a warpath. My brother had to be hiding within these walls. There was nowhere else for him to go—his own home thought him traitor, the other kingdoms despised him, and this was the home of the woman he trusted most.

My guards pushed forward, sending streams of flame through the hall. It was harder for the warriors to deflect and avoid our attacks inside the confined space.

I was growing impatient, following the guards and getting nowhere. At every turn, we found more resistance and no answers in the maze of hallways.

I pushed my way forward in front of the guards and ordered them to fall behind me.

"But princess—" one argued.

"Unless you want to find yourself at the mercy of my father when we return, you will not argue with me," I commanded.

I knew the threat of my father would be enough to bring any man to his knees. I wanted them to respect me in that same manner, but respect was earned, and I still had to prove myself.

I stormed through the halls, not letting a single warrior stand in my way. Each time one rushed toward us, I took them out in the blink of an eye using my flames. I could feel the hot stares of the guards behind me, mesmerized as I led them. A smile formed on my lips, knowing they were already regretting not trusting me to lead.

We rounded a corner, and I saw exactly what I had been looking for: the grand doors. I'd finally found the throne room.

I hoped the water kingdom wasn't foolish enough to give my brother refuge behind their walls. Part of me wanted to walk through those doors and find him on his knees as a sacrifice to the fire kingdom. The other part of me still hurt for the brother I knew, and I'd hate to see him like that.

I was teetering on the brink of sanity. I could feel the fire inside me, begging to be let out and burn everything in its path. Everything I knew, everything I had been, tried to contain it, but the betrayal and torture had been too much. My mind could barely handle reality any longer.

I marched toward the door, on a warpath. My heart pounded in anticipation of what I would find behind it, not knowing if I would see my brother or an empty room. My hand shook as I reached for the handle. I took a deep breath before pulling on it. The moment I flung open the door, I let my hands turn to flames and stepped through.

Inside, I was met with a wall of warriors standing in front of a single man.

The king's eyes met mine, and I knew I was too late: Bellamy was long gone.

"Where is he? We had a deal," I growled.

"Abelon never seems to honor its deals, so why should I?" the king stated.

A man stepped through an open doorway just beyond the throne and joined the king at his side. I recognized him instantly, even with his dark hair that was such a contrast to hers. He was the spitting image of his daughter, Koraine.

"General Nero. I've heard so much about you," I said.

I knew it was hopeless. Bellamy was already gone. I noticed the princess of the water kingdom was missing and imagined the king would not have left her go far from his side. If both she and my brother, along with Koraine and my prisoner, were all missing, it meant they fled further into the water kingdom or to another . My instinct was the later, the other kingdoms being able to provide them the protection they would not find in the countryside of Morwen.

"If you do not retreat, we will wipe out your army," the general threatened, his eyes narrowing on me. I could feel him reading every aspect of my body.

"Since you do not have what I came for, you are useless to me," I stated. I didn't hesitate before I let my flames lash out.

I let them explode in a burst that blinded the room. The general stepped in front of the king to protect him, using his own water manipulation to shield them. Many of the warriors were not as quick to act.

Flames struck them, knocking them to the ground, burns mottling their skin.

Balls of my flames flew through the air, igniting curtains draped along the walls and the various portraits hanging there. I made a promise: hand over my brother or watch Morwen burn.

I knew I didn't have time to fully bring the capital city to heel, but I could leave them with a reminder of the strength of the fire kingdom. My guards joined in burning anything we could along our way out of the palace. Not a single warrior had tried to stop us or follow.

I expected a bit more of a challenge but was disappointed when I found a clear path back to my ships. The water kingdom was a disappointment, and it was a shame they didn't put up more of a fight. My heart was looking for someone to take the anger I held so close out on.

I wanted a battle, wanted to be able to release the fire inside me. Letting it go would bring back some semblance of who I was. It felt like I was at war with myself, two halves of me no longer compatible. Every time I thought I could put it aside and be the person I was before, that feeling, that rage, crept back in, and all the pain of those days spent in my father's dungeon played over and over in my mind. He had turned me into a monster, and I would never let them forget it.

CHAPTER 8

KORAINE

THE SHIP WAS SMALLER than most but spacious enough to fit the five of us. My brother helped me aboard, grasping my hand and pulling me up onto the deck. There was no time to wait or process everything that had happened; the fire kingdom had already breached the city.

Bellamy climbed up onto the ship behind me and helped Ervin. The princess refused to accept help and pulled herself over the siding of the ship. There was no ramp to make things easier; the ship was there as a fast escape.

Caspian whistled loudly, the sound piercing my ears, signaling to the sea serpent where we were. If Elios was summoned by Caspian's call, Talay would be close behind. The serpents had an uncanny ability to know exactly when and where we needed them.

Beneath the deck of the ship were two rooms, each sporting a single small cot. There was also a small space with a hammock and minimal crates of supplies.

Bellamy followed me beneath deck and helped me open the crates. One contained dry and plain clothing; another held bland food preserved to last. Bellamy opened a crate with blankets and handed one to me. I wrapped it around my arms, cold from the chilling autumn weather. There had been no time to grab our belongings, and my makeshift cloak was not meant to protect the cold at sea.

"Thank you," I whispered to the prince.

His bruised face was swelling, a few cuts on his body scabbing over. There was dried blood on his skin, and I called on my water to help wash it away. My hand moved over the wound, close to his skin, only letting the water touch it. The dry blood washed away, and I caught the gratitude on the prince's face as I dared to look up. Everything he experienced was my fault, and my heart hurt with the consequences of my choices.

"Stop," the prince commanded, and I froze, letting the water disappear from my hands. "That's not what I meant," he corrected.

I looked up into his eyes and saw the sadness behind them. I dared to gently reach out a hand, letting my thumb trace over one of the bruises on his cheek.

"This wasn't your doing," Bellamy said, and I shook my head. "Koraine, look at me."

I swallowed hard and let my gaze meet his.

"This wasn't you," he said again. "You couldn't have known and we needed somewhere to flee. The fire kingdom would have killed you. We made the right choice."

"Why does it still feel like the wrong one then?" I asked.

"Because sometimes, the right choice isn't the easiest one. Sometimes, the right choice is the one that hurts the most," he said, letting his gaze drop.

The prince backed away and walked over to one of the doors. He opened it and beckoned for me to follow him.

"Shall we?" he asked, a small smile forming on his lips.

I nodded, following him through the door. The space was small and cramped, but it was better than the boat we traveled on to get to Morwen. Bellamy crawled into the cot and dozed off shortly after, his body tired and defeated.

I stayed with him and curled up next to him until he finally fell into a deep sleep. My mind was wandering far too much to rest. The day was still early, and even though I had spent the entire night rescuing Bellamy, I was still not tired. Adrenaline coursed through my veins, and I could feel myself growing anxious.

I climbed out of the bed slowly, careful not to wake the prince. I found Ervin in the hammock and tried my best to quietly sneak past him, climbing the stairs leading to the deck. They creaked beneath my feet, and I froze when I heard Ervin let out a deep, grumbling noise. I waited a moment but realized he was still asleep when he rolled over.

On the deck, I glanced around, noticing we were entirely surrounded by the sea. We'd already made it far away from shore, Caspian still manning the ship. It was small enough for one person to manage, and I knew we would have to take shifts to keep the boat on course.

Princess Asena was hovering close to Caspian, watching his every move.

"Are you always like this?" Caspian asked her.

"Like what?" she demanded, her dark gaze glued to my brother.

"A complete and utter pain," he grumbled.

The princess moved quickly, but I was faster. Water rose

from the sea at her will, and I quickly placed myself between them.

"Enough," I scolded. "We are all already exhausted and unhappy with the situation, but fighting amongst ourselves will not help us reach the earth kingdom."

It would be a few days' travel, and we'd never make it if we fought amongst the group.

The princess rolled her eyes and stormed off.

"She's a delight," Caspian muttered.

I punched him playfully in the arm. "You're no better," I scolded.

"What are you, my mother?" Caspian asked, and I noticed the way the word *mother* hung in his mouth.

"Tell me," I demanded. His eyes fell as he realized what I was asking.

"She's not well," Caspian said. "It's why we were at the palace when you arrived. Father had her moved there and asked the king for a favor. He wanted the best healers in Morwen to be by her side. Even then, not a single one of them could help her. The illness is consuming her too fast," Caspian said, his voice trailing off.

"There's nothing they can do?" I asked, even though I already knew the answer.

His eyes remained on the wooden planks of the deck.

"By the time this is over, it might be too late," I said, realizing I might never get the chance to say goodbye to my mother.

Memories of helping her at the apothecary and running through the snow with her during the winters flashed through my mind, and I couldn't help the tear that escaped.

"Don't think that way," Caspian said. He quickly pulled

me into a hug, and I let him. He was the only family I had right now, and I knew he was hurting just as much as I was.

"She'll fight, and she'll keep fighting until we get home," he assured me.

I let my head fall against his chest and prayed to the goddesses he was right.

I found Bellamy beneath deck in our shared room a short while later.

I willed water around my hands and lowered its temperature. The cold pressed against the prince's skin would help alleviate the swelling of his wounds.

We sat in silence, our bodies barely touching while I did my work. It felt like the longer we sat there, the more the silence grew between us. I couldn't stop thinking about the prince's words from earlier that day. None of this was my fault, but no matter how many times I tried to convince myself to believe them, I couldn't.

"I never realized you could do this," Bellamy noted.

"Do what?" I asked, snapping out of my own thoughts. I found my eyes meeting Bellamy's dark gaze, the ember of determination just barely still there. It broke my heart seeing him losing hope. He put on a brave face in front of the rest of the group, but I knew him.

Deep down, he was sinking further away from being able to win control from his father. Seeing his sister manipulated by the king took a toll on him.

"Manipulating the temperature of the water," he said.

"Can you not will your flames to burn a little hotter or brighter?" I asked. My hands wandered over his arms, touching every bruise and cut I found.

I saw his mind wander and, finally, he nodded slowly.

"I suppose I could," he said. "I never thought about it like that."

"I learned how to do this when I learned how to heal the warriors during the war."

Memories of my father at war came rushing back. I could feel the kingdoms heading toward the same fate again, and a lump formed in my throat. Each time the kingdoms clashed in war, it left devastation in its wake.

"You were only a child?" Bellamy questioned.

"We had no idea how long the war would last, and my father was one of the most respected generals in Morwen. It was expected that the rest of us would follow in his footsteps, my brothers becoming warriors, and myself becoming a healer to help the war effort."

My future has always been decided for me by someone else until I left for Abelon. It wasn't until then that I finally took control of my life and decided what I wanted.

"They prepared children for war?" Bellamy whispered, horrified. It wasn't until now I realized how horrifying the realization was.

A knot formed in my stomach at the memory of how my mother used to heal the warriors during the war. She had a gentle touch and knew all the best herbal remedies to mix with her healing water. I'd caught glimpses of the ghastly injuries the men would come back with. It made my stomach turn, the sight of burns and the smell of charred skin, but my mother had never once faltered in doing her part.

I had wanted to be just like her.

"Where did you just go? Bellamy asked.

The memories of my mother and my childhood in Morwen were too painful. Nothing would ever be the same, and I would never be able to go back to the simple times when I thought I would follow her footsteps.

"Caspian said my mother is not doing well," I admitted. Bellamy's face dropped. His hand slid to my lap, and he gave my upper thigh a gentle squeeze.

"The goddesses will look after her. If she's anything like you, she will fight through illness, and you will see her again," Bellamy tried to reassure me.

"I just fear…" I couldn't bring myself to say the rest.

"I know, my moon," Bellamy said softly.

He pulled me closer, wrapping an arm around me and holding me tight. I let my head rest on his chest, listening to his heartbeat, the sound soothing me.

The prince ran his fingers through my white hair and let me stay wrapped in his arms for a while. It grew darker outside, and soon, the moon would be well above us.

At sea, I felt safe. It was the first time in a long time I could truly say I felt that way.

I would've remained wrapped in the prince's embrace for the night had there not been a large thud from above us. The startling sound was followed by commotion on deck. My eyes widened, and I looked at Bellamy, whose mouth fell open.

I grabbed a nearby blanket, wrapping it around me to protect from the cool night, and hurried from our small room, Bellamy following behind. We raced up the steps and onto the deck, where I found my brother staring down a large beast.

"What is this thing doing here?" Caspian asked, horrified.

My brother, caught off guard and frantic, paced in front of the dragon. His eyes were narrowed on the beast, and I could see his skin had paled slightly. I tried not to laugh.

"She can only fly for so long," Bellamy said. "She needs rest."

Imry let out a huff that sounded like an agreement.

"Well, tell this thing to rest elsewhere. I can't concentrate on navigating the ship when there is a fire-breathing beast staring me down," Caspian complained.

Imry let out a snort, her eyes remaining on my brother.

"The dragon stays," Bellamy said. "And I suggest you be kind to her if you do not wish to end up a pile of ash."

I couldn't hold my amusement any longer, and a slight chuckle escaped my lips. Both Bellamy and Caspian threw me glares before I rolled my eyes and walked over to the dragon.

Holding out a hand, I let the beast come to me. Imry nuzzled her large head against my palm and let out a gentle sound. I smiled, comforted by the dragon's presence. The first time I met her, I'd been terrified. I'd come to appreciate the beauty of the beast and knew how much she meant to Bellamy. I owed my life to her and would forever be in the beast's debt.

"Why don't you go get some rest, Caspian?" I asked. "I can take over manning the ship."

"You don't know how to man the ship," Caspian accused.

"You've already set the sails. All I need to do is make sure we stay on course. Go get some rest, and you can take over in a few hours," I demanded.

I could feel Caspian's frustration building with the lack of sleep and now having to share a space with the dragon. My hope was that Imry would be able to fly by the time Caspian took over again.

"Fine," he said. "Where am I sleeping?"

Caspian hadn't been below deck since we set sail, busy making sure the ship was on track. The only room left was the one the princess had already claimed, Ervin still asleep soundly in the hammock.

"You can share with me."

The princess' voice startled me. Turning, I found her watching in the shadows at the top of the steps. Her arms were folded, and the scowl on her face had me glad I was not the one sharing her company.

"No, absolutely not. I'm not sharing with her," Caspian argued.

"You have no choice—unless you'd like to sleep with the dragon," Asena pointed out.

Caspian glanced to Bellamy, and I watched the prince quickly put together where his mind was heading.

"Absolutely not. You're sharing with the princess," Bellamy said.

Caspian rolled his eyes. "Fine," he growled as he followed the princess down the steps beneath the deck. Bellamy wrapped his arms around me from behind, placing a gentle kiss on my cheek.

"Do you think they'll last till morning?" I asked, and Bellamy let out a low chuckle.

"I think we'll be lucky if we make it to the kingdom without one of them killing the other."

My heart fluttered at the warmth of Bellamy holding me tightly. The smell of him brought me comfort and made me feel at home.

I shifted to turn around, but he held me firmly in place. I tried to fight him, but he let out small moan of pain, and I stopped.

"Sorry," I whispered.

"I'm just still a little sore," he admitted.

I took a step forward, leaving Bellamy's embrace and walking closer to the dragon that had curled up in front of us. I sat down close to her and leaned back against her large torso. Bellamy followed, and I could tell how relaxed he felt in her presence. I wished I could find that same peace with my serpent, but I knew he was well beneath the ship, traveling under the waves.

"Do you think they'll help us?" I asked.

"I think we have to try," Bellamy said.

It wasn't an answer to my question, but I knew what he meant. The earth kingdom was our best hope at having an advantage in the coming war. If we could convince them, we'd be able to sway the water and air kingdoms to join.

"I'm tired," I admitted.

Bellamy shifted to glance over my face, his brow raising. "Didn't you just volunteer to man this ship for the next few hours?" he asked, teasing.

"That's not what I meant," I started. Reaching out, I took his hand, curling our fingers together and giving it a light squeeze. "I'm tired of running. I'm tired of always having to fight. All I want is peace. I thought our marriage would finally bring that to the kingdoms, but I was wrong. Now I'm running and fighting for my life and kingdom yet again," I explained.

"When this war is over and my father is no longer on the throne, I will ensure that the kingdoms have lasting peace," Bellamy promised.

He leaned in, cupping my face with his free hand. Kissing me lightly, I closed my eyes and gave into him. The feeling of his lips on mine drove away all my fears and doubts. When I was with Bellamy, nothing else mattered. Only him. It would always be him.

I pulled back, noticing the growing dark circles under his eyes. This close, I could see the exhaustion weighing on him.

"You should get some sleep," I said softly. "Even though, selfishly, I want to keep you here, you're no good to us if you don't rest."

He didn't try to argue. "I'll be right below deck, my moon. Wake me if you need me," he said.

He pressed a gentle kiss to my forehead before standing and heading to the stairs. I watched him disappear beneath deck.

I was alone with the dragon and the ship. Leaning back against the beast, I settled for watching the sea, cuddled up against the dragon. The more I let my body relax, the heavier my eyes felt. I was fighting against the call of sleep, trying to keep my eyes open. They burned, and I could feel myself slowly dozing. The last thing I saw before I shut them for just a moment was the glow of the moon high above me.

"Aren't you in charge of the ship?" a deep, gruff voice asked from above me.

I startled awake, glancing around and realizing it was still well into the night.

"I didn't mean—" I glanced up spotting the man looking down at me. "How long was I sleep?" I asked, my voice groggy.

"I don't think you've been asleep long," Ervin admitted. "Your brother came down not long ago, and I've been awake, listening to him argue with the princess ever since."

I laughed, knowing how stubborn both could be.

"I'm sorry," I said.

"You do that a lot, don't you?" the old man observed.

"Do what?"

"Apologize for things out of your control," he stated.

He held out a hand and pulled me up. The dragon shifted behind me but settled quickly.

"I guess I do," I admitted sheepishly. "Why are you up here?" I asked. "I know I may not look it, but I can handle manning the ship. I never should've sat down and let myself doze off."

"I came up because I cannot sleep and thought you might want some company," the old man admitted.

" I can handle it. I know everyone thinks I'm not capable, but I am," I argued.

"I know," he said gently. "I came up here solely because I wanted to, not because I thought you needed me."

"Well," I started with a smile, "then you're welcome to stay."

"I found this in one of the crates down there," he said, pulling out a small satchel of something. He pulled the little drawstring on it, opening it up before pouring the contents into his hand and holding them out to me. Leaves filled his palm, and I recognized them instantly. Peppermint.

"If you can get us water, I can boil it," he said.

I found an empty container and filled it with water that I manipulated.

Ervin took the metal container from me, letting his hands ignite with flames. I watched intensely as the water slowly begin to bubble. His flames were mesmerizing, and the way he held such control over them... I was able to manipulate and control water, but I could not bend it to my will with the precision he could his flames. Each movement was intentional, and I held myself back from asking the old man about it.

Ervin found a small bit of netting woven tightly enough that the leaves would not fall through. He cut a section using a knife from one of the crates and tied it with a piece of twine he found.

He plopped the makeshift teabag into the bowl and let it sit for a few minutes as I hunted around the deck of the ship to find two empty cups. He poured the hot liquid into each of our cups, and I waited a bit before taking a sip, afraid to burn my tongue. The taste of peppermint warmed my core from the cool night breeze when I finally did indulge.

"You really love your tea," I said, looking to the old man.

"There is nothing better than getting to know someone over a piping hot cup of tea."

He let out a deep belly chuckle, and I found myself genuinely smiling. Ervin made me feel safe and welcomed, a feeling that was hard to find during a time of war, one I wanted to hold tightly.

My heart ached for him, ripped from his home and used by the princess as a way to lure the prince. He never asked for any of it. Ervin wanted a quiet life doing what he loved most: cooking for people.

"Do you miss it?" I asked.

"I don't think I'll ever fit into the fire kingdom under its current rule," he said carefully. His brows furrowed, and his eyes remained on his cup of tea. "I think I always knew the only thing keeping me there was the prince, and the moment he left, it didn't feel so much like home."

I knew what he meant. I knew wherever the prince was would feel like home for me. It didn't matter which kingdom I was in.

"Well, you're home now. You found us," I said.

"More like you found me," Ervin chuckled.

"I suppose you're right," I admitted.

He sat with me for a few hours, telling me stories about the fire kingdom and the prince as a child. I felt my smile coming back, happiness spreading the longer I spent with the old man. His happiness was contagious, and I craved more of it.

He finished telling me one of the more scandalous stories from Bellamy's childhood, and I let out a true belly laugh.

"What's so funny?" Caspian asked from the stairs, pulling both of our attention.

"Nothing," I said, trying to suppress my giggles.

"Go get some sleep, sister. I can take it from here," Caspian said. The slow trickle of dawn was just peaking beyond the horizon.

I wanted to argue and spend more time with Ervin, but I knew I needed sleep. My body was exhausted, and if I stayed longer, I would fall asleep while manning the ship again. I took a step toward the stairs but turned back to Ervin one more time. I quickly threw my arms around him and hugged him tightly.

"Thank you," I whispered.

When I pulled back, the old man smiled and nodded.

I made my way beneath the deck and found my room. Inside, Bellamy was still sound asleep. We were quickly approaching the sunrise, and I knew he'd stir soon. I carefully crawled into the bed and tucked myself against him. My head had barely hit the pillow before I drifted to sleep in the prince's arms.

CHAPTER 9
NYLA

My ship was full of strangers, guards I barely knew. I felt alone, a failure. My brother had been so close, and I let him flee. I flinched at the thought of the punishment I would face from my father if I returned home empty-handed.

That wasn't an option.

I would find Bellamy, or I would die trying. The scars on my back were enough to keep me going. They reminded me of the pain and suffering I would face tenfold if I let myself fail.

Frustration swelled inside me, and I clenched my fists. It always led back to my brother—my father's fixation on having the perfect heir, Bellamy not living up to that. It didn't matter what I did. I would never be enough for him. He would never let me have his throne. Even if I proved my strength and let my flames burn brighter and fierce than my brother's, it still wouldn't be enough.

I wasn't Bellamy.

Instead, I'd be punished for letting him leave the kingdom, for him being a disappointment to my father.

Hatred built in my heart and in my mind, and I found it harder and harder to see the possibility of forgiveness. Bellamy had yet again chosen to leave me, knowing what the consequence would be if he did not return. My father would not allow such insubordination. He would tear the kingdoms apart until he had Bellamy back under his grasp.

I growled in frustration, wanting to melt away.

If my father would not accept me as his heir and never see me as an equal to Bellamy, I would prove myself more ruthless and powerful than he was. Anyone who stood in my path was my enemy.

I walked down the steps leading to the belly of the ship. My chambers were not far; I walked down a narrow hall to find the door to my room. Two guards trailed me, standing post outside the room.

The heavy metal door slowly opened, and I quickly shut it behind me. The room was much smaller than I was used to, but it was still comfortable.

It was designed for Bellamy to use if he led the army someday. Instead, I found myself the one occupying it.

A small bed was tucked into the corner, a desk beside it filled with stationary. I sat down at the desk, letting out a sigh. I would need to update my father on the failed siege and inform him that we would be moving forward with finding the prince regardless.

There was a second dragon traveling with our ships that I could use to deliver the letter. I started writing, my pen hitting the paper, but none of the words felt right. Countless pieces of parchment littered the floor beneath the desk as my attempts piled up.

I held the newest attempt in my hand, and fire sprung to

life, consuming and burning the paper until it was a pile of ash.

I pushed out of the chair, frustrated, and walked to a wardrobe across the room. My hands fumbled with the latch but eventually opened it, finding clothing inside. I needed to rid myself of the armor I wore and the clothing that smelt of the salty air.

I found a nightgown hanging in the wardrobe and pulled it out. The armor was difficult to undo myself, but I managed to pull it off. I loosened the corset of the dress I wore before letting it fall to the ground. It was cold on the ship without the comfort of a fire in the hearth of my room. I'd been too distracted to remember to light one.

"Shit," I murmured as a shiver ran up my spine.

I quickly pulled on the nightgown to cover my bare skin. It left my arms exposed, and I sent a stream of flames into the fireplace to warm me.

A knock came to the door, and I whipped my head in its direction.

"I wish to be left undisturbed," I called out.

The guard would soon leave, and I would have my solitude once more.

I walked over to my bed, but before I could crawl into it, the door opened.

"I said, I wish—" I stopped before I could finish the sentence. Cyrus stood, with the cruelest smile on his face, in my doorway.

"Why are you here?" I snarled.

"Are you not happy to see me, my betrothed?" Cyrus asked.

I clenched my fists. I knew he was taunting me, and I still let it get to me.

Deep breaths calmed my unease before I repeated, "Why are you here?"

I would fight with everything in me to prevent my marriage to Cyrus. If Bellamy came back, there would be no need for the marriage. He would take the throne, and he could end the marriage agreement. My father only forced this pairing because Cyrus was the next best thing to an heir he believed he had.

"Your father sent me," Cyrus stated, moving further into the room and letting the door slam behind him.

"Why?" I asked. "I have this handled."

"Oh, do you?" Cyrus asked. "Because the failed siege, lack of a prisoner, and lack of the prince on your ship, which is sailing away from Abelon, tell me otherwise."

My cheeks grew red, and I tried to avert my gaze.

"Your father sent me because he did not trust you to lead this army. The moment you set sail, he knew it was a mistake and asked me to follow. I was going to give you a chance and let you have this siege, but I waited and watched and realized your father was correct," Cyrus said, every word calculated and precise.

He brushed past me, opening the wardrobe I had been at moments before. He pulled off his white shirt, exposing his skin, and tossed it inside.

When he turned back to me, I spotted the mark on his neck, the burn scar a vibrant red. Seeing his burns made my own ache, and I instinctively reached my hand to my shoulders.

Cyrus walked over to stand beside me, looking down at

me. His hand reached for my own burns, and a shiver raked down my spine as his fingertips brushed them. I tried to lean away, but his hand caught my shoulder and gripped it tightly.

"You and I are alike," he said. "And with my help, you will undo the dragon shit you have dragged us into," he growled.

He passed by me and climbed into my bed. My heart raced; I could still feel the spot on my shoulder where his nails had dug into me.

I opened my mouth but let it fall shut just as fast. There was little sense in arguing with him. I knew I needed his help, and pushing back would only irritate him further with my failures. Regardless of my distaste for the captain, he knew how to lead an army and had talents I could make use of.

I stormed out of the room, eager to put distance between us. I didn't know where I'd go or where I'd stay for the night, but there was little chance I would sleep in the same room as the captain of the guard.

I hurried up steps of the ship and called out loudly to my dragon. Veros appeared, breaking through the clouds. Her massive body soared through the sky and landed on the ship gracefully before she knelt and curled up at my feet.

"Rest here," I said.

I walked over to the beast, running my hand along its torso. I slid down beside it and curled up into the dragon to cover myself from the cold. I let my head rest against its belly, and could feel the rise and fall of each breath it took. The beast and I dozed off together, letting our problems melt away..

I woke to the sound of men's shoes banging against the deck. I startled away from my dragon, who shifted in response. Quickly, I stood, smoothing out my nightgown and holding my head high.

My cheeks reddened when I caught sight of the guards before me glancing over my body. I tried to stand tall, but I could feel my confidence wavering. Behind me, Veros let out a guttural sound. The guards warily eyed the dragon, and I realized it was silly for me to feel ashamed. I was their princess, their commander. I had nothing to be ashamed of.

I was the princess of fire, now heir to the throne, and goddesses damned, I had a dragon that would incinerate them at the blink of an eye.

"What are you staring at?" I hissed, crossing my arms to cover my chest. I narrowed my gaze on the men and watched them frantically glance between each other. "Shouldn't you be attending to your duties?" I asked.

They shifted nervously.

"Their duty was fetch the princess," Cyrus' voice rang out behind them.

I rolled my eyes as he stepped in front of the guards.

"We have plans we need to discuss today," Cyrus said, his eyes on me with a predatory focus. I let out a small huff and followed him back beneath deck.

I quickly found myself in the room I had been occupying before his arrival. He motioned for me to sit at the desk, but I remained frozen in place.

"Fine," Cyrus growled.

He walked over to the wardrobe and pulled out a simple red dress. He tossed it at me, and thankfully, I caught it before it was able to hit the ground.

"At least get dressed," he commanded.

I had no desire to listen to him, but the hairs standing up on my arm craved warmer clothing, and the sleeves of the dress were far too tempting.

I quickly slipped out of the nightgown, my eyes remaining locked with Cyrus. His gaze never left mine, no desire in it. Cyrus despised me as much as I detested him. He only agreed to marriage to gain power.

At least I felt more comfortable with the long red gown on, the dress made perfectly for my frame.

"We need to decide which kingdom they're heading for. There is far too much sea for us to cover it all. If we pick wrong, we will be set behind by days," Cyrus said, suddenly switching into his role as captain of the guard.

As much as my stomach couldn't stand him, he at least knew what he was talking about when it came to war.

"They won't go to air," I said with certainty.

"Perhaps they'd go to Luheo, just for that way of thinking," Cyrus suggested.

"No," I said firmly. "I know my brother, and he'd never seek Luheo's help first if he didn't have to. They slaughtered his men; he won't forgive that so easily."

Cyrus stroked at the stubble covering his chin. His hair was lighter than most from the fire kingdom, but the rest of his features labeled him an Abelonian.

"I suppose you're right," he admitted. "Your brother is

stubborn, unwilling to bend his morals. It will be his downfall."

I nodded firmly. I hated the idea of turning Bellamy over to Cyrus. The burn marks on the captain's neck were still fresh, and I knew, deep down, he sought revenge for them. I wouldn't be able to protect Bellamy from his wrath. If the prince refused again to come with us, Cyrus would use force to make him bend, and accidents could easily happen in the process.

If I could get to him first, convince him to come peacefully, I could protect him. I knew the thought was a distant fantasy. Even my own fury and confusion begged not to give him another chance, but it was hard to let go of the people you loved.

"Then we send a scout toward Zetron," Cyrus said. "They couldn't have made it far ahead of us. We will know before the end of the day where they are."

A lump formed in my throat as I listened, making it hard to swallow.

The following day, I would need to face my brother once again.

CHAPTER 10

BELLAMY

I woke up to my arms wrapped around Koraine. My body ached, but there were parts that felt less sore after the long rest.

Pressed against her back, I could feel my cock hard and aching for her.

Her white hair was in my face, and I took a deep inhale, taking in her scent. It was a comfort, one I had come to rely on. The more my own kingdom slipped away from me, I desperately grasped for anything I could consider home, somewhere I belonged. Koraine had never faltered in giving me that. She was my home, and I would protect my home at any price.

The way she shifted under the blanket had my arms wrapping tighter around her. I wanted to savor every second of this moment. It was too soon to give in to the call of the sunlight pouring through the small window.

The quarters were no bigger than a large closet, and the ship itself was designed to be easily manned without a large crew. Even the cots lacked space, and too much movement would send one of us rolling out of it onto the hard wooden floor.

Koraine stirred a bit, and the movement of her ass against me cast me further into discomfort. I tried to adjust, but selfishly, I wanted to stay pressed against her for the rest of my life.

She turned around, rolling over on the cot, and her eyes fluttered open to meet mine as she sleepy lifted a hand to my face.

"How are you feeling?' she asked, worry coating her words.

"I was feeling a lot better when you were grinding against me, but now, I'm not too sure," I teased.

"I could fix that," she said, the gleam in her eye mischievous.

"I'd like to see you try," I said.

Koraine wrapped her leg around me and moved quickly. Before I could react, she had me on my back, sitting on top of me. Her thighs pinned me down, and already, I could feel my cock swelling beneath my pants. The pants were irritating, and I ached to remove the layers between us.

"Does this help?" she asked, brushing strands of white hair hanging over her shoulders as she glanced down.

"I think I feel a little better," I admitted, and she laughed. The sound of it was contagious, and I wanted to imprint it on my memory forever.

She tugged off the white shirt I wore, exposing my body. I'd still been wearing the cut up shirt from my time in the dungeon. With the layer removed, my cuts and bruises were exposed to her, the scars on my arms vibrantly red, more irritated than usual.

She bent down to trail kisses gently along my torso, making sure to stop at each cut and bruise before she sat back and manipulated water to form over her hands. I watched as she worked across my skin, washing away any remaining dirt or blood. The cool temperature of the water felt blissful on my swollen and irritated skin. Watching Koraine heal was enough to make me feel at ease.

"Do they hurt?" she asked as she worked over the mutilated skin. My body was almost unrecognizable through the new cuts and bruises.

"Not as much as they used to," I admitted. "But they are still sore."

I placed my hands on her thighs, gripping tight, like she might slip away at any moment. It had been a while since we left Abelon and stayed on that island, where we had a moment of peace to ourselves. Selfishly, I wanted to keep her where she was.

I knew we were of more use on deck, helping sail to Zetron, but the rest of the group could do without us for another moment or two. The water disappeared, and she stopped tending to my wounds.

Already, I could feel her attempted healing was helping. A few more days' rest, and I would be back to full strength —it would be the same time we would reach Zetron, and I needed all the energy I could muster.

Koraine tucked her fingers under the waistband of my pants and tugged on them. My hand slid further up her thigh and rubbed lazy circles at the top of it.

She shifted her hips and adjusted, sitting so close to my cock, I thought she might drive me crazy. Every small movement made it flinch and ache to be inside her.

"This probably doesn't help," she said.

"Oh no, it most certainly does help," I said, biting my lip to hold myself back from tearing off bit of clothing she had on.

If I didn't find release soon, I would lose all my sanity. I could feel the tension building in my muscles, begging me to grab hold of her and pin her under me.

Koraine shifted to remove her skirt, and I helped pull off the blue fabric. All that remained between us were her undergarments and my pants. I let my hand drift closer to the edge of the undergarments and slipped my thumb under the fabric. She moved at my touch, and a small groan escaped from her lips.

"Quiet, or they'll hear us," I warned.

"If you keep teasing me like that, I don't know if that's possible," she admitted.

I let my finger slide along her center, felt her writhe against me, unable to sit still. I made teasing circles, and her body reacted to each movement. The way she arched her back, hoping to get more, had me ready to lift her from our cot and pin her against the wall.

The boat lurched, and my fingers slid partially inside her.

"I guess the sea is working in my favor for once," I growled close to her ear.

"I don't know. I think that's still in my favor," she said with a smirk.

I grabbed her hips and quickly flipped her around, pinning her beneath me. My abdomen burned at the quick movement, but I pushed the pain away, distracted by the woman before me. Koraine was a welcomed distraction from the tenderness of my wounds, the sister I betrayed hunting us like prey, and the inevitability that I would need to return to the fire kingdom to confront my father.

Her hands wrapped around my neck, and I leaned in to kiss her. Our lips collided, hard, and I bit gently at hers.

Each kiss felt like bliss, her delicate lips pleading for more. I obliged her request, this one thing the only gift I had to give her. We'd been through every nightmare imaginable, and still, Koraine came through stronger than before.

She was my solace.

The ship lurched again, and I swayed away from Koraine's touch. I cursed under my breath, the sudden disruption causing my abdomen to flare up.

"We shouldn't be doing this," Koraine breathed.

"We should," I countered.

She squirmed out from beneath me as her bright blue eyes stared into my soul. The look on her face said it all.

I had lost this fight.

I may have been the prince of the fire kingdom, the one most feared for his fiery temper, but the woman before me had more flame to her than most under my rule.

"Bell—" she started.

"Come here," I said instead of arguing. There would be no convincing her once her mind was set.

She moved closer to me on the cot, and I wrapped my arm around her, pulling her tightly to me.

I breathed her in, resting my chin on top of her head, her white hair soft against my stubble.

"Soon," she promised.

"Soon," I agreed, placing a kiss on her head.

KORAINE

THE REST of the day dragged on, the hours at sea growing long. I helped where I could, but I wasn't as well versed in sailing as my brother and Bellamy.

The princess remained distanced from the rest of us, quieter than she had been. I watched as she leaned over the railing at the head of the ship, distantly watching the waves.

Ervin used what we had to cook up small meals for us. Even with the little supplies he had, the food still tasted delicious, the best I had eaten in days.

I glanced over the side of the ship, hoping to see a fish or two to catch for our dinner, but with two sea serpents trailing the ship, there were none to be found.

If I sent Talay away to hunt for us, he'd bring back plenty, but the idea of my serpent wandering far made me uneasy.

A hand slipped on top of mine that was gripping the railing of the ship. I glanced over to find Bellamy standing beside me. The prince's clothing was no longer the tattered pieces he'd worn for days, but items from the crates below.

Already, his injuries were healing, and I could see the blacks and blues of his bruises starting to fade into green.

"How long until we find Zetron?" I asked, glancing back out in to the sea.

"I don't think it's much further than a day or two away," he stated, following my gaze into the water.

"Have you met them?" I asked. "The royal family of Zetron?"

"Yes," Bellamy answered. "I met them many times when I was young. The royal family is large and resides together in the palace. I believe I've met the princess' betrothed."

I glanced over to Asena, who still sat at the head of the ship. I tried to picture what the nephew of Zetron's king might be like. I wondered if the princess even wanted to be married off. If she had any say, would she choose this fate for herself?

A small part of me empathized with her, knowing what it was like to be sent to an unfamiliar kingdom to marry someone you barely knew.

I sighed.

"I can't stop thinking about the possibility that they'll turn us away," I admitted.

"We have her," Bellamy said, nodding to the princess. "It will be hard for them not to join us against my father."

I prayed to the goddesses that he was right.

I stood at the head of the ship, gazing at the stars above, each one like a shining crystal in the sky. The moon was bright, and its light cast upon the deck of the ship. Basking in it made me feel alive, like I could soak in every drop it had to offer and conquer the four kingdoms.

It was a whimsical dream, one that came toppling down around me the moment my brother placed a hand on my shoulder.

"Drink?" he asked.

He held out a tin can filled with amber liquid that I accepted, hesitantly raising the glass to my nose. The liquid swirled in the glass as I examined it and inhaled. A gag left my mouth, and I immediately regretted the choice, the pungent scent of liquor reaching my nose.

"Caspian," I coughed out.

"I figured after today, you might need something stronger," he laughed.

"Where did you even find this?" I asked.

"In a crate shoved in a corner beneath deck." He shrugged.

I let out a small laugh. The glass reached my lips as I decided to let my cares slip away. The drink was a much needed relief.

Each sip was like liquid fire pouring down my throat. I coughed, handing the tin back to my brother. "This stuff is awful."

"The right amount of awful to make you forget just how much serpent shit we are in," Caspian retorted, raising the tin cup to me.

I nodded, but already, my mind was wandering. We still had a few days at sea, and then everything would become uncertain again. The king of the earth kingdom may not help us, and Abelon would never give up its hunt.

Caspian walked off, and I watched him pour another tin of his liquor to offer Ervin.

The princess had disappeared beneath deck earlier in the night, and I hadn't seen her since. She was private, withdrawn from the rest of us. Her icy surface remained intact, and I had no desire to break through it.

I was still trying to come to terms with being thrust into traveling with the princess.

Everything happened so quickly, there was no time to process any of it.

I turned back to the sea, watching the dark waves roll across the surface and crash against the sides of the ship.

Surely, we couldn't be much further from the earth kingdom. I tried to envision its shorelines, covered in vast fields of green and the most colorful flowers. The night was eerily silent as we sailed across the Vitrum Sea. My eyes scanned the night for any sign that our journey would end soon.

A slight movement in the clouds caught my attention. I leaned into the railing, my chest hovering over the sea below me.

A shooting star?

No, it moved too slow to be a star traveling across the sky. I sighed, realizing luck wouldn't come that easily. The sign of goddesses' luck was far rarer than that.

I squinted, trying to make out what I saw. Clouds were scattered across the sky, obscuring part of my view.

My heels lifted off the deck as I leaned in further, hoping to get a better glimpse.

Strong arms pulled me back, and I let out a curse under my breath.

I turned to find Bellamy searching my face. His brows furrowed as he looked me over. I opened my mouth to argue, but he beat me to it.

"Are you insane?" he asked.

"I saw something out there," I argued.

"You almost went overboard," he accused. "You could've fallen in, my moon."

His eyes looked me over again, his expression worried. I took a breath, holding in my laughter over the absurdity. I flicked a wrist, summoning a stream of water from behind me, and then let it fall just as quickly.

"I'm okay," I said, but it did little to soothe the concern on his face.

"Bell—" I paused, taking his hands in my own.

"I just—" he started, his eyes seeming distant. "Just be careful."

"I will," I assured him. His hand brushed back white strands from my face. "Are you okay?" I asked.

"I don't think I will ever forget the memory of you falling helplessly from that ship into the ocean," he admitted.

My stomach sank, and dread washed over me as the pieces fell into place. I'd never once stopped to think how Bellamy felt after saving me from drowning. He had faced his biggest fear, all to save my life. I could never repay him for that.

"I'm right here, Bellamy," I said. "I'm not going anywhere, I promise. I'm sorry for everything I have put you through."

"It's not your fault," Bellamy said. "I couldn't protect you."

I watched his shoulders sink, his entire body shifting.

"Bellamy, don't do that," I tried. "You'll tear yourself apart thinking like that. There is nothing you could have done to stop it."

"I never should have shoved you away or been so hard on you in Abelon," he said.

"We are born enemies. I don't blame you," I argued.

"It doesn't matter. I couldn't protect my mother from my own father and the tragedies of war, and I couldn't protect you from smugglers," Bellamy admitted. "How can I ever stand before my people as king and promise to protect them?"

"You will never be able to protect everyone from every horror of this world, but you can be there and hear their plights, find ways to make Abelon a safer and prospering kingdom. That is how you protect your people," I said, bringing my own hand to his cheek.

He leaned in and placed a gentle kiss on my lips. His arms quickly moved, scooping me off my feet with surprising strength.

"For tonight, I will protect you, my moon," he whispered in my ear. "And right now, that means taking you beneath deck, away from any edges you can fall over."

I giggled, and Bellamy gave me a warm smile back. His confidence returned to his features, and he gave me a quick wink. I let out a deeper chuckle, wishing every moment could remain just like this.

CHAPTER 12

NYLA

"Prepare the dragon," Cyrus ordered.

I watched one of the guards climb onto the dragon traveling with our group as a messenger to Abelon. It was never intended to be used for scouting, but Cyrus insisted this way was the best plan.

I sighed, watching from a few paces away as Cyrus whispered instructions to the guard. He only needed to fly ahead of the ship to scout if he saw the group we sought and then return straight to the ship.

It was a simple plan, one that would work, I kept assuring myself. Each moment Bellamy fled further, my hopes of capturing him grew more distant. I need something tangible, a hope to grasp in my hunt.

"The scout will be back with news of your brother soon," Cyrus said, his voice deep and unsympathetic.

"And then?" I dared to ask.

"We burn their ship so nothing remains and take the prince back to Abelon," Cyrus stated, not an ounce of care coating his words.

"And the others?" I asked, raising a brow.

"We leave them to drown or become food for the serpents that roam these seas," Cyrus scoffed.

I swallowed hard. I despised Koraine, but the idea of leaving the others to die in the middle of the sea left me unsettled. Before all of this, I never would've have accepted such a fate. I closed my eyes and remembered what I was fighting for. My freedom and power were at risk, and I couldn't let anyone strip me of that.

"You won't kill Bellamy?" I questioned, nerves washing over me. My brother needed to atone for everything he had caused, but the idea of him dying at our hands was enough to amplify my sea sickness.

"No, the king ordered he be returned alive. I have no intentions of defying an order," Cyrus said, his eyes narrowing. "But do not think me a fool. Bellamy will pay for his traitorous crimes. Your brother will find pain at my hands," he promised.

I tried to hide my disgust. My only reason for cooperating with Cyrus was to save my own life and take back my freedom. If I returned without Bellamy, I faced certain death. Cyrus was my best chance at preventing that.

"And after he returns to Abelon and the king is satisfied?" I questioned.

"Enough questions, princess," Cyrus snapped. "The scout is leaving."

I glanced over as the dragon took off. It was a runt, a smaller black dragon carrying a single guard. I watched the beast's powerful wings carry it high above the clouds.

It quickly disappeared from sight, and I squinted as the

bright sun shone in my eyes. I looked away within seconds, my eyes no longer capable of bearing the light.

Cyrus stalked off and disappeared beneath deck, leaving me alone with guards busying themselves. I need a distraction, something to pull my mind away from the scout locating my brother. If I sat idle on the ship, I would slowly lose my sanity.

I whistled loudly, hoping Veros would hear my call. If anything could keep my mind from focusing on the unknown, it was my beast.

Something large moved just beyond the clouds and covered the sun's light from my eyes for a moment. I glanced up to find the dragon already descending toward the ship. It did not take long for her to land on the deck.

Many of the guards anxiously steered clear of the beast. I didn't blame them. Many of them had never rode or worked with a dragon. It was an honor bestowed only on those my father deemed worthy. He controlled everything related to the beasts that inhabited the waste lands of Abelon.

The guard scouting the sea was one trained to carry messages between kingdoms and ships. If my brother spotted the guard and beast and attack, the man would be useless in a battle.

My heart raced at the idea. I didn't want more innocent people dying. Too many had given their lives already for the acts of Morwen against Abelon, and now, my own brother was aiding them.

I walked over to my dragon, reaching out a hand to stroke her face. The beast nuzzled into my touch. "Want to go for a fly?" I asked.

It let out a low but gentle sound, kneeling to allow me to climb on to its back. I pulled myself up, gripping its neck.

The dragon took off only seconds later, leaving the ship well behind us. I held tightly to the beast, afraid to slip off and be lost to the ruthless sea below. Even as a strong swimmer, I would be helpless against the unruly waves. Odaesia had no mercy on those without the blessing of water manipulation.

I leaned against the strong body of the beast, putting all my trust into Veros as she sped up. The cold wind slammed into my face the faster we moved, and I regretted allowing my dark red hair to remain down. It was hard to see as it whipped over my face.

I risked letting go with one hand to brush it behind my ear, and my hand quickly returned to the dragon's neck. I let myself sit up a little to catch a glimpse of the view as we soared above the ship. The sea below reflected the sun, causing the surface to shimmer.

I smiled for the first time in days.

"Faster," I commanded, feeling alive.

The way flying made my heart race and excitement course through my veins had me aching for more. I had no desire to return to the ship. This was the distraction I had been yearning for.

Veros tucked her wings, letting us fall beneath the clouds at a rapid speed. She extended them out seconds later, catching us and stopping our descent as I let out a sound of pure joy.

My dragon coasted across the sky, slowing our speed again. It gave me a chance to sit upright and loosen my grip. For a moment, I held my arms out and let the wind meet me. It sent my long hair blowing behind me, and the cold increased the adrenaline I could tell was feeding my euphoria.

"I could stay here forever," I whispered, not a soul around to hear.

Away from the watchful eyes of the guards and my betrothed, I could be myself. The princess who never asked for this responsibility. The girl who had dreams of traveling the kingdoms and roaming the moorlands of Zetron. I wanted to live my life to the fullest, beyond the bounds of just Abelon.

All of that came crashing down around me the moment Bellamy left.

Veros let out a huff of pure steam, sensing my displeasure.

"Easy," I reassured the beast.

Her temperament was a reflection of my own. If I lost my composure, the dragon would react and grow frustrated or aggressive. I didn't want to return to the ship with an unruly beast.

I let my icy façade fall back over me, needing to remain tranquil and focused. My chest rose and fell with a deep breath, and I could feel myself letting go of the resentment driving my frustration. I shoved them deep down where they would not affect me. Finding Bellamy was my only focus; I couldn't let my personal grievances sabotage that.

If I let my emotions control me, I would never find my brother.

I directed Veros to turn back toward the ship, and I could see it appear as a speck in the sea beneath us. Veros turned her nose down and began lowering us toward the deck, guards rushing around below.

In the distance, a splash of color just beyond the ship caught my attention. I could just make out the colors of a faint rainbow painted across the sky.

I let myself smile for a moment before forcing myself into my cold demeanor as Veros landed gently on the ship.

I still found my mind wandering for hours, trying to avoid the guards and Bellamy, trying to keep my mind off the scout who had yet to return. It was growing dark, and I had finally wrapped my mind around the truth that we would not locate my brother until the next day.

I let out a defeated sigh, heading beneath the deck.

"Can I help you, princess?" a guard asked as I passed them in the hallway below.

"No, I am fine," I answered, knowing the words were false.

There were many things I wanted to ask for or find but felt I couldn't express them.

I was meant to be the leader the guards looked to on the ship, but the moment Cyrus came, that all changed. Every move I made was closely watched, and the guards were loyal to him. If I asked for a single item, he would know. If I showed any weakness or incompetency, he would know.

Instead, I ate my meals and kept mostly to myself.

I continued through the hall until it opened into a larger

room at the end. Many guards sat at small tables, playing cards and drinking. I caught a few throw glances in my direction, their brows furrowing at my arrival. I ignored them.

Instead, I pushed into the room and found an empty seat at a table in the corner. I tried not to glance at the others in the room. My own room was no longer a safe haven from the pressures of my role on the ship; Cyrus had commandeered the room as his own.

"This seat taken?" a deep, gruff voice asked.

"Yes," I said, unable to lie. I tried to keep my voice uninterested.

"You mind?" the guard asked.

My eyes widened at his informality. Not many of the guards were bold enough to speak to me in such a manner. I nodded slowly, admittedly curious about the man before me.

His dark brown eyes seemed curious as they searched my face. His short, dark brown hair reminded me of my brother's, and his light tan skin was a similar complexion.

"Shazo," the guard said, holding out a hand.

I narrowed my eyes on his hand, hesitating. "Nyla," I said slowly, and he let out a chuckle.

"I know," he said. "Drink?"

"No, I'm good. I came down here to be alone," I noted, crossing my arms and sitting back.

"You came to the wrong place," he noted.

It was a fair point. I had walked straight into one of the busiest rooms on the ship. It wasn't that I minded being surrounded by the men, but I wanted to sit in peace without having to be the princess for a moment.

Shazo pulled out playing cards, the symbol of the fire

kingdom painted on the backs of each. The cards were made for Pyrelum, a game of strategy and deceit. Bellamy had taught me to play as a child. He always won when we were kids, but I still enjoyed the game.

"One game," I said, nodding to the cards. "Then, you go."

If one hand of Pyrelum was what it took to earn back my solitude, I was willing to play through once.

Shazo smiled, shuffling the cards. He passed out ten to each of us and watched as I picked up my own. I tried to hide my face as I analyzed the cards. It was a game catered toward liars. If I could keep my thoughts from my face, that would be the key to winning.

"I can tell you have the Ember," he noted, raising his brows in a challenge.

I kept my face neutral. The Ember was the highest scoring card in the game. To have it essentially secured half of the player's victory so long as they could lie through their teeth.

I shrugged. "And if I do?" I challenged.

He sat back, frowning. Had I won so quickly?

Then, he leaned forward, placing his cards down without beginning the game. They remained facing down to the table, but Shazo seemed uninterested in them.

"So tell me, princess," the man continued, leaning his elbows on the metal table, "how does someone like you end up here with us?"

A distraction to throw me off guard. There it was. The entire reason he had worked up the courage to come sit with me. I knew there was more to it. The question every guard was wondering hung in the air.

I noticed men at a nearby table stopped talking, trying hard to still look engaged, but I knew better. I took a few breaths before attempting an answer. It was not a single guard's business why I was assigned to the task, and I had no plans of revealing my father's threats to complete strangers.

"Does it matter?" I tried, hoping the man would take the hint and leave.

"It does when this is the most battle this crew has seen in years," he rebutted.

"I—" I paused. What was I going to tell a complete stranger?

My father cast me aside. He would kill me if our crew did not deliver my brother to him. I was a failure, abandoned by her own family. I wasn't strong enough to face the king and had broken to him in only days.

None of it mattered. All of it made me pathetic.

I hated myself for it.

I wanted nothing more than to find my brother and restore my own peace.

Before I could answer, a guard came rushing into the room. All eyes fell on him as his boots echoed across the floor. He put a hand behind his neck, his eyes darting around nervously until they landed on me.

"They are back, princess," he stated.

I let out a sigh of relief, thankful for the interruption. I stood immediately from my seat and stalked across the room, leaving Shazo behind, the pile of Pyrelum cards on the table un-played.

A pain stabbed at my chest, and I tried to brush it aside.

I rushed through the hallways, eager to make my way

back to the deck. Other guards followed closely behind, allowing me my space.

I made it to the stairs and hurried up them. On deck, I found Cyrus already standing beside the messenger dragon and its rider, nodding as the rider gave him the debrief of his findings.

I couldn't hear the pair from where I stood, but I hesitated to continue toward them. It was the answer I had been waiting for, and suddenly, I found my feet unable to move.

Guards brushed by me, joining Cyrus and standing ready for orders. I forced myself to move forward. I had to know.

The messenger dragon took off to a nearby ship to rest. Trapped on my own ship, it was easy to forget the multiple others following our command.

I stood next to Cyrus, waiting patiently as he finished speaking with the guard who had been assigned rider to the dragon. He nodded firmly to Cyrus before giving me a short a bow and walking off. I watched as he disappeared beneath deck without a word.

"Did he—" I cut myself off.

"They are not far ahead of us," Cyrus said.

"Can our ships catch up?" I asked, my heart pounding in my chest. It felt like I could hear the noise of it ringing in my ears. My hands remained clasped behind my back as I fidgeted with the rings I wore.

"They could, but they would see us coming," Cyrus noted.

"Then how do we take them by surprise?" I asked, growing impatient with his lack of eagerness to share what he'd learned.

"We take our dragons ahead of the ships tomorrow. We will have the advantage of the sky and can burn their ship so they have nothing left. That is how we capture your brother and then leave the rest behind," he explained.

My mind ran wild. I had no desire to fly Veros into a battle. "I think we should take the ship," I argued.

"We are taking the dragons. It is the most strategic option."

"The ships are the safer option," I pointed out.

"Nyla, do not push me," he pushed.

"I just think—"

Cyrus took a step closer, grabbing my hand. He pulled it to his chest, squeezing hard. To anyone else, it would appear he was comforting his betrothed, but I knew better. His hand warmed and became hot. I tried to pull my hand away, but he held tighter.

"I will say this once," he growled in a low tone. "I do not care that you are the princess. You are nothing to your father. I do not care what you think. I am the captain of the guard, and I make the decisions on this ship. You will ride with me at dawn, and we will take the dragons," he stated.

I pulled my hand again, and finally, he let go of it, allowing me to take a step back.

There was no use in arguing. Once Cyrus gave the order, it was set.

He had the favor of my father; I knew the moment he had helped whip me with flames that he would never betray the king. If Cyrus gave a command, the entire crew would listen. Their loyalties remained with him.

"We leave at dawn," he said sternly before stalking off.

He left me staring ahead at the sea beyond the ship. I

could barely move, realizing the one thing I cared about in the world had been dragged into the mess I created. Veros would be forced to fight, and that reminder made my stomach drop.

I ran over to the railing, allowing myself to be sick over the side of the ship. I quickly moved my hair from my face and stepped back to catch my breath.

My hands gripped the long red skirt of my gown as I tried to calm my nerves and steady my breathing. The thought of Veros being injured—or worse—sent my mind reeling. I tried to push the thought away, but it remained. Each time a new scenario ran through my mind, the urge to be sick again grew.

I stepped back from the railing and slid down to sit against the ship's side. I knew I had limited time to wrap my mind around the reality.

In only hours, I would fly my dragon across the sea and meet my brother once more.

CHAPTER 13

KORAINE

I woke to the pounding of a fist on my door.

My entire body jumped into action, throwing myself from the bed and pulling open the door to find my brother, his eyes wide with panic.

"What?" I asked, my heart racing.

"We're under attack," Caspian said before turning and rushing off.

I turned back to the room to wake Bellamy but realized the prince was nowhere to be found. Had he snuck out from our room during the night?

There was no time for questions; I needed to get above deck to help the group.

I heard Caspian pound on the princess' door before sprinting off, and Asena appeared in the doorway as I slipped out of my own room.

"What is going on?" she demanded.

"I don't know," I admitted, my voice soft.

I feared the worst. I knew the princess of the fire kingdom would catch up to us, but I wanted more time.

I rushed past the princess to the steps my brother had taken moments before. Above deck, I spotted Caspian rushing to adjust sails and turn the ship, Bellamy and Ervin watching something in the back of the ship. I hurried to meet them, and Bellamy looked relieved to see me as I stood beside him.

"What is going on?" I asked.

"She found us," he answered gravely.

"Nyla?" I asked, knowing the answer.

He nodded his head. Asena joined us, glancing back to my brother a few times. Her presence was unnerving, and I shifted uncomfortably away from her. To have her so close to Bellamy brought back far too fresh of wounds.

"We need to move faster," she said, her voice wavering.

Was this the one thing the princess feared? She wore an icy shield, but even fire could melt through it.

"The ship can't go any faster," Bellamy explained. "The wind is not in our favor. We have been fighting it all morning."

The princess glanced back to the clouds. I followed her line of sight, spotting what had everyone panicking. Well above the waves, dipping in and out of the clouds, was a large mass. The closer it got, the more I could just make out the shape of the beast.

A dragon.

I couldn't see the ships in the distance with the heavy fog, but I could see the beast moving quickly in our direction. I held my breath, waiting for someone to have an idea. I knew the warships wouldn't be far behind.

"Can your dragon fly us out of here?" Caspian shouted to Bellamy.

"She can't hold all of you," Bellamy said, and I heard the defeat in his voice.

We still had no idea how far we were from land, and risking the ocean was too much of an unknown.

"Bellamy, take over for Caspian," I commanded, nodding to the wheel Caspian was controlling. "Caspian, help me manipulate the water to make this thing go faster," I demanded.

We each took one side of the ship, trying our best to manipulate the waves around us to propel us forward. I could sense my serpent beneath the ship, swimming along with it, and felt a slight wave of relief. Knowing my serpent was there if we needed him was the one thing I needed to calm my nerves.

The princess joined on my side of the ship and helped manipulate the water. The boat lurched forward and moved an impossible speed.

"They're gaining on us," Ervin shouted.

I dared to glance back to the sky and could just make out the shape of someone riding the back of the dragon. This close, I could see the navy blue scales and knew exactly who the rider was.

"How did she catch up so quickly?" I asked, but no one answered.

Frantically, we tried everything in our power to get the ship out of reach of the dragon. We poured our energy into fighting against the direction of the waves. I manipulated them to propel us forward instead of slamming into the body of the ship, and a bead of sweat dripped from my forehead.

"It's no use," the princess said.

She moved away from the ship's edge and stopped manipulating the waves, turning to face the incoming dragon.

"What are you doing?" I hissed.

"Do you really think we're gonna be able to outrun that?" she accused.

I knew she was right, but everything in me screamed to keep trying. I didn't want to fight the princess, and I knew Bellamy wasn't ready to confront his sister either.

"There's another one," Ervin shouted.

I stopped manipulating the waves and glanced to the sky. Faintly behind the first dragon, I could make out the shape of something large. The closer they got, the easier I was able to see it was a second.

I walked across the deck, closer to where Bellamy stood, now staring up into the clouds.

"They must be using the messenger dragon," Bellamy stated, but his voice wavered. "The army always brings one of my father's dragons to deliver messages back-and-forth."

I could just barely make out the shape of a rider on the dragon's back, but the color of the dragon felt familiar. "Would someone ride the messenger dragon into battle?" I asked. The way Bellamy had sounded so unsure before had an unsettled feeling washing over me.

"It's possible," Bellamy admitted. I still couldn't shake the feeling there was something more.

"But unlikely?" I finished, my gaze holding his. I wanted him to disagree, to chase away that dreadful feeling taking hold of me.

"Yes," he said in a low tone.

"What do you mean?" Caspian asked. We all stood at the back of the ship now.

"I mean exactly what I said: it is unlikely that the dragon with my sister is a messenger," Bellamy stated.

"But you said—" Asena started.

"I know what I said," Bellamy snapped.

I held my breath, knowing the prince's fiery temper would be of no help with the approaching threat. The group needed him calm and focused.

"It doesn't matter," I interrupted. "What matters is that any minute now, those dragons are going to be within range, and we have no plan."

"Our only option is to fight," Caspian said, his voice grim. "We can't lose this ship."

Without our ship, we had almost no hope of reaching Zetron. We'd be stranded in the middle of the Vitrum Sea with no sense of direction toward land. My brother used the sun and stars to guide the ship, but lost to the waves and trying to stay afloat, it would be easy to get turned around.

The dragons were seconds from reaching the ship. I could make out Nyla's vibrant red clothing and the way her hair blew behind her in the wind. Cyrus wore golden armor, and his eyes were entirely focused on Bellamy.

I lifted my hands in the air, the sea following my motion. A column shot upward, aimed for Nyla's dragon. She narrowly dodged, forced to turn away from our ship. Cyrus attacked from the front of the ship, where Bellamy and Caspian fought side by side. Their power was a flurry of blues and reds.

I let out a huff of air, realizing I'd need to be faster to hit the elusive dragon. My hands moved at a speed I could barely comprehend, sending the water flying in each direction.

The dragon was equally as skilled. Each attack missed its mark. I poured more energy behind my attack. A stream of water that was not my own flew toward the dragon, and I added to it, directing a stream close behind it.

The first attack missed, but my own locked with the dragon. The beast dropped from the air before gracefully catching itself.

Nyla let out a growl of fury. Fire flew toward our ship, but I doused it with water.

I glanced to my side, finding Asena standing only feet away.

I didn't have time to thank her or process her presence. I'd take any help I could.

Fire flew past us in a powerful attack, narrowly missing the beast ascending back above the ship. Ervin threw balls of fire that zipped past my head; I could feel the heat close to my scalp. Suddenly, pain filled Ervin's eyes, and I knew attacking the princess went against everything in his nature.

Movement to my right caught my attention. Cyrus wrapped around the ship and passed by Nyla as he avoided attack after attack. I watched him lower his dragon to almost the surface of the water.

My arms went up in defense, ready for any attack he threw our way. Instead, he aimed his beast straight for us.

Bellamy and Caspian had run across deck to follow him, but they were too late.

"Fuck," Caspian hissed, taking quick steps back.

I realized too late why he'd cursed.

Cyrus turned his dragon at the last second and let the beast's body slam into the ship.

It was impossible to stop him. Had we been too close to the railing, we would have fallen over as the ship's deck lurched with the attack.

The dragon's wings cut through the air with ease. He directed the beast back to the bow of the ship, letting fire rain from the sky as they went.

Bellamy redirected the flames, and Caspian worked to extinguish anything he missed.

I had to trust they could handle it.

Nyla had already focused her attention back in our direction, and fire barreled toward us.

Ervin stepped in front of Asena and me, waving his hands in one fluid motion and redirecting the flames. I watched in amazement at his control, but my surprise was short lived. New flames followed quickly, and I threw up a wall of water before they could reach the ship.

Nyla's dragon, Veros, let out an aggravated roar when it lost sight of us temporarily.

I let the wall of water drop when I saw Asena raise her own hands. A column of water rose from the sea and quickly froze over. She flicked her wrist, and the column cut into discs of ice that flew at the beast.

It veered left, but one managed to clip its wing.

The beast let out a terrible sound of pain that pierced my ears.

Nyla looked physically pained when her beast was hit. I knew what dragons meant to their riders—it was the same deep connection I had with Talay.

Veros dropped lower and hovered over the sea after the injury forced her to dive down.

Something washed over me, and I held off on my next attack. It was like being able to sense what would happen next.

A moment later, the surface of the water broke.

Talay burst through the waves, jumping toward the dragon. My serpent came close to grabbing hold of the dragon's wing but missed.

I tried to follow with an attack, but Nyla pulled up.

I growled my frustration. Ervin moved his hands faster than I expected in his old age, and I watched as his fire danced and then shot into the sky at the two circling drag-ons. His strength was unmatched comparatively, and his control was like nothing I'd ever witnessed. The way he could control the flames with ease and make it look like a dance had my jaw dropping. I matched his attacks with my own water, a blur of fire and ice.

His flames soared through the sky and narrowly missed the princess, but I watched as part of her trailing gown became singed. I followed with my own water, and even as the dragon dodged, it still partially connected. The splatter of my attack soaked the princess.

We needed to drive them away from the ship. It was our only resource, and to lose it would be our demise.

"Koraine," Caspian shouted, "we can't keep this game up much longer. They are coming in close enough to draw out our power but keeping their distance until we exhaust ourselves."

He was right. They were wearing us down, waiting for the best time to strike. I didn't know how to draw them close enough to strike them down, and pushing them back was not working.

All we were doing was wasting energy.

Fire flew past my head during the distraction, and Ervin caught it before it made contact with the wood of the ship. Without fire manipulators, we would have been screwed.

"Thank you," I managed.

"He's going for the mast," Caspian shouted.

I turned to see Cyrus pulling his dragon well above our ship, aiming directly for the mast.

If he burned it, he knew we'd have a useless ship.

It was hard to believe I'd ever thought the ruthless captain a friend.

He wanted nothing more than to see me dead.

I tried to manipulate the sea to knock him off course, but it was no use. He was too high above to effectively aim.

"Shield it," Caspian ordered, nodding to the mast.

Fire leapt from the dragon's mouth, and Nyla's beast quickly changed direction, aiming for the same central pole.

They both let fire pour down onto us.

I quickly urged water above the mast, and Asena and Caspian followed while Bellamy and Ervin threw attacks of fire at the dragons to slow them.

The three of us forced the water to harden into ice and held it in place over the mast. When the fire finally reached the mast, it collided with our shield of ice.

The ice shattered, raining down onto the deck.

"It's no use," Asena shouted. "We can't continue like this."

"We have to," I argued, my eyes tracking the beasts overhead.

"No, we can't," she pushed back. "We will drain through our power before they come close enough for our attacks to matter."

It was the same strategy I knew my father would've picked. It was brilliant.

Cyrus was a skilled captain, as much as I hated to admit it.

"What do you suggest we do then?" Caspian asked. I saw him glance to Bellamy, and the gesture had me raising my brows.

Had the pair finally accepted each other's presence?

"We jump," Asena said firmly before the prince could answer.

"Are you out of your mind? Do you not see the dragons hunting us?" Bellamy asked. "They won't let up unless we stop them now."

"Are your wife's water abilities so incompetent, she can't control the sea?" The princess raised her brows in challenge. "We stay beneath the waves and use the serpents to travel away from the ship faster than they'll be able to track."

"On three," I interrupted, knowing there wasn't time to debate.

Another large stream of fire narrowly missed us, the heat brushing against my side. Another attempt, and the vengeful princess may find her mark. A heap of rope went up in flames as we failed to extinguish the attack.

"That's going to be our ship soon," I noted. "One," I counted, taking Bellamy's hand. "Two."

I spotted the beast opening its mouth, the red glow inside promising death.

"Three!" Asena shouted, and we all jumped overboard.

The sea slammed into me, the fall making the impact sting. The three of us plunged deep into the water, its cold welcoming. A bubble of air formed around me, and I threw my own ability into keeping it there. The princess beside me looked concentrated, and I knew she'd formed it.

Talay rushed from the depth of the sea, allowing me to grab on to his back. I pulled the prince on with me. Before I could reach out for the princess, a dark mass rushed toward us, catching my attention.

"Asena—" I began to warn but stopped. The closer it came, the better I could see the familiar length of a serpent.

Its white scales caught shimmers of light breaking through the water's surface. White horns curled out either side of its head.

Without any more delay, we took off, the serpents guiding us through the depths of the sea. My powers were growing weaker with every passing minute. Keeping out the entire sea and adjusting every inch we moved was taking its toll. I could tell the princess was tiring by her furrowed brows. We wouldn't last beneath the waves.

KORAINE

THE SEA SERPENTS wouldn't last much longer, pulling all of us along under the waves. Elios carried Caspian and Irvin while Talay supported Bellamy and me. The princess was a few feet ahead on her own serpent.

On top of the serpents, Caspian and I wielded the water to create a safe bubble for us all to breathe. I wouldn't be able to last longer than a few hours, functioning on minimal sleep and my powers still exhausted from the events of the few days prior.

If Zetron wasn't close, we would need to surface and figure out a plan. Perhaps Imry could carry some of us the rest of the way, but that still left about half the group behind. Not a single one of us would agree to that plan.

I tried not to think of the inevitable, but I needed to be realistic. My arms weighed heavy, and I could feel my muscles cramping the longer we went.

Bellamy's soft touch grabbed my waist from behind. He sat behind me on Talay and had been silent for most of our journey underwater.

"We aren't that far from the earth kingdom," he assured me.

"Traveling has been a blur of confusion. I can't tell how far we've made it, and under the waves, it's impossible," I said.

His fingers tightened on my waist, and I felt his thumb rub a circle on my lower back. I tried to relax my muscles and focus on his comfort.

"We will have to surface soon," I said. I hoped he didn't catch the wavering in my voice.

I glanced over to Caspian and Ervin. My brother caught my gaze, a grim look on his own face. He had been the one with the least amount of rest, manning the ship for so many hours. Expecting him to wield water for any longer was almost impossible. I could see the strain on his face and the weighing bags under his eyes. Even Asena's serpent had slowed its pace.

"How much longer?" I asked Caspian. He shook his head in response, and I knew the answer wasn't what I hoped to hear.

If we surfaced, there was a chance we'd be able to spot how far land was if we were getting close. Anxiety rattled in my chest, and I found it hard to breathe. I didn't want to find more disappointment above the waves.

Bellamy leaned in close to kiss my neck. I tipped my head back, resting it on his shoulder. I could feel the heavy rise and fall of his breathing, sensing his worry.

"Are you ready?" I asked.

His head dipped close to my ear, and he whispered, "Take us up."

The shift in my weight to prepare for the serpent to rise

was enough to cue the beast. My thighs gripped the serpent body; I couldn't use my hands to balance myself, and I prayed to Odaesia I wouldn't slip off its back. Even as an experienced rider, serpents were still unpredictable.

Caspian followed, and I watched Elios aim his large blue body upward.

In front of me, the princess' white serpent changed direction the same as ours.

"She really is that far gone," Bellamy said, and I knew he meant his sister. It was the first he'd mentioned her since seeing her with Cyrus.

"You know she's not with him by choice. We have to help her," I insisted.

"I'm starting to worry she's beyond our help," Bellamy said.

"Don't give up on her," I insisted. "She's your sister."

"And I will fight for her every second I can," Bellamy answered, his fingers tightening on my waist. "But I can't help the crippling fear that sinks in each time I see her, realizing the hold my father has on her."

I understood. Seeing her with Cyrus by her side, she had not been the same princess we left behind. Each time I saw her, I was reminded of the pain of having to leave without her. If I could take back that day, find a way for her to come, I wouldn't hesitate. I never imagined she would turn into a monster.

The surface approached, and I prepared myself to break through. I let my arms drop and rest, no longer needing the air bubble around us. Talay was the first to poke above the waves, with me and Bellamy following. The beast swam along the surface, allowing us to sit upright and view our surroundings.

My eyes burned at first, and I had to squint to adjust to the sunlight. I watched Caspian and Ervin break through beside us, the princess following close behind them.

I sucked in a breath, meeting everyone's wide eyes. There wasn't much to notice, only the daunting endless body of water surrounding us.

My heart sunk at not seeing any land nearby.

I could see the disappointment written across everyone's faces.

"Come on," I encouraged Talay. The beast started to slowly move in the same direction we had been heading.

"We go as far as the serpents can carry us," I said. No one argued, knowing it was our only option.

I prayed again to Odaesia that she would allow our serpents to move a little faster through her sea.

The princess caught up beside Talay and glanced at my beast. "This is Ryn," she said.

"Talay," I answered, motioning to my own beast. "I didn't realize yours had followed us."

"Is it that hard to imagine when your own serpent followed?" Asena asked. Everything from her lips was a challenge. "You didn't really think the Princess of Morwen would leave the kingdom without a serpent, did you?"

"I guess I didn't have the time to consider," I said, shaking my head.

My long, white hair clung to my shoulders, still wet from when we dove off our ship. My clothing was damp, and the cool breeze sent a shiver through my body.

The prince wrapped his arms around me, trying to warm us both.

He let go suddenly, and I felt intense heat from behind me. I risked a glance back and saw Bellamy's hands full with flames.

"Put those out," the princess scolded.

"Do you want to freeze today?" Bellamy shot back.

Ervin copied Bellamy's actions and created his own flames, warming my brother.

"Do you want them to find us faster?" the princess asked, her brows raised and arms crossed.

"No, but it will make no difference if we freeze out here," Bellamy assured her. "If you move as close as possible to our serpent, my flames can keep you warm too," he offered.

"I'm good," the princess said with a scowl.

I found myself watching her, worrying whether we could get her to Zetron alive.

The king of Morwen would never help us if any harm came to his daughter.

I didn't like the princess, but our fate was riding on her safety.

"Move closer to us and warm yourself," I demanded as everyone's eyes fell on me, watching me challenge the princess. "If you do, they'll agree to use the flames sparingly. We will only have them out for short periods of time," I tried to compromise.

"Using the flames at all is foolish," she said.

"Foolish," I agreed, "but necessary. We are no use if we succumb to the cold out here."

I watched her consider the offer, her eyes narrowing on

the prince. Without a single word, she nudged her serpent closer to Talay. If I wanted, I could've reached out and touched her.

I noticed the way her muscles relaxed, letting the fire warm her. Her shivering slowed until it was no longer. I hadn't noticed, but my own shaking had ceased, and I could feel myself relaxing.

We let the serpents carry us for what felt like another hour until we could feel their pace slowing. With each passing minute, our hopes for reaching land felt more and more distant.

"We need a plan," Caspian said, breaking the long silence.

"We're out of options," Bellamy answered.

"What about your dragon?" Caspian asked.

I felt Bellamy freeze behind me. "Imry can't carry us all," he explained. He said the same back at the ship, but I could tell my brother was grasping for any slither of hope.

"Could Imry carry some of us to Zetron and come back for the rest?" Caspian asked.

"We don't even know how far the kingdom is," I pointed out.

"I'm not sitting here, waiting for some beast to fly me to Zetron," the princess snorted.

"Ervin shouldn't have to sit out here either," Caspian argued. "And I'm not leaving my sister here with *him*," Caspian snarled toward Bellamy.

"Caspian—" I warned.

"I'm old, not fragile," Ervin mumbled.

"Then send Koraine first," the princess argued.

"I'm not leaving here at all!" he snapped. "I almost lost

her to a different kingdom once. I am not making that mistake again.”

I felt torn. “Imry can only carry three people, and not far.”

“I’ll stay,” Ervin offered.

“No,” Bellamy snapped.

“This is pointless. No one is staying behind,” I argued. “It could be a day or longer before the dragons would come back for the rest of the group. We have no food, no dry clothing, and nightfall is approaching rapidly. It won’t work.”

“We’re out of options,” Caspian said, his voice rising, growing more frantic. The pressure of being the one to lead the group was weighing on him. Everyone naturally looked to him for an answer, but there were none. “We wait here until our serpents sink to the bottom of the sea to rest, and then what? How long can we keep them breathing under the waves?” Caspian continued, motioning to the others.

“I don’t know,” I whispered, knowing he was right.

“We take a ship,“ Ervin suggested.

“What?” we said in unison, looking to him.

“We sail the rest of the way,” he said, as if the answer was obvious.

“If you haven’t noticed, we lost our ship,” Caspian said.

“Thanks to him,” the princess muttered, glaring at Bellamy.

I felt my gaze fall on her like icy daggers.

“That ship,” Ervin pointed.

We all followed his gaze, noticing the distant blur on the horizon. I could barely make out that it was a moving ship.

Our bickering had almost caused us to miss the opportunity in front of our faces.

"Do you think it could be…?" I started, but Bellamy cut me off.

"We can't think like that," he said.

The ship was our last sliver of hope. If it was the fire kingdom, our attempt at fleeing was over.

We directed the serpents toward the ship, their long bodies slithering through the waves. Their pace was slow but still gaining on the ship.

The closer we got, the more details I could make out. Its flag was adorned with a green crest. I made out the shape of mountains and instantly felt a weight lift off my shoulders.

These were not fire kingdom ships—it was the earth kingdom. With this ship came the promise that the earth kingdom was not much further.

I spotted men running to the side, shouting commands in response to our arrival. A new sense of panic washed over me, and my heart raced. How would we convince them to take in stowaways from both the fire and water kingdoms?

This was our last hope.

CHAPTER 15

BELLAMY

As we approached the ship, we had our arms raised in a surrender, hoping to not provoke the guards we saw on board. Each was dressed in a matching uniform bearing the crest of the earth kingdom, mountains embroidered onto the left side of their chest over their heart.

"Be calm, my moon," I whispered into Koraine's ear.

The way she rigidly held her hands up, I could sense her panic. If any trained guard caught sight of her when we boarded, it would put them on edge.

"We seek safe passage to the earth kingdom," Caspian shouted.

"Your trespassing through our waters, and by the looks of it, you're Morwenian. What business do you have in our lands?" one guard shouted. "If we had half a sense at all, we'd take you prisoner for not entering through the port."

"You're right, we are from Morwen, which also means we have the advantage out here in the open sea," Caspian noted, and some of the guards shifted uncomfortably. "We have surrendered ourselves to your mercy and come peacefully."

"We are escorting the Princess of Morwen," Koraine shouted, and all eyes whipped to her.

My heart sped up when the guards leaned over the railing, eager to weigh the truth of her words.

"Why would you tell them that?" Asena hissed.

"We need to give them a reason to help us," Koraine said.

I didn't agree with her lack of hesitance to share information, but she had a point.

"She's right," I added. "Why would they help us if they gain nothing? We clearly aren't traders straying from the port."

"You're using me as bait," the princess accused, her eyes widening.

"No, a trade," I corrected. "One that will get you exactly what you want. Regardless of if they escort us or take us prisoner, you will arrive to your betrothed."

She crossed her arms and scowled. Her long dark hair fell over her shoulder, and I swore, if the brown of her eyes could grow darker, it did.

The waves rocked the serpents while they sat idle. My stomach lurched, and the desire to be aboard the steady ship grew. I would do or say whatever it took to gain their trust.

"If they take you safely to the earth king, they gain his favor," Koraine said. "It's a bargain almost any guard would be foolish to pass up."

The princess remained unmoved, her eyes flashing to Caspian. He listened carefully while we exchanged hush whispers.

"It's true," he added, shouting toward the ship. "I was assigned personally by the king to ensure her safe travels. Our ship was attacked by Abelon, and we narrowly escaped. We are asking for your help escorting her safely to land and to your king."

The guards glanced between each other, exchanging curt nods and whispers I couldn't quite make out. One guard bent over, grabbing something off the deck. He tossed it overboard, and a rope ladder slapped the side of the ship.

"Come aboard," he shouted.

I still felt on edge enough not to jump in celebration. We made it out of the sea alive and the serpents could rest, but my instinct was to not trust another kingdom. Their only motivation was the princess we transported. The rest of us were disposable.

"I still don't like this," Asena growled. "It's too easy."

"Men will do anything for power," Caspian assured her.

I let Koraine climb before me and followed closely behind her up the rope ladder. After a short while, we all stood on the deck of the ship. Ervin moved closer to me, and I could tell he felt as uneasy as I did.

Guards stood before us, taking in our every move. Their pale green shirts matched the emerald green trousers they wore. Each of their boots was covered with mud that had to be at least weeks old.

Their golden skin was a similar tone to Koraine's, only slightly lighter. Many of the guards had short, curly hair that I knew to be rare in my own kingdom.

I hoped my looks alone would not raise any flags to the guards. My complexion was far different from Koraine and Caspian. My only hope was that Ervin shared a similar appearance to me, and if these guards were unfamiliar with Morwen, they may assume we hailed from a different region.

I felt my legs sway and couldn't tell if it was the building anxiety or the moving ship. Even after days of sailing, I had not gained my sea legs.

"It was a short sail to land from here," one of the guard said, stepping forward. It was the same guard who had tossed us the ladder.

All the others looked to him for direction, and I pieced together that he was the captain.

"Thank you for allowing us safe passage," Caspian said. "I am trained to sail a ship. If I can be of any service to you, please let me know," he added.

I kicked myself for not thinking to offer similar sooner. The more we made the crew grow to like us, the more likely we would safely arrive to Zetron.

"There's no need. We have plenty of hands on deck," the guard assured him.

"Rodrir."

"Caspian," Koraine's brother said, holding out a hand and firmly shaking Rodrir's.

"There will be time to get to know the rest of you, but from the looks of it, you've been traveling for a while. You look exhausted. Why don't I show you to your quarters?"

"Quarters?" Koraine asked.

Each time I had set sail from Abelon, our ships had been packed, with little to no spare room.

"I'm sure you're hungry and want a warm place to sleep. It won't be much, but I will have some of my men shift around to allow you to share a room," Rodrir finished.

"Thank you," Caspian said, a grateful smile spreading across his face.

Maybe it was the benefit of traveling with the princess betrothed to one of their own, or maybe it was sheer luck, but the hospitality came as a shock.

Rodrir led us beneath deck, showing us to a room a short walk down a hallway. The ship was built slightly larger than any of the warships Abelon had in its fleet.

"Here's the room," Roger said, opening a solid metal door. "It's not much, but I'm sure it will work for the night."

I glanced around at the other doors in the hall, all similar. It was an odd structural choice; a wooden door would have been more efficient and easier to build.

"Why such solid doors?" I asked, unable to help my curiosity and needing to put the growing anxiety in my chest at ease.

A quick movement of Rodrir's arms had the door across the hallway bending at the top. The metal shifted at his will, and just as quickly, it was put back into place.

"Some of us are able to control certain metals," he explained. "It made more sense to build as much of the ship under our control as possible. Think of it as a precaution in case we were to be attacked. It gives us a resource on the ship."

My muscles relaxed, and the tightness in my chest drifted away.

"That's incredible," Caspian said.

Even the princess looked slightly impressed, her brows raising.

Koraine reached out and grabbed my hand, giving it a reassuring squeeze.

"Why do your uniforms only bear the crest of the kingdom and not the symbol of your king?" Asena asked.

"What do you mean?" Rodrir asked, his forehead creasing.

"Every guard I've met on my visits to Zetron, their uniforms look like yours, but also bear the symbol of the crown. Why don't yours?" she asked.

She crossed her arms. Again, my head swam with thoughts, the accusation bringing back the anxiety I had only just soothed.

Rodrir chuckled. "You're observant," he noted. "Only guards who work in the palace bear the symbol of our king. We are guards assigned to patrol the nearby waters. Therefore, we do not wear that honor," he explained. He gave a sad, longing smile, like the question drew up painful memories.

The princess remained quiet, satisfied by the answer. She was the first to move inside the room, and we all followed quickly behind her.

"I'll have one of them bring you warm food, but until then, make yourself at home," Rodrir said, closing the metal door behind him.

I heard it click into place as it shut and turned back to the room, taking it in. It was small, containing only two cots. There were no windows; otherwise, the room was sparse. A few blankets sat on each of the cots, and Asena moved to grab one. The princess wrapped it around herself, warming her still-damp body.

We divided the blankets amongst ourselves, coincidentally having the perfect amount for everyone. Our bodies were still cold and wet from traveling beneath the waves;

we needed warm and dry clothes. I made mental note to ask whoever brought us food if they had any clothing to spare. They'd already given us more than we asked for, and I hated to be a burden, but I knew if any of us caught ill, we would be at a disadvantage when the fire kingdom came.

It was inevitable that my sister would catch up to us.

"We should all take turns resting," Caspian suggested. He motioned to the two cots. "I'll rest first before the food comes. You should take the other cot," he said, looking to Ervin.

"Again, I'm old, not fragile," he protested.

"You have some of the greatest control over an element I've ever witnessed," Koraine said.

Ervin looked doubtfully toward her.

"I saw the way you made the fire dance and bend to your will without hesitation when you fought those drag-ons," she said.

"If that's true, then we need your strength rested," Caspian said, crossing his arms.

"Please try to rest," I offered. "We all need it at some point."

Ervin climbed slowly into the cot with his eyes narrowed on Caspian, but he didn't protest any further. The two men turned away from the group, closing their eyes to rest.

That left only Koraine and me, plus the princess who sat in the corner, scowling at us.

"Trust me, I don't want to be here with you as much as you don't want me here," she spat.

"I never said—"

She cut me off. "You didn't have to," she hissed.

"You know, it'd be easier if you just worked with us," Koraine argued.

"My home was left burning because of you," she said. "I had months before I was set to leave for Zetron and my wedding. Now, I'm fleeing my home, unsure if anything even remains to return to, and I am meeting my betrothed earlier than expected. Excuse me if I'm not groveling at your feet," she said, unable to hide her disgust.

I watched as Koraine flinched at the words.

"I'm sorry," Koraine said softly.

The princess refused to meet her eyes and rested her head against the wall, her eyes fluttering shut.

I motioned to Koraine to sit against one of the empty walls with me. We slid down to the floor, and she leaned in close. I wrapped an arm around her, holding her to my body and wrapping my blanket around her for heat.

"You don't have to do that," she said.

"I want to," I said.

Even trapped aboard a foreign ship with our spirits depleting, Koraine still looked like a goddess. Her vibrant blue eyes sparkled the way that the sun danced across the sea. Each time I found myself staring into them, I was truly wrapped up in her existence.

Fate had a cruel way of giving you your one desire and testing you at every turn. When the war ended, I knew it would be her and me standing together at the end of it. I would make her my queen, and she would help me restore the fire kingdom to what it once was.

CHAPTER 16
NYLA

Each day at sea made me long for Abelon. I missed the mild fall breeze compared to the freezing gusts of wind slamming into my face as I stood at the edge of the ship.

My dragon remained on deck, resting from chasing my brother.

Again we had failed, and I found myself growing far more bitter and frustrated. With each failure grew the inevitable fate that my father would punish my inadequacy.

Verus stirred behind me, and I turned to find Cyrus, cross-armed and watching me. His dark eyes bore into me, his permanent scowl enough for me to keep my distance.

He was the last person I wished for company from on this ship and certainly the last person I ever wished to marry.

I'd grown up watching his quarrels with Bellamy. The pair had despised each other, always vying for my father's attention.

Cyrus had lost his father, I knew, but ever since, it felt like he'd sought the approval of my own father. Beyond his duties as captain of the guard, his need for power and to stay in my father's good graces always outweighed his need to do what was right.

My stomach turned at the thought of marrying someone like that.

"They'll still be heading for Zetron," Cyrus said, walking up beside me.

"I know," I muttered, wishing he'd leave the moment he settled against the ship's railing.

"And what will you do then?" Cyrus asked, staring down at me.

"Do I even have a choice?" I asked, rolling my eyes. "If I return home without Bellamy, I am asking for my own death."

"You always have a choice," Cyrus answered.

I let out a breathy snort. My choices were nonexistent. I either returned home to face torture having failed, or I continued to chase my brother across the four kingdoms and drag him home to face our father's wrath.

For a moment, I knew what Cyrus felt, standing in Bellamy's shadow and begging for my father to see me was draining. Nothing I ever did would be good enough because I wasn't him.

I would never be powerful enough for his throne in his eyes.

My very being wished to prove him wrong. Even if, deep down, I knew it wouldn't matter, I needed this for myself, for everything I had endured and been through.

"We sail for Zetron," I said, turning back to face the sea.

Cyrus nodded and walked away, leaving me again to my peaceful solitude.

The longer Bellamy kept me from home, the more my resentment grew. It festered inside me, driving me to the brink of madness.

My knuckles turned white as I gripped the edge of the railing. I was sick of the ship and sick of being a prisoner to my own punishment.

Without my brother, I was nothing, but with him, all I felt anymore was agony.

I stood there, watching the mesmerizing waves, for what felt like hours until the sound of boots behind me broke my concentration.

"Princess," a guard said, timidly behind me. I turned to find the man watching me, body rigid. "Cyrus has asked that I escort you to dinner," the guard said. His eyes darted around nervously, waiting for my reaction.

The crew may not be privy to all details of our hunt, but they were not blind. They knew exactly how I felt about the captain joining.

"Dinner?" I echoed back.

"He's arranged for a meal with you, princess," the guard explained.

I let out a long sigh.

I moved away from the railing, allowing the guard to lead me.

It was easier to give in, to let go of the argument. I needed all my strength and energy focused on finding Bellamy. Cyrus was a thorn in my side I would deal with later. For the time being, I would play along as the helpless princess he had been promised.

The empty space at the end of the hall had been cleared

of guards. Only Cyrus sat at a table made for two people in the center of the room.

My escort quickly left my side, and I watched him hurry off down the hallway. He didn't remain longer than he needed.

I took a few steps forward, my sleek black dress dragging along the floor. I had changed the moment we got back from our failure into clothing that was not drenched from the Morwenian attacks.

Cyrus watched me with predatorial focus. I shifted uncomfortably but tried to regain my composure quickly.

The seat across from the captain was empty and pulled back. I took my place at the table and slid myself closer.

Plates were already set with the first real food I had seen in a long while.

"How?" I asked.

"My men respect me and would do anything I asked," Cyrus said.

My cheeks reddened. In my entire time aboard the ship, not a single guard had offered me a warm meal. I ate the same as the crew: the minimal food packed for the journey. I didn't mind, but the warm food had me missing home.

I pushed out the thought, remembering another of my failures—allowing the chef to escape with my brother.

"Why am I here?" I asked, crossing my arms. I left the plate untouched as Cyrus dug into his food. It was a form of rice and vegetables, steam rising from his plate. It was hard to tell what exactly made up the dish, a dark sauce covering it.

"Because you and I can help each other," Cyrus said, wiping his mouth with a nearby cloth.

He lifted a glass bottle from the center of the table and poured red liquid into his cup. He held it up to me, but I shook my head. Ignoring me, he continued to pour wine into my glass. I left it in its place.

"I doubt that," I scoffed. What could I have that Cyrus would want?

My father had promised him my hand in marriage, affording him the power he craved. He was captain of the guard, the honor of a dragon bestowed on him. There was not much more he could possibly need.

"What could I possibly help you with?" I ventured.

"Revenge," he said, sipping his wine and watching me closely.

I tried not to react, but my eyes naturally wandered to his neck. The scars were still vibrant and raw.

No matter how much power Cyrus managed to collect, he would never be Bellamy.

"I want your brother to pay," he stated.

"I won't help you," I stated. Even on my own journey, sorting through my anger, I did not wish to aid Cyrus on his warpath.

"I think you will," he said, leaning in, his dark eyes settling on me.

His light brown hair was swept back, and I found myself eyeing the crest on his shirt marking him captain of the guard.

"You don't want to be trapped in this marriage to me as much as I do not," Cyrus went on. "If you aid me in killing your brother, I can help you."

"You have nothing I desire," I snapped.

He sat back and let out a short laugh. His arms crossed

over his chest, covering the captain's crest. "Oh, but I do," he went on. "Your freedom."

I straightened my shoulders, watching Cyrus as he toyed with me.

"You're wrong," I said.

I didn't want him to think he had any control over me. My freedom was the thing I valued most, but to allow Cyrus to hold it in his hands would be damning myself.

"I don't think I am, princess. I think you would do anything for your freedom, the autonomy your own brother stole from you. We are alike more than you know. Your brother stole from me as well. Help me deliver the punishment he deserves. Help me, and I will give you back your freedom."

"What do you mean?" I asked, unable to stop myself. The temptation was far too great.

"I do not want to marry you as much as you do not wish to marry me, but neither of us has the power to act against your father. If Bellamy is no longer the heir to the throne, you would be next in line, making me prince consort. We could rule side-by-side, and you would never have to give up your freedom. You can take all the lovers you wish. We just need to be a united front in front of Abelon. Keep the nobles satisfied and solidify our power over the other kingdoms."

"My father would never allow you to kill him. He has ordered us to return Bellamy to Abelon," I started.

"War is coming, princess, and there are always casualties in war. I have no desire to disobey your father's direct orders."

I went to open my mouth, but Cyrus stopped me, leaning forward in his seat.

"Think on it, princess," Cyrus said. "I do not need your answer now."

He slid his chair back and stood before stalking from the room. His boots clattered against the floor, and I was left in eerie silence as their echoes trailed off.

I didn't wish to marry the captain, but was I willing to sacrifice my own brother for that freedom?

Would Cyrus even uphold his end of his promise?

My eyes stung, and I squeezed them tightly shut, imagining what everything would have been like had Bellamy stayed in Abelon.

I wouldn't be forced into chasing him across the kingdoms, and I wouldn't be forced into marrying someone I despised.

Every single time I tried to convince myself to give my brother a chance, it always circled back to the same thought. All of this was Bellamy's doing. Everything that happened was because of him. I couldn't ignore that sinking feeling in my gut.

One thing remained true. My brother was the reason for all my pain and suffering and the restraints placed on me.

Every single dream I ever had was washed away in one moment when that whip of fire hit my skin.

I cringed, thinking about the strike.

I tried to bottle up the feelings and push them away. I could not allow Cyrus to get to me the way he already was. My only task was to find my brother and bring him home to my father.

If I did that, there was a chance he'd give me back my

freedom. The rightful heir would have returned, and Bellamy would make things right. My father would punish him, but he couldn't truly kill his own heir, could he?

Without Koraine in the picture, Bellamy could be the balance Abelon needed again.

All I had to do was separate him from the woman who had dragged him away.

KORAINE

Aboard the ship, we waited patiently in the confinement of the room the crew had provided us. My brother didn't sleep long before waking and insisting someone else rest. Ervin snored away while Asena finally agreed to take a moment.

I still sat beside the prince, my stomach occasionally growling. "When did he say he'd be back?" I asked.

"He should have sent food by now," my brother muttered.

Bellamy's thumb stroked my hand, and I watched as his eyebrows furrowed deeply.

"They should've come," he said quietly.

"Something isn't right," I said, my stomach growing queasy. It wasn't the swaying of the ship over the waves causing my unease.

Bellamy stood, walking over to the door. His hand found the handle and gave it a light tug.

"He said stay out. I don't think—"

I froze as Bellamy tugged again on the door, harder this time.

It didn't budge.

My heart stopped and my breath hitched, waiting for it to be some type of mistake. There had to be a simple explanation as to why we were locked in.

Bellamy pounded a fist on the door. "Excuse me," he shouted.

I pulled my legs in close, hugging them to my chest. The wood against my back felt cold, and a shiver ran down my spine. We may be stuck, and it was entirely my fault. I'd led us straight to the danger.

The shouting woke both the princess and Ervin. Asena sat up in her cot, her eyes frantically finding the door.

"Are we locked in?" the princess asked, her tone turning dark and accusing.

Bellamy didn't answer; instead, he tugged on the metal door, but it did not budge.

"Not a single one of you tried the door before now?" the princess asked, sliding off the cot and stalking over to the door.

"I didn't see you rushing to try it either," I accused.

I was sick and tired of being blamed for every little thing that inconvenienced the princess. We'd saved her from a siege on her kingdom, protected her from multiple attacks by the fire kingdom, and we were on our way to the kingdom where her betrothed awaited her.

She folded her arms and scowled.

"Fighting won't help us," Caspian scolded. He moved to stand by the door with Bellamy, and together, the two combined their strength to push and pull, but still, it didn't move.

I glanced around for way out, but there were no windows or other doors.

"Can we break through the wall?" I asked, realizing the walls were made of wood and not metal.

"By the time we broke through and made a big enough gap for us to fit, they would know what we were doing. They'd certainly be awaiting us on the other side," Caspian noted.

"What about your fire?" the princess asked.

"No," Bellamy said, his eyes narrowing.

"We would burn this whole ship down," Ervin chimed in. "The wood would spread the flames faster than we would be able to control by the time we burned a hole big enough to escape."

"We can't be trapped. This has to be a mistake," I said. Surely, we'd missed something, an easy explanation for why the door was kept locked.

"Why would they want to trap us? We already wanted them to take us to their king. It doesn't make sense," I added.

Bellamy paced the room, and I could see his fire rising to the surface. He was growing frustrated, and his fiery temper was doing nothing to soothe that.

I stood from where I sat and walked over to the prince.

I quickly took Bellamy's hand and spun him to face me. The wild look in his eyes told me he was struggling to keep all his frustration bottled inside.

"These feelings are only temporary," I whispered, reminding him of the same words his mother used to say.

His eyes quickly found mine, and I saw his features soften. He nodded and slowly took a step back.

"They didn't bear the king's crest," Asena said, her eyes widening.

"You believe they aren't guards for the king?" Caspian asked

"I've never encountered a guard from the kingdom of Zetron who didn't bear the crest of the crown. I'm just saying it's a possibility," Asena explained. "One I do not wish to discover the consequences of."

"Do you think they're from the fire kingdom?" Caspian asked.

We all glanced to Bellamy, but it wasn't the prince who answered.

"No. I've lived in the fire kingdom for many years, more than you've all been alive. I've never once encountered an Abelonian with features like theirs. They're definitely from Zetron," Ervin said, his voice low.

"We need a way out of here," Caspian said, cursing beneath his breath. He ran a hand through his longer black hair—it was the first I noticed that my brother did not have his hair tied back.

He looked less like the proper warrior my father groomed him into and more like himself.

Before we could continue arguing and debating, the metal door opened. Each of us raised our arms and stood ready in defense.

A tiny, slim woman slipped through the door, and it slammed behind her just as quickly as it had opened. She carried a tray with bread and fruit. Her eyes widened when she saw each of us ready to attack, and the tray of food dropped out of her hands. She backed up toward the door and fumbled to regain her composure.

"Wait," I said, reaching a hand out.

Her eyes darted between us, and she stood as close to the door as possible, closing herself off.

"What do they want with us?" I asked, realizing we had yet again found ourselves captured like prey.

"I shouldn't," she mumbled softly.

Bellamy moved faster than I could comprehend and grabbed the woman's arm, pulling her away from the door. His hand quickly ignited with flames, and he held them close to the woman, tugging her tightly against him.

"Bellamy," I said, my eyes widening.

"She knows something," Asena chimed in. "If she won't answer our questions, we'll force it out of her."

Bellamy glanced from the princess back to me, my face filled with horror.

"I don't know anything," she insisted, her voice quiet and small. "Please, I am indentured to them."

"Indentured?" I asked.

Bellamy held the flame close to her face, and I watched her eyes nervously glance between it and myself.

"Let her go," I insisted.

Rage still filled his features, and I saw the internal struggle he faced. "You aren't him," I said, seeing bits of the ruthless prince the world knew.

His eyes softened as if he finally truly saw me playing for him. Memories of our final days and Avalon flashed through my mind, the battle between him and Cyrus, Bellamy, unable to tame flames that live within him.

I didn't want this woman to end up the same as Cyrus.

The flames quickly extinguished, and he let her go. She scrambled back toward the door.

"Wait, please," Caspian insisted. "We won't hurt you," he added, glancing toward Bellamy with an icy stare.

My brother had finally been growing used to the idea of Bellamy, but now, I saw that washed away within seconds. His distrust for the prince had come rushing back.

"They're taking you to the market," she said in a hushed tone.

"Market?" the princess asked, and my stomach felt heavy.

"I've said too much. If they know I've spoken to you, I'll lose my tongue for it. Please," she begged.

I recognized the terrified look on her face and knew she wasn't lying.

Whoever these men were, they were ruthless, and they certainly weren't guards for the king.

The woman quickly moved her hand, and I heard metal click out of place as the door popped open. She quickly opened it and slid through, shutting it tightly behind her. I heard the same metal sliding, and the door locked into place.

I knew it was hopeless; we would never be able to break through the door. Only someone able to manipulate metal could open and close it.

"What market are they taking us to?" Caspian asked the moment she disappeared.

"They are taking us to auction, aren't they?" Ervin said, his tone stern. "They're going to sell us to the highest bidder on the underground market.".

Smugglers.

My heart sank, and I felt like someone had stabbed me in

the chest. All the memories of smugglers and Abelon came rushing back. I felt like I couldn't breathe, my hands scrambling to my chest and neck, pulling at the damp shirt clinging to my skin. I felt like I was choking on water again as the feeling of being thrown overboard and left to die came rushing over me.

My breath picked up as the feeling sank its claws into me.

Bellamy quickly rushed to my side, wrapping an arm around me and pulling me close into his body. I managed a single deep breath and inhaled the smell of the prince holding me. His touch brought me back to reality, and slowly, I chased away anxiety that had threatened to consume me.

"It's okay. It's going to be okay," Bellamy assured me quietly.

My cheeks reddened as all eyes fell on me.

"Our best hope is to escape when they move us from the ship to the market," Caspian assessed.

"And if we don't?" I asked.

"Then they'll sell us to the highest bidder for whatever twisted reason they wish to purchase us," Bellamy growled.

"I have a feeling they know exactly who they have on this ship," Ervin said, his head hanging.

I watched all the joy drain from the old man's face.

It was a full day before we saw another crew member. The

group was growing impatient and frustrated after a full night's rest on small cots or sleeping on the hard floor.

I'd curled up against Bellamy for warmth on the floor while Ervin and Asena took the cots.

Caspian had slept sitting upright, prepared to spring into action if the door opened once again. He'd remained in that same position until the door slowly cracked open the following morning.

Water sprung to life in his hands, and I watched him lash it forward to grab hold of whoever was stepping through the door.

"Ah—" the woman yelled, stumbling forward.

"You're back?" I asked, recognizing the same woman as the day before.

She held a tray of breakfast foods and lowered it to the ground, sliding it toward us.

"I already explained: I work for the crew on this ship. I do whatever they ask, and that includes serving meals to the prisoners."

"Are there more like us?" Caspian asked, withdrawing his water.

The woman rubbed at her wrist where it grasped her. "That's not for me to say," she answered, her eyes narrowing.

"And what is for you to say?" Bellamy snapped, joining me by my side and hovering protectively behind me.

I knew this woman wouldn't hurt us—I felt it deep in my heart—but I still relaxed at Bellamy's protective presence.

His hand found the small of my back, and I leaned back slightly into it. His touch was warm against the skin exposed between my skirt and tank top.

"They'll punish me if I say anything more," the woman argued. "I must go."

She hurried toward the door, unlocking and quickly slipping back through it.

Bellamy let out a loud sigh.

"Useless," Asena muttered, pulling her knees to her chest on her cot. "We are never freeing ourselves from this."

"We just have to wait for our opportunity," Bellamy said.

"For once, I agree with the prince," Caspian added. "If we wait until they move us, we will have an advantage. We will be able to use the sea, and we will no longer be trapped in the confines of a wooden ship where fire would consume us all if we used it."

"And if it doesn't work?" Asena asked.

"Then they sell us to the highest bidder," Bellamy muttered under his breath.

I sucked in a gasp and grabbed his hand. I needed the comfort, the reassurance that no matter what, he wouldn't leave my side. He was my husband, and I did not care to find myself separated from him again.

"We cannot be much further from where they plan to take us," Caspian noted. "They may move us off the ship today."

"And when they do? What is our plan?" Asena asked.

"Get as far from these smugglers as possible," Ervin snorted.

"Fight with everything we have left," Bellamy said at the same time.

I shifted uncomfortably, knowing most of us were still drained from fleeing. Without proper rest, we would be lucky to last long in a true fight.

My own energy felt drained just from safely navigating under the waves the day before.

Our elemental abilities were like a well of energy, and when we spent that energy, it needed time to replenish. The harder we pushed without rest, the more we approached drying up the well of power.

Asena rolled her eyes, turning her body to rest against the wall the cot sat against.

I watched as she became withdrawn. I wanted to assure her we'd still safely deliver her to the earth king, but I knew I couldn't promise that. Even after all her resistance to helping us, I never wished for her life to become uprooted.

I'd gone through the same, and even though it brought me Bellamy, I knew there was a piece of myself I'd never get back.

"Rest," Caspian ordered, walking by me. "We all need it."

"How can I rest when I know what's coming?" I asked, meeting his gaze.

"We have to try," he sighed.

Bellamy placed a hand on my shoulder. "He's right."

Caspian moved to pick up the tray of food left behind and passed it out to our group.

I gladly accepted an apple, turning it in my hand before taking a bite. Bellamy took the remaining apple and followed me to sit against the wall again.

I felt useless. How could I sit there knowing the fate we'd meet in the near future?

I wanted to protect the people around me, but I couldn't keep them from this. We'd walked straight into the smugglers' grasp, and they'd welcomed us with open arms.

Our exhaustion and desperation had made us naive.

I leaned against Bellamy, biting my way through the apple.

"If we make it through this alive, I want a proper wedding," he whispered, his voice low.

"What?" I asked, glancing to him with my eyes wide.

"You deserve a proper celebration, one where everyone from Abelon and Morwen comes to celebrate our love. When this war is over, that is going to be the first thing I do," Bellamy said.

"Since when do you care for weddings or celebrations?" I asked, furrowing my brows.

"Since I met the woman who made me see there was a way out of the darkness."

My heart stopped for a moment, and I fumbled to respond.

Bellamy filled my stomach with butterflies. Every moment spent with him, I fell harder for the prince.

He leaned in to kiss my forehead.

"Now rest," he ordered. "I want you by my side when we fight our way out of here."

It was a few hours before we heard men gathering outside our door.

Their boots gave them away before we saw them, echoing against the wooden boards of the floor.

I tried to listen for voices but heard nothing. It was impossible to tell how many gathered outside the door.

"Now's our chance," Bellamy hissed, jumping to his feet.

I scrambled to stand beside him.

"We should wait until we are off the ship," Caspian argued. "We have no idea how many men stand in our way of getting off this ship, and we still have no idea where they've brought us."

"If we wait, we may never be able to escape. We have no idea how secure we'll be once they come in here to move us. This may be our only chance," Bellamy countered.

I nodded my agreement. If we waited, we risked not being able to escape our new confines.

Caspian gave a single firm nod, and both Asena and Ervin moved from the cots, ready to fight.

An icy chill ran down my spine as I remembered her torturing Bellamy.

The metal door clicked open, and everyone glanced wildly at each other, backing away from the door. My back hit my brother as he pushed in front of me.

I raised my hands defensively, ready to protect myself if needed.

I didn't get the chance to try—the moment the door opened, we were restrained. Metal shackles flew through the air, manipulated by the smugglers come to transport us. My arms were pinned to my side, a metal band wrapped tight around my body.

I struggled against the restraints, but it was no use.

I had no power over metal.

Rodrir laughed as he stepped through the doorway, and

his men moved into the room behind him. More metal flew through the air and wrapped around our ankles. The tight metal knocked me off balance, and I fell to the floor, a familiar feeling washing over me.

I'd been a victim of smugglers before, and I knew how ruthless they could be.

"What do you want with us?" Caspian demanded.

Many of the men in the room snickered as they watched us with pure amusement. My heart raced, and my arms and ankles burned as I wiggled against the restraints.

"Did you genuinely think it would be that easy?" Rodrir asked. "The moment we spotted Abelonians and Morwenians together, we knew exactly who was approaching our ship. Word travels fast from the fire kingdom. There is a hefty price on your heads," Rodrir drawled the last word.

"Let us go," I demanded.

"Quiet, or I'll gag you," he threatened.

"Why would you do this? You know who we travel with. You know the king would pay a hefty price for her. Why would you take us to the market when you could've had that?" Caspian asked.

I could hear the last bit of hope slipping away with his words.

"There are many willing to pay far more than our useless king ever would for the princess of Morwen. Her father is responsible for many Abelonian deaths, and there are many who wish to see his pain when his daughter's head is sent back to him. I could say the same for the prince here," Rodrir snarled.

I managed to sit up, my eyes widening. It was a struggle

to back away, scooting myself across the wooden floor. Bellamy sat watching the men surround us. It was no use; there was nothing we could possibly do.

CHAPTER 18

BELLAMY

I FOUGHT against the men as they carried each one of us from the ship. My arms were restrained, but I could still manage to make small balls of fire with my hands.

I lashed out, letting the small flame grow and fly toward the guard picking up Koraine.

My flames found their mark, hitting the man and knocking him over. He clutched at his side, a large, singed hole burnt through his clothing. The skin underneath was vibrant red from the burn.

Another smuggler quickly manipulated metal that shaped around my fist, covering my hands. I tried and failed to resist, my flames no use with my arms so close to my body, my hands left useless.

Silently, the guards help the old man to his feet, walking him out the door.

It took two men to carry me off the ship. I continually fought, making it difficult for them to contain me. A guard close behind carried Koraine, and I let out a sigh of relief knowing she was nearby.

We let our exhaustion blind our judgment. The promise of land and the earth kingdom had outweighed our logic. We never should have trusted a stray ship in the sea.

I should've prevented it. My temper and frustration rose the more I realized I could've stopped everything.

The ship was tied to a makeshift dock jutting out from the beach. I caught a glimpse of the vast green fields to the west and the forest line to the east, just beyond the small strip of beach.

The greenery of Zetron was more stunning in person than the stories made it out to be, like walking through a dream during the day. I looked around, soaking in the sight of plants and other vegetation.

It would've been easy to admire, had I not been restrained and dragged through the sand.

I ventured that the market could not be far; the established dock suggested they traveled by foot. Five prisoners would be hard to move a long distance without any form of transportation.

We moved up the beach at the direction of the smugglers, and once all five of us were removed from the ship, the men sat us down in the grassy area bordering the sand.

"Do not move," one of the men commanded.

Rodrir stalked up the beach, his earth-toned clothing the same uniform as the day before. At quick glance, anyone nearby would believe these were royal guards.

Rustling in the nearby tree line caught my attention, and Koraine gave me a nervous look.

"Bellamy," she said, her voice trembling.

My heart ached at my inability to reach out to her. Her

face appeared distraught, which was only heightened by the sound of foliage crunching as something approached.

"I know, my moon," I said softly.

"What was that?" Caspian asked.

"I heard nothing," Ervin said.

"It's likely an animal," Asena scoffed, any warmth the princess had found in our company far gone.

A stray tear slipped down Koraine's cheek. I wanted to reach out and wipe it away, but the metal on my hands made it impossible.

"This is your fault," Asena accused. "If you hadn't told them who I was, they never would have realized the value in selling us."

"I know," Koraine said, hanging her head. "This is my fault. I just wanted to help and find us refuge from the sea."

"It's every last one of our fault. Any one of us could have recognized everything wrong with that ship, and not a single one of us did. We all agreed to board that ship. We believed what we wanted to see," I snapped.

More rustling had all five of our heads snapping toward the trees, and the argument dissipated.

I heard the low growl and snapping of twigs before I saw it.

The green glowing eyes were the first feature I could make out as the beast stepped out of the woods.

I tried to slide myself closer to Koraine as Caspian moved himself in front of Ervin and Asena.

The large feline stepped out of the forest. It stood at least seven or eight feet tall, its black fur as dark as midnight, its eerie green eyes boring into me.

The moment it took us in, the beast let out the deepest growl.

"Hold," Rodrir shouted.

The feline stopped in place and knelt to the ground, waiting for its next command.

I swallowed hard, realizing the beast was a pantherus, the beast gifted by Aeris.

Those worthy of the creatures in Zetron were gifted the fierce feline, similar to the dragons that roamed Abelon and the sea serpents of Morwen.

Two fangs dipped just beneath the creature's lips. I knew if the pantherus sank them into one of us, there would be no surviving it.

Rodrir walked over to where the beast knelt. He placed a hand against the creature's side, and a smile grew on his face.

"You've never seen one, have you?" he asked, staring directly at me.

I kept my mouth shut, refusing to answer his question. Instead, I spat on the ground in front of him. He jumped back, eyes narrowed with fury.

He lifted a hand, ready to strike, but dropped it just as quickly.

"I think she'll ride with me," he drawled, his eyes landing on Koraine.

I immediately writhed against the metal that held my arms and feet in place. I couldn't let him touch Koraine, my temper once again getting the better of me. And now, Koraine would suffer for it.

"No," I shouted.

"We have long travels. We should get started," he answered, ignoring my plea.

"Don't you dare touch her," I growled.

Caspian balked at his own restraints, almost successfully standing but falling to the ground once more when Rodrir stalked over and kicked at his lower leg.

He grabbed Koraine's arm and dragged her across the grass. She protested and tried everything to escape his grasp, but it was no use.

It pained me to watch.

Asena observed in silent horror. I cursed and threw myself forward, attempting to reach her, but it was no use.

Smugglers made their way up the beach and restrained each of us. More creatures emerged from the forest line, and the men dragged us, lifting each of us onto the backs of the beasts.

Two men lifted me, draping me over the feline. My legs and head hung over either side. On my stomach, there was nothing I can do but allow myself to be transported. Even if I could find my way off the feline, I was still restrained by metal, and it would be impossible to rescue the rest of the group.

We had missed our chance.

The jostling on the pantherus made my still-healing wounds ache. I could still feel the faint bruises scattered across my chest and rib cage.

A man sat behind me on the back of the beast, smelling of the sea. The lingering stench of fish filled my nostrils, and I gagged at the nausea washing over me, amplified by my growing dizziness, my head hanging. I tried to take deep breaths and use what little energy I had to lift my head and search for Koraine.

Each attempt was a failure.

"Where is she?" I hissed at the man behind me.

"Shut your mouth," he barked.

"What did you do with her?" I asked.

I managed to set my gaze on Caspian, Ervin, and Asena, but I could not see Koraine. Panic washed over me, and dread filled every inch of my body. I knew they would've separated us regardless, but I still felt responsible. He could be doing anything to her, and I had no way of stopping it.

I felt powerless.

One of the beasts trotted beside the one I was on, and I lifted my head to find Caspian glaring back at me.

"She's okay. I can see her," he mouthed.

My muscles relaxed only a little, but the reassurance did help.

To my displeasure, Caspian went back to ignoring me. I knew gaining his trust wouldn't come easily, but I had seen hope when I fought by his side. All of that had faded the moment I showed who I truly was. Letting my temper out for even a second broke that bit of trust again.

The journey through the forest felt like it took hours. I was hungry and exhausted, and the bumping up and down did nothing to help.

Occasionally, I lifted my head to catch Caspian's gaze, but each time, I found no words would come out. There was nothing I could say that would change his mind.

A high-pitched yell came from the front of the group, and my heart stopped. The voice that carried through the air sounded like Koraine.

I thrashed on the back of the beast, trying to get a better look. It was near impossible to see her, my head unable to catch a glimpse in the direction of where she traveled. The neck and head of the pantherus blocked my view.

I needed to know she was okay.

I used all my strength to throw myself backwards. I slid off the back of the pantherus and managed to connect my feet with the ground first. Without balance, I fell over, and as quickly as I could, I sat up, searching for Koraine.

The entire group halted their travel. Already, the smuggler was jumping off the back of the beast to grab me.

He directed me up onto my feet and waited for another smuggler to help him lift me. Finally, I was able to get a good glance at my surroundings. That was when I spotted her on the back of Rodrir's pantherus. I saw the pink handprint on her cheek and knew instantly it had been her cry of pain.

"You bastard," I shouted, throwing myself forward.

I fell over again, and my face slammed into the forest floor.

Pain shot through my face, and when I rolled over, I felt sticky, warm liquid dripping down my cheek. I felt the sting of a cut right near my brow.

Two men yanked me off the ground and lifted me swiftly. I found myself back securely on the panther.

The smugglers resumed our travel, and the group remained silent the rest of the journey. My mind was reeling, anger threatening to consume me.

I wanted to kill him for what he had done.

My temper was hard to extinguish. It would fester until I was no longer able to bottle it up inside me. The moment I

broke free of my shackles, I would find Rodrir, and I would
make him pay.

CHAPTER 19
NYLA

I WAS CALLED up at the sighting of a ship our fleet was on track to meet. My guards ran across the deck, frantically preparing to make contact. Cyrus had ordered we board the ship to search for my brother and to demand any information they may have.

I agreed it was the best strategy.

The ship across from us bore the flag of the earth kingdom. My father was not at war with Zetron, but I knew he would be soon. There was no reason to suspect we would be received hostile, but Cyrus instructed the men to be ready to burn the ship to ash if needed.

I tried to train my face to give nothing away. I need to be the Princess of Abelon, the fierce princess of fire who would incinerate every last one of them if needed.

I reminded myself why I was doing this. My life and freedom were the price. If I did not locate Bellamy soon, my time would run out.

That wasn't a chance I was willing to take.

"I do the talking," Cyrus command.

"You are not the Princess of Abelon," I noted.

"And you are not trained in strategy or negotiations. I do not trust that you will do what's necessary if it comes down to it," Cyrus said.

"You do not trust me at all, and that is why we can never help each other," I sneered, crossing my arms.

The captains forehead creased as his brows furrowed. I knew I had hit a nerve.

The ship came close enough for us to place a short plank across and board. Two guards held my hands and helped me climb. I refused to glance down at the sea underneath my feet, my steps quick as I crossed.

I rushed to the other side and leapt off the board onto the ship.

The crew that greeted us was smaller than I expected. The ship, at a glance, looked large enough to house at least thirty men, but only ten to fifteen stood in front of us.

"Good evening," Cyrus started, his voice deceivingly welcoming.

I frowned as all the men looked to Cyrus. Not a single one nodded in my direction.

"We are searching for stowaways," he explained. "We would like to know if you have any information, and I would like to search your ship," he stated.

I let out a soft scoff. Why would these men allow us search their ship unprompted?

A dreadful feeling started building in my chest, anticipating that they would force our hand. "And what would the stowaways look like?" one of the men asked, breaking the silence.

"I search for the Prince of Abelon and the Princess of Morwen, who travel with a small group."

One of the guards across from me shifted uncomfortably. He shoved his hands into the pocket of his brown trousers and kept his eyes glued to the deck.

"I think we would know if we had a prince or a princess among us," the guard chuckled.

I caught the way his voice went up at the end, and I knew Cyrus did as well.

"And I think you know something," Cyrus drawled. I heard the underlying threat, and the others did too, their demeanor shifting.

"We don't want trouble," the man said.

"Tell us where they went," Cyrus demanded.

"We don't know of a prince or princess," the man said once more.

"You know something," I cut in.

I was sick of being treated like I couldn't handle the responsibility. I was the Princess of Abelon, the most ruthless kingdom in the world, and I would be damned if I stood aside and let the men do all the talking.

"I know nothing of stowaways," the man hurriedly said.

His hands fidgeted in front of him, and I watched as the other man glared at him.

"Search the ship," I commanded.

Many of my men had filed across the plank behind us, filling the deck of the ship. They hesitated to move at my command.

I cast a glance to Cyrus, and he studied me. The captain seemed to weigh my disobedience over my willingness to do what it would take to find Bellamy.

He gave a slight nod, and the guards instantly spring to action.

They spread across the ship, searching every corner. Nothing and nowhere would be left unchecked. If Bellamy had taken refuge on the ship, we would know soon. I paced the length of the deck, waiting for my guards to complete their search. The ship was large, with a plethora of rooms.

Agonizing minutes passed until one of the guards appeared on deck and stood close to Cyrus. He whispered his report, and I impatiently waited. It irked me that the guards consistently ignored my existence, only acknowledging me when Cyrus was absent.

My foot tapped on the wooden boards of the deck.

"He isn't here," Cyrus stated.

I watched as relief washed over the men huddled together at the side of the ship. It was like a large weight had been physically lifted off their shoulders. Their muscles eased, and they stood straight and confident.

I watched the same man who had nervously fidgeted before go back to picking at his knuckles, like no one would notice the involuntary movement.

If these men knew nothing, why did they look relieved at our failure?

Something inside me snapped, and red fury filled my vision.

I stormed across the ship, grabbing hold of the nervous man's collar and tugging him away from the group. Before he realized what was happening, I already had flames in my palm, held to his neck.

"Where is he?" I snarled.

"Nyla," Cyrus warned.

The lack of my title did nothing to soothe my anger.

"Where is he?" I repeated, holding the flames closer.

The fire licked at his skin, and I could see him flinch each time the scorching flames hit his neck.

"Nyla," Cyrus warned again. "Let the man go."

His command infuriated me. Instead, I ignored it. My flames grew hotter and more unruly, reacting to my temper.

Impulsively, I let my fire touch his skin for far longer than I should've. It burned him, leaving behind blisters I knew would fester if not treated immediately.

The man still held his tongue. Torturing him would get me nowhere. The man would end up dead long before he gave me the information I sought.

I would not give him that wish or turn him into some martyr for these Zetronians. I would not be the final piece that incited war between our kingdoms.

I tossed him aside, and he fell to the ground, clutching at his neck. The other men began to rush forward, but I let my flames grow in both of my palms.

"Do not move," I said.

My moves were calculated. I needed to uphold the façade to get the information I wanted, to buy myself time to think of a new tactic, one that would finally lead to my brother.

"I would listen to her," Cyrus warned, a smug look on his face.

A movement behind Cyrus caught my eye, metal flying through the air—a small band that hurled toward Cyrus.

"Cyrus—" I started, barely getting the warning out in time.

He noticed the way my eyes glanced behind him and

side stepped while turning around. The metal flew past him and landed harmlessly next to the group of men.

I watched closely for any sign of movement, but they remained still.

Cyrus stepped forward, stroking the stubble on his chin. The moment he caught sight of the man I had burned, a satisfied smile grew across his lips.

"If you do not give us the information we seek, you will end up far worse than him," Cyrus warned. "And if a single one of you tries something like that again, I promise, I will personally burn each of you staked to the helm of this ship, slow and painfully."

No, that hadn't been the plan.

Flames ignited in his fists, and his eyes narrowed on the crew.

What was he doing?

My heart stopped as nausea washed over me, realizing what I had done to the man on the ground.

It truly sank in.

His skin was mutilated by my hand.

I had let my flames act in anger.

"Tell us where the prince and princess went, and we will guarantee your safe passage," Cyrus stated.

"We don't know," one of the men growled.

Each of the men stood tall before us, but I saw something else behind their eyes. Terror took hold of them as they realized their lives hung the balance.

"If you do not tell us where they went, you and the ship will be reduced to nothing more than ashes," Cyrus threatened.

His menacing tone sent a shiver down my spine.

Everything silently fell into place. I'd been used.

Cyrus had nudged me into embracing my fury. He used me to elicit the fear he wanted from the crew. My stomach turned, realizing I had been nothing more than a pawn.

He never had seen me as an equal.

I kept my mouth shut, unwilling to show the crew any weakness. I was committed to seeing this through and finding my brother, regardless of my naive mistakes.

My eyes darted nervously between Cyrus and the men. I didn't want to see them burn, but I knew he would uphold his threat.

None of the men answered his demand. Instead, they watched him in silence.

Cyrus's hands moved faster than I could track, a stream of fire flying toward the mast. Ignited, it rapidly began to burn.

"No," one of the men shouted.

"Are you remembering something?" Cyrus asked, toying with the men. The cruel amusement in his eyes had me backing away a step.

The man held his tongue.

"Goddesses damn you," another man growled through gritted teeth.

Cyrus sent more streams of flame across the ship, burning it little by little. I watched as horror washed over each of the crew member's faces. I wanted to cry out and stop him, but it'd be futile.

The threat had gone too far. I wanted to return to our ship.

"Just tell us where they are," I said, trying hard to hide the pleading behind my words.

I felt torn inside. The hunt for Bellamy was dividing me in half. I no longer recognized the monstrous piece of me that tortured that man for information.

"Tell us where the prince went," I demanded, more force behind my words this time.

I tried to keep my voice steady and hide the growing panic. Silence hung in the air, and more small fires appeared. The ship wouldn't be able to handle much more.

"The market," one of the men blurted out, earning glares from the others.

My eyes widened as I glanced to Cyrus. He cocked his head, flames still alive on his hands.

"What market?" I asked, my words rushed.

"They're being taken to the market in Zetron to be sold to the highest bidder. If you want them so bad, go buy them yourself," the man spat.

A cruel and wicked grin was plastered on Cyrus' face. I couldn't tell if his satisfaction was from knowing where Bellamy was or watching as the crew finally caved to our demands.

"I suppose we are continuing our way to Zetron," Cyrus said, and I hated the way his words made me feel vile. "I will keep my promise and allow you safe passage."

My brows raised; I could hardly believe what I was hearing. Never in my life had I known Cyrus to show mercy.

He beckoned for me to follow him back over the plank to our ship. I walked carrying the skirt of my dress, careful not to trip on it as I climbed up onto the plank. He was the first back on our ship, and I followed behind him. Our guards made their way across and pulled the board back, the rest of the fleet awaiting our command.

Cyrus gave the signal that we would continue.

"Wait," one of the men on the other ship called out. "You promised them safe passage. Put out the fires."

I looked back toward the ship, realizing the mast was almost completely destroyed, other portions of the ship still burning. Surrounded by flames was normal for me. It hadn't even crossed my mind to put out the fires before we left.

Cyrus ignored their plight. He stalked across the ship and demanded one of the guards have our ship sailing for Zetron at an impossible speed. I followed, my heart racing as I listened to the men behind me call out. Our ship began to move, putting distance between us and the earth kingdom ship.

"Why aren't you helping them?" I asked Cyrus.

"I upheld my promise. It is not my fault they cannot put out their own fires."

"Cyrus, their ship will burn," I said, my voice shaking.

"You should've thought of that when you threatened them with your own flames," he snarled, not a hint of sympathy on his face.

My eyes narrowed as I clenched my fist. I stalked back across the deck to the railing, facing the ship that was now burning.

I held up my hands and tried to feel the flames I could still see dancing in the distance, but strong hands grabbed my arms and pinned them to my side. I was pulled back from the railing, and I kicked out as someone lifted me off my feet.

"Put me down," I demanded indignantly.

"No," Cyrus snarled in my ear.

"I am not a child, Cyrus. Do not treat me as such," I argued.

"You are acting childish and ignoring my orders," he said. "These are my ships and my men, and I will not have insubordination."

I writhed in his grasp, but it was no use. Cyrus was far stronger than me.

I was forced to watch as the flames grew out of control on the ship. Minutes passed, and the further we went, the smaller the ship became until it was but a small speck in the distance. When Cyrus finally let me go, all I could see was the smoke that rose in the air.

CHAPTER 20

KORAINE

THE MARKET WAS NOT what I imagined. I had envisioned a place built underground by earth manipulators, dark and filled with secrets.

Instead, as the pantheruses approached, I held my breath as I took in the palace-like structure in front of me.

It was built atop a hill, the estate surrounded by a silver metal wall. I saw no gate to access the inside but spotted men wearing similar uniforms positioned across the wall.

The beasts approached, and I startled when Rodrir held up a fist, signaling for us to halt. I waited anxiously, Rodrir signaling to one of the men posted on the wall.

Suddenly, solid metal shifted as a slice of the wall sunk into the ground and left enough room for us to pass through. The moment our group was fully inside the confines of the wall, it went right back into place.

I craned my neck to catch a glimpse at the rest of the group.

Bellamy was draped across one of the beasts, similar to my brother on his own. Asena sat watching, taking in her surroundings, pure fury written on her face. My stomach sank when my eyes landed on Ervin on the back of the final beast, this head hung.

Our group was met by men again, dressed in the same uniforms. Rodrir slid off the back of his pantherus and grabbed my arm, yanking me down. I barely caught myself, my feet landing on the ground as I fell against him. The rest of my group were dragged off the creatures and handed off to the men before us. One stepped forward to take me, but Rodrir held up a hand.

"I will deliver them myself," he demanded.

"That's not how this works," the man in front of us said.

He spoke in a calm and steady tone, but I heard the stern command behind the words.

Rodrir's grip on my arm tightened.

All the stories I had heard about the market were false. It was not the horrifying and grimy place many spoke of. Instead, it was a fortified estate, hosting only the richest of patrons.

"I'm taking these ones to the Warden myself."

"Fine, but it's your life you're gambling with," the man sneered.

A cold feeling washed over me, and I shivered. I had no desire to meet the Warden, and I had a sinking feeling nothing good could come from it.

Earth manipulators removed the metal bindings from our ankles, allowing us the freedom to walk. I noticed the redness that now adorned my skin, my ankles burning with each step I took. My arms, though, remained pinned to my side.

We were forced inside by the men who took possession of us. I tried to move closer to Bellamy, but Rodrir kept a tight grip on my arm and guided me away from him. The others were afforded the freedom to walk on their own, but we remained boxed in by men surrounding us.

Inside, I found a pristine white room with high ceilings and a staircase in front of me. The white and black marble floor was polished enough that I imagined I could see my reflection in it if I tried. Men and women walked freely in the grand entry, all wearing the matching uniforms. It made me nauseous to realize how many impersonated Zetron guards were praying on innocent people.

We were guided to the staircase and directed up. The marble steps echoed our footsteps, and the sound rang through the entry. For such a large estate, it was oddly quiet.

Where were all the people who came to buy illegal goods? Where were the prisoners they kept at the market?

I couldn't shake the awful feeling that had my chest constricting.

Asena walked close beside me, and I caught her giving me a side long glance. I snorted under my breath.

"What?" she demanded, catching it.

"Are you ever going to stop fighting us?" I asked. She bit her lip, and her forehead creased.

"I'm going to lose my head because of you," she growled. "If you had never come back to Morwen, none of us would be here."

My cheeks flushed and my breath caught.

"Don't listen to her," Caspian whispered.

It was too late, guilt spreading its roots and eating at me.

All I ever wanted was to keep my family and people safe,

and all I had done was bring them destruction. Every time I tried to do what was right, it only made things worse.

"Shut your mouth," Rodrir growled, his sharp nails sinking into my upper arm.

I let out a wince at the pain, but the man did not care.

We walked down the hall to the left to face multiple doors. We passed many that were shut, only a few cracked open. I caught a glimpse inside one as we passed, a tiny, empty bedroom hidden behind the door.

I wondered what type of person would reside in such a place.

I paused at a disruption behind me. Ervin cried out as he tripped, and I tried to move to help, but Rodrir held me firmly in place. One of the men closest to Ervin kicked his side as he lay on the ground.

"Get up, old man," he hissed.

Bellamy threw himself forward, headbutting the man with his forehead. The man fell over, his face now a bloody mess. A hand reached up to cup at his nose and contain the blood.

Another man rushed forward to detain the prince, but Bellamy kicked out at him. Again, he connected with his target, and everything broke out into chaos.

Rodrir pulled me away from the group, and I watched helplessly as Asena tried to hug the side of the hall, Caspian and Bellamy fighting against the men.

More people rushed up the stairs and out closed doors. It was over as soon as it started.

A thundering voice at the end of the hall ceased the commotion. Ervin was standing on his feet once more, and I caught the glimpse of a quick, satisfied smile before he trained his face to neutral. He had purposely tripped and caused the commotion that broke out?

"And what do we have here?" the deep voice echoed through the hall.

Bellamy and Caspian were thrust forward, two men holding each of them.

"A new prize for your collection," Rodrir said proudly..

"The Prince of Abelon and his companions," the man said, his eyes glancing between Bellamy and Caspian.. "To what do I owe the pleasure?"

Caspian struggled in the man's grasp, and I watched as he broke free, rushing forward. His arms were still contained, but his legs were free to run. Before he made it far, something collided with his chest.

A branch shot through the hall before I could understand where it had come from.

The man stood still, and a woman stepped in front of him. Her short brown curls complemented her golden tan skin. She was short, but I could see from the muscles in her outstretched arms how strong she was.

Caspian dropped to his knees in pain, the branch retracting into the woman who controlled it.

"Caspian," I cried out.

"I've told you before, don't spoil the goods," the man scolded.

We were ushered to the end of the hall, where a heavy wooden door opened into a study. Old books lined the walls behind an oak desk, the two front legs of the desk carved to look like trees.

Blood soaked the front of my brother's shirt, and I tried

to position myself next to him. Our shoulders touched as we were crammed into the room.

"Are you okay?" I whispered, leaning in and away from Rosie.

"It hurts, but I'll be fine," he groaned.

The man, who I assumed was in charge, moved to sit behind the desk.

Rodrir straightened as the man's eyes fell on him

The Warden.

"What have you brought me, Rodrir?" the Warden drawled.

"The Prince of Abelon and the Princess of Morwen and their companions," he said.

I fidgeted as the man looked me up and down, as if he was weighing my value.

"I know all about you, Koraine," he said.

My heart stopped beating in my chest, and I couldn't find the capacity to breathe. The sound of my name on his lips raked over me.

"Don't look so surprised. I have men and women spread across the four kingdoms. Of course, I know about the woman from Morwen set to marry the ruthless fire prince," he said.

"As for you two," he looked between Caspian and Ervin, "I do not know your names, but I am confident I will fetch a fair price for the pair of you."

I swallowed hard.

The woman who attacked Caspian slowly made her way behind the desk. She backed up to the shelves of books and remained quiet.

"Why are you still here?" the Warden asked, turning to

Rodrir.

He shifted his weight and struggled to get his words out. In front of the Warden, he was no more than a terrified servant. I watched the once confident and ruthless smuggler crumble under a single question.

"I—" he started.

"Did you think you would be rewarded?" the Warden asked.

"I, sir—" Rodrir tried again.

"You work for me. I own you," the Warden began. "Your job is to bring me the most valuable things I can sell in my market. I admit, you have outdone yourself here, but you would do well to remember your place."

Rodrir's eyes fell to the floor.

"Sir, I was hoping you might reassign me," he began. "I'd like a position away from the sea."

The Warden's face remained stoic, giving away nothing. The woman behind him pursed her lips. Tension hung in the air, and the silence was overwhelming.

Suddenly, the Warden broke it with a deep, menacing chuckle.

"I have tolerated you because you remain on that ship at sea, but I am losing my patience," he snarled as Rodrir's eyes widened, instant regret plastered on his face. "You are simply replaceable."

He flicked his wrist, signaling to the woman behind him, and before Rodrir could react, she moved.

The sharp branch spread like a vine, faster than my eyes could track. It stabbed straight into his chest and pierced his heart. I watched, horrified, as Rodrir dropped to the ground clutching his chest. The branch retracted,

and the woman went back to standing against the book-
shelves.

No one said a word.

I was afraid to move or speak, my heart pounding in my
chest. One wrong move, and we were all dead.

"Take them below," the name commanded, and the
woman moved.

A shiver ran down my spine. The power this woman
held, that he entrusted her to take all five of us, made my
stomach twist. I knew the others could sense it too.

She brushed by me toward the door and held it open.

We shuffled our feet, heading out of the study, but Ervin
turned one last time. Before I had a chance to stop him, his
hands moved. Flames danced from the palms of his hands
and flew toward the Warden.

"No," I shouted.

Caspian tried to move to stop him, but it was too late.
The stream of fire rushed toward the Warden.

It was inches from colliding with him, but it stopped. He
moved his arms in one fluid motion, and the flames
wrapped around him. He commanded them to swirl around
his body and then extinguished them.

My mouth fell open, and Ervin appeared speechless.

"You're Abelonian," Bellamy said.

"I abandoned that title long ago," the man said. "Many,
like I, have suffered at the hands of your father for far too
long."

CHAPTER 21

BELLAMY

THALIA MOVED us beneath the estate, following a set of stairs at the opposite end of the hall to an entire floor below the main entry.

Underground was cold and damp, the walls made of stone, its long halls lined with cages filled with prisoners. Some were stacked above each other and made of pure metal. I caught a glimpse in between the narrow gaps of the metal bars at the people behind them. Defeated men and women sat inside, awaiting their fate.

Every last one of us had lost our fight. We had put everything into one last attempt, but it had been futile. I watched Koraine walk beside her brother, her shoulders sinking inward.

The princess remained silent the entirety of our walk.

We were lead to the end of the hall, where a single metal cage sat. Thalia manipulated the metal, creating a space large enough for us to pass through. We filed in one by one and moved toward the back of our new cell.

"This is where you will remain until the auction," she said sternly.

"What about our shackles and his wound?" Koraine asked.

Thalia waved a hand, and the shackles fell to the ground with a clatter. The ache from the tight metal already pestered me, unreachable to soothe with my metal-covered hands.

"And these?" I held up my fists.

"Those stay," she stated.

She shut the metal behind us, closing us in. I noticed there were a few others already inside the cage.

I groaned, the metal weighing my hands down.

With the metal cage closed and blocking the minimal light, it was dark, hard to make out the others inside. The market held those from all four kingdoms and every age as its prisoners. An older man had his arm wrapped around a woman young enough to be his daughter huddled against a wall of the cage.

"Bellamy?" a quiet female voice said from the corner.

"Koraine?" the woman answered immediately.

My eyes settled on the thin woman, hugging her knees and staring up at me from the corner of the cell. Her eyes looked sunken and her skin pale, but I recognized her long brown hair instantly.

The priestess, Oleena, the one who had married Koraine and me, sat before me, trapped in the cell. A moment of disbelief came and left; I had thought I would never see her again.

"What are you doing here?" Koraine asked, also recognizing the priestess.

"Smugglers raided our island and rounded up as many as they could during the night."

"Kamari?" I asked, remembering the other priestess.

A somber look washed over her. I swallowed hard, prepared for the words I knew she would say.

"She died protecting the temple."

"I'm sorry," Koraine said, her voice wavering.

She moved beside the priestess in an effort to comfort her.

"Who is she?" Caspian asked me in a whisper.

"A priestess from an island not far from Morwen," I explained.

Caspian easily put the pieces together in his head and nodded slowly.

Asena moved to sit on the other side of the priestess, and it was the first act of compassion I'd ever seen the princess make. It was odd to see her care about anything other than herself.

"How long have you been here?" I asked.

"Only a day," she said.

It was unlikely we would get any more information from her than we already knew. She was trapped here like the rest of us while we awaited the auction.

"We need to find a way out," Caspian growled, frustrated.

He stalked over to the metal bars, trying to catch a glimpse between them.

The metal cage that held us left little room for us to peer through its bars. The gaps were only large enough to allow us to breathe inside its confines. My fire was useless inside a prison like this, even if my hands were free. I would need to create a torrent of flames and will them to be hotter than anyone within the confines of the box could stand. If I melted the metal, I would end up burning everyone else alive.

I stood facing the side of the cell where we entered, looking for any weakness in its integrity. I could feel the growing tension from the group and let out a sigh realizing, that escape was hopeless.

The market itself was not underground at all. I'd managed to catch a glimpse at the large estate as they dragged us inside. We were in some form of building only slightly smaller than a palace. It didn't surprise me that the wealthy were the ones who operated the market.

A guard passed by our metal cage, whistling a low tune.

I let anger take hold of me and impulsively slammed my metal fist into the bars.

The guard, dressed in the same uniform as the others, let out a quick noise of surprise and spun on his heels. He faced the prison cell, his teeth gritted.

A smirk grew across my lips, and I crossed my arms, satisfied.

"Keep laughing," prince, the guard snarled. "But in a few days, you'll be sold to the highest bidder. There are many who will travel far to seek their revenge for what you've done to them."

A lump formed my throat, and I swallowed hard at the thought.

Koraine watched, her deep blue eyes filled with worry, and her forehead creased with concern. I knew there were many who despised my father; he was responsible for the deaths of hundreds across the kingdoms. No one would believe me if I claimed I had no hand in his doing so. They thought me to be a ruthless and heartless prince, the heir to the throne of fire, just as cruel as his own father.

My mind wandered, realizing how many wealthy nobles would pay to see my downfall. Had word made its way to the fire kingdom that I was here?

My chest tightened, knowing if any Abelonian saw and recognized me, they would receive a hefty prize to return the traitor prince to his father. It also meant Cyrus and Nyla would not be far behind us. I shook my head, afraid to venture down that path.

"We have to escape," I muttered.

"No shit," Asena grumbled, rolling her eyes.

"If this auction happens, then we've already lost the war," I said. "If I am not there to take the throne at my father's downfall, another will step into my place, and there's no telling if they'll be just ruthless. You may win the war without me, but no other elemental manipulator will be able to rule the fire kingdom. Only one who commands flames can. I need to take the throne and put Abelon back on the right path."

"A wrath far greater than your father's is coming," Oleena said quietly from the corner.

"What?" I asked.

"The goddesses are stirring, and they will bring destruction to us all," she murmured. "Kamari believed it when she was alive, and now I see it clearly. The kingdoms are out of balance, and the elements must be restored."

"What is she rambling on about?" Caspian asked, glancing to Koraine and me. His sister shrugged, and I remained quiet.

"If the king tries to burn the world, the goddesses will not allow it. When nature falls out of balance, only then do the goddesses interfere," the priestess explained. "Your father's war will bring destruction far greater than we can imagine."

"There will be no one left to see such a destruction if my father has his way. We must escape," I insisted.

Koraine's face fell, and Caspian slammed his foot against the metal bars.

"Last time we tried to escape, we failed before we even tried," Ervin muttered.

"This time, we can't fail," I said, my voice darkening. "The fate of all four kingdoms rides on this."

A day passed, and no one came to check on us. The other prisoners noted not a single person had opened the cell before we had joined them. It didn't give me hope that would change any time soon.

We passed time getting to know the others, hearing their stories and where they came from. Every kingdom but the earth kingdom was represented within the cell.

"They keep those who are earth manipulators in cells made of a material other than this metal. I've heard passing guards discussing it," one man explained.

The day felt like it had already passed for the most part, but it was impossible to tell without any windows. My body felt tired, and my eyes already were growing heavy. Was the lack of food pushing me toward exhaustion?

I moved closer to Koraine, who was tending to her brother, both seated on the ground. Her hands were covered in water as she worked at tending to his wound. It was a shallow stab wound, but it still needed treatment. If Caspian did not keep it clean or heal it, the wound would fester.

"It's still bleeding slightly; you can't handle much more blood loss," Koraine said.

I caught a glimpse at his face, his usual tan features much paler.

"She's right," I noted.

Caspian scoffed, lifting his eyes to me. His brows furrowed, and he tensed as Koraine let her hands touch the tender skin around the wound's opening.

The makeshift bandages they'd made from scraps of our clothing were no longer enough. The wound needed to be closed, and soon, or Caspian risked infection or too much blood lost.

"We need to cauterize," I noted.

"With what?" he growled.

"You can't be serious?" Koraine asked, glancing between us.

I walked over to the metal pieces of shackles left on the ground from our restraints. It was the only metal we had to use. My hands were still covered and unable to heat it.

I glanced to Ervin.

"No," he started.

"Ervin, we have no other option. We can't let him die," I said.

"I won't die," Caspian scoffed.

"Only an idiot would think that," I argued.

"Says the one who almost got my sister killed and earned himself metal hands," he pushed back.

I went to open my mouth, but Koraine jumped between us.

"Enough," she snapped. "Fighting will get us nowhere."

The other prisoners watched in silence. I felt fire boil in my chest at Caspian's accusation. No matter how much truth it held, the idea that I would ever put Koraine's life in danger enraged me.

"We are cauterizing this wound," Koraine said with a glance to Caspian that dared him to challenge her.

He frowned, glaring past her at me, but slowly nodded.

I brought the metal over to Ervin and held it out for him to heat. He warmed the metal enough for it to glow a faint red. Carefully, I carried it back toward Caspian, who still sat against a wall of the cell.

His body tensed at the sight. Koraine knelt beside her brother, her eyes filled with terror.

"Hold him still," I ordered.

"What—" she started.

"I need you to hold him still. I will make this as quick as possible, but we need to make sure the bleeding stops," I said.

I hesitated, Caspian watching me with deadly focus. The burn would be excruciating, and I knew too well what that pain felt like, the way hot metal felt against one's skin. Painful memories came rushing back.

"Do it," Caspian demanded.

I snapped free of the torturing thoughts.

Stepping forward, I quickly pressed the metal to Caspian's wound. He let out a scream of agony, pulling away, but I knew it wasn't enough.

"Hold him tight," I demanded.

Koraine winced.

Again, I moved with the metal. Koraine's knuckles turned white, clenching to hold her brother still. I held the metal to the wound only long enough to be sure the bleeding would cease. The burn would ensure Caspian stopped losing any more blood.

He let out another agonizing yell. Others in the cell shied away, holding to each other and avoiding watching. My stomach turned seeing the work I had done.

The skin was raw and red, a fresh burn mark now on his shoulder.

"He will need you to treat that still," I noted to Koraine.

She nodded, all the color drained from her face.

"He needs rest now," I said to her.

Caspian's eyes were barely open, and I could see his chest rising and falling heavily. I grabbed the nearby shirt he had removed to let Koraine work before. Placing it beside him, I motioned to it.

"Rest," I ordered.

Slowly, he lowered himself to the ground and used the shirt as a cushion for his head. A man from the far side of the cell walked over and handed me another piece of spare clothing, a yellow robe.

I dropped the clothing over Caspian like a blanket. Already, his eyes were shut, and I could see him focused on slowing his breathing and willing himself to sleep. The once fierce Morwenian warrior was reduced to the sight before me in the matter of moments.

I sympathized with him. It pained me to see him in such agony from the wound and healing process. I knew what that journey was like, remembering every horrid burn my sister and then Koraine had treated.

The thought of Nyla caring for me filled my mind.

The same woman who now hunted me across the kingdoms.

I felt ill and walked over to a wall to sit. The world came crashing down around me, and all the weight of everything I was running from felt like it was crushing me. I could barely breathe or think straight.

Koraine joined me after checking her brother was alright to leave.

She slid down next to me and placed a hand on my outstretched leg. We sat in complete silence for a few moments. I could feel the way her muscles went rigid.

"What's on your mind?" I asked.

"What's going to happen to us?" she asked.

"I don't know, my moon," I admitted. "But I will not leave your side."

"You can't promise that," she retorted.

"I would capture you a star if you asked," I promised. "Nothing is impossible when love is involved."

She leaned her head against me, and we watched the others in the cell as we sat there for a while. It was all we could manage, exhaustion and hunger slowly claiming us.

The cell was cold, and our minimal clothing did nothing to keep us warm. Keeping close together was the only way to preserve warmth.

"I miss it, you know," Koraine whispered.

"Miss what?" I asked, leaning my head onto hers.

Her hair smelt faintly of the salty sea, and I imagined we were anywhere else. I closed my eyes, letting the distant illusion consume me.

"Abelon," she said, forcing my eyes back open.

I sat up straight and glanced down at her. Her head moved back to meet my gaze, and those curious blue eyes sank into me.

"I was finally starting to feel at home there," she explained. "I'd created new family and was just starting to find my place."

"And then, that all was ripped away again," I finished.

She sighed. I wished I could bring her back.

"I found everything I ever wanted with you, love I could never imagine for myself," she continued.

I placed a gentle kiss on her head and pulled back again.

"I love you, my moon," I whispered and pulled her in close to my body.

"I love you too," she whispered back.

We cuddled together for rest for a while, and the rest of the group managed to find comfort leaning against the walls and shutting their eyes. The cage was silent, but sounds still echoed throughout the underground. Metal clanged and voices rang out in the distance. Some moaned in agony and others pleaded for their lives. Prayers were made to the goddesses, but none would be answered.

The goddesses had abandoned us long ago.

"Can we go back someday?" Koraine asked sleepily.

"To Abelon?"

My eyelids felt heavy, but I managed to get the question out.

"To Abelon, to the waterfall, and that special home we carved out in the fire kingdom."

I let out a soft chuckle.

"Rest, my moon," I said, "while I tell you a distant tale of that waterfall."

She rested her head down in my lap, curling her legs in. Her breathing became slower and heavier, and somehow, I knew she'd already shut her eyes.

"Many in Abelon believe that when the goddesses created the four kingdoms and our gifts, Mavalu and Odaesia were caught in the middle of a feud: water and fire, the two elements always at odds with each other. Mavalu wanted a kingdom made of fire and ruled by those who wielded it, while Odaesia wanted the opposite. As a final affront toward her sister, Odaesia used her influence over the sea to carve out a piece of Abelon, a small part of the fire kingdom that reflected the power and influence of the water goddess."

Koraine's head started to feel heavier in my lap.

"I like to think she already knew one day, one of her people would find their way to the fire kingdom and be the key to our long awaited peace," I trailed off.

My fingers ran through Koraine's soft waves, her white hair falling into my lap.

Across from me, Caspian still slept. The princess had moved unusually close to him, keeping a watchful eye. I didn't question it, nor did I think she would share with me.

Ervin spent his time taking care of the others in the cell; he rested against the wall across from me. His eyes were shut, his head leaning back into the wall, and his hands sat on his round belly.

I let my eyes close, knowing my group was alright for the time being. My mind wandered, and I tried to direct it toward happier times, ones that wouldn't steal my sleep from me.

Instead, I found my thoughts riddled with our problems.

Two days after they put us in the metal boxes and starved us, the men in uniforms came. There was one to escort each of us. I knew it was useless trying to fight them; we were outnumbered. Again, our best hope for escape would be when they moved us out of the estate to wherever we had been sold.

They moved the entirety of our cell, and I saw other guards emptying a few nearby ones as well. My stomach sunk, knowing the day had come. The auction would run whether we wanted it to or not. The Warden had sent the men to retrieve his prizes.

It was a short walk from underground to a spacious room on the first floor. Metal chairs lined the room for an audience to sit in. Men and women dressed in finery entered , wearing all types of masks to hide their identities, cowards afraid to be caught.

I spotted a few dressed in red and black, a sinking feeling building in my gut, knowing they traveled from the fire kingdom.

The men lined us against a wall to the left of the small, raised platform, big enough to hold only two people at a time. I knew they would take us up onto it one at a time, selling us off like livestock. A pit formed in my stomach as the wealthy took their seats.

The line in front of me approaching the stage was filled with many people. It would be a while before it was my turn

My fists remained enclosed in metal. I wanted to burn the entire building down with all these bastards trapped inside. The moment I returned to Abelon, I would hunt down each and every one of the men and women who participated in the market, and they would *burn*.

Koraine moved close beside me and linked her arm with mine. Her touch was enough to settle my growing rage. I needed to keep my mind focused and find a way out.

The Warden appeared from a door off to the side. His presence silenced the room, and the wealthy waited for him to begin the auction.

CHAPTER 22

NYLA

OUR SHIP MADE land in no time after a full day of travel. A small beach sat along the southern shore of Abelon. Cyrus had known exactly where to find it.

His knowledge about the market sent a shiver racing down my spine.

He'd instructed our men to wait at the fleet of ships while we ventured across Zetron. He'd explained that the market was private and invitation only. There would be no way for us to bring our guards. If we wanted to enter and confirm Bellamy was being held, we needed to play by their rules.

The market was filled with influential men and women, run by a man they called the Warden. I tried committing all Cyrus' notes to memory, but it was useless. I was out of my element.

I could play the part of princess, fit in with nobles at a party, but venturing to an illicit market and finding my way in was not in my skill set.

A market as notorious as this one would not be the place

to use brutal force. I'd found a new ruthless side of myself, but I could not break through the market on my own. Instead, I would walk in through the front gates with Cyrus by my side.

The pair of us left the ship and made our way up a beach. Beyond the sand, vast fields were set against a forest. My heart ached to explore the land, but I knew those dreams would never come to be.

Bellamy had ripped that away from me.

"It's not far from here," Cyrus stated, barely waiting for me to trail behind him.

"The market?" I questioned, my heart racing.

It had been non-stop since leaving Abelon. I barely slept, my mind filled with the chase, the hunt for my brother. I could barely eat or even breathe without the thought crossing my mind. It was consuming me, pushing me to the brink of madness.

"The checkpoint," he said.

"Checkpoint?" I echoed back, but he ignored me.

My feet picked up their pace, forced to keep up with the captain. A permanent frown had been plastered to his face since leaving the burning ship. I could see his fuse running shorter and shorter. In no time, Cyrus would explode and take out everyone in his path.

The captain was strategic, but like my own brother and recently myself, he had a temper, a side too hard to control. I didn't want to be a victim of it when it finally did come out.

I walked for a bit a few steps behind Cyrus. We crossed the beach, walking through the field. Flowers grew around us, and the lush green grass was soft under my feet. I tried to soak in everything around me while keeping an eye on Cyrus.

We ventured deeper and deeper into the field until we found a path that veered off to the right. Cyrus turned and followed it; I could tell many had traveled the same path, the ground flattened, no flowers growing. The path lead straight into the forest. The brush was thick on either side of us, but the ground ahead was clear.

Cyrus remained silent, expectantly pushing forward as I let out a frustrated huff.

"Where are we going?" I demanded.

"Enough, princess," he growled.

"Cyrus-"

He turned, letting flames fly toward my head. I ducked, letting the fire soar well past me.

"Dragon shit," I cursed under my breath.

"Enough questions," Cyrus demanded.

I stood frozen in place, waiting for him to demand more. Instead, he turned away, and I forced myself to follow, my forehead slick with sweat.

An hour later, a small cottage appeared ahead in the woods. I smelt it before my eyes located it: a chimney carried puffs of smoke from a fire I knew I would find burning inside.

We walked up to the cottage, and I spotted a pen off to the side of it. Multiple horses were roped up, drinking water from a trough.

"Wait here," Cyrus said.

I didn't argue. He disappeared inside the cottage after knocking three times on the door as I walked over to the pen of horses.

Four were roped to the fencing closest to me, and I reached out to touch one. I went slow, letting my hand hover in front of its face for it to see me first. As I outstretched my hand to the horse now glancing up at me, the door to the front door opened.

"Untie him," Cyrus commanded.

"What?" I asked.

"Untie that horse. We are taking two," he said without any further explanation.

I listened and untied the horse, leading it through a nearby opening to the pen. I climbed up onto its back with Cyrus' help and clung tight to the reins.

"We have a long travel ahead of us today," Cyrus noted, and I nodded my understanding.

"Whatever it takes to find Bellamy," I answered.

It didn't take long before Cyrus and I reached the estate housing the market. Not once on our journey nor on the ships did I question how Cyrus was so familiar with its location.

We rode up to the tall silver wall on our horses and waited to be let inside. Cyrus made a signal with his hand, and one of the men above the wall nodded before manipulating the metal to part for us. The moment we trotted inside, another person handed us golden masks.

"Why do we need these?" I asked, already pulling mine onto my face.

206

"One of the rules of the market is anonymity. If you'd like to bid today, you must wear it," the man explained.

Cyrus snorted, annoyed at my innocent question. I thanked Mavalu for the opportunity to remain hidden inside the Estate. If a single Abelonian spotted me, word would reach my father within days. It would be grounds for stripping my title, and the nobles would have every excuse to pull even more power away from my father.

"You've brought someone with you today?" another man asked, looking at Cyrus.

"She is my wife," he lied.

"Sir, you know only those with an invitation to the market can enter," the man said, glancing between us. If he recognized who I was, he said nothing. It was not his job to question who was invited to the market and why they came.

"Invitation?" I muttered under my breath.

Tales of the market and its outrageous acts and items traveled all throughout the four kingdoms. No one knew its inner workings, and no one knew who ran it. I'd never imagined it to be what was before my eyes now.

What type of people were they inviting to participate?

"Will you really send my wife off?" Cyrus drawled. "I am loyal, a longtime customer and supplier. I do not believe the Warden will mind her accompanying me."

I saw how the man tensed at the mention of the Warden. I tried my hardest to bat my eyes innocently at the man, playing the naïve wife. Inside, though, I was slowly tearing myself apart. My stomach sank knowing Cyrus had been here before. Had he been here on orders from my father?

"You know the rules, sir," the guard insisted.

"Then fetch the Warden for me," Cyrus said. The man glanced nervously to the entrance and then back to Cyrus. "Although, I cannot imagine he would be happy to be disrupted for something so trivial."

The man extended his hand out to me. "Welcome, miss," he said, his voice unsteady.

I took a deep breath before climbing off my horse.

Inside was grand, though everyone was ushered into a room off to the side. Workers in matching earth-toned uniforms greeted us, and I nodded a slight greeting back. The plan was to remain unnoticed and wait until we found Bellamy.

It wouldn't be long before the auction began, and I knew soon, they would parade out each of the prizes up for purchase.

Whispers carried through the room, and I tried my best to listen. The words prince and princess starred in many conversations, but I couldn't make out any reliable information.

Cyrus grabbed my arm and tugged me toward the far side of the room. I tried not to let my surprise and frustration show; we were supposed to be the happy couple. It was all part of the ruse to get what we wanted.

Chatter picked up, and I found myself falling deeper to my own thoughts. I imagined finally seeing Bellamy again and being able to return home. When I pictured traveling to Zetron, it was never on my father's orders. My dream had been to see vast and beautiful fields, to drink wine and spend a day roaming through them, not a single care in the world. Instead, I found myself in the most notorious, despicable market to exist.

Movement from the back of the room took hold of everyone's attention, and I followed their stares. Men and women proceeded into the room, escorted by workers. The heels of my feet rose, my toes lifting me to catch a glance. I craned my neck to spot my brother as the end of the line entered the room. Then, I finally saw him.

He stood behind Koraine as the rest of his group trailed in behind him. I almost felt guilty at how defeated they appeared. Hope was gone from their eyes, and each one of them hung their heads low.

I took a single step forward, but Cyrus' grip on my arm tightened, holding me back.

"We wait," he hissed.

"But he's here," I said. "Let's get him and go home."

"Impatience will get you nowhere," Cyrus said.

I rolled my eyes before falling back into place beside him. I knew he was right, but I couldn't bring myself to admit it. If I acted on impulse, we risked losing Bellamy yet again. I had minimal time until my father grew sick and tired of waiting.

At the front of the room, the Warden entered through a side door. A hush spread, and I took a seat beside Cyrus. Imprisoned people from each of the four kingdoms were guided onto a small platform. The process moved slowly as the wealthy purchased men and women like they were nothing.

Every second I spent sitting in the auction, watching the horror of it, I felt myself slipping further and further from who I was.

This was never me, never something I would have stood for.

I wanted to be ill and swallowed hard to keep the bile rising in my throat down.

These were people. Men and women with families and lives. People who found themselves in the wrong places or trusted the wrong people. It was unthinkable that others viewed them as so little. I tried to move from my seat, but Cyrus grabbed my thigh to hold me down. I shifted uncomfortably away from him.

"Don't cause a scene," he hissed under his breath.

"I need air," I insisted.

"No," he commanded.

I couldn't argue further with him, afraid it would draw far too much attention. We had a singular goal, and I would not be the reason we failed.

I forced myself to sit and watch as each person was sold. I tried to block out the horrid sight, but each second spent there, it burned further onto my mind.

They slowly made it through the line of people, and Bellamy and his group were only a few away from the platform. My heart sped up with anticipation, and I felt my skin growing warm as jitters ran through my body. My foot tapped, and I wanted to spring from my seat.

"What is our plan?" I asked Cyrus. He still had not given me a hint to how we would obtain the prince.

"We wait and see who places the winning bid on your brother," he said.

"What?" I asked. "You're going to let someone else take him?"

"No, but we cannot bid on him."

"You are risking him getting away again," I warned. I

could feel myself sweating, heat rising in my gut. I was a mix of nerves and growing fury.

"I warned you impatience would get us nowhere. I want to see your brother dead. I want to drag him back to Abelon and watch him suffer as the traitor he is, but I know I need patience to do so."

I folded my arms, scowling. I would not be told what to do any further by Cyrus.

CHAPTER 23

KORAINE

My turn to be dragged up on the platform came faster than I hoped. A man stepped forward and tugged me up onto it. My feet felt heavy and incapable of moving, my mind racing.

Everything screamed at me to pull away and run back to the safety of Bellamy, but I knew even there, I wouldn't be safe from this fate.

"The bidding starts at a hundred gold coins," the Warden announced. "This fine young woman is the daughter of a prominent Morwenian general. She is young, healthy, and fit. She is still in prime condition to bear children."

Each fact the Warden rattled off made my stomach sink. The idea that someone would buy me to bear their children made me nauseated and dizzy.

"Two hundred," a deep voice from the back of the room called out.

My knees trembled.

"Three hundred," another voice from the front of the room chimed in.

My hearing turned fuzzy.

I could barely hear as more voices joined in, shouting numbers. This was all I had been reduced to, no more than something worth gold coins, my autonomy no longer my own.

My eyes drifted to the side of the room where Bellamy stood. I could see the fire in his eyes, like he may rush up and save me himself.

Impossible.

My eyes combed over the crowd of people, all wearing extravagant masks to hide their faces. They landed on a woman to the far side of the room, and something felt oddly familiar about her, the way her dark eyes born into me like she recognized me.

I swallowed hard, still unable to hear what was going on around me. I had to get myself out, and I needed to take everyone with me. If I attacked, there were at least fifty to one hundred manipulators in the room. I'd never make it out alive.

My anger alone would make them get rid of me. I'd never be suitable for being the obedient woman one of these nobles purchased. I needed to wait and bide my time, the way we had planned, but it was growing more impossible by the minute.

"Smile, dear," the Warden hissed.

My insides boiled at his suggestion. How could I smile when my life was being taken from me? The most hopeful I could be was for a noble to purchase me as a woman to care for their home or their children. At worst, someone from

214

Abelon could purchase me to take their anger with my father out on or use me to get to him. He had been the reason Abelon did not win the war. He was the reason for many deaths, the reason my people lived in peace for all these years.

"Sold," the Warden called out, and the crowd clapped.

I searched the room for who had placed the winning bid, but no one stood out. I was grabbed by strong hands from the other side of the platform and dragged off it, forced to sit and watch as Bellamy was also sold. A new wave of fear filled me, and I prayed to any goddesses who would listen that Bellamy would make it through this. He never deserved to be held responsible for his father's actions.

I pushed my own troubles aside, my eyes unable to leave the platform as he stepped up. His hands were still covered in metal, his eyes narrowed on the crowd. I could tell he was soaking in every detail of the people who sat before him.

If I made it out alive, I'd come back someday. I'd never leave these people to continue such heinous acts. The market needed to be destroyed, and if we all survived the war, it would be the first thing I did.

"Alright, settle down," the Warden shouted before opening bidding.

The bids grew higher and higher, a ridiculous amount of gold being thrown around, the kind the only the wealthiest had. My own family had never seen anywhere close to the amount these men and women were shouting to purchase the prince.

In the chaos of everything, the familiar woman I'd noticed stood. She took a few steps forward before her eyes locked on Bellamy.

A new type of dread washed over me; she was giving him a look promising death. The man with her slowly held out a hand to pull her back.

The man himself felt familiar as well, and I tried to reach deep inside to chase that feeling. The movement had caught the prince's eye, and I looked across the room to Caspian, hopeful to gain his attention.

My brother looked up and saw the worry on my face. He nudged the princess and Ervin standing on either side of him. Oleena followed their gaze, and the group watched as I nodded toward the couple, who had set their focus on Bellamy.

Were they going to bid?

Before I could consider any theories, the woman moved with trained speed, flames flashing across the room in a flared burst. The wealthy ducked their heads, and panic ensued. Many remained close to the ground, trying to quickly flee. The Warden's men rushed from the outskirts of the room toward the woman, but she held them off with a wall of flame.

I used the chaos as an opportunity to hurry over to my brother and the other two. Bellamy was still firmly in the Warden's grasp and unable to use his own flames.

With my own hands free, I manipulated water to appear and rush toward the Warden. He dodged my attempt, letting go of Bellamy in the process.

Bellamy leaped off the platform and joined us to the side. Men closed in around those of us who were meant to be prisoners. The wealthy crowded the door, making it impossible to get out as the woman with the flames stalked across the room, her fire attacking anyone who stood in her path.

Again, she felt familiar. I caught a glimpse at the dark red hair pulled away from her face, and instantly, my stomach sunk. The man who followed had sandy brown hair, and instantly, I knew why I'd recognized them.

Nyla ripped off her mask, letting out a snarl as our eyes met. She sent fire racing across the room in our direction. Caspian threw up a wall of water to protect us, and it collided with the flames in an explosion that filled the room with steam.

"Let's go," Bellamy shouted.

There would be no escaping through the single door toward the entryway that all the fleeing souls blocked. There were small windows up high, but they weren't large enough for us to climb through. The only other option was the door across the room. The Warden had already disappeared behind it, but there were still his men and women in the way.

We'd have to fight our way out.

We raced across the space, and Nyla stepped in our path.

"Go," I insisted.

"No," Bellamy answered.

"There's no time to argue. Take them and get them out of here. I'll be right behind you," I said.

He hesitated, but he nodded slowly, trusting me to find my way back to him. Caspian was in no shape to fight, and Ervin and Oleena needed someone to guide them safely out. I knew Asena could look after herself.

I quickly sent a stream of water toward Nyla, and she

sidestepped my attack, but it allowed the rest of the group to hurry by her without challenge.

Cyrus closed in, approaching from behind Nyla, and I cursed under my breath when he locked his sights on the group. Taking on one of them was manageable, but I started to doubt that I could hold them both off.

The steam managed to provide cover but was fading fast. The group ran for the door, and Cyrus turned to follow, but I manipulated my water to block him. Nyla used the opportunity to throw flames in my direction, but I dodged them.

Bellamy paused and held open the door for the others. His eyes filled with sorrow the moment they connected with mine.

He went to step back toward me, but someone stopped him before he could make it far.

Asena held the prince back and shoved him through the doorway. I could barely hear from the commotion around me and the attacks Cyrus and Nyla threw my direction.

Asena closed the door behind the others and stayed.

"No," I whispered under my breath. That wasn't the plan. Bellamy and Asena needed to make it out. They were our only hope of the kingdoms surviving and winning the war.

What was she doing?

"Koraine," she shouted, pulling me from my thoughts, just in time to dodge the fire barreling toward me.

I raised my hands into the air, a shield of water flying up in front of me before I shoved it forward. A tornado of water began to form and hurried across the room toward Nyla, but she cut through it with a slice of flames.

Many of the wealthy had made their way out of the estate, a few stragglers finally exiting the room. Chairs were littered across the floor, making navigating the room hard. Not only did I need to dodge, but I needed to avoid tripping over the littered furniture left behind by the stampede of people.

Asena distracted Cyrus, caught up in her own battle with him, and a small feeling of thanks filled my chest. The selfish princess had sacrificed her own escape to ensure the others would make it out. I knew the rest of the group wanted to stay and help and fight, but if they did not make it out, then all of this would be for nothing.

Asena and I closed in on Cyrus and Nyla, forcing them back to back. They were sporadic and disorganized in their movements, and our water abilities worked together to douse each flames that shot in our direction. I caught a short smile from the princess as a stream of her water collided with Cyrus' chest, knocking him back a step.

The princess of fire let out a frustrated growl, unruly flames flying in my direction.

Again, I dodged and sent my own attack her way. We were locked in, and only one pair could escape.

Another few rounds of attacks were exchanged, and I was growing tired. We'd been starved and deprived of suffi-cient rest in our metal cells. The lack of sleep and food was starting to get to me. I could see the concentration growing on Asena's face across from me, each attack seeming to pull more out of her. Fire brushed against my skin, and the heat made me whimper. Nyla's attacks were getting closer to finding their mark. I dove to the ground, ducking as flames flew above my head.

I sucked in a breath, preparing for the worst as more fire followed. Before it could collide with me, a wall of stone flew up in front of me. The stone grew and circled Nyla and Cyrus, trapping them in.

I glanced at the doorway to find Thalia standing there with her arms outstretched.

I prepared for her to detain us, but she did not. Instead, she nodded toward the door to the side. "Go." She nodded.

"Just like that?" I asked

"Koraine," Asena warned.

"Go before I change my mind," Thalia said through gritted teeth.

I nodded my thanks and hurried across the room, following the princess. We rushed through the hall until we found a door leading outside. We burst through it, and light slammed into us.

CHAPTER 24

NYLA

"Damn Aeris," I cursed under my breath.

My flames chipped away at the stone in front of me, but it was a thick wall and taking longer than I had.

I'd wanted to follow Bellamy, but his wife had stood in my path. She made it impossible to go after him. I let my anger blind me, wanting to finish her off once and for all. Again, I gave into my temper, refusing to listen to Cyrus and wait until the auction was over.

I wouldn't sit by and watch my brother be sold to someone else. He belonged to Abelon, and he was rightfully mine to take home. If we waited, we risked losing him, and that was not something I was going to let happen.

Cyrus tried to stop me, but he was too late, and now we both paid the price of my ignorance.

Those who ran the market trapped us inside a stone wall.

"You bitch," Cyrus hissed. "If you had listened to me, we wouldn't be here. We would've had the prince and been back on our way to Abelon, and now, yet again, he escaped, and it's your fault."

"He would've found a way to escape if we waited much longer. You were going to wait until whoever purchased him took him back from the market. How would we keep eyes on him the moment they removed him from this room? Would you follow whoever purchased him? Would you remain here, waiting for a horse or a ship to arrive back at the beach?" I shouted.

Cyrus scoffed, throwing a large burst of flames at the wall. Again, pebbles broke off from it, but it did not budge.

We waited, knowing that, eventually, they would need to let us out. By that point, though, Bellamy would be long gone. I groaned, knowing I still could not return home. The other kingdoms were vast, and now, we had no idea where my brother was heading.

"We return to Abelon," Cyrus broke the silence after a few minutes.

"No," I said rapidly.

"We do not know where the group is heading, but I do know Bellamy knows far too much of your father's plans. If he wishes to live, he'll have to stop your father, which means eventually, he will have to return to Abelon."

"I cannot return home without him," I argued.

"That is something you should've thought of before you sent flames flying through this room like a child throwing a tantrum," Cyrus growled.

"If you weren't so incompetent—" I started.

Cyrus closed the distance between us with impossible speed. His forearm slammed against my neck and pushed me back up against the stone wall. I let out a cry of pain as my back collided with the rock. He ignited his fist, flames licking dangerously close to my face.

"Do not test my patience, princess," he growled.

"Or what?" I spat.

"I will reach my limit, princess. When I do, I will have no further use for you," he threatened. The flames came closer to my face, and I tried to turn away from them.

I knew his threat wasn't empty. He'd always wanted Bellamy gone. I knew he'd helped with all the torture my father inflicted. I was no more than a pawn to reach my father and brother.

If I did not help him, then I was useless to him.

He'd find a way to rid himself of me, and I knew my father would look the other way.

My hands were against cool stone, but I let little embers flicker to life in my palms. Quickly, I let the fire spring to life and jabbed into his side, shoving him back. He hissed in pain and clutched his side, letting go of me.

I backed away to the other side of our prison. My breathing was rapid, and my chest felt tight. Cyrus was a dangerous creature, and I wouldn't let myself fall prey to him.

"They'll go to Gralar," I growled, knowing my brother would still go to the earth king for help.

Before Cyrus could answer, the walls dropped, and I stumbled backward, landing on my ass. My cheeks reddened, and I stood as quickly as I could.

I was met by a woman with short, curly dark hair. Her gaze set me on fire, and before I could move, metal wrapped around my body, pinning my arms to my side.

Cyrus stood still, watching, his eyes narrowed. She

turned to look at him but just shrugged, leaving him as he was.

I supposed that was the benefit of frequenting the market.

She nodded to the entry door and grabbed my arm, tugging me toward it. Cyrus followed behind silently.

I was forced into the entryway, my mask long gone. Many of the wealthy still remained, huddled together and whispering. Their words barely reached my ears, but I knew what they spoke of. The Princess of Abelon had just made an enemy of many.

I swallowed, trying to clear the lump forming in my throat, but it was no use.

Cyrus kept his head bowed as we walked. The woman led us to the main staircase then down the hallway at the top to a room at the end. I was shoved inside a study, finding the Warden sitting behind his desk.

"The Princess of Abelon threatens to ruin my market," he drawled. "I traded one royal for another."

His nails tapped on the desk, and I shivered.

Cyrus stood, carefully observing, his demeanor similar to when he stood before my father, respect and understanding written on his face.

"I only came for the prince," I growled out.

"You could've bid like everyone else," the Warden noted, unimpressed.

"He belongs to Abelon, and I will not pay for him," I argued.

"Because of you, he belongs to no one," the Warden said, and I heard the threat behind the words.

I held my tongue.

"Warden," Cyrus started, "my apologies for the princess' rash behavior. It was never our intention to disrupt your market. You know Abelon has provided many loyal customers. We are here on the king's orders to bring the prince home to serve justice for his crimes against the crown. Allow us to leave freely, and I promise, you will reap the benefits."

The Warden held Cyrus' gaze, and the men sat in silence, studying each other. I wanted to cut in to tell the Warden that if he didn't let us go, I would burn his market to the ground. I was done taking orders, done being prisoner to everyone else. My father would never agree to what Cyrus was proposing.

"Abelon has always contributed rather nicely to the market," the Warden agreed. "But I fear I've had enough of the king's games."

Cyrus reacted quickly as the Warden moved. Fire shot from his hands towards us, and my mouth dropped open, but Cyrus controlled the flames before they hit us. The Warden was Abelonian, and I had been blind to it.

The woman who had dragged me to the study moved quickly, already filling the room with her vines. I let fire form in my hands, pointed at the ground, my arms pinned to my side by metal. It shot forward across the room, burning her moving vines. Cyrus grabbed my arm and pulled me toward the door, using the distraction of flames to flee.

Neither the Warden nor woman did not have time to react as we burst through the door. The Warden was already taming the flames consuming his study.

Cyrus pulled me along, down the hall as if he'd already memorized the entire floor plan of the estate. He aimed for a room at the other side of the hall, trying the door knob and finding it unlocked. Inside was a simple set up, made for housing those frequenting the market. On the far side of the room, two glass double doors led out to balcony.

I looked at Cyrus with a quirked brow. "Cyrus, I can't even use my hands."

"You only need your legs to jump," he stated.

I could tell there was no winning the argument as his brows furrowed and he moved toward the balcony.

"Let's go back out the front," I pushed.

"There will be dozens of men waiting down there for us. Would you prefer to become one of the prizes he sells off?"

I knew he didn't actually care whether I was captured and sold at the market, but it would harm my father and aid in taking power away from Abelon.

"Fine," I hissed.

Dragging me over to the balcony, he opened the doors and didn't hesitate as he climbed over the railing. He lowered himself, hanging on to the edge of the balcony and letting his legs dangle. He let go and hit the ground, letting himself fall and roll to absorb the impact.

How hard could it be?

All I had to do was copy Cyrus.

The only issue was, I had no control over my arms.

The door to the room flew open, and the woman with short brown hair stepped inside.

"Let's go," Cyrus yelled up.

I hesitated.

The woman stalked over to me, but I was frozen in place.

She grabbed hold of my clothing, my top bunched in her fist. She held a metal dagger in her hands, placing the blade as close to my neck as possible without cutting me. I searched her eyes, surprised by what I found. There was no anger and no hatred. It was nothing like the way people usually looked at the Princess of Abelon.

Instead, I found hesitation and what I thought to be a glimpse of sympathy.

"Don't," I whispered. "Let me go."

My voice was soft. Cyrus couldn't hear me below; the balcony obscured his vision as he waited for me to join him.

"I can't," she said. "He'll have my head."

I saw the distant fear written on her face. She was more like me than anyone I'd ever met, stuck somewhere she never asked to be and forced to follow everyone else's orders.

"You can," I continued. "You never found us. We were gone before you got here."

She bit her lips, thinking it over for a moment. I thought she might just slit my throat and save herself the hassle, but the metal clattered on the ground as my shackles fell from my wrists, the dagger still sat pressed to my throat.

She was frozen the same as me, caught between betraying those who commanded her and finally doing something for herself. It was the same war I fought with myself every single day.

I thought of my brother and my father. I knew what awaited me in Abelon if I did not reach Bellamy—worse than the simple, swift death this woman promised.

I had to try. I had to take Bellamy home. Everything

came rushing back, and that ruthless monster I tried so hard to push down came barreling to the surface.

Quickly, I moved my hands with fire in my palms, throwing up a wall of flames between us, forcing her back as her eyes widened.

I didn't wait until the flames died down. I threw myself over the edge of the balcony, quickly lowering myself and jumping down. I tried to minimize the shock of the landing, but I didn't roll fast enough.

My ankle twisted, and I almost buckled over when I tried to stand back up. It ached, but as I looked down, I knew it wasn't broken. Cyrus was already moving quickly across the open green fields.

I limped as I followed him, moving as swiftly as I could. The land behind the market was vast and empty. I couldn't see where the furthest wall of the metal that protected the market stood.

"Let's go, princess," Cyrus snarled.

"How—"

"I don't want another word from you," Cyrus hissed. "In the matter of a day, you ruined everything I've worked for here. You rid Abelon of any power it held at the market, and you forced us to follow after Bellamy yet again. If you wish to make it back to Abelon with your life, I suggest you keep your mouth shut."

I opened my mouth to argue but closed it, thinking better of myself.

I wasn't afraid of Cyrus, but I *was* afraid of my father, and I knew he would trust Cyrus' word over mine. If I truly lost Abelon power, I already knew my father would punish me the moment I stepped foot in the fire kingdom.

The burn scars on my shoulder blades served as a reminder of what happened when I stepped out of line. It wasn't enough to just bring the prince home. I had failed many times already at that. My father's hand would be waiting with the metal chains for all my failures. I wasn't confident I could survive another lesson.

CHAPTER 25

BELLAMY

EVERYTHING in me screamed at me to stay and fight. Asena had forced me out the door and promised to protect her. Her words still rang in my ear as we hurried out of the estate.

"Let me help, just this once," the princess had said.

It was the first she had offered to do anything of the kind for the group, and her selflessness had stunned me. She'd pushed that Caspian was in no shape to protect Ervin and Oleena, that the three needed me to guide them.

I knew she was right, but it still pained me.

I had to trust Koraine. I had to put my faith in my wife.

I'd left her, helping the other three navigate the halls. We received little confrontation, aside from a couple of men I took care of.

It wasn't long before we found a door out.

The land behind the estate was vast, like the fields that covered Zetron. We ran, heading for the distant far end of the estate, and I knew Koraine and Asena would follow closely behind.

We needed a head start to find a way off the estate.

Screams still rung in the air from panicked nobles, but I refused to look back.

Ervin held pace, pushing himself to keep jogging through the field. I let surprise wash over me for a moment at the old man's stamina. Oleena trailed close behind, next to Caspian.

I could tell his shoulder ached by the way he kept letting his hand drift to it. He was slower than normal, and his breathing was labored. The short few days in the cage without food or water had done nothing to help him heal.

We continued running, the land full of endless hills and grass. The sun shone in our eyes as we ran directly into its brightness. It shrouded the far wall of the border.

"Bellamy," a voice called from behind me.

I paused, turning to realize just how far we'd made it.

Koraine and Asena ran side by side toward us, waving their arms. They were faster, easily able to catch up. Relief washed over me at seeing my wife's face.

A knot formed in my stomach when I realized what that meant for Nyla.

They joined our group, only pausing for a second to catch their breath before we pushed on.

I let silence hang for a bit before I forced myself to ask the question.

"Nyla—" I started.

"Captured by the market," Koraine said quickly.

Pure relief again washed over me. I never wanted my sister dead. I'd tried so many times to save her, to keep her from my father and in the end, it was no use. He'd sunk his claws into everything within the fire kingdom. My heart ached for the sister I'd lost, but I wasn't sure I could survive knowing she was completely gone.

"How are we going to get out of here?" Koraine asked.

Our pace was slowing, and we still hadn't found an end to the walls.

"It'll be dark soon," Ervin noted, glancing up to the sun. "And he needs rest."

The last part, he said quietly with a quick nod to Caspian.

"I know, but we can't stay here," I answered.

Koraine and Asena walked side by side ahead of us, but I was certain the two hadn't exchanged a word since fleeing the market.

The longer we spent with her, the more I felt Asena started to trust us. Even with her icy front she put up and how she acted as though she despised us, I could see she was slowly coming around.

"If we go much further, who knows what we will find if we make it outside these borders?" Ervin pointed out.

"We traveled far north to get here. From my understanding, we shouldn't be too far from Gralar. Possibly just a bit further north and east," I calculated.

"You think we'll make it there tonight?" Ervin asked.

"I think we must try," I said, watching the women in front of me striding through the field.

I knew Nyla couldn't be far behind. Even if the market captured Cyrus and my sister, I knew they wouldn't contain them long.

Koraine's white hair fell in perfect waves down her back. I was enamored by her, every second I spent near, it was hard to take my eyes off her. She was like starlight.

Mountains rose distantly around us. I hadn't noticed them before, too focused on escaping, but they felt like another barrier holding us in.

I spotted something in the distance with a gleam. The metal shone like a distant piece of jewelry.

"Be smart, my prince," Ervin warned. "These people look to you, and so will the entire fire kingdom one day. You know need to know what's best for the group and lead them."

I shuddered at the thought of leading an entire kingdom when I could barely lead the small group of people with me. They didn't trust me, so how would I lead them?

I caught a gentle smile from Oleena, who walked close to Caspian, keeping a watchful eye on him and his shoulder.

"I just want to protect them," I said to Ervin. "But I don't know if I can even do that."

"I have faith in you, my prince."

The title sent a chill down my spine. He almost never used my title. It made the reality all the clearer. Soon, I would have to lead an entire kingdom. People would look to me for answers and guidance. They'd rely on me for their safe keeping and well-being, and I wasn't sure I was ready to take all that on.

I had no choice.

The sun was dipping and the sky was growing dark when we finally found the far side of the estate.

"How do we get out?" Asena asked.

I ran my hand along the cold metal wall. It stood at least ten feet high, too far to climb. We had no supplies to help us over the wall.

"I don't suppose you're from Luheo?" Caspian said with a slight chuckle to Oleena.

"I have no ability to manipulate the elements," she said. It was the first time I'd ever met someone without the ability to control one.

"What about Imry?" Koraine asked, her eyes full of hope.

"I could call, but I don't know how long we have and if she will hear. I have no idea where she found safety on land when we were taken captive," I said, my chest heavy.

"Do you think the patrols come out this far?" Asena asked.

"I think the Warden is too meticulous for there not to be any out here eventually," I said.

The reality that, sooner or later, his men might find us out here was sinking in.

We could try to force them to open the wall, but I worried their fear would outweigh their willingness to obey. We saw what he was capable of in the blink of an eye. His men were disposable.

"There has to be way over this wall," Koraine grumbled.

"Could you melt it?" Caspian asked.

"It would take longer than we have, and I'm not sure I'd be able to melt a hole big enough for us to escape through," I answered.

"I have an idea," Koraine said. "But I'm not sure you guys will like it."

We all stared blankly at her, waiting for her to elaborate. She shifted uncomfortably before taking a deep breath.

"We could use water to lift us up onto the wall and lower us over the other side. I would need the princess' help, but I think we could manage it. We use streams of water to lift you one by one up the wall and then follow closely behind. And then we do the same going down to lower you gently."

Asena stared at Koraine but didn't argue.

"Are you sure?" I asked.

She frowned at me, and I tried to take back the hesitation I'd shown.

"I trust you," I assured her.

"I can help," Caspian said.

"No," we collectively said. His face dropped, disappointed by the denial.

"You need to rest and heal that shoulder," Koraine scolded her brother.

"Who's first?" Koraine asked, watching us all.

"I'll go," I said, stepping forward, hoping to make up for doubting her abilities before.

Koraine was strong, and I knew her control over water was unmatched, but allowing myself to be consumed by the element was still off-putting.

I stood close to the metal wall, and she moved behind me.

"Bend your knees like you're about to sit," she instructed.

I followed her guidance and waited.

A stream of water appeared slowly. The water pressed against my legs and behind as it rose, and my feet lifted off the ground. I was completely carried by the water as it moved higher and higher. Putting my hands out in front of me, I could just barely touch the metal wall for balance.

It only took a few seconds before the water had me at the height of the wall. I leaned forward and grabbed ahold of the top, pulling myself away from the water and quickly scrambling to sit.

I glanced down with a nervous grin. The idea had worked.

Koraine smiled back proudly, and my chest swelled.

That was my wife.

The woman who would one day lead my people by my side.

She quickly got to work, lifting the others with Asena's assistance, and soon, we all sat at top of the wall.

The water lowering us was easier than lifting. It went much faster, and within minutes, our feet were all on the ground on the other side.

Darkness approached above us, and I realized we stood before another open range of land. There were trees scattered about, but there were no villages in sight.

Ervin's voice echoed in my head, and I knew, looking at the rest of the group, they were exhausted from days without food or proper rest.

To push them forward would be sentencing them to more pain and suffering.

"We camp for the night," I stated.

"What?" Koraine asked.

"No," Caspian argued. "We need to get to Gralar."

I took a deep breath. I imagined not what my father would say to his people, but how my mother would speak to the people she ruled.

"We are exhausted and hungry, and it's almost dark. It is safer and wiser for us to rest the night. Ervin will get a fire made, and I will find food."

I directed the group to a patch of trees not far in the distance.

"We rest there for the night. The trees will give us coverage, and we will leave first thing after sunrise for the capital."

Asena shifted uncomfortably at the mention of Gralar. I knew a single sleep separated us from leaving her in the safety of the kingdom. It wouldn't be long before I was forced to return home. It was finally time to face my father.

CHAPTER 26

KORAINE

BELLAMY DISAPPEARED to gather food for the rest of the group.

I helped Ervin break branches of the trees to use for firewood. He called forth his flames, small orbs forming in the palm of his hand and floating to the pile of sticks, igniting them for warmth. The cold autumn breeze nipped at my skin and sent a shiver down my spine.

I couldn't help but glance at the wall not far from us. The silver did not shine as much under the moonlight. I wondered whether the market sent the pantherus after us. Would we run into more of the large beasts beyond the wall?

My stomach sunk. The large felines left me unsettled.

Before long, Bellamy returned with hands full of berries plucked from bushes.

"It isn't much, but it's something," he said.

My stomach felt empty, and I was grateful for any chance to eat. I'd lost track of the last time I had a full meal, feeling weaker by the day.

Lifting everyone over the wall had taken most of my remaining energy. I felt lightheaded by the time we all stood on the ground outside the estate.

I didn't know how Asena did it.

She never showed weakness, and nothing seemed to bother her.

I sat on the plush ground close to the fire and hugged my knees. The prince joined beside me, and I watched Oleena and Caspian chatting across from us. Asena remained quiet, leaning against a tree.

An unlikely group.

I ate my portion of berries in no time at all.

The capital would have food and supplies for us to stock before our journey onward. It felt odd, knowing we would leave the princess behind. I knew everyone had thought about it, but not a single person had mentioned it.

Regardless of how stubborn she could be, Asena had become part of our small family, and it was like leaving a piece of us behind.

I knew we didn't have a choice, but my stomach still twisted.

None of us argued when Bellamy volunteered to take the first watch for the night. Everyone felt the effects of exhaustion.

The prince let me put my head in his lap as he sat awake, keeping a lookout. It wasn't long before my eyes felt heavy, and I heard Bellamy whisper, "Goodnight, my moon."

I woke the next morning to Bellamy gently shaking my shoulders.

"Why did you never wake me for a watch shift?" I asked.

"Caspian and Ervin took turns as well," Bellamy said. "It wasn't needed."

I let out a drawn out sigh, wishing I could've contributed.

Oleena was already standing, and Asena sat up in a sleepy haze. Her eyes looked heavy, like she hadn't gotten much sleep at all.

"We need to get going," Caspian said. "We still don't know if anyone is behind us."

The memory of the stone wall enclosing the princess inside kept flashing back. Somehow, it didn't feel like enough. I knew Nyla would still find a way to hunt down Bellamy.

It was what the rest of the group was thinking.

I stood, brushing off my clothing. The group cleaned up camp quickly. We tried to disperse the ash pile from the fire, hoping no one would realize we'd been there to follow us. I knew it was futile; it was impossible to rid the ground of the small scorch marks that remained.

I used my water, manipulating it, hoping to wash away most of the remnants, but at a closer glance, I could still see the remains. We needed to move and start our journey to Gralar; we couldn't spend more time at the camp.

"Come on," Caspian said to me as the rest of the group began to walk away.

I stared at that single spot where the fire had been, imagining the hot flames flickering during the night. I shook my head and snapped myself out of the daydream, turning to follow the rest of the group. We continued walking, and the further we went, the more confident Bellamy became that we would soon find the city.

We spotted small cottages in the distant fields but never got close enough to know who inhabited them.

A few hours, and my feet burned from walking, the prospect of finding the capital feeling grim. I let out a sigh from the back of the group, and Bellamy peered over at me, raising a brow.

"I'm just tired," I said, trying to reassure him. He looked unconvinced, his eyes narrowing.

I needed to push forward with everything I had. My friends and family were relying on me. I needed to do whatever I could to protect them. It was my responsibility to keep them from the war that was coming.

A war I had a hand in starting.

We climbed over a hill filled with tall grass. Strands brushed against the sides of my legs.

"Gralar!" Ervin shouted from ahead.

My heart sped up, and I set my eyes on the top of the hill. He had found his way ahead of the group, leaving us still quite a ways behind him. The rest of us began to run.

We found that small bit of energy left to hurry to the top of the hill, hoping to catch a glimpse at the capital we longed for.

Bellamy took my hand and ran beside me.

My eyes found the capital in the distance the moment I made it to the top. The palace was the first thing I spotted, green and gold, standing out amongst the rest of the city.

Tall, emerald spires marked the capital even from where we stood.

"Finally," Caspian said, letting out a sigh of relief.

"I told you we couldn't be far," Bellamy said.

"Maybe next time, I'll believe you," Caspian said with a slight chuckle.

It warmed my heart to hear him at least speaking to the prince again.

I gave a reassuring squeeze to Bellamy's hand, and my free hand went up to my forehead to shield my eyes from the bright sun.

"It won't be long now," I assured the rest of the group.

It was another hour before we stepped foot into Gralar. Our feet moved faster with the capital in sight. My foot found cobblestone instead of dirt and grass. It felt like a weight had been removed from my shoulders.

Men and women hurried through the busy streets, wearing different shades of green and other earth tones. I knew we stood out in our assortment of clothes. I tried not let the lingering stares get to me.

Our only focus was making it to the palace. Nothing else mattered.

Merchants stood outside shops, trying to entice

customers to come inside. Smells from bakeries drifted into the streets, and I let out a groan after realizing we had no money.

I wasn't willing to steal from the hard-working people within the city just to fill my stomach.

"Fuck," Caspian muttered.

"You smell it too?" I asked.

He nodded, and I noticed the way he held his shoulder.

"Let me look at it," I said.

"No, we need to keep moving," Caspian said.

"It will only take a moment," I assured him.

We moved off to the side of the street, the rest of the group continuing without us. I moved Caspian's shirt aside and peeled back the makeshift bandage. The quick glance I was able to catch, I sucked in a sharp breath. The skin around the wound was vibrant red and irritated. I knew it wouldn't be long before infection set in.

"We need proper supplies," I said gently.

"We will find them soon," he assured me. "First, we deliver her," he said with a nod toward the princess.

If we could make it to the palace and get Asena there safely, there was a chance for us to get Caspian to a healer.

"Let's move," I said.

The closer we got to the palace, the more I spotted green flags and banners with the crest of mountains embroidered on them. I never noticed if Alua had something similar the few times I'd been to the capital.

Gold gates sat the top of the road we followed, six guards posted outside. They carried metal weapons, and I swallowed hard, imagining what they could do manipulating them.

Every passing second, my nerves grew.

What if they turned us away?

What if they didn't believe who Asena was?

It had taken everything our group had to ensure her safety. If it had been for nothing, then we lost the war.

We made our way up to the golden gates of the earth king's palace. There was no plan. We had nothing left besides the princess by our side.

She stepped forward, marching up to the guards.

I watched as she talked to them, signaling us to stay back. I couldn't make out what they were saying, only that the guards kept shaking their heads.

I fiddled with the skirt I wore. It was old and tattered from everything we endured.

Somehow, pulling at the fabric helped keep my nerves at bay.

I could feel Bellamy's presence behind me. I wanted to take a step back and lean into him, but I knew I couldn't always rely on him to find solace, I would need to be my own strength.

Asena raised her hands quickly, and water formed around her. I sucked in a breath as I watched, streams of water flying toward each of the guards, covering their bodies. The water quickly freezing. The metal weapons poked out of the ice, useless without the ability to move.

"What are you doing?" Caspian scolded.

"Talking was getting me nowhere," she said and rolled her eyes. "Let's go."

She brushed by the guards and pushed the metal gates open. I had a feeling security would be increased at the gates after the princess made easy work of six guards.

I quickly ran after her, following her into the courtyard behind the gates.

Guards poured into the courtyard from the palace, and our group stood frozen in the middle.

"That got their attention," Bellamy huffed.

"Wasn't that the point?" Asena asked innocently.

"We need them to help us win a war. We're trying to make allies, not enemies," Caspian stated.

That is no help," I scored at him.

His chiseled jaw went rigid.

"Are we supposed to bide our time? Caspian asked Asena.

"No, this will get their attention," she said. "Take me to King Roan," she yelled.

Guards pointed metal spears at us. Not a single one moved at her command. I tensed, flexing my fingers, ready to call on my water if needed.

Asena remained relaxed as she stepped forward.

"I am Princess Asena of Morwen, betrothed to Sora. Bring me to King Roan, or consider yourselves at war with Morwen," she demanded.

She called on her water and let it swirl around her, ready to take on anyone who challenged her.

The guards exchanged uneasy glances as they weighed the truth of her words, seeing her control over water.

A man stepped forward, dressed in a slightly different uniform. Instantly, I noticed the crest of the king Asena had described. "I'll take you."

Asena nodded and stepped forward to follow him. The rest of us made to follow, but the man held up a hand.

"Not you," he commanded.

The guards closed in around us, their weapons raised.

"They come," Asena said.

"No, only you speak with the king. They remain here for now."

"It's okay," I said.

"No, it's not," Caspian countered as I swatted his arm.

"We will be here," I promised.

I trusted the princess. She'd proven to us she had the group's best interest at heart. It had taken a while to gain her trust, but I knew she wouldn't abandon us. She had every chance to abandon me in the market, but never once did she leave. She fought fiercely by my side.

She nodded with understanding.

We just had to wait and put our faith in her.

An hour later, the same guard from before returned.

We'd given in to sitting on the cobblestone ground. Time had ticked by painfully slow, waiting for the princess' return, and the guards never once let up their stance.

The man stood in front of his men and motioned for us to stand. We scrambled to our feet.

"Follow me," he said.

"Where is Asena?" Caspian asked.

He ignored him and instead walked inside the palace, his strides long and quick.

"We made the mistake of too easily trusting before. Can we trust this was not another trap?" I asked before moving.

"We have no choice," Bellamy said, understanding my hesitation.

"We have to trust Asena," I said, nodding and trying to push away my own growing nerves.

Our group followed the man inside the palace.

I let out a breath, stepping foot inside. It was the third palace I'd been inside in only a few short months. It might have been the most beautiful of them all.

I was drawn to Morwen's palace, with all its water features, but the earth king's palace was exquisitely unique.

The entry was predominantly green and gold. The dark forest green walls matched all the gold detailing. The white marble floors held specks of gold within them. Stone statues sat on either side of a long hall before us.

Instead of some grand staircase leading up to other floors, the palace expanded down the hall, all on the same level. I'd seen the green spires in the distance before, so I knew there were other floors to the palace.

The guard continued down the long hall in front of him, never once turning back to us.

We followed, and my eyes grew wide at the oil paintings that decorated it. Vibrant fields filled with flowers were depicted. I spotted one canvas that held the foliage of autumn, the oranges and yellow standing out.

At the end of the long hall, doors opened into a courtyard, similar to the entry to the palace. It still had the cobblestone ground, but around the edges, flowerbeds lined the walls.

Women dressed in tan gowns and men in brown trousers tended to the flowers using their manipulations to bloom and grow them. A few women hurried over to our group, holding vines in their hands.

The man leading us paused, and the women walked up to each of us, placing the vines that were woven into necklaces around our necks. The woman placing mine on gave me a warm and welcoming smile.

It still all made me feel uneasy. There was something nagging at the back of my mind.

We continued to the other end of the courtyard and into another identical hall. At the end, it opened into a room with high ceilings and two parallel staircases that spiraled up to another floor. I glanced up and noticed the entire ceiling was painted. Floral fields stretched across the space, and I had to crane my neck to get a look at the entire piece.

The man led us up the golden metal steps. At the top, the landing overlooked the large room we had just walked through, a large glass window on the same wall as the door. I hadn't noticed it when we walked in, but now, I could see perfectly out it. It held a view of not only the courtyards, but the distant capital city.

The sight was breathtaking.

Bellamy stood close to me, and I felt his arm brush against mine. My heart fluttered at the touch of the prince.

Caspian joined on my other side, and I heard him wince a bit as he brought his hand up to his shoulder, reminding me of the wound that still needed to heal.

"Come," the man said from behind us as he pushed open doors before him.

We walked through, and I instantly realized we'd entered the throne room. At the opposite end, Asena stood next to a man. He was tall and handsome with dark curly brown hair, his golden skin far darker than hers.

On the throne next to them sat an older man, his long, dark curls mixed with strands of grey. A golden crown graced his head, and I recognized the crown crest embroidered onto his green finery.

King Pilor Bramden.

"Thank you, Kai," he said, his voice echoing across the room as he dismissed the guard. "Come forward," he commanded, waving us toward the throne as he stood. "My captain of the guard tells me you travel with the princess."

My head turned side to side, taking in the beautiful trees that lined the edge of the room. They were short but perfectly trimmed. The golden throne the king sat on had metal vines wrapping up the front and sides of it.

The king moved forward a few steps, forcing us to pause.

"You safely escorted the princess to my nephew," he said. I didn't detect a single hit of anger or disgust behind his words. "She also speaks of a coming war," he continued, his voice deepening and his eyes turning to Bellamy. I watched the prince shift uncomfortably.

Bellamy's father's crimes were not his, but I still saw the shame he bore.

I instinctively shifted, ready to protect him. I'd seen the way my own kingdom had turned on him, blaming his father for the deaths of hundreds, ready to use the prince as revenge.

"Be calm, child," the king said, his head snapping towards me. "I do not wish the prince harm. The princess spoke highly of him and has told me of the alliance he has offered to the other kingdoms."

I glanced past the king to Asena, unable to read her face.

"Asena has asked on your behalf for my aid in the upcoming war against your father," the king spoke.

"My father will destroy the other three kingdoms," Bellamy said.

"The earth kingdom does not fight another's battles. Luheo has already come to me, begging for my assistance in their assault on Abelon," he explained.

That was one less kingdom for us to convince in joining the fight.

"My father will burn the earth kingdom to the ground. There is no stopping him unless the kingdoms work together," Bellamy completed.

"We've already seen what a small portion of his army can do," Caspian chimed in. "They led a siege on the capital of Morwen. We narrowly escaped, but most of the port and much of the city was burned in their wake. That was only a portion; imagine what the full strength of the kingdom could do."

The king narrowed his eyes on Caspian. "I've already made my decision, and as I've told the princess, I have no desire to join a war if I do not need to. You are welcomed guests of the kingdom; that is the furthest I can do. My hospitality goes only so far. I will not set sail for Abelon for a fight that has not come to our shores yet."

"But it will come to your shores," Bellamy said.

"And when it does, the kingdom will be prepared to protect their own," he said. "I am throwing a ball tomorrow night to welcome the princess. You are welcome to stay in the palace and attend. After that, I kindly ask you leave and take your battle elsewhere."

He turned away and walked past the throne to a door behind it.

"I'll show you your room," a voice said behind us.

We turned to find Kai waiting for us.

I turned back once more to glance at Asena, and she peered back over her shoulder, pleading with me before the king's nephew ushered her out of the throne room.

I recognized that woman.

I was that woman only months before, trapped in a marriage I didn't ask for, in a new kingdom I'd been forced to call my home.

She turned away, and I rejoined our group, following them out of the room.

CHAPTER 27

NYLA

"Someone stayed here," Cyrus said, kneeling on the ground beneath the trees.

He swiped a hand across the dirt, remnants of ash coating his fingers.

It had taken us a full day before Nondaar made it to the estate to carry us over the wall.

We'd fallen behind pursuing the escaped group. I knew by now my brother would've made it to Gralar. Once he was under the protection of the king, there was little I could do.

Still, I insisted on tracking their route and following them. If we could catch up in the city, we stood a chance of still being able to capture them. Otherwise, we could bargain for a small ship and sail back to our fleet.

I spent the day following Cyrus' lead, afraid to make another misstep.

When I finally saw Gralar, I wanted to collapse. We hadn't caught up, which meant he made it into the city and would not have wasted time finding the king.

All my anger and frustration came boiling to the surface.

I could no longer hold it in and let out a scream. Fire grew around me, closing me in and blocking out Cyrus before I could catch a look at his face. I let the fire build until it raged high above me.

I remained hidden behind the flames, shrouded from the captain's judging stare.

I'd been the reason we failed. I let the war inside me tear me apart. I'd been holding back, unable to embrace the unforgiving side of me to become the fire princess my father expected.

Every seed of doubt took root in me, and every part of me that ever had love for my brother held me back from being the monster I needed to be.

Maybe I had sabotaged myself. Maybe I never wanted to find Bellamy. Deep down, everything was holding me back.

I had to deal with the consequences.

I took a deep breath and started to shove all of it aside. I could no longer be that woman. I knew I finally had to let it go.

Standing on this hill where I knew my brother must've stood not long before, I knew I needed to do whatever it took to bring him to Abelon alive. If not to satisfy my father, then to preserve myself.

No longer could I continue to shove my wellbeing aside. War was coming, and if I did not act now, it would destroy me. I needed to survive.

I stood up, letting the tears I hadn't realized were falling dry up. I wiped my eyes and dropped the flames around me. Cyrus stood, facing me, watching my every move.

My sanity was slowly slipping from my grasp. Each

second I spent with the captain infuriated me further. I was trapped in a nightmare, one where my father controlled my every move, manipulating me the way he had my brother for years.

The only thing I could grab hold of was bringing Bellamy home and fixing the imbalance. Abelon would never survive without its prince. Cyrus could not ascend the throne as my betrothed. I'd do whatever necessary to bring Bellamy home. He would follow in my father's footsteps, and then I would have my freedom back.

I took a step forward away from the now scorched ground and met his eyes, holding his stare. Before I could change my mind and go back to being the helpless princess who was her own worst enemy, I held out my hand to Cyrus.

"I'll help you," I said. "I'll do whatever it takes to get Bellamy home."

I'd find a way to betray Cyrus later. For the time being, I had to do what was necessary to capture the prince.

Cyrus wanted revenge. I knew he wanted to see Bellamy dead, and I still wouldn't let that happen. With him by my side, I could avoid my father's punishment and save the rest of Abelon. I would worry about the rest after. It was one simple goal at a time.

Cyrus took my hand and pulled me closer as his devilish grin spread across his face. I swallowed hard at the delight in his eyes.

"It's too late for that, princess," he whispered.

Before I could even register the words, he pulled me in and spun me around, wrapping a strong arm around my neck. The pressure on my throat was too great, and I couldn't squirm from his grasp. I choked for air, but nothing came. My eyes grew heavy, tired of fighting and tired of running. I gave in to the darkness and allowed myself to slip away.

I woke aboard a small ship, surrounded by the sea.

My head pounded.

I took deep breaths, savoring the ability to breathe.

Cyrus sat at the head of the small boat. Thankfully, the sails were enough to carry us across the waves.

"Where—" I started. I tried to sit up but found it hard, my hands completely tied up behind my back.

"Do you really think I can't burn through this?" I asked, cocking my head at Cyrus.

"No, but it will slow you down enough. You'd be a fool to try anything," he growled. "I'm not letting you out of my sight until we make it to the shores of Abelon."

My heart sank. Cyrus had abandoned the hunt for Bellamy, forfeiting the prince to return home.

"But my father—" I said.

"Your father ordered me to watch you and clean up after your mistakes. He would not wish for me to allow you to make the fire kingdom look any weaker than you already have. I'm taking you home before you ruin anything further for him."

I pulled against the ropes that held my arms, but they were tight, with little room to move.

"We confirmed the prince made it to Gralar. We know what he's after. He wants to build an army against your father. There's nothing more we can do but return to Abelon and ready our own army. War is coming to our shores, led by your brother, thanks to you."

"My father started this war," I spat.

I wasn't sure what came over me, the words tumbling out of my mouth before I could stop myself.

Bellamy was a fool to march armies against our father, but I was not naïve enough to think it was not my own father who started the war first.

We needed the land. We had nothing to build on. The entire kingdom was a wasteland of flames and ash. Our resources were dwindling. If we didn't act soon, we would be left without anything. If bringing Bellamy home would've stopped that and restored my freedom, I would've done anything to make it happen.

All of that was impossible now. He had forced me to give up.

I craned my neck to look past him. Our fleet of ships sat in the distant water, and I recognized the red flags on them. My personal army awaited my return. I shook my head with the thought. The fleet did not wait for me—it awaited its captain.

Defeat overcame me as we were welcomed on board. Cyrus set the course for Abelon immediately, and we wasted no time.

The sail home was uneventful. We met no ships in the sea, and Cyrus held true to his promise, never letting me out of his sight. He forced me to sleep in the same room as him and followed me everywhere on the ship.

I felt like a prisoner to Abelon once more.

Dread filled my body when I spotted the shores of Abelon a few days later. We docked in Raden, where the royal guards met us with horses. Cyrus and I rode separately, leaving behind the fleet and the army on it. My time at sea was over. I knew they'd instantly jump into preparations for the approaching war. I overheard Cyrus already beginning to prepare on our journey back.

Whispers had spread quickly across the ship. The prince was coming home.

Even on my own horse, away from Cyrus, I was no fool to think I was finally free. Cyrus was marching me straight back to my father.

My nerves grew, my chest tight.

My father would force me to pay the price, to learn my lesson and never repeat these mistakes again. My brother wasn't here to save me from his wrath this time. I had to face it alone.

I'd become lost in my thoughts and hadn't realized when we stepped through the front gates to the palace. The flames parted for us, and the guards welcomed us back.

Overhead, I watched Veros and Nondaar fly past the palace, heading toward the mountains of fire where they resided. Cyrus had barely allowed me to see my dragon on the journey home. He knew if I could climb onto Veros, I would take off and never come back.

Every single night, I had tossed and turned in bed, praying to Mavalu for the moment I could reunite with my beast. I'd fly to another kingdom, or further. I'd push myself to the brink of the Vitrum Sea, discover what lies beyond it.

Maybe the world just stopped. Maybe there was something larger waiting for us.

I climbed off the horse and made my way inside the palace I was so familiar with. The walk to the throne room was mindless. Every second spent walking, I dwelled on the punishment I would face.

I failed at bringing my brother, the traitor of Abelon, home. The failure alone made me as much a traitor to my kingdom as him. I knew my shortcomings were unacceptable, and the punishment may be my death, if my father so chose.

It was a short walk to where I knew my father waited, but my feet felt heavy, dragging along the floor. Cyrus stood beside me and took hold of my arm, pulling me along.

"Do not keep him waiting," he hissed in my ear. I pulled my arm back and kept my eyes ahead.

Back on the ship, Cyrus had forced me to dress in a long black gown, taking away every choice I had. I was forced to eat when he ate, forced to dress how he saw fit, and forced to follow his command.

I knew I looked the part he wanted: the princess who'd become a monster, her soul black as the night sky.

A guard stood post at the doors and opened them wide. I strode through, walking straight across the room. My father already sat in his throne, scowling, eyes settled on me.

I diverted my gaze to the ground and continued my walk while Cyrus remained at the entrance of the room. I stopped only feet away from the steps to the dais, my head bowed until my father spoke.

"You failed."

I looked up to find he was already standing from the throne. I swallowed hard.

"You have returned without your brother. You have failed at your one task. Why do you stand before me now?" he asked.

"Please," I started. "I need more time."

"You've had plenty of chances. Do you not think the captain of a guard would not send a report ahead of arrival?" the king asked.

I quickly turned to look at the smug look plastered on Cyrus' face. He got word to my father, guaranteeing what I said would not matter. He told the story he knew my father would want to hear, the one that painted him as the glowing hero of Abelon and me, the failed princess.

"I-" I started, turning back to my father.

"You have made Abelon look weak," my father stated. He stepped down the steps toward me. Fire trailed behind him, and I felt my body go rigid.

"You will learn from what you've done," my father said in an eerie, steady tone.

A wall of flames circled us, closing in and blocking out the guards.

"Kneel," my father demanded, and I listened without hesitation. My knee dropped to the floor, and I bowed my head. "Hold your hand out," my father commanded.

I outstretched my non-dominant hand, afraid of what my lesson would be. I'd always seen the results of Bellamy's shortcomings, forced to take care of them after. Punishment after punishment came, and he never reached the impossible standard our father set.

I should've let myself succumb to the darkness. I

should've poured everything I had into bringing him home, to escape fate.

It was selfish.

I knew if it wasn't me, it would be Bellamy, but he had always been able to handle it. I knew my father wouldn't kill him, but I was disposable. I was not the heir he wanted.

If I had poured all the fire inside me into bringing him home instead of waging a battle inside my own head, I wouldn't be kneeling before my father. Regret washed over me the moment my father took my hand in his own. My eyes held the floor, staring at his black leather boots.

Instantly, pain seared through my body, my father's hands lighting with flames. He held my hand tight as I tried to pull it back. My flesh burned, and the stench of my skin reached my nose, nauseating me.

He held tight as I screamed in agony. The flames around us trapped us inside, but I knew everyone outside could hear as I let out another scream of agony.

He let the flesh on my hand burn until it was useless. When he finally let go, the flames disappeared around us, and I collapsed to the floor, grabbing my wrist. The limb was mutilated. My throat ached, and I threw up the contents of my stomach.

Darkness trickled into my vision, and I couldn't bear the pain any longer.

"Take her to a healer," my father hissed at Cyrus.

The last thing I saw before everything went black was the captain lifting me into his arms, a satisfied grin stretching across his lips.

CHAPTER 28

BELLAMY

My fist hit the wall for the hundredth time, and I let out a sound of fury.

I watched as Koraine's eyes widened, afraid to stop me. The terror on her face was enough to snap me out of my anger. I moved across the room and sat next to her on the bed we shared. I felt her slight flinch away from me.

"I'm sorry," I said gently. "I let my temper control me."

"You've been at this for hours. These feelings are only temporary," she reminded me.

"I know," I said, remembering the same words from my mother. "I know it's no use. There's nothing I can say that'll change his mind until my father shows up in Zetron, but by then, it will be too late."

She's slowly nodded. I'd been over it a thousand times with her.

"I'm sorry," I repeated.

"I'm just worried for you," she said.

"Worried for me?" I asked, sliding closer when her

muscles finally relaxed. I let my temper slip away and felt my skin cool down from its fevered pitch.

"I'm worried about what happens if the kingdoms don't join us. I'm terrified your father will bring you back to Abelon and you won't survive. I'm terrified of being separated, and I'm afraid rage will slowly consume you," she said, her eyes darkening.

I reached a hand to her face and gently stroked my thumb along her jaw before placing it on her cheek as her hand came up to meet mine. I needed her to trust me, not to fear me.

"I'm afraid Cyrus will catch up to us and you will destroy each other," she admitted, her eyelashes fluttering, deep blue eyes meeting mine.

I slid back onto the plush bed, inviting Koraine to crawl further onto it. She pulled her legs up onto the bed and nuzzled into my chest as I held her tightly.

I didn't want her to worry for me.

"Cyrus will never stop until he has the revenge he seeks," I said.

"Why does he hate you so much? Your father favors him, and he sees the way he punishes you. Why does he want to hurt you further?" Koraine pushed.

"It's long story," I said, dreading the history there.

"We have time," Koraine said, motioning around us.

I didn't know if I could. I struggled opening up about our past. I'd never told anyone the truth beyond those who were there. Cyrus wanted me dead, and it went further than rivalries or being power-hungry.

I swallowed hard as she patiently waited. "I'm the reason his father is dead," I said.

"What?" she gasped.

"He blames me for his father's death, and he will never forgive me for that," I continued.

"How can you be the reason he's dead? His father died in the war. We were only children," Koraine said.

"He's right," I said, hanging my head. "I am the reason he's dead. The war broke out when I was still a child, but I was expected to train as the prince who would take the throne one day. Every battle was an opportunity for me to learn, to practice. My father didn't care about my age. He didn't care if I was ready for more responsibility. I was forced to sit at his table while strategies were reviewed and plans were made. My father also used it as an excuse for punishment. Every mistake or wrong suggestion I made, he would burn the right answer into my mind."

Koraine's eyes widened in understanding.

"The Battle of Gila was never supposed to be a huge offensive. My father made me weigh in on how to approach. I was asked to compare our warriors and decide who would be best to lead the affront. It was a harmless task. A king should easily be able to make the decision. I spent so long going back-and-forth comparing our best to send to that island. I never expected the decision would have all the men slaughtered. I couldn't have known what your father would do that day."

Tears streamed down space Koraine's face, and I hated how she looked at me like I was broken.

"I sent Cyrus' father to his death. I chose him. The decision was completely on me, and when those men didn't return, my father made sure everyone knew who to blame,"

I said. "Cyrus has never let that go. He wants me to pay for the wrong decision I made."

I could feel my voice starting to break. I swallowed hard and could feel my body trembling at the memory.

"You were only a child," Koraine said softly, reaching out to grab my hand.

"It doesn't matter. A prince never gets a childhood, and I was the prince of the most ruthless kingdom. I was expected to follow in my father's footsteps. I am the reason his father is dead."

My words broke her. Koraine was shaking, trying hard to be a steady hand for me, but she was crumbling at the realization of everything I had lost to my father's rule.

I never got the childhood my mother wanted for me. I was never allowed to be carefree.

My heart broke for my sister. Now, the burden I carried for all those years, the burden of making my father happy and bending to his will, was hers. I tried to open my mouth to speak, but nothing came out.

Koraine wrapped her arms around my center and held me tightly. I returned the comfort, trying to shove the feelings aside.

"No one should ever have to carry a burden like that alone," Koraine whispered softly.

"No, my moon," I agreed. "No one should ever, and no one ever will again."

CHAPTER 29

KORAINE

I woke to the loudest explosion of my life. Bellamy had already jumped out of our bed, running over to the balcony, and I followed quickly, searching for the threat.

I flinched as another explosion rang out, and fire rained from the sky, fizzling out as it approached the ground.

"Did they find us?" I asked Bellamy, my heart racing.

He turned back to me from the balcony, a smile growing on his face.

"What?" I asked, feeling like I could barely breathe.

"No, my moon. No one has found us. Come see for yourself."

I walked out onto the balcony, and Bellamy pointed to the sky. Another bang rang out, and I watched as a flaming ball of rock hurdled into the sky. Then, it broke apart, the fire exploding into a beautiful display across the night sky.

"It's a celebration, not an attack," Bellamy said with a soft chuckle.

A movement caught my attention, and I spotted Ervin and Caspian on a balcony a few rooms away. I gave a slight

wave to my brother, my arms still trembling as my body realized we were safe.

"I've never seen this before," I admitted to Bellamy.

"I don't imagine Morwen often allows flames in their
lands," he said.

"No, we certainly do not," I laughed.

We stood on the balcony, Bellamy's arm wrapping
around my shoulder, watching the fire display continuing to
rain through the sky.

The amount of flame used was small enough that when
it fell from the sky, it trickled out before any embers could
catch on the ground below. I watched in awe, amazed at the
sight.

Guards below littered the grounds of the palace, helping
manipulate the display. I imagined the king would be
watching from his own balcony, somewhere far off in the
palace.

I shivered as my body finally settled.

"Come inside," Bellamy directed, heading back in to our
room.

"It'll be a while before I can fall back asleep after that," I
joked.

Bellamy sat on the bed and grabbed my hips, pulling me
in close. "I can think of a few ways we could spend the rest
of the night," he said, his voice sending a shiver down my
spine.

"And how would you have me, prince?" I asked.

"In every way," he said slowly. "I would savor you, please
you in all the ways I could think of for the rest of the night."

My cheeks reddened at the promise behind his words.
"And if I wish to please you?"

"Seeing your pleasure come from my touch is the only thing I ever need."

He pulled me in swiftly and pressed a hard kiss to my lips as I met him with as much desperation as I could. I'd been waiting since that night behind the waterfall to finally feel the prince pressed against me like this again.

"Your wounds?" I asked, remembering the barrier that stopped us last time.

"Thanks to you, they are completely healed."

"Are you sure?" I asked, not trusting him, if I was honest.

"Even if they hadn't, you would never be able to stop me from claiming this," he answered, pulling me onto the bed and guiding my legs to straddle him.

I leaned into his touch, his wandering hands. I still couldn't get enough. I wanted to live in this moment forever. I let myself take a deep inhale as I tilted my head back.

The prince's hands wandered up my torso, and I removed the layer between us. I'd slipped into a nightgown before crawling into bed to sleep. Now, that decision was hindering me from allowing the prince to explore my body fully.

"Remove it," I demanded. Bellamy tilted his head and glanced over the thin gown covering my body.

Torturously slow, he pulled up the material. My breath hitched as he pulled it over my head. My body was fully exposed, only my skin before him. I could feel my nipples harden against the cold of the room, and I missed the warm fireplaces of Abelon.

He pulled me close, his own warmth lighting my skin on fire. Kisses trailed down my neck before he took my breast into his mouth, nipping at my skin. I clawed his clothing, desperate to pull off the shirt he wore. My hands fumbled clumsily with the material.

"Let me help," he said gently.

His hands slowly pulled his shirt over his head, and I was comforted seeing the way his skin had healed. I found no new bruises or remaining cuts. Still, I ran my hands over his chest, as if I needed to confirm it with my own touch.

"I told you I was alright," he assured me.

"None of us are truly okay," I said, and he nodded. "It'll take time for us to heal, but I wouldn't wish to do it with anyone else. Some wounds are deeper than just the skin," I whispered to Bellamy.

"I know," he said. "I'd spend every moment I can chasing away that darkness," he promised. I kissed him, and my lips felt like they were on fire.

Bellamy slid back further into the bed, pulling me with him. I remained on top of him, and my hips ground against his body. I could feel the way he ached to be with me, his cock hardened through his trousers.

"Why did you sleep in this?" I asked, annoyed by another barrier between us.

I saw his eyes, and I regretted the teasing question immediately.

"I wanted to be ready in case they found us," he admitted.

I swallowed hard and let my hands wander gently over his skin, I couldn't keep myself from cracking. All the pain and uncertainty had molded us into new people. Our peace was no longer intact. Every night, we had to sleep knowing it could be our last rest before war.

The prince found my hands and slowly pulled them down to his waistband.

"We could go back to sleep," I said sheepishly.

"Is that what you wish?" he asked.

"No," I admitted.

"Nor I," he said

My hands made quick work of his pants, pulling them off, and I found him hard and ready for me beneath. I slid my hand down his torso to the base of his cock, and it bobbed at my touch.

Bellamy's head fell back into the pillow, his chin tipping up as he let out a breathy moan, my hand moving along his shaft.

I stroked slowly up and down once.

I paused at the bottom.

"Do that again," he moaned.

I stroked again and again, listening as his breathing grew more feral.

I let a small amount of water form around my hands, the slight wetness providing a lubricant to the friction of his skin. He let out another sound of pleasure before suddenly flipping us, pinning me beneath him.

I had no time to react.

I laid beneath Bellamy, his legs straddling me, holding me to the bed. I tried to move and flip him back, but he held me down with his legs.

"You're going nowhere," he growled, and the way the words washed over me made my core warm.

He kissed along my torso, stopping to savor my breasts. Every inch of me warmed and begged for him to move lower. I bucked my hips, hoping to encourage him to continue his trail downward, and Bellamy flicked his tongue over my nipple.

"So impatient, my moon," he scolded. "Sit still and let me do my work."

I let my muscles relax and stop fighting, allowing him to savor and explore every inch of my body. He left no amount of skin untouched.

His mouth continued its way down, and soon, I found him between my legs. I had everything I wanted and more.

Bellamy continued to pleasure me, sending my mind spinning. His lips found their way to my center, and his hands pulled off the thin lace undergarments I wore.

I could feel my center slick and ready for him. His fingers found my opening and slid in effortlessly, his tongue sending me into a spiral of pleasure.

I tipped his chin up, forcing him to look at me. His dark eyes settled on my face as his tongue grazed over his lower lip.

"I need you," I whispered.

The prince moved then, climbing up and over me. His hands rested on either side of my shoulders as I reached down to guide his cock to my center. The wet of his tongue and my arousal allowed him to slide easily into me.

At first, it stung, the length and size of him stretching me. I let out a quiet moan, and Bellamy lifted a hand to brush my hair from my face.

"Only a moment more, my moon," he promised, and I knew what he meant.

Just hold on a second, and the pain would melt into pleasure.

He was right. Another few seconds, and the stinging

receded. My center was slick and wet, helping guide him in and out of me. Bellamy brushed a deliberate path with his hand along my side, landing on my hip. He held tight as he continued to pump into me.

Suddenly, he slowed his pace, pulling his cock out at a painfully unhurried rate. I bucked my hips, but he continued the torture.

"You're teasing me," I accused.

"Or am I savoring you?" he asked.

He returned to his faster pace, a small moan escaping his lips. I could tell he wasn't giving me his everything. He felt reserved, like he was keeping something from me.

"Don't hold back," I panted.

That was enough for him to snap. He pulled out and grabbed my waist. His strong hands flipped me over and guided me to my hands and knees before he took my hair in his hands, tugging softly on it.

I let out a heady moan as his cock slid easily inside me once more. I arched my back at the feeling, the new angle wringing new amounts of pleasure from me.

I wanted everything he had to offer, to spend the entire night finding new ways to explore each other in bed. We only had hours before we would sail for Abelon. The moment we left the shores of Zetron, there was no guarantee we would come back. War was brutal. It ripped away the people you loved with no mercy. When the fighting began, it would take everything in us to protect each other.

Bellamy's skin slapped against my back side. The sound echoed through our room, and I blushed at the prospect that anyone in the hall could hear us.

"Shouldn't we be more discreet?" I asked.

Bellamy tugged on my hair again. "No one is stopping us from having this moment."

I tried to push the worry aside, focusing on the feelings coursing through my body. I could feel myself approaching a climax. My body was trembling, barely holding on.

"Come for me, my moon," Bellamy demanded.

That was all I needed to hear. I let my body relax and toppled into pleasure. Every part of me felt like it was on fire, the pleasure tingling across my skin.

Bellamy's hands moved to my hips, his nails digging into me as he gripped my flesh. I felt his body tense and knew he was close to joining me. He thrust into me again, and a deep moan rumbled through his chest as he finished inside me. His cock slowed, and eventually, he pulled completely out.

I turned around, sitting before him as he leaned in and kissed me again. His tongue brushed against my lips, and I moved closer. I lost my balance, and we both toppled into the bed.

Our naked bodies tangled, and I wrapped a leg around Bellamy, trying to hold him close.

"We could do that again," Bellamy offered between labored breaths.

'We really should sleep," I pointed out.

"What fun would that be?" Bellamy noted.

I shoved playfully at his arm. I could feel myself grinning wide, my cheeks still warm from my climax.

"We need all the rest we can get," I answered, rolling my eyes.

"As much as I dislike it, you're right, my moon," he agreed, pulling me in.

His arms wrapped around me, and I spun in his grasp,

pushing back against him. I wiggled until my entire backside was pressed into the prince's body.

"You're teasing me," he said with a laugh.

"It's your punishment for teasing me earlier," I laughed.

He gave me a gentle squeeze. "Goodnight, my moon," he whispered in my ear as I dozed off. Exhaustion washed over me, and I found no struggle giving in to the sleep that called for me.

CHAPTER 30

NYLA

I woke on a rock solid cot. My body arm ached, and I moaned in agony. I tried to blink away the darkness, but my vision was blurry.

I glanced around, barely recognizing the room. The space felt familiar, but my memory was clouded. It was small, the walls made of stone. The single window across from me poured light into the room, and I prayed I hadn't been out more than a few hours.

"You're awake," a woman's gentle voice said.

I tried to sit up, but my head pounded.

"Rest, princess," she insisted.

"Where am I?" I asked.

"The infirmary," woman answered.

I squinted and was able to make out the dark haired woman. Again, I tried to sit, and it took longer than I hoped, my muscles tired. The ache in my arm felt unbearable, and I let out another moan of agony.

I glanced down where my father had burned my hand. A large bandage covered the area, and my stomach sunk as I saw it fully covered my hand. I couldn't see my fingers or anything beneath.

"How bad is my hand?" I asked.

The woman bit her lip and took a step back. I felt nauseous.

"How bad is it?" I asked again, my body trembling.

"I —" she started. "I'm sorry, princess."

"What do you mean? Will I be able to use it again?" I asked, my voice broken.

"No," she said, and my heart shattered. "I couldn't save it."

"Couldn't save what?" I was shaking.

"Your hand," she said. "I'm sorry, princess. We had to remove it. There was nothing left to save."

Again, I threw up the little remaining contents of my stomach. My vision turned spotty, and I could feel my heart racing.

"Lay back down," the woman commanded.

She helped me down, and I pulled my arm close, hugging it. The bandage where my hand would've been was all I could stare at.

"It's gone?" I whispered.

She nodded slowly. "I'm sorry, but it was too bad. There was no way for me to save what remained. If I tried, it would've left you susceptible to infection, with little functional limb left. It was safer this way. Your father demanded you be ready for war. This was the only way I could guarantee that," she said, her voice trembling.

I knew it wasn't her fault. My father had threatened her. This was his doing. He knew exactly what he'd done the moment he called those flames to his hands.

I had failed and made the fire kingdom susceptible. I'd opened our shores for attack. This was a mercy.

This was the only time I'd known my father to do so—because I was his own flesh and blood. He spared my life but left me a reminder of what happened when I failed. There was no other way to explain why I was still alive after my embarrassment.

"He asked I send you to him when you woke," she said. "I can give you few more hours."

I closed my eyes and let the darkness consume me again.

"Thank you," I whispered, grateful for the kindness. I wasn't ready to accept my fate. I needed more time.

When I woke again, the woman from before was gone, and a new woman stood beside my cot.

"I'm sorry, princess," she said softly. "Your father's counsel is meeting, and he has requested your presence."

She held out a hand to help me sit up. I slid my legs off to the side, standing as my vision instantly went fuzzy again.

I fought back a wave of nausea and lightheadedness but managed to take a few steps to a basin nearby. It was already full of water, and I splashed some on my face. A mirror hung above it, and I looked up into it.

My skin was a shade lighter than my usual warm tone. I looked like a ghost.

I splashed water on my face and cupped some into my hand to use to slick my hair back. I reached up to pull it back but realized I couldn't manage with only my left hand.

"Let me," the woman said gently, stepping forward and pulling my hair back. She tied it with a ribbon from her pocket.

"Thank you," I said softly.

Worry crept in, and already, I feared how useless I'd become. I'd be of no use to my father if I could not wield fire.

I called on my flames in my left hand and sighed, knowing it would be a long journey before I relearned how to tame my fire with only a single hand.

I nodded to the woman as I left the infirmary, knowing I had to find my father. If I kept him waiting, it would be another lesson to endure.

I made my way to the throne room where he held most meetings. If Bellamy was bringing an army to our shores, my father and Cyrus would waste no time preparing.

The infirmary sat in one of the spires, and I walked down the spiral steps, making my way to the throne room. It took longer, the need to pause every few steps forcing me to lean against a wall. Nausea and faintness plagued me.

I finally arrived and pushed through the doors to find a table set in the center of the room, my father's top generals around it. Cyrus stood directly behind my father, his eyes shifting up to watch me.

I saw the sickening grin grow on his face the moment he watched me walk through the room. I wanted to kill him. My punishment was his fault. I never would've come back to Abelon without Bellamy. I would've died trying to return my brother home rather than face my father's wrath. Cyrus had taken that choice away.

"Nyla," my father's voice boomed across the room. "Join us," he said, nodding to a seat next to him. I hurried across the room, all eyes watching me. My legs trembled, but I managed to make my way into the seat.

I sat quietly, listening to the men around the table argue over strategy, where to station different portions our fleet, and when to expect the forces coming.

The voices soon drowned out, and a buzzing rang in my ears. I found my eyes wandering over to Cyrus, unable to stop myself. I thought of all the ways I would make him suffer for this.

My arm ached, and I bit down hard on the inside of my lip to keep myself from wincing.

My mind fell distant and hazy. I ventured that the healers had given me a form of tonic to numb the true extent of the pain. I knew it would wear off eventually. I was afraid I wouldn't be able to handle the pain when it did.

I tried to sit through the rest of the war meeting, answering my father's questions when I could.

Where would I position are men, the docks or the beach?

How many patrols should we send out?

How often?

The questions were numbing, and I barely heard my answers. I tried to mimic what Bellamy would say.

I started to feel the beginning of the pain coming back. It was odd. My mind had not fully registered that my hand was no longer there. Each time I went to move it or thought about it, my mind took a few moments before I realized it was gone.

I pushed back my chair, knowing I had to get myself out of the room. I couldn't let these men see my weakness. I couldn't give my father another reason to get rid of me.

I stood without thinking.

"Sit down," my father growled.

My cheeks reddened, eyes boring into me.

"Excuse me, my king," I started. "I must tend to something."

I kept my head lowered, waiting and praying for my father to dismiss me. My heart pounded, hoping he wouldn't question me further.

I was unnecessary to the meeting. I led no armies. He trusted me with no amount of power. I was a pawn in his game, and whatever they decided today, I would be forced to follow.

"You are dismissed," my father said insincerely.

He immediately moved to focus his attention back on a map sprawled across the table. It reflected the entirety of Abelon. I noticed the small pawns all over the map to represent our armies.

Had those been there before? I hadn't noticed them until now. I shook my head, the cloudiness slowing my thoughts.

I raised my head further and found Cyrus' eyes narrowed on me, studying me instead of the war strategies.

I rushed from the room, my remaining hand holding the bandaged arm. I felt tears welling in my eyes, stinging as I tried to push them away. I made it into the hall, hurrying back to where I knew the healers' quarters were.

Exhaustion started to sink in, and I prayed for mercy from Mavalu.

Movement behind me caught my attention, and I froze, trying to train my face back to neutral.

"What is so important that you leave a war meeting?" Cyrus asked.

I turned to find him waiting, his face infuriating. My fist clenched, and my nails dug into my hand. Everything that happened was because of him, because he gave up our search for Bellamy.

"Back to the healers," I spoke.

"Then I will escort you," he said. "I am to be your husband. I want to make sure my wife is okay."

The way he said wife made my insides turn. It was a façade, a way to stay in my father's good graces. Play the helpful and caring husband, tend to the princess and protect her, and my father would grant him more power.

More power for him to abuse.

I scoffed. A new wave of adrenaline kept me from collapsing in pain.

"Okay?" I asked. "I am not okay. Because of you, we lost Bellamy. We lost the one thing that would've gave us power here. The one thing that would've freed us from this ridiculous marriage. Because of you, I lost this." I held up the bandaged arm.

"That was your doing," Cyrus sneered.

"I would've found him," I said.

"You were making fool of yourself. Everything you do reflects on your father. I was not going to let you make the kingdom look weak any longer."

I swallowed hard, tears threatening to stream down my face.

I turned away from Cyrus, expecting him to follow, but

he never did. He chose to return to my father, the single person he had the capacity of caring an ounce for.

I was nothing to him.

I continued back to the healers' quarters and stumbled through the door, the pain finally starting to return in full. The healers helped me back to the cot where I woke only hours before.

They rushed a tonic over to me, seeing the sweat beading on my face and the desperation staring at them.

I got it down quickly and let myself slip into oblivion.

Darkness called to me. I just wanted to slip away.

CHAPTER 31

BELLAMY

THE NEXT MORNING, Koraine and I slept in well past sunrise. I quietly snuck out of our shared bed and into the halls, trying to find any of the palace workers. After a few wandering turns, I stumbled into a woman dressed in a pale green gown.

"Are you lost?" she asked, concern in her eyes.

"I was just wondering where I might find food for breakfast?" I asked.

Her face softened, and she smiled. "I will send some to your room."

I headed back to the chambers to find Koraine already seated on the bed. Vibrant blue eyes watched me as I stalked across the room. She fiddled with her hair, pulling it back from her face and braiding it down her back.

I walked over to the curtains tied back away from the glass balcony doors and pulled the ribbon holding one. It easily slid out of place, and I walked over to Koraine, handing it to her for her braid.

"Where'd you go?" she asked, her eyes filled with curiosity. I loved the way her brows furrowed ever so slightly.

"To find food," I said.

Her hands wandered unknowingly to her stomach. A smile grew across her face. "I can always trust you to prioritize what's important," she teased.

"Well, since I don't have Ervin to rely on for a hot meal, I figured I'd settle for the next best thing," I said playfully. "Although, don't tell Ervin I've sought out another chef."

Koraine pretended to consider the idea, laughing softly.

She stood and walked over to me, her hands wandering up and around my neck. "Actually, I take that back," I said, and her eyes widened. "I settled for the third best thing."

"And what would be your second choice of a meal?" she said, raising a brow.

"You," I said, leaning in and playfully nipping at her neck.

Her hand moved to bring my face toward her, and she pressed her lips against mine.

"I think I might just love you," she said, pulling away from my lips.

"And I think I just might love you too, my moon," I answered.

After food arrived to our room, I ventured out to check on the rest of the group.

Ervin and Caspian were settled into their own room, and the pair explained Oleena had chosen to reside with the other priestesses in the palace.

I had no way of checking on the princess or knowing if Asena had settled into Zetron. It was no secret she missed

Morwen, and I empathized with her. As destructive as my home was, I still found myself wanting to return.

"If the earth king won't help us, we need to sail to the air kingdom next," Caspian said.

"There's no need," I said. "Luheo already wants my father dead. They've already declared war on Abelon after my failed invasion. We don't need to convince them to fight by our sides. We just need to pray they are ready in time."

"Will they sail on Abelon?" Caspian asked.

"I have no doubt," I answered.

"But there won't be enough of them. We still need more," Ervin noted.

I nodded my agreements.

The door open to their room opened, and Koraine slipped inside. She walked over and sat on the bed where her brother was already seated.

"I asked for clean bandages," she said, holding out her hand. "They said you could see their healer if you wish."

Caspian scoffed. "I don't need a healer."

"Let me be the judge," Koraine huffed.

I watched as she pulled back her brother's shirt, unwrapping the old bandages. The wound underneath was still raw and red. She manipulated water to her hands and worked it over the wound, causing Caspian to flinch. The movement was enough for her to decide to finish and re-wrap the wound with new clean bandages.

"Seeing a healer doesn't mean you're weak," I said, and Caspian whipped his head toward me.

"I don't need-"

"Just go see them," I stated. "Even if you don't think you need it, you need it. We need you and your strength. I'll feel better about sailing back to Abelon if you have that looked at," I stated.

"Fine," Caspian said, standing. I caught the quick look of gratitude on Koraine's face.

"I'll show you to them," she offered and held out her arm to her brother.

The pair disappeared from the room, and I was left in silence with Ervin.

"I know that look," he said gently.

"What look?" I asked, even though I could feel my muscles in my face tense and my brows furrowing.

"The one that tells me you're thinking of doing something rash," Ervin said.

"We need to try something else," I said. "Without the king's help, we stand no chance. We do not know if Morwen will stand with us, and the kingdom is still recovering from my sister. We need the strength of the earth kingdom," I explained.

"I know we do, but force is not how we get it," Ervin said.

"Then how?" I asked. My skin grew hot, and I could feel my patience slipping. No matter how hard I tried to control my temper, it still came at the worst times.

"Would your mother have forced the earth king's hand? Would she have forced his people to help in a war they didn't wish to be in?" he asked.

"She wouldn't need to," I said. "Her people would've done anything for her."

"Be that type of ruler," he said." The kind other kingdoms look too. The one they seek for help in times of need. A firm but gentle ruler."

"I still don't see how that gains support for our current war," I said.

"I'm sure you'll find away," Ervin said.

He walked over to the balcony of their room, pulling open the doors. The breeze hit me, and I shivered as I stepped out to join him.

"Soon, snow will come, and the kingdoms will be forced to turn back to their own lands. This war is coming faster than any of us would like, but if it is not now, then it will be months from now. Your father will never stop until we remove him from the throne," Ervin explained, staring out at the sun and the city beyond us.

"This ends now," I said. "This war will be his last."

The promise sent a shiver down my spine, anxiety and nerves rushing through my veins. Whatever came of the war was fate. There was no running from it. I had to face it, whether I was ready or not.

The door clicked open, and I turned to find a man stepping into the room. His emerald green uniform with the king's crest settled my racing heart that was always prepared for the worst.

"Prince," he addressed. "I've been sent to escort you."

"Escort me?" I asked.

"To training," he said.

"Training?" I asked. Ervin shrugged when I glanced to him in confusion.

"Go," Ervin said softly as I hesitated to follow.

I left the balcony and trailed behind the man as he led me down into the courtyard.

It was filled with men, all sporting metal weapons and matching uniforms. At least fifty guards filled the courtyard.

I knew it was only a small portion of the king's army—more would be on patrols or stationed throughout the kingdom.

The captain of the guard stood at the opposite end of the courtyard, in front of the men. I could see he was giving them orders, but I could not hear what.

I walked closer, and the man who led me disappeared.

The men spread out across the courtyard, and I spotted a few females amidst their ranks. Each jumped into different training exercises; some sparred while others worked on strength. Every aspect of their training was meticulously organized. I watched in awe.

A hand on my shoulder startled me, and I turned to find the earth king behind me.

"What is this? Did you bring me here to me to show me exactly what you wouldn't give us?" I demanded. Again, that same anger inside me rose.

I could feel my fury building, the flames ready to spring to life.

"No," he said firmly. "I brought you here to show you why I cannot give you my army."

"What do you mean?" I asked.

"These men and women trained tirelessly to perfect their skills and build their strength. They are ready at a moment's notice," he explained. He began to walk the outskirt of the courtyard, and I followed. "My army does not need to march on Abelon. We have always defended ourselves, and every single time, we have emerged stronger."

I swallowed hard.

"If your father comes to my lands, my army will meet him. We are stronger within this kingdom. Aeris gave us these lands to draw our power from. This kingdom is suited for the manipulators who live here. I will not march my army on a kingdom where they hold little power over those we battle."

My mind reeled as I thought of Abelon, of the desolate lands that provided nothing for its people. How could the fire kingdom be built by Mavalu for my people?

"They'll burn your kingdom to the ground before you even realize what's happening," I said.

"Let them try," the king said.

"You don't understand–" I started.

"Stay a bit, train with my men. I think you'll realize I do understand what it means to stay. I trust my people to protect their own," he said, turning and walking off.

I opened my mouth to argue but closed it as he put distance between us.

I turned back and found the captain of the guard watching me. He made his way across the courtyard to me, stopping only feet away.

"Do you spar?" were the only three words he spoke.

"Yes."

"Then today, you will be my opponent," he answered.

The fires within me jumped with excitement. I knew they needed to be released. All the tension and anger was building up, and I needed a way to let it out. I was thankful for the opportunity to channel it.

We stepped into the center of the courtyard, and most of the men and women paused to watch.

"Let's see if you can uphold your reputation," he stated. His eyes settled on me hungrily, and I knew the fight would not be an easy victory. "Can the future king of Abelon beat me?" he taunted, loud enough for the rest to hear. "Just a mere guard." He held his arms wide.

I knew he was trying to get into my mind, weaken me before the fight even started.

My fists clenched, at the ready. I could feel them warming, begging for me to release my flames.

I circled around my opponent, but he made the first move, sending a wall of rock rushing toward me. I dove to the side, rolling and standing back up quickly. I knew his abilities would push my endurance and speed to their limits.

Instantly, I threw fire back his direction. Flames barreled across the sky, and many who surrounded us took a few steps back. Again, another wall of rock wall barreled toward me, and I tried to sidestep but found another wall jutted up from the ground, slamming into my side.

I stumbled and regained my balance quickly.

I needed to get closer. The more space I allowed him, the easier he could manipulate the earth around me.

I threw flames in his direction, trying to push my way forward. Walls of rock flew up before him, blocking them. I continued my assault. If I could keep up the speed of my attacks, it would force him to defend.

Before I could take another step, the ground in front of me parted, and I dove back onto my ass to avoid falling into the growing pit. It was enough time to allow the captain to make his move. Another pillar of stone slammed into me when I tried to scramble to stand. I choked out a cough, the air leaving my lungs.

I stood quickly as another came my way. It narrowly missed.

I let my hands grow ablaze again and threw more fire in

his direction. The captain side-stepped and blocked each. I wanted to end the fight. It was useless spending all my energy on proving a point.

I wasn't even sure of the point I wanted to prove any more.

The spar had been a way to release the growing fury inside me, but all it was doing was draining my energy. What did I believe? That the king would help us if I won? That I would prove he was ill-prepared? The captain was one man. The king had hundreds more. He would not be persuaded by my one spar.

I pushed forward, needing the rush of adrenaline the fight was fueling. Letting all my rage out would clear my head, provide the clarity I needed to find a solution.

I threw more flames, and the captain raised his arms, pulling the earth upward in a dome-like shield. The fire struck the wall with a deafening sound as it shattered, sending dust and bits of rock flying.

He slammed a foot into the ground, and a large crack rapidly grew in my direction. I rolled to my right and cursed under my breath.

I was growing tired and needed to stop soon. I knew I had to. It was for my own good. My group needed me; I had just said the same to Caspian, and now, here I was, wasting my energy.

Distraction was my weakness,

A boulder flew through the air in my direction, and I couldn't move fast enough to dodge. Instead, I threw up a wall of fire in front of me, pouring all the rage I had left into it.

It was enough to stop the boulder, the stone exploding in

the air. I ducked and covered my head. It was the only thing I could do to protect myself from the falling debris.

When I glanced up, the captain stood mere inches from me,

My heart stopped. I knew it was over.

I prepared for the final blow, a punch to the face or kick to the gut, but it never came.

"Not bad," the captain admitted.

"Not bad?" I repeated. "That's all?"

"I know when to end a fight. There is no use in injuring you or wearing you down any further," Kai stated, the men and women around us already returning to their own training. "I'm Kai."

I stared, confused.

My father never would've left a fight ended so easily. There would have been some form of lesson, some pain to suffer for my mistake or failure. It was never enough to just yield.

I certainly did not allow Cyrus to walk away so easily. I'd let my rage consume me, burning him and leaving my mark.

"Train with us," Kai offered. I opened my mouth, but he cut me off. "There is still much you can learn from us, prince," he said as he walked away.

I debated leaving. I could find Koraine and spend the rest of the day regaining my energy. Still, something about the training around me made me reconsider. The temptation to stay was far too strong. It had been weeks since I last did any form of training.

If I didn't push myself too hard, it could only help us. We needed to be at our very best to face my father. Last second training would help me re-focus.

I spent a few hours in the courtyard, walking through exercises and allowing the guards to show me the weapons they trained with.

"This is a glaive," a woman said, handing me a long weapon. "Most of us are trained to carry and use them, although some prefer something shorter."

I held the pole in my hand, examining the large, sharp blade at the end. It felt bulky in my hands. I'd trained with daggers and swords but never something as large or long.

I handed it back, and the woman laughed. "It's not as easy as it looks at first," she said. "But after time, it gets a lot easier to wield, a lot like learning our elements when we are younger," she explained.

I barely remembered when my training had started as a child, likely starting before I even had the capacity to form coherent memories. The king had been preparing me since the day I was born to be king.

"Maybe someday, I will come back to learn," I said.

She smiled warmly. "If you do, I would be honored to teach you," she said, her eyes lighting up with passion.

This had been what Ervin meant. It was the same way my mother led her people, getting to know them and spending time learning their crafts.

If only I had the time to do the same with the rest of Zetron.

"My prince," a voice interrupted from behind, and I turned to find the same man from earlier standing behind me. "I have come to escort you back."

I was led back to my room in a hurried fashion. The first thing I did was search for Koraine, but she was nowhere inside our shared room. Koraine was missing, and my heart sped up, wondering where they had taken her.

"Not to fear. She is getting ready for the ball," the man said. "You'll meet her there."

I let out a quick sigh.

A bath was drawn, and I quickly washed my skin of the sweat plastered to it from training. The moment I stepped out of the bath, I was greeted by new people in my room. They carried pieces of finery and ushered me toward a mirror in the room.

I was forced to watch as they helped dress me in the outfit that had been chosen for me.

CHAPTER 32

KORAINE

A WOMAN ARRIVED at my room while Bellamy was gone and ushered me out of it. She led me down the hall to a new room, one filled with gowns.

"The king had them sent for you," she explained.

Each was a different shade of blue. It reminded me of home.

Of Morwen.

My mother would've loved them. My heart stung, wishing I could be home at her side as she grew sicker, but I knew I was doing this for her, to protect those like her who could not fight when the fire kingdom inevitably invaded their home.

I walked through the room, combing through each of the gowns.

"This one is my favorite," the woman said, holding up a dress for me.

It was fancier than I would've never chosen it for myself, but as a guest of honor, I knew it was important to uphold certain appearances. If an extravagant gown could help gain us support for the war, I'd do it.

I held out a hand to grab the gown, but the woman pulled it closer to her body.

"I'll help you," she assured me.

I turned and watched in a mirror as she helped me dress. It was tighter at the top, and it laced up in the back to hold it in place. The sparkling sleeves puffed ever so slightly near my shoulders, and the gown itself was large and fluffed out. I ran my fingers along the tulle material that gave it the extravagant look. I swayed in the mirror, watching how the gown sparkled as I moved. The woman untied my braid and worked quickly, pulling half of my hair away from my face and tying it back.

It was hard to believe that only days before, I had been trapped and beaten down. I'd come close to giving up. War was coming, and my hope was dwindling.

Looking at the woman who stared back at me in the mirror, I found a little spark of that hope once more.

My corset felt tight, and for a second, I fought to get a deep breath.

We were running out of time.

The ball was our last chance to win the king's favor and secure the peace I dreamt of. He promised us no support for the war, but that couldn't be the end of it. There had to be more I could do or say to convince him.

"Finished. Would you like me to escort you down?" she asked.

"Can Bellamy?" I asked, remembering the missing prince. My heart ached at his absence; he'd been missing most of the day, and already, the sun was close to setting.

"He's already being led down. You'll find your prince in the ballroom," she assured me.

My stomach felt unsettled; I hated being without Bellamy. I wanted to cling to his comfort, but I knew I couldn't.

I let the woman lead me down to the ball. She left me at the top of the steps that signaled the entrance to the ballroom. A crowd had gathered outside, waiting to enter with their partners.

I glanced around for familiar faces but found no comfort in the people around me.

"Do you need an escort?" an older gentleman asked, approaching me. His green suit was over the top, decorated with golden designs head to toe. I held back a giggle at the absurdity of the extravagance.

"I have one," I assured him.

The gentleman frowned, glancing around.

"He's already inside, I believe," I said, my confidence wavering and my voice shaking.

"He left you out here?" the man asked, bewildered as many around us began to stare.

I sank further into myself, losing the confidence all together. My cheeks reddened, and I could feel heat building throughout my body. My corset felt too tight, and I wanted to tug at it, to peel all the layers away from my skin. I couldn't bear the eyes on me.

"I'm here," a deep voice said behind me, and for a moment, I was confused at who had stepped in.

Caspian stood behind me, dressed in deep royal blue finery. His hair was slicked back into a bun, and he held out his arm for me to take. I grabbed on, grounding myself with his presence.

I took a deep breath.

"My apologies," the man muttered as Caspian led me away.

"Where's Bellamy?" he asked when we were further away from the man.

"Inside, apparently," I muttered.

"Don't be so harsh on him, sister," my brother scolded at my tone. "I am sure he was dragged around the same as you and me today."

I rolled my eyes, knowing Caspian was right. He was far more logical than I was.

"Since when do you defend the prince?" I asked, raising a brow.

"I don't," he said. "But I do sympathize with him."

I paused and glanced up at my brother. "Why?" I asked skeptically.

"Because he has put up with your attitude for this long," he teased, a grin spreading across his lips.

I knew he was joking. I smiled and nudged his side.

"You know father would be proud," he whispered, and I felt my breathing stop for a moment.

"Father?" I asked. I'd barely let myself think of the man, the memory of him and my brother Emmett far too painful. They'd abandoned me, turned their backs on me. When I begged for their help, they'd denied it. Only Caspian had been there.

"You're becoming the daughter he always hoped you would, whether you wish to or not," he explained, waving a hand at my gown.

"This?" I exclaimed, my eyes widening. "This was not a choice I made."

"But you love it," Caspian accused.

"I do not," I said, letting go of his arm and placing my hands on my hips.

"You look like you are fighting it so hard," he teased.

"I didn't have a choice, the same as you," I said, frowning.

"Oh, make no mistake, sister. I love what they've done to me," he said, spinning around to give me a better look at his entire outfit.

"Enough," I complained.

"You don't like it?" he said, partially frowning and pretending to be disappointed.

"I swear, Caspian," I huffed and grabbed his arm again.

"You love me and you know it," he said, walking toward the steps.

I paused. I knew he was still joking, but my heart swelled. It'd been so long since I felt so comfortable with him. I'd missed his presence in Abelon.

"I do. I truly do," I admitted as we came to the top of the steps.

CHAPTER 33
BELLAMY

KORAINE STEPPED out at the top of the stairs, and my heart stopped. It was like that night in Abelon when I first saw her at the ball. It was when I knew that no matter if our people were enemies, my heart would never stop yearning for her.

She walked down the pale gold steps, Caspian by her side as her escort. I made my way hastily to the bottom of the steps, holding out my hand as she reached the last one.

"May I?" I asked. Caspian stepped aside, allowing me to escort his sister.

I felt out of my comfort zone. My entire life, I'd been trained for war and fighting. Though I'd received lessons on how to interact at these events, here in another kingdom, with everyone genuinely enjoying themselves and not attending solely for the politics, I felt uncomfortable. No one was here to win my favor or bore me with their attempts for power.

Koraine accepted my invitation, taking my hand and glowing with a widespread smile. Her cheeks were a pale shade of pink, and I noticed the slight glimmer in her eyes.

"Where did you find all of this?" I asked. "We certainly didn't have this with us on the ship," I tried teasing.

"I could ask the same of you," she noted, looking up and down at the finery I wore. "The king had this all brought to me."

The king had sent the clothing I wore to me as well. He dressed each of us in our respective kingdom colors, making sure we fit the part of guests.

"How does he find the time for all of this when there's a war approaching?" I muttered under my breath.

I glanced to where he sat on his throne on the opposite side of the room. Emerald green and gold covered him in every aspect, and his thunderous laugh echoed as he entertained nearby nobles. Asena stood to the right of the throne with whom I assumed was her betrothed. The nephew shared similar features to his uncle.

Curly, dark brown hair held a golden crown in place, and I breathed out a slight chuckle at the oddity of it. He was no king or prince, yet he wore a crown like the prince himself, who stood to the left of the throne.

His wife was a noble's daughter; I could tell from her appearance that she was from the earth kingdom. She wore a long, shimmering pale green dress that complemented her golden skin and brown eyes. Tight coils of curls fell down her back, pinned perfectly out of her face.

I turned back to Koraine, still leading her into the middle of the ballroom to dance.

Regardless of all the nobles in the room, she was the only one person who mattered.

I turned her to face me and grabbed her other hand, my opposite one moving to her waist. Upbeat music flowed through the room, and I began to guide us, recalling the lessons I had taken as a child.

She kept up easily, matching every step I took. Her long blue gown swirled around us. It was different from anything she normally wore, more frivolous than I knew she gravitated toward. The tulle skirt of the dress glittered with silver sparkles, and the pale blue drew out the vibrant colors of her eyes.

"This all feels rather pointless," I said. "We brought the princess safely here, the king amused our plea for help, and now, he has us dancing before him at this ignorant ball. What more could he want before he wakes up to the reality the fire kingdom will wage terror on his shores?" My brows furrowed. I was trying to enjoy the moment of peace, but my mind kept wandering back to my father and my sister who hunted me across the kingdom.

"It gives them hope," Koraine answered, a gentle look on her face, calming my growing frustration. "If people don't have hope, why would they fight?"

"You're right," I answered, shaking my head.

I hated the reality, but the truth was, many of these people had been protected from the horrors of war. They hadn't been on the front lines or lost people when the fire and water kingdoms last fought. They needed a reason to protect their kingdom when the next war came.

"I know you're anxious to put your father's terror to an end, but we need these people. Without them, we have no chance of standing against him. If the king doesn't give these people something worth fighting for, why would they join us?"

She had a point. She always had a point.

"I was trained all my life to lead an army, studying tactics, spending hours training, yet somehow, here you stand, more eloquently spoken then I'll ever be," Bellamy said.

"I'm just rattling off what my father would have said if he were here," Koraine answered. I caught her eyes quickly wandering to her brother and then back to me.

"No," I started. " You are rattling off what any good queen would tell her people."

Koraine's eyes widened, and I saw a corner of her lips tip up. "I am no queen," she argued.

"You are my queen."

I whisked her away across the dance floor then, letting the people around us melt away. The king sat perched on his throne, but I paid him no mind. My only focus was on my wife.

My stunning wife, who gave me a reason to push on. A reason to fight. She was worth fighting for.

I would give her a world where she could live in peace, one where she could roam the fire kingdom safely as a Morwenian without fear of hate. And one where my father no longer threatened to burn her own home to the ground.

After our dance, Koraine and I ventured around the ballroom, and part of me hoped I would get another chance to speak to the king. I knew the others anxiously awaited a chance to change his mind.

I wasn't sure when that chance would come. Time was running out.

We found Caspian and Ervin retrieving drinks from nearby servers, and they raised their chalices in our direction as we approached. It was an odd sight, seeing a

Morwenian and Abelonian sharing a drink on peaceful terms.

"I never would've had these together," Ervin snorted to Caspian, waving his drink, and I chuckled as I walked up.

"Have you seen Oleena?" Koraine asked her brother.

"No, but I did hear the priestesses would be in attendance," he answered.

"Where did you hear that?" Koraine asked, her hands on her hips.

"I heard the healers discussing it when they looked at my shoulder today. I asked if they were coming, and they commented that everyone, even the priestesses, would be joining tonight," he said shrugging. "I guess they do not attend most events the king hosts."

Koraine hung her head, disappointment on her face.

"I'm sure she's okay," I assured her.

"We just saved her from one cage. I do not want her to end up in another," she whispered softly.

"She won't, my moon," I promised.

We carried on with the night and tried desperately to enjoy ourselves. The music was festive, and the food was undeniably good. Each one of us never seemed to be able to fully smile though, at least not the kind that reached one's eyes. It was impossible to ignore what would come the next day. This was our farewell, not our welcoming.

We'd be sent away on our own to this war. We delivered Asena safely to the kingdom, but would that be enough for Morwen to be persuaded to join us?

"I sent word to my father," Caspian said after a while.

"You wrote to Father?" Koraine asked.

"I told him the princess arrived safely and of our plans

to sail to Abelon next. I asked for support and armies to join us."

"Do you think they will?" I asked

Caspian remained silent, his eyes cast down the floor.

War was coming, we knew. I remembered Oleena's warning at the market, the way she'd been frightened by what the goddesses would do when they realized another war threatened their balance.

I spotted movement from around the king and his family. Asena and her betrothed walked down the steps of the raised platform and ventured into the crowd of people.

"We should speak with the princess," I said, motioning to where she moved.

Before I turned to lead Koraine away, new movement at the top of the ballroom steps held her attention. A group of woman stood at the top, and I quickly realized Oleena was among them. The priestess made her way down the steps, smiling. She looked at home amongst the other priestesses in their matching tan gowns.

"I'll make sure she's okay," Caspian said. "You go check on Asena."

I nodded, taking Koraine's hand and leading her back into the crowd.

As I navigated the room, the chatting attendees made me think of Abelon and my father. I had done the same at many of his events and parties.

This time, I was able to just be myself, but in the past, I would've had to make small talk or win over nobles to our side. It was exhausting. There was always someone new to convince, to persuade to support my father's rule, to lend him any power they possessed. He built his army to be feared by all, and it became almost untouchable.

It took a few minutes before we found Asena and her betrothed speaking with another couple in the ballroom. Her eyes were on them, but she wasn't giving them her full attention. She looked distant, her mind completely somewhere else. Her eyes flickered over to where we stood, and she placed a gentle hand on her betrothed's arm. He gave her a subtle nod, and she left his side to join us.

Koraine quickly gave the princess a hug, and my eyes widened for a moment. Koraine had found forgiveness in her heart for the princess, he same forgiveness I had found long before her. I was at peace with what the princess had done to me. I knew what it was like to have your father control you and to try to live up to their expectations.

I could not fault her protecting her family and kingdom.

"Are you okay?" Koraine asked Asena.

"They treat me well," she said.

Her eyes flickered back to her betrothed. She spoke the truth, but I saw no adoration behind her gaze when she looked at the man. They were practically strangers.

"I'm sorry," Koraine said, catching Asena's glance.

"He is kind," she said, as though trying to convince herself. "He will protect me, help make Morwen stronger."

"I just-" Koraine started and placed a gentle hand on her shoulder. "I just know what it's like not having a choice."

"Everything turned out perfect for you," Asena said, a slight hint of sadness in her voice.

"And I thank the goddesses every day for that," Koraine started. "But that does not mean you should be forced into something you never wanted."

The princess opened her mouth, but she quickly stopped as movement from behind her caught her eye. "I have to go," she said quietly.

The princess rushed off without another word. It left a pit in my stomach—the emptiness in her eyes, the way this foreign kingdom had already drained so much of who she was. Even if they treated her fairly, it would never be her home. It would never be Morwen.

Before I could offer to lead Koraine back to her brother, a small tremble shook the floor. Koraine grabbed hold of my arm, her fingers digging in tightly, a wild look on her face.

The trembling only lasted a moment, like the after effects of an explosion.

Could they have found us?

Again, the ground started to shake. Other attendees took notice, and cries of fear broke out. The guards moved quickly toward the royal family, Asena's betrothed dragging her back to where the king had sat, joining his family as they were ushered out of the room.

The trembling intensified, and the guards abandoned us. Soon, it became hard to keep our balance to stand. Decor around the room fell from the wall, and glasses on tables shattered as they hit the floor.

I pulled Koraine to the wall, watching helplessly as destruction made its way through the ballroom.

CHAPTER 34

KORAINE

T HE FLOOR SHOOK VIOLENTLY, and I clung to Bellamy to stabilize myself as others within the ballroom screamed. Portions of the tile floor cracked, and I moved toward the outskirts of the room, the prince beside me.

I glanced around the room, looking for the rest of our group, but I could not see them through the panic.

"Is it an attack?" I asked Bellamy.

The more the floor shook, the harder my heart raced. It was impossible to walk or escape the trembling. Others tried and failed to run from the room, stumbling and falling.

"I don't think so," Bellamy said, his voice quiet. "The amount of power and control needed for an attack this size, they would need multiple earth manipulators all nearby. The guards would've found them by now."

We stood near a window, and I tried to slide myself along the wall, letting go of Bellamy. I reached out, grabbing onto the edge of the window to peer out it.

Outside, guards knelt on the ground, unable to stand. The ground around them shook, and I watched portions of it sink inward. Being able to manipulate the earth at such a magnitude could only be the power of one type of entity. I heard many nobles around the room muttering prayers to the very same goddess.

I looked to Bellamy with wide eyes. "Aeris," I said in a whisper.

His brows raised, but he didn't deny what I said. There was no other explanation. The goddess was punishing us for something, and I prayed to the others I never had to know the true magnitude of her strength.

Staying put wasn't an option. The floor near us cracked and the walls shook. I grabbed Bellamy's hand; the trembling paused for a moment, and I took my opportunity.

We fled from the ballroom, and I spotted Ervin and Caspian on our way out, who followed close behind us. The Earth ceased shaking for only a few minutes before it erupted into tumultuous destruction once more.

I ran up the steps of the ballroom as fast as I could, Bellamy trailing slightly behind me. I kicked off the blue heels that had been so carefully selected for my ballgown.

Only a few steps away from the top, the shaking started again.

The steps shook like a volcano, ready to erupt. It made the battle uphill even harder. Others rushed up the steps around us, scared and hopeful of fleeing. Caspian and Ervin had caught up and joined beside us, but I had no view of Oleena or Asena.

In front of me, a step cracked and sunk in as I prepared to ascend it. Bellamy pulled me back, saving me from the gaping hole that remained. My heart raced as I stepped over it quickly, making my way up the rest.

We made it out of the ballroom and fled from the palace. People poured out into the courtyard, watching pieces of the building crumble down the sides.

Guards arrived, flooding the courtyard, some riding pantheruses. We were corralled and penned in like trapped animals. The more people who shoved out of the palace and into the courtyard, the harder it became to keep our group together.

Someone shoved themselves between Bellamy and me, and I reached out for the prince but was unsuccessful. Bellamy was pushed further and further from me as I tried to wade through the sea of people.

The world around me became harder and harder to keep a hold on. Everyone needed to cease their panic, or the problem would only grow. We needed to be united.

I tried again to push through the crowd to Bellamy. I could see the prince slipping from me, trying his best to get back to my side.

"Bellamy," I shouted, fear slipping into my voice, but it was no use.

People tried to leave, but the guards blocked the entrance, forcing us all to stay put. My mind raced, and I could feel my anxiety growing. My breathing became labored, my palms clammy.

Desperate to end the panic, I shot my hand into the air. Water spring to life on my fingertips and shot into the sky in a stream. I stood in the center of the courtyard, letting my water soar high and rain down on us.

People froze, their gazes rising to the sky. They were stunned by my water raining down over them, the cold liquid in the already freezing night grabbing their attention.

The explosive noise of shouting and arguing died down. Everyone froze in the courtyard, silent as I let the water die out, thankful for a moment peace.

The show of power had drained what little energy I had left. I could feel myself growing faint, and Bellamy found his way back to me. He pulled me into his arms and held me tightly against him. I tried not to let it show, but I leaned into the prince for support. He was the only thing keeping me from collapsing.

"Wrath." Before anyone else could speak, a voice rang out across the courtyard. "This is what happens when we anger the goddesses." Oleena's voice carried through the air, echoing off the walls.

Whispers broke out, and people huddled together in fear.

I'd never heard the soft-spoken priestess raise her voice, but I found her at the opposite end of the courtyard, standing on the base of a statue, no longer the innocent, frail priestess we found in that cage.

"This is what happens when the world is out of balance. The goddesses are punishing us. They're taking away the blessings they gave us."

Guards quickly seized her, pulling her off the statue and ending her speech.

I tried to move towards her, but Bellamy held me back. "Wait," he said softly. "They won't hurt her."

"I know, but she's right; these people need to hear it."

Before Bellamy could answer, guards pushed through the crowd toward us. There was nowhere to run or flee. We were trapped.

I spotted guards escorting Caspian and Ervin out of the

courtyard and back into the palace. The shaking had since stopped, and the palace still held firm. Pieces were missing from the walls and spires, but the structure itself stood tall.

"Let's go," the captain of the guard said, grabbing both of our arms. We had no choice but to listen. There was no way to fight with the courtyard as crowded as this.

We followed the guards inside, and I recognized the path we took only a day before. They pulled us along across the throne room the moment we arrived. The king sat in his throne, Asena beside him, her betrothed nowhere to be seen. I saw the worry in her eyes, and she tugged anxiously at the long blue skirt of her dress.

"Did you think destroying my palace would force me to help you?" the king asked, his knuckles white as he gripped the arms of his throne.

I swallowed hard.

"This was not us," Caspian said firmly.

"You asked me to go to war, and only a day later, my palace is attacked. What do you expect me to believe?"

"No manipulator could have orchestrated this themselves," Bellamy said. "Multiple manipulators would have had to attack to cause this."

"It was the goddesses," Oleena's voice shouted across the room as a guard dragged her in behind us. Relief washed over me knowing she was safe and unharmed.

"You expect me to believe our goddess would harm her people like this?" the king scoffed.

"Ask any one of your priestesses," she challenged. "The elements are out of balance, and the goddesses are unhappy. They thrive on balance. When one element holds too much power, chaos reigns. The goddesses cannot exist without balance. They will tear apart these lands and start over," she explained, her eyes full of fiery determination.

"What she says is true," I added quickly. "We do not wish your people more suffering; we only wish to prevent the destruction that's coming."

"Your palace is in shambles, and I'd be willing to venture the city below is also suffering," Bellamy said.

The king stared at our group, his features remaining stern. "Get me a priestess," he demanded of the guards.

Multiple guards rushed out of the room, and we were left to wait.

My eyes met Asena's, and I saw the pleading behind her gaze. A plead for us to live? A plead for us to make it out of the earth kingdom? I could feel sense her tension from across the room.

I gave a subtle nod to her, which seemed to settle her nerves slightly.

A few minutes later, the guards walked in behind a woman dressed in a light tan gown. It was simple yet beautiful, and her dark hair was pulled back into a perfect bun.

"What do you make of the attack on the palace?" the king asked slowly.

She glanced around the room and walked closer to where the throne sat.

"You are sworn to the goddesses. Is it possible this was the work of Aeris?"

She glanced to where Oleena stared desperately back at her. I didn't pretend to understand the commitment the priestesses made to the goddesses and their will, but I'd always been taught they were the closest connection we had to those who blessed us with power. If the king did not believe Oleena, he had to believe this woman.

"I believe only the power of a goddess could conduct such a showing of earth manipulation, my king," she answered, bowing her head slightly.

"So you believe the ramblings of this woman?" he asked, nodding to Oleena.

She didn't look back this time. Her eyes remained forward on her king. Even if her loyalty was to the will of the goddesses, she still resided under the king's rule and lands.

"Every priestess is taught the most important principle to our land. Balance must be upheld, or we will face the wrath of our creators," she spoke.

Her words rang with the same warning of Oleena's.

"Our goddess' power is displaced, and there will be no stopping her until balance is restored," the priestess warned.

I watched the king take in her words, leaning back into his throne. "You are dismissed," he said sternly.

The priest hurried from the room, a few of the guards trailing behind her, leaving behind only the captain of the guard.

"Kai, what do you make of this?" the king asked, glancing to his captain.

He looked us over, his eyes narrowing, a scowl plastered to his face.

I held my breath, knowing if our fate was in his hands, we were never making it out of palace. He despised us from the moment we stepped foot inside the palace. He was loyal to his king.

"You know this wasn't us," I said, trying to plead with him.

"Koraine," Bellamy said quietly, and I heard the warning in his tone.

"Please," I tried again.

I glanced around at my group and saw the defeat on Oleena's face. Bellamy stood close to me, but I could feel the tension in his body. Ervin's eyes fell to the floor, and my brother's gaze settled on the princess, who stood atop the dais.

I caught the quick look of sadness and concern that flashed behind his gaze. What would become of the princess if the king blamed us for the attack? What would become of Morwen? Would he blame our home for everything, for sending us? Would the princess no longer be safe?

"My men and women found no one within the walls of the palace or nearby who could have conducted the attack. The damage done would have taken multiple manipulators. Already, word is coming from the city that they felt the effects as well," Kai stated, his tone even.

I froze, my heart stopping as Kai's words rang through throne room.

"I do not believe they did this," he said firmly.

The king's brows ticked up slightly. "And if there is truth to the priestesses' words? Would you have me go to war and endanger our people?" he asked.

Tension filled the room, and I didn't dare move or speak. I knew the king was only protecting his people.

Kai tipped his head, studying the king and thinking. "If what the priestesses predict is true, I do not see another option, my king," he answered.

"We can stop my father before he destroys the other kingdoms. We can restore balance," Bellamy promised. "When I ascend the throne, Abelon will help rebuild. We will restore what was broken tonight."

He reached out, taking my hand. I gave it a tight squeeze of reassurance.

The king stood from his throne and stalked down the steps as Asena remained frozen in place. He walked up to Bellamy, glancing down at the prince. Bellamy held his stare, and the sheer power between the two sent chills across my skin.

"My army is yours," he said, placing a hand on Bellamy's shoulder. "The fate of the kingdoms is in your hands."

Bellamy shook his head firmly. I swallowed, trying not to let fear creep into my features.

We could not fail.

If we failed, the kingdoms we cared dearly for would be destroyed.

CHAPTER 35

BELLAMY

I watched as men and women worked on repairing the palace—decor ruined, statues shattered, walls and floors with cracks in them. I knew it would take a while to rebuild what the palace once was.

I hated seeing the destruction my father caused without even raising a hand. He had thrown our world out of balance. No power was enough. No amount of land was enough for him to cease his terror.

My stomach turned each time I thought about it, and I tried to push him from my mind.

The king had agreed to lend us a ship. I made my way to the council chambers, where the king and his council were planning to meet. He had invited me to sit at his table while they discussed war preparations.

I spotted Kai standing at the door and knew I found my way to the meeting. He let me in, stepping aside as I passed through. I noticed the entire council seated around a circular table, a mix of men and women all dressed in green clothing.

I shuffled in and found an empty seat waiting for me. I pulled out the chair and sat down with the council watching me in silence. The only person missing was the king.

We waited a few moments before Kai opened the door once more and trailed in behind the king.

Everyone at the table rose quickly, and the king motioned for us to sit down.

"Abelon is only a few days travel away," the king started. "We need time to make preparations before we can sail. I will not have our men sent unprepared."

Everyone around the table nodded.

"If I may, Your Majesty," one spoke up, an older gentleman with jet black hair and dark eyes. "Wouldn't it be wise to wait for Abelon to attack on our lands? Even if we know the king of the fire kingdom is ready to wage war, would it not be wiser to fight him on our own lands? Here, we have more power, an advantage over him."

The king glanced to me and back to the man before answering. "Destruction is upon us. You all saw the effects of the quake. That will continue to happen if we let war come to us first. Our goddess is angered, our kingdoms are out of balance, and if we do not restore it, our goddess will destroy us before the king has a chance."

All heads swiveled with hesitant glances, as though they had something to say, but they held back.

"I will sail to my father's kingdom first. I will fight by Zetron's side, and at the end, he will no longer be on the throne," I assured them.

"How do we know you won't be exactly like your father?" a man in a green tunic asked.

"All I can do is give you my word and fight by your side.

My power is yours in this war. I will take on my father, and I will restore the fire kingdom to peace," I said.

"I still do not trust you will not turn out just like him," the man said. "I imagine no one at this table trusts that."

They were right. They had no reason to trust me. All the kingdoms thought me ruthless like my father. The prince of the fire kingdom had no regard for the other kingdoms. A few months prior, they may have been right, but all of that completely changed the moment *she* came into my life.

"I will take a Morwenian as Queen Consort," I said.

I watched as eyes widened. Even the king raised his brows a hair and tilted his head.

His eyes wondered diagonally to a woman dressed in light tan, her hair pinned back.

"It's true," she confirmed. "The priestess they travel with told me the same," she said. "They were married in a temple."

Whispered voices broke out in the room, and the king held up a hand to silence them.

"Having a Morwenian as Queen Consort in Abelon would fix the balance," the king said. "For far too long, the fire kingdom has been left unchecked. It has been allowed to grow far too strong and incite wars. We would change all of that with this."

I gave a firm nod. "She is the fire kingdom's last hope."

"If all you say is to be trusted, then our kingdoms may have hope after all," the king said. "I will provide you a small ship to sail ahead as we discussed. My men will follow a few days behind and will meet you on the beach near Raden. I expect you will find us a path to your father by then."

I nodded again.

"Then it is settled. You are all dismissed," the king said. "Kai, Prince Bellamy, you both remain," he instructed before I could leave my chair.

I stood, pushing in the chair. Men and woman filed out of the room, but I stayed behind with the captain of the guard. He walked rigidly and stood tense next to me.

All the others had left from the room, and the king turned to us.

"Kai, I want you to set sail with them," he ordered.

"Your Majesty-"

"I've already decided this is my command. You will sail with them. I need someone to make sure Abelon is ready to receive us," the king said. "I need someone I know I can count on there when we arrive."

He nodded slowly, keeping his mouth shut. My nerves grew, and I felt unsettled as the harsh reality began sinking in. I would be back home soon. Abelon awaited the return of its prince.

I soon found the rest of my group after meeting with the king and shared everything that had been discussed. The king gave us access to supplies for our journey back to Abelon, and we spent the remainder of the day packing up food for our journey.

I packed a set of black clothing I found in the piles sent for us. I imagined it'd help us blend on the shores with a night sky when we arrived. We needed to remain undetected within Abelon for days; otherwise, all our efforts would be useless. We could not allow for Abelonian scouts to find us before the king's army arrived.

Luheo was also preparing for war with my father, but every inch of me was worried they would not arrive in time. It would take every additional bit of strength we could gather to conquer my father and his army.

We were bringing the battle to his land, and Oleena had insisted the goddess, Mavalu, had built the lands to give us strength and more power. We could draw from the land. All our desolate land had ever done was starve us.

I shook my head, still unable to believe it. My father had dragons and the strongest army the kingdom. We hardly stood a chance.

"I will be back shortly," I said to the group. Koraine tilted her head, and I gave her a warm smile.

I made my way into the courtyard of the palace. I trusted the rest of the group to finish packing for our journey, but one thought kept plaguing me. I had to resolve it before I could continue.

I let out a loud whistle as I waited, hoping my effort was not useless. It had been days since I last saw her.

Minutes passed by, and nothing. I tried to let out another whistle. My heart raced, considering if something happened to her. Another few minutes passed, and I turned to walk back, my head hanging.

I prayed she had returned to Abelon, the home she was familiar with.

I would find her the moment I was back.

Before I set foot inside, I heard a few guards monitoring

the courtyard shouting. I turned to find a large mass moving through the sky, aimed directly at us. Imry barreled from the clouds, closing in on the ground. I ran back into the middle of the space, holding up my hands to the guards.

"Don't harm her," I shouted. "She won't hurt you."

Many looked confused. The guards remained with their weapons raised, but I managed to convince them to hold off on their attack.

The beast landed gracefully in the courtyard and pulled her wings close to her body. She brought her head down as I approached, and I held a hand out for her to nuzzle into my touch.

"I missed you too," I said to her.

It felt like a piece had been returned to me, one I had been longing for and felt empty without. I knew I'd ride into Abelon to meet my father in battle, and somehow, that made me feel more confident.

"I should've known the commotion was you," a voice rang out from behind me.

I turned, finding Asena watching me, her arms crossed. Her dark hair was tied back from her face, but it blew in the breeze, the skirt of her teal gown blowing with it.

"I heard the guards shouting when I was walking," she said.

"And you thought to run toward the shouting rather than away?" I asked, raising a brow.

"I can't resist," she shrugged. She took a few steps forward, sizing up my dragon.

"You can touch her," I said.

The princess held out a hand slowly, her fingertips

inches from Imry's side. She hesitated before letting her fingertips run along my dragon's scales.

"Similar to Ryn," she noted.

I knew what she meant. I'd ridden on Talay multiple times. Each time, I had the same thought: the serpent's scales reminded me of my own dragons. Perhaps they had all started as part of the same family. Perhaps the goddesses had made them that way on purpose.

Exact opposites more alike than they ever thought.

"I'm going for a ride. Would you like to come?" I asked the princess before I could stop myself.

"I shouldn't," she said softly.

The hesitance killed me. I wanted to see the fire that once burned deep in the princess.

"It will be quick," I promised.

"He wouldn't like it, she said."

"The king's nephew?" I asked.

I saw the light usually in her eyes completely extinguished. Only days in, and already, she was becoming a shell of herself.

"You belong to no one," I assured her.

They were the same words I once told Koraine, and now, I knew the princess needed to hear it more than ever.

"You make your own choices. Do what makes you happy," I said softly to her, my face relaxing and my features turning gentle.

She nodded and glanced back at the palace. For a moment, I thought I saw the fire in her gaze, but only for a second.

"Okay," she agreed.

I walked over to Imry and climbed onto her back,

holding out a hand to Asena. I helped her climb in front of me, moving close to steady her balance as she held tight to Imry's neck.

The dragon stood, ready to take off, extending her wings. She pushed off the ground and carried us into the sky as guards scattered beneath us.

It was mere seconds before we entered the clouds.

Asena's knuckles turned white, holding onto the dragon, and I let out a soft laugh.

"Not used to being in the sky?" I asked.

She shook her head. I could tell she was nervous, barely able to relax on Imry's back.

I glanced ahead and realized we had a perfect view of the sea. The sun reflecting off it made the surface sparkle from this high up.

"Look," I said to Asena, trying to give her something of comfort.

The princess glanced out to the sea, and I saw the longing in her gaze.

I directed Imry toward the water, and as we approached, I commanded her lower. The dragon flew just above the surface of the sea, and I could sense the delight filling the princess.

Before I met Koraine, I never would have imagined the happiness I would feel seeing the water and watching a Morwenian feel overjoyed by it.

Yet, I found myself filled with a new feeling. I felt warm, but it was not the usual rage that fueled my fire.

Ahead of us, I spotted movement along the surface of the waves. A familiar white head broke through the water, and Asena shifted to get a better look.

Two more rose on either side, and all three serpents raced through the sea. I watched as Ryn led Talay and Elios across the waves. It had been days since I'd seen any of them, and somehow, they had still found us. Asena's body finally relaxed.

We spent a few minutes flying above the serpents and following their path. After a bit, the princess turned her head.

"We should head back," she said sadly.

I nodded, knowing I had already pushed her outside her comfort zone.

"Take us back," I commanded, and Imry carried us away from the sea.

She landed only minutes later at the palace, and I found Koraine waiting in the courtyard, her face filled with a genuine smile. She walked over, holding out a hand to help Asena off the back of the dragon. I heard her whisper a greeting to Koraine before hurrying back inside.

"She missed you," I told Koraine.

She walked over to the front of the dragon, and Imry placed her head into Koraine's outstretched palm, nuzzling against her. She stepped forward and wrapped her arms around the dragon's neck, hugging the beast tightly. The sight only reaffirmed what I already knew: Koraine was destined to lead Abelon.

CHAPTER 36
KORAINE

AFTER A FULL DAY OF PREPARATION, the group was ready to set sail. The king had allowed us one last night in his palace before we would depart early the next morning, before the sun rose fully in the sky.

I felt nervous knowing I would once again be returning to the kingdom of fire, but seeing Imry soaring through the sky and being able to wrap my arms around the beast had calmed some of my nerves.

I barely slept wrapped up in Bellamy's arms, knowing that only a few hours later, we'd be back on a ship.

I spent the prior day preparing warm clothing and food with Caspian and Ervin. I'd barely spoken with Asena since we'd been in Gralar, and I was only briefly able to see her when she returned on Imry with Bellamy. She'd rushed off without a word. It felt like all the passion and fight she once had was drained from her.

I hadn't seen Oleena either since the night in the throne room. She returned to the priestesses, and I wondered if she would join us to Abelon.

I woke Bellamy when I saw the first signs of light in the sky through our balcony glass doors. He turned over, rubbing sleep from his eyes and finding my gaze on him. His hand brushed my hair from my face.

"Ready, my moon?" he asked, his voiced filled with sleep.

I shook my head.

He leaned in, pressing a gentle kiss to my lips, and then pulled back quickly before sitting up. I wanted to pull him back, to throw the sheets back over us and hide from all the responsibilities on our shoulders.

It was useless.

No one could run from fate.

I followed him out of the bed and found some clothing the king gave us. It was a plain black shirt, long sleeved, and a simple pair of black trousers. It was far from the normal blues and silvers I wore, or the skirts and dresses that had filled my wardrobes over the past few months. I slid the clothing on and found Bellamy watching

"What?" I asked Bellamy, his gaze burning a hole straight through to the most vulnerable part of me.

"I've just never seen you in anything other than your usual clothing." He shrugged.

"Is it so ghastly you can't tear your eyes from me?" I guessed.

"Quite the opposite, my moon," he said.

His words made my core warm. He stalked toward me and grabbed my waist, pulling my body to his. I could feel each rise and fall of his chest. Even in the early hours of the morning, my heart was racing, every bit of me awake.

"You look fierce and strong, like you are ready to lead us into battle."

That wasn't what I expected to hear. All my life, I wanted someone to call me beautiful or fall in love with my looks. My hair made me stick out and deterred men from pursuing me. I never looked like the other Morwenian women.

Somehow, his words filled me with more confidence than I ever expected.

I stood on my tiptoes and pressed a kiss to his lips. "I would follow you to war any day," I promised.

"And I would wage a war if it meant I could protect you always." His eyes darkened, and for a moment, his hold on me tightened, like he never wanted to let me go.

We left our room, supplies stuffed in our satchels, and met the others at the entryway to the palace. We'd make the journey through the city together, down to where the ships were docked. The king had a small crew ready to meet us. The plan was to get us as close to Abelon as possible undetected and then utilize Elios and Talay for the rest of the journey. It would be a few days before we arrived. We had plenty of time to rest and prepare.

I found Caspian and Ervin already waiting with their own bags. To my surprise, Oleena stood beside them, her own small satchel slung over her shoulder.

"You're joining us?" I asked her, shock in my voice.

"I couldn't abandon you all," she said. "Not after all you've done for me."

"You fought enough; you deserve to rest, to live amongst other priestesses," Bellamy tried.

"It's no use. We've already tried," Caspian said, a gentle smile on his face.

I was thankful for Oleena's company, but I still worried for her. War was brutal, and I feared she wouldn't have the ability to fight back against Abelon's army.

"I plan to stay far from the fighting," she said, reading my face. "I can help tend to the injured and provide supplies."

I remembered my mother doing the same during the last war. She'd worn herself thin, taking care of the injured who came back to Morwen. Caspian's brows furrowed, and I knew he had the same thought.

This was different. Oleena would not end up sick the way my mother had. Generations of women on my mother's side all fell ill with an unexplained sickness.

That wouldn't happen to my friend.

It wasn't the same.

"Thank you," Bellamy said softly from beside me.

The sound of heels echoed on the tile floor, and I glanced over to find Asena standing in the entry to the hall. Her arms were crossed, and she watched in silence, her eyes raking over each one of us.

Her lips parted slightly, like she wanted to say something, but she closed them.

I was the first to make my way over to the princess. I stopped just short of her, wishing I was anywhere else. My heart ached to know we had to leave her behind.

I threw my arms around her, taking her by surprise. She let out small gasp, and Ervin followed me, wrapping his arms around us both.

Her muscles relaxed, and although she didn't say

anything, I knew there were a thousand things she wanted to tell us. In a short time, we'd all become close. We saved each other's lives multiple times and been through the worst. It pained me to have to say goodbye to someone who'd become a part of our small family.

Bellamy walked over slowly, his hand falling on her shoulder. She gave him a simple nod.

Never in my life did I think I would see the prince of the fire kingdom and the princess of the water kingdom growing close enough to become allies. In truth, it was more than just an alliance. Asena was our friend.

I felt tears stinging my eyes, and I tried to hold them back—not for my sake, but to protect the princess from feeling worse.

It wasn't right.

I knew she was unhappy, and I knew she didn't want to marry the king's nephew. It sucked the life from you and forced you to become someone you didn't recognize.

Caspian was the last to join. He walked over, and we all stepped back from our hug, allowing him access to the princess.

I thought he may just walk away. I could see the pain in my brother's eyes. He cared for the princess, cared about her the way any assigned protector would.

She threw her arms around his waist, hugging him tightly. Slowly, his arms wrapped around her neck and held her close. It only lasted a moment before she stepped back. Still, they said nothing, but I could see the water starting to fill her eyes.

"Come with us," I said before I could stop myself.

It was insanity. She'd found safety. I was asking her to give that up to throw herself into war.

"Koraine…" Bellamy said, placing a hand on my shoulder.

I knew it was a futile attempt. She was a princess and had her responsibilities to uphold.

"I can't" she said, sadness filling her voice.

"You can." I was shocked to hear Ervin's voice. "You decide your happiness."

"You don't want to marry him," I added.

"I don't have a choice," she said. "My father arranged this, and I have to follow through."

"No, you don't," Bellamy said, surprising me further.

I raised my brows toward him and saw the smile that flashed across his face. I knew I had his full support.

We couldn't leave Asena behind.

"I followed my father's orders blindly and look where it got me. We will find other way to make sure Zetron remains an ally. A way that won't sacrifice your well-being and joy."

A million thoughts clearly raced through her mind, and I could see her brows starting to pull together. From the grimace on her face, I knew she was torn.

It was an impossible position, choosing between her happiness and her obligations to her kingdom.

"Please," I tried.

"I'm sorry. I can't," she said and turned to hurry down the hall.

My heart broke into shattered pieces. It was like I was stabbed in the chest and someone twisted the knife further and further.

I saw Bellamy's face drop and knew the sadness extended beyond the princess denying us.

It was only weeks before that he left his sister behind in Abelon. He hadn't been able to convince her, and now, he'd failed again.

I moved to his side, grabbing his hand.

"I thought she'd leave," he told me softly.

"We all did," Caspian said, clasping a hand on Bellamy's shoulder.

My mind couldn't accept the harsh reality that we failed. Not again. It couldn't happen again. I'd seen the rage and pain that filled Nyla's heart when we left her. She blamed Bellamy and me for it all.

She was right.

We never should've left her behind. I wouldn't make the same mistake again.

I pulled away from Bellamy and raced down the hall. Before I could explain to the group, I took off running. In just trousers and boots, I moved more swiftly.

I could hear the echoes of Asena's heels against the floor ahead of me. I followed the sound, determined to catch the princess. I didn't care if it cost us our alliance with the earth kingdom; Asena was family, and I wouldn't leave her. I finally spotted her ahead in the courtyard on the other side.

"Asena," I shouted.

I saw her flinch at my voice, hesitating before starting to walk again.

"Please," I shouted again.

I made it through the hall and courtyard, standing directly across from her. Her back was still to me, but she stopped.

"Come with us," I panted.

I saw the way her shoulders tensed. "I can't," she managed to choke out.

I walked carefully across the courtyard, afraid she'd leave. I knew the moment she stepped foot out of the courtyard, I'd lose her. This was my only chance to convince her.

"I was you once," I said softly. "My father forced me to Abelon to marry the prince." I knew she knew the story better than anyone—she had been at that table that day, after all.

"I arrived in Abelon with so much rage in my heart. I felt hurt and no longer myself. I let myself start to slip into something I didn't recognize. I don't want that for you."

"But you found Bellamy," she said. "You found love and happiness in the prince."

"Do you truly believe you'll find that in him?" I asked.

She paused. "I can learn to love him."

My heart and chest ached for her. I could see the desperation and desire to please her father, to do what she thought was right. I hated seeing her shattered from the warrior I knew she was.

"No," I said. "You can't force yourself to love him. He may protect you and give you a comfortable life, but you can't force those feelings. You'll never be able to."

"But you did with Bellamy," she insisted.

"No," I said. "I think part of me always knew. There's a piece of me that always longed to be around him, that wished he might linger a little longer. I found myself searching for him, even when I thought I hated him. Don't accept a life void of true love," I said. "Do something for yourself. Choose your happiness. The decision is yours. I can't force you to come."

She took a step forward, only inches from the other hall. My hands shook, and I felt my knees go weak. I wanted to collapse in the courtyard. I was barely able to suck in a breath, watching her begin to walk away.

Again, I failed.

I forced myself to take a step, to begin to turn. I knew we had to leave. There was a little time to make it to the ship and set sail to Abelon. I started to walk away across the courtyard, my feet felt as they dragged across the cobblestone. I could barely hear anything, my heart racing in my ears.

The look of disappointment I'd see on the group's faces when I returned without the princess had my stomach sinking. Before I could make it to the other hall, though, a hand slipped into my own.

I paused, glancing to the side to find Asena standing beside me, a small smile on her face.

Before she could speak, I hugged her, filled with relief.

"I choose to be happy," she said. "I choose to fight by your side."

CHAPTER 37

NYLA

I STOOD in the courtyard where we held our annual bonfire. It was fitting as I tried to manipulate my flames, same as I always had. Every time I lit the flames in my hand and tried to move them to the residual limb, the flames died out.

I let out a frustrated growl. I'd been out here for hours. Over and over, I forced myself to try to control my flames with the limb that no longer had a hand, feeling more and more hopeless by the second.

If I didn't find a way to wield my fire at full strength, I would die quickly in the war approaching our kingdom. My father's spies reported they were preparing to sail for Abelon. The battle was coming to our shores, and I was ill-prepared.

That would be no excuse for my father.

He expected me to help lead his armies, to fight by his side.

He didn't care if I couldn't wield my fire. He would force me to die trying.

There was no honor in hiding from war. I would fight and die a warrior's death.

I could feel the pain coming back to the base of my wrist. The wound was still fresh, the tonic wearing off. My body was becoming reliant on it. Each day, I ventured to the healers, convincing them to give me more. They tried and failed to convince me stop taking it. The pain was too much.

Without the tonic, I couldn't focus. All that consumed me was agony.

The tonic washed away the memories, my father burning me in the throne room. It made Bellamy's betrayal feel like a distant thought. I barely remembered the hurt and sadness in my heart. Instead, all I felt was numbness.

That's what I wanted.

To feel nothing.

I continued my attempts to grow and control the flames. The closest I came for a moment was flames at the tip of my arm that extinguished just as fast.

"You'll find a way," Cyrus' voice echoed across the courtyard from behind me.

"What do you want?" I snarled.

"Can I not check on my future wife?" he asked.

I rolled my eyes and turned away from him. He stalked across the courtyard, his boots thudding on stone. He grabbed my arm, turning me to him, his nails digging into my arm.

"You will treat me with respect," he said. "I am done entertaining your games. We are about to go to war. I will not have a disobedient wife getting in my way."

"Respect? You should've thought about that before you let my father burn my hand from my body."

He let go of me, and I thought I saw sympathy flash across his face.

"Believe it or not, I never wished for that to happen," he said.

I scoffed. "You should've taken the deal," I said. "We would've caught up to Bellamy and brought him back to Abelon to please my father."

"You should've taken the deal when I first offered it. Follow my command and learn obedience, or you will die in this war," he said, and I couldn't tell if it was a threat or warning.

"Your father is searching for you," he added. "I suggest you find him."

Cyrus' eyes narrowed on me, his lips drawn thin.

He turned and stalked away, leaving me alone in the courtyard once more.

My stomach sank, and there was not enough tonic in the world to prepare me for facing my father. I had not been with him alone since he took my hand. I'd left the meeting too fast to face him, and I spent my time avoiding him since.

I walked slowly through the halls of the palace, willing myself to slow my heart rate. If I walked into the throne room flustered, the king would know.

I found my father sitting on the throne, a column of flames on each side. Entering the throne room, I walked closer and bowed my head.

"Nyla," he addressed me, and I glanced up, noticing his hands gripping his throne tight.

"War will be upon us any day," he started. "My men tell me you've been training tirelessly since your return home."

What he meant to say was since he removed my hand. I held my tongue.

"You have always been loyal to your kingdom and to me," he said, and his relaxed tone surprised me. "Loyalty is always rewarded. It's how your future husband worked his way up to captain and why you will one day become Queen of Abelon."

My heart stopped, and I thought I'd misheard. Never once in my existence had my father ever acknowledged the chance of me taking the throne. Bellamy was his pride and joy, always the perfect son.

"Bellamy has betrayed this kingdom. He married a Morwenian, our enemy. He made me look a fool. I am not so naïve as to trust him again. He formed an alliance with the other kingdoms. There's no hope for returning the promised prince. You are our hope now," he said and stood from the throne.

My father walked down the steps of the dais, the column of flames dying out behind him. I stood unnaturally still as he approached me. I prayed he couldn't hear the beating of my heart or see the way I could barely catch my breath as he towered over me.

"I have an important role for you in this war," he said and glanced to me with his dark gaze.

I hid the fear from my face as I spotted the rage and fire in his eyes.

"You will kill Koraine," he said.

My lips parted, but that was the only surprise I let myself show.

"Bellamy is no longer welcome in this kingdom. He is not the son he once was, and his loyalty lies elsewhere now.

If he wishes to turn his back on us, then I will be forced to end his betrayal. Killing Koraine is the first step to weakening him. If we remove her from the war, it'll be a wound large enough to stop him.'

I barely heard most of his words. The monster in me bagged for revenge, to be let out, and I finally gave it permission. Everything I had been imagining was becoming a reality. Koraine was the reason Bellamy turned his back on Abelon. She was the reason he left me behind and betrayed his family. She was the reason for all my pain and suffering. Finally being able to face her, to fight her, was what I needed to start healing.

Nothing else mattered.

I needed this like I needed air.

I felt fire growing inside me, begging to be let out.

I grew my flames in my hand, pushing them over to where my other hand once was, letting my rage fuel the strength of my fire.

Flame caught, licking up my arm and wrapping around it as it replaced the missing limb.

I turned off all other feelings, hesitation nowhere to be found. The war inside me was finally over as I embraced the monster I'd been forced to become.

"I will not disappoint you," I vowed.

KORAINE

THE TRIP down to the docks was fast. We had no time to stop and admire the beautiful city that was the earth kingdom's capital. We couldn't risk anyone spotting the princess. We'd left the moment Asena had agreed to come with us.

If we could just make it to the ship, we stood a chance of getting her out of here.

The captain of the guard would be waiting for us, and I wasn't sure how we would convince him to allow the princess to join. Kai was the one person who took orders from the king. If he thought anything was off, he would stop us.

We raced through narrow roads, getting a glimpse of the water ahead. I crossed my arms and urged my feet to move quickly, the cold of the late autumn morning brushing at my skin. My nose stung, and I pictured the vibrant red it would be.

"This is mistake," Asena mumbled.

"Don't start with that now," Caspian scolded her. "We're

breaking you out of this kingdom whether you like it or not."

His tone sounded half-joking. I genuinely imagined he'd sling her over his shoulder and carry her out of Zetron if that was what it took.

"That's the ship," Bellamy called out, pointing to a small ship amongst the others.

It was docked the furthest right in a row of ships. We made our way quickly to it, climbing the wooden ramp.

As much as I loved the sea, I'd been on far too many ships in the past few weeks. Every time I boarded one, a new issue arose. The crew was on deck, dressed in the king's uniforms as they waited for us.

"Where's Kai?" Caspian asked, his tone firm. My stomach sunk with nerves.

I glanced around but didn't spot Kai. Would he force Asena back to the palace when he arrived? Would he believe us if we lied?

"Where is the captain?" Caspian asked.

"Beneath deck," one of the men commented.

"We have orders to set sail the moment you arrive," another stated.

I stiffened, realizing this was our chance. We could make it into the Vitrum Sea before Kai even realized who was on board.

"I can let the captain know you've joined," one of them offered.

"No need," Caspian said. "I can help you get the ship sailing. No need to disturb the captain in his preparations."

I almost had to stifle a laugh. My brother played the role so well. The lies rolled easily off his tongue. I caught the wary glance Bellamy threw in Caspian's direction, but my brother ignored him.

Ervin and Oleena were already settling on deck, sitting on crates near the edge of the ship. Bellamy and I followed Caspian's lead, drawing in ropes that tied the ship to the dock and pulling up the anchor that kept us there. I organized a rope and passed it off to Bellamy to store in one of the crates on deck. The ship was larger than the one we used to escape Morwen but smaller than the ones I'd seen from the fire kingdom. Within a few minutes, Caspian and the rest of the crew had us drifting away from the dock.

Asena was standing at the back of the ship, watching as the earth kingdom became more and more distant. "Do you think he's realized yet?" she asked me.

"Maybe," I said to her. "But I still think you made the right choice."

"I know," she said." But why does the right choice have to make me feel like such serpent shit?"

"Did the princess of Abelon just use the phrase *serpent shit*?" I giggled.

She let out a soft laugh. "I've been spending too much time with you and your brother."

I smiled and leaned against the railing of the ship, watching the kingdom drift off with her.

A breeze rolled across the waves, and I watched Asena shiver. She still wore her gown and heels from the palace.

"We have spare clothing. Let's get you into something warmer," I offered. Our supplies contained extra clothes, among the other items. I turned around, and I regretted it immediately.

At the top of the stairs leading beneath the deck, Kai

stood, his eyes wide with fury. "Why is she here?" he accused.

His presence caught the attention of the others. The rest of the group hurried over, standing protective around Asena.

"We're turning around," he said.

"No," I argued.

"She is not supposed to be here!"

"The king—" I started.

"Do not lie to me," he yelled. "The king did not send her here. I know the king well enough to know he would never risk her life at war."

"Worth a try," Caspian muttered under his breath.

"She stays," I said, letting my control tug at the sea behind me. I would do what I must to protect Asena.

I started building the water behind the ship, a large wave growing. Everyone broke into argument, shouting, their words drowning each other out. The more I tried to listen, the more distant I grew, and my focus remained on the wave.

My vision was slowly turning to black, little specks creeping in and setting me on edge. My heart was racing, and no matter how many deep breaths I took, it wouldn't slow.

"Bellamy," I said faintly, reaching a hand out to the prince. The water behind me fell as quickly as it had built up.

He didn't hear me over the sounds of everyone's discourse.

I grew out of breath, and my chest felt tight. I could feel my knees wobbling, like my body was a swaying ship. I couldn't stop what was coming. I knew I was going to lose consciousness. Before my vision turned completely black, I grabbed tightly to the prince's sleeve, trying to slow my fall.

"Bellamy," I said with a little more force and panic behind my plea.

I collapsed, losing control of my limbs and vision. My body hit the deck with a hard thud. My hearing was fuzzy, and I could barely make out the sounds of growing panic around me.

I was drifting in and out of awareness. Someone knelt beside me, cradling my head, and I could feel them softly running their fingers through my hair.

"We need to move her below deck," the priestess said.

Someone walked closer and hovered protectively over me.

"If any of you touch her, you will all burn," Bellamy growled protectively. I could barely make out the blurry green figures backing away from the prince.

It was the last thing I heard and saw before I completely gave in and let my mind sink into a deep darkness.

When I woke, my eyes felt dry, barely opening enough to see pale sunlight pouring in. I tried hard to recall how I had gotten to this room, this bed, but it all came back a blur—collapsing, the priestess moving me.

"How often does this happen?" the priestess' voice asked from beside me.

I turned my head to find her sitting in a wooden chair beside my cot. From the look of the room, I was in her quarters on the ship.

A small, circular window let light in, making the space bright during the day and offering a sliver of moonlight at night. It was still daytime, but had I missed multiple days, or had I only been out a few hours?

My brows narrowed, and my head ached the more I thought about it.

"You've only been out an hour," the priestess assured me. She tilted her head, examining me. "Does this happen often?"

"This was the first," I admitted.

She frowned, and the wrinkles on her forehead grew deeper.

"What?" I asked.

"Your brother seemed worried, like he'd seen this happened before," the priestess noted.

A knot formed in my stomach, and a dreadful feeling washed over me. "Where is Caspian?" I asked.

"I sent him away," the priestess said. "You needed rest, not a brother doting over you."

I let out a weak chuckle, but before I could ask her to find him, the door burst open without warning. Caspian and Bellamy stood in the doorway, both sharing concerned looks. The pair tried to step through at the same time but didn't fit. Bellamy was able to slip in before Caspian could move, and my brother trailed behind him.

"I'm not dying," I huffed out. "I just fainted."

Both men crossed their arms, watching me with concern in their eyes.

"You had us worried," Bellamy said. "It came out of nowhere. We've been out there waiting for you to wake because she wouldn't let us in."

The priestess scoffed.

"Not nowhere," Caspian said, and my eyes instantly found his.

I narrowed my gaze and tried to discourage him from bringing up what I could see he was thinking. I didn't want Bellamy to worry about me, and if Caspian shared the information I suspected, it would only cause more panic.

"I'm fine," I said in a stern tone. Caspian went to open his mouth, but I cut him off. "I'm *fine*," I repeated, sitting up in the bed. "I'm completely alright."

Bellamy sat beside me in the bed and pulled me close into his chest. The priestess shrugged and watched us with curiosity.

"Can I have a moment with my sister?" Caspian asked, refusing to drop my gaze.

"Caspian," I warned.

"This isn't a debate," he warned, and Bellamy glanced between us, waiting for my answer.

"It's alright. I'll meet you on deck," I said.

The prince reluctantly left the room, closing the door behind him. I glanced to the priestess, waiting for her to get up from her chair.

"I feel it's important I hear what he has to say," she said, firmly planted in her spot.

"Fine," I grumbled, rolling my eyes.

"You know what I'm going to say," Caspian said.

"And what's that?" I bit out, my impatience growing.

"Mother started with dizzy spells," he noted.

Her illness had not always been as debilitating as it'd grown to become.

"I know," I admitted. "But this isn't like Mother." I couldn't tell if I was trying to convince myself or Caspian, my voice shaky.

"Her mother started the same way as well," Caspian continued.

I noticed the priestess took in every word. Our grandmother had passed away at an earlier age than most from a similar illness no healer could figure out.

"I'm not them," I insisted. "I was likely dehydrated."

Neither the priestess nor Caspian looked convinced.

"You look just like them. There are far too many similarities between you all to think this illness might not be something you inherited," Caspian argued.

Each of us had the same rare white hair that made us stand out the rest of the Morwenians. Our people had dark features with golden tan skin. I was the outlier. My white hair and blue eyes stood out in every crowd.

"Your mother shares the same appearance? The same white hair?" the priestess asked, and I noticed how she sat forward in her chair, could see all the possibilities running through her mind.

"What?" both Caspian and I asked.

"And you've never had this happen before?"

"I haven't," I said firmly.

Caspian looked unconvinced, but I was telling the truth.

"I saw you that day we escaped the market. You look ghostly when you finished lifting everyone over the wall," he recalled.

"And you've been using your powers of water manipulation a lot more in the past few months?" the priestess asked immediately after hearing Caspian's addition.

"What does that have to do with it?" Caspian started, but she held up a hand.

"Answer the question," she stated.

I nodded weakly.

"Before she fell sick, did your mother use her powers a lot?" she continued.

I thought of all the years my mother helped our people. She never used her manipulation for violence. Instead, she was a talented healer. She helped anyone and everyone she could. She controlled water to tend to the injured, especially during the war. When I noticed her beginning to use her water manipulation more than I'd ever seen in my life, the sickness began.

"Yes," I answered.

"How is this related?" Caspian stated.

"I never imagined the stories to be true," the priestess said in awe.

"What stories?" I demanded. My heart raced, and I could feel every inch of my body growing tense.

"The stories of the moon goddess," the priestess said, as if it should be obvious.

There were four goddesses our kingdoms looked and prayed to. I had never heard of more than that, and certainly not a goddess of the moon.

"There's no such thing," Caspian said quickly.

"There is," the priestess insisted.

"Then why have we never heard of this goddess?" Caspian argued.

My stomach turned, and I felt like I could be ill. What

did any of this have to do with my mother's illness or my own dizzy spell?

"Because she was a goddess who has long been lost in our history. It has been a decades since her name has been spoken within these kingdoms," the priestess continued.

"How is that related to this?" I asked, my anxiety increasing.

I moved to sit on the edge of the bed, feeling like I wanted to escape the confines of the room. I felt like I might be sick, and my breathing picked up as I waited for her answer.

"You're moon touched," she said, and I held my breath. "It explains the illness that runs through your family and your odd features," she continued.

"Moon touched?" Caspian asked.

I let out a breath, realizing my hands were shaking.

"What is moon touched?" I dared to ask.

"Moon touched is a blessing from the moon goddess herself. It is a power so great, it will either give the blessed the most power we've ever witnessed in our kingdoms in a millennia, or it will kill them. The more they use their other powers without giving in to the call of the goddess, the greater the toll on their body."

"But my mother just healed people. She wasn't going to war or using her water manipulation than more than in its simplest form," I argued.

"It doesn't matter. The blessing from the goddess needs to be released; it feeds on your power. If you do not embrace it and learn to control it, it'll deteriorate you, burn through you from the inside out."

I swallowed hard. "So the more I use my water abilities, the more this will happen?"

"I'm afraid so. It will continue until there's a point of no return."

"What is that point?" I asked.

"When your body grows too tired, too ill to house the blessing any longer, you will grow sick beyond any healer's ability," she said.

"Like our mother?" Caspian asked.

"I have not seen her and cannot say for certain, but if what you tell me is true, it sounds like her body has given up."

My stomach sank, my hope squandered.

"Is there any way we can help her?" I asked, unwilling to give up on her just yet.

"It depends how ill she is," the priestess said. "She could try to fight it, take on the power of the moon, but it is no easy task. It would still take a toll on her body and mind."

I shook my head, unwilling to believe it. My mother was a fighter, and I would make it back to her and help her through this. First, though, I needed to learn myself.

"How does Koraine gain control of this curse?" Caspian said, hissing the last word.

"She needs to find somewhere sacred to the moon goddess, somewhere she can be directly connected to her. Only there will she be able to call on that connection and allow the moon goddess to bestow full power and control on her," the priestess explained.

A feeling of familiarity washed over me. Had I already been to such a place? Why couldn't I place the thought? Something nagged at my mind, but I pushed it aside.

"That is super helpful," Caspian muttered.

"There isn't a lot in our textbooks on this," Oleena muttered. "I am recalling what I can."

"And we appreciate it," I said, throwing a glare at my brother.

The door pushed open, and Bellamy stood with Asena outside of it.

"I tried to stop her," he said with a frown, glancing at each of us. "What?" he asked, his face falling.

We spent the next few minutes catching the entire group up on what Oleena had explained. Caspian had found Ervin, and everyone sat around me, listening with worried looks plastered across their faces.

"I will be fine," I assured them.

"You don't know that," Bellamy said, and I heard the fear in his voice.

"I will find a way to control this after the war," I said.

"That kind of power could win us the war," Asena said. "Maybe we should sail to Morwen."

"We don't have time," Caspian said, his arms folded.

"What if she doesn't have time?" Bellamy said, motioning to me.

Everyone again broke into chaos, shouting over each other. The noise made my heart race. I was sick of listening to others speak about me like I was already dead.

"Enough!" I bellowed. "It is my decision to make. We sail to Abelon, and I deal with this after the war."

Everyone slowly turned to me and nodded reluctantly. The room fell into silence before Oleena finally broke it.

"Come. She needs rest," she said, standing and motioning to the group to follow.

Everyone rose and followed toward the door. Bellamy was the last, trailing behind everyone.

"Wait," I called to him. "Stay."

His dark eyes turned and found mine. His hand held the door, and he slowly closed it behind the others.

"Of course, my moon," he answered. "I will always stay."

CHAPTER 39
BELLAMY

I SELFISHLY CHOSE TO STAY.

She had asked, and I refused to deny her.

Even though I knew she needed the rest, I needed to be by her side. Instinct refused to let me leave through that door. Koraine was slowly dying, and there was nothing I could do to stop it. I knew war would speed up the sickness.

I crawled into the cot, pulling her in close. It was the middle of the day, but I didn't care. There was a crew manning the ship, and the others could wait for anything they needed. We had days stuck aboard the ship.

Before Koraine woke, I had confirmed with Asena the serpents followed us through the sea.

"Talay is beneath us," I said, whispering into her ear.

"How do you know?" she asked.

"Asena."

"I should've known," she said with a weak laugh, but I could tell her heart wasn't in it.

"Where'd you go, my moon?" I asked. Her mind was clearly elsewhere.

"My mother," she admitted.

I'd heard stories of her mother, even knew of her illness no healer could fix, but I'd never seen Koraine reflect so sadly upon the woman.

"I just want to save her," she said. "But how can I save her when I can't even save myself?" she asked.

"You aren't alone," I told her, hugging her tightly. "You have us to help. The moment we figure out how to deal with this curse, we will help your mother," I promised.

She took a deep breath. "I just hope we aren't too late," she sighed.

"You can't think like that," I said. "Have hope."

"I have just about run out of that lately," she murmured.

It was hard to argue. Each day, our fates became grimmer and grimmer. We were sailing into the deadliest kingdom to begin a war. The tides were carrying us fast, and before long, we would be surrounded by death and tragedy.

"I know, my moon, but you have to hold on to something," I told her. "Otherwise, why are we fighting in the first place?"

She let out a huff. "I hate when you're right, you know," she said, turning to face me.

"It happens often," I joked, and she rolled her eyes.

She nuzzled her head to my chest, and I placed a light kiss on her head. The smell of her hair filled my nose, the slight hint of sea salt and citrus mixed together.

Her body relaxed, and she glanced up to me, an entire ocean of blues in her eyes. I could see the exhaustion she hid. Even in her bright-eyed stare, I spotted it shoved deep down.

"Sleep, my moon," I stated.

"Sleep? It's the middle of the day," she said, starting to slide herself up.

I wrapped my arms fully around her and pulled her back down.

"At least try. For me?" I asked.

She tilted her head and studied me. "Fine," she said, admitting defeat. She let herself sink further in my hold. "Tell me that story again, the one you told me in the cages of the market." Her voice was a soft plea.

"The one of the waterfall?" I asked.

"Yes. Something about it feels like home," she started, her eyes distant. "I can't explain it, but I just need to hear it again."

So I started, speaking of when the four kingdoms were created.

"Each goddess built a kingdom suited for their element. Mavalu built a land ruled by fire, mountains that spread flames across the lands and beasts that breathed fire. Aeris built a kingdom of all the beauties the land had to offer, vast fields and tall mountains spread across what is now Zetron. Isleen built a land suited for air, with tall cliffs and tress, cities built high only those with control over the winds could reach. And Odaesia built her kingdom of water, one that let the rivers run straight through the lands and housed cities on the coasts."

Koraine nodded along with the story. We'd heard it a million times before. It was what every child was taught.

"But Mavalu and Odaesia were caught in their own battle. Each wanted more than they had."

It was the same rhetoric the kingdoms spewed now about each other. Fire and water could never exist in peace.

But that wasn't true.

Koraine and I had proven that.

"Odaesia wanted more than she had, so when Mavalu finished creating Abelon, she carved a piece of the land out. She created a small oasis of water tucked into the fire kingdom, a final way to win the fight they'd been locked in," I said.

"That doesn't make sense," Koraine said.

"What?" I asked.

Her voice was soft, sleep dripping from it, her eyes growing heavy.

"The story doesn't make sense," she said.

"How?" I asked, my hand running through her hair.

"I had never once heard of the feud or a piece of land carved out by Odaesia. We are taught from a young age the history of creation and the lore of the water goddess. I have never once heard this story. Would this not be a story worth keeping alive in Morwen?" she asked.

"I suppose," I started, confused.

"It has been bothering me since you first told it," she said. "Something about it feels so familiar, yet I have never once heard it."

She adjusted in my arms, and suddenly, the exhaustion there moments before as replaced with curiosity.

"What do you think then?" I asked.

"I don't-" she started, her mind racing before me.

I followed her thought, the way she'd felt connected to the story. I agreed, it didn't add up that she never once had heard the story. I had never shared the lore the very first night we visited the waterfall, but I had always known it was a place meant for Koraine.

"What if it wasn't carved out by Odaesia?" she asked.

"You think Mavalu?" I started.

"No," she said quickly. "I think a different goddess." She shook her head. "It's silly."

"It's not," I insisted. My hand reached for her face, cupping her cheek and forcing her to meet my gaze. "Go on."

"What if it was the moon goddess?" she asked.

"You think the waterfall is the answer to all of this?" I asked.

"The moment Oleena mentioned I needed to go somewhere connected to the moon goddess, I knew I'd been before. It was like an instinct washed over me."

"The moon and sea are connected," I noted.

"What if the moon goddess wished for her own sanctuary? Her own bit of a kingdom to claim as her own? It would make more sense than Odaesia carving out the land. What if this was the piece the forgotten goddess created for herself when the others made their kingdoms?"

"It would make sense," I admitted.

I remembered the night I took Koraine to the waterfall, the way the moon beamed down on us as we swam in the pool, the way it reflected off the surface and illuminated my wife. She'd seemed more alive, more herself than I had ever seen her.

"I think we need to go back to the waterfall," I said.

"What if I'm wrong?" Koraine said.

"We need a place to wait," I said. "The earth king ordered us to find a way for them to arrive safely, a path straight to my father. This is it," I said. ""And if you are right, you just may be the key to saving us all, my moon."

CHAPTER 40
KORAINE

Nine days at sea.

Nine grueling days at sea.

Kai forced us to take the longest route to Abelon.

We sailed close to the sea bordering Luheo and followed the route until we were able to head toward Abelon from the south.

On the ninth day, we finally sailed close enough that we could call on the serpents. I stood at the helm of the ship and called out to Talay.

Caspian and Asena stood on either side of me, watching for Ryn and Elios.

The three serpents broke through the surface, their beady eyes staring us down. They could sense the anticipation, the tension we each held for the war we were walking into.

The last leg of the journey was the hardest.

There were three of us to wield the water and protect us beneath it, but we needed to keep air bubbles around seven people and keep our supplies dry. The task alone would require hours of rest to follow. Luckily, the sun was approaching setting. Kai timed our arrival with sunset to allow us the cover of darkness to remain unnoticed.

I climbed down the side of the ship on a rope ladder and climbed onto my serpent's back.

The distance to shore wasn't far. I'd take Bellamy and Ervin. My brother would take Oleena, and the princess would take Kai.

I adjusted the satchel slung over my shoulder. We'd each carry our own supplies.

"Ready?" Bellamy asked, his eyes full of promise.

We hadn't told the rest of the group of the waterfall.

If I was wrong, I couldn't face the idea of letting them down further.

I'd visit the waterfall and spring when the moon was high and the group was sleeping. It was like a siren's call, beckoning me home. I wouldn't rest until I knew for certain.

"My moon," Bellamy said gently, and I realized I'd been so lost to my thoughts, I had not seen the other serpents descending into the water.

I nudged Talay forward, and the serpent dove beneath the waves, my hands rising to manipulate the water around us on the dive downward. The water shifted to form a bubble around us, and I held it in place, allowing us to breathe and protect the supplies.

The swim was not long. We barely had time or the capability for discussion.

I knew the sun was setting by how dark the shallower parts of the water were becoming.

There was increasingly less distance between the surface

and the sand beneath us. Soon, we'd be forced to send the serpents away and walk the remaining distance.

"As close as we can get, we go," Caspian stated, and I gave a firm nod.

The supplies remaining dry was a priority. Winter was only weeks away, and the cold during the night was dropping to freezing. With wet clothing or supplies, we risked catching ill.

Another short distance, and the serpents struggled to go further. Talay swam slow and careful, avoiding dragging his body on the ground and trying to keep us beneath the surface as long as he could.

Eventually, it became impossible. All three serpents broke through the surface, our bodies fully emerging from the water.

I prayed there were no patrols on the shore. Bellamy had sworn this portion of beach was left unwatched most times, the king more occupied with the docks, a direct route to Raden.

This beach was where we planned to usher the joining forces to make their arrival.

My heart raced as we climbed off the serpents, spotting the shores of Abelon only a short distance away. They'd swam us as far as they could possibly go.

This was the last home I had known, a kingdom I had found a way to love. It gave me hope for a better future before ripping it away.

Our legs were submerged in the water as we trudged forward, but we kept the dry satchels well above the waves. We'd change the moment we found our spot to camp.

The waves splashed against the back of my thighs, and I

turned back to watch the serpents disappear under the water. My heart ached, and I knew Talay felt similar. I wished I could wage the war on the sea, riding the back of my serpent, but I knew it was impossible.

Our feet finally left the water and made it to the pebbled beach. There was enough of the strip of shore left for us to walk on, but it was growing shorter. I knew the tide would soon cover it. That reason alone was why Bellamy was confident patrols would not come out this far. It was useless during high tide.

We walked along the pebbled beach, and I recognized the area that would lead us to the waterfall, the place Bellamy had once referred to as my home.

It was odd how true that could become overnight. The urge to return was growing stronger with each passing second, and I knew there was something more to the small oasis carved into the fire kingdom.

I couldn't be wrong.

I needed this to be right.

"How much further?" Oleena asked after a few minutes. The priestess had insisted on traveling with us, but already, I feared for her safety. We couldn't protect her when war broke out. I prayed to every goddess she would make it out.

"Only a bit more down the beach," Bellamy assured the group.

I walked close to Ervin and Asena, the pair both shivering from the wet pants we all still wore. The princess has taken the old man's satchel at some point, and my heart ached imagining the pair walking in to battle.

It was hard to imagine any of us facing battle. This was my family. I couldn't lose them.

"There," Bellamy said, raising a hand to point.

I spotted the greenery that marked the river I knew would lead us to the hidden cove. The water raced into a hot spring naturally heated by flames deep beneath Abelon.

I pushed forward, following the prince, and the group trailed behind us. Only a short walk further, and we could rest.

The walk through the brush did not last long before I heard the familiar sound. Water toppled over the cliff and crashed into the pool below. The group's eyes widened seeing the waterfall in person. It was still an odd sight set against the backdrop of the fire kingdom.

"This way," Bellamy said, directing them to the narrow stone path leading up and behind the waterfall.

We walked in a single line on the path only wide enough for one person at a time. I stepped behind the waterfall, manipulating the water away from myself and the rest of the group.

Oleena sucked in a gasp as the last person to enter. The cavern was as I remembered it: large enough to hold us all, the remnants of the last to stay still scattered on the ground.

I thought back to that night only weeks ago, to the fire the prince had built for us and the way I'd slept safely in his arms.

It was the first time I realized Abelon had become my home.

Ervin and Bellamy worked to build a fire while the rest of us pulled out warm clothing from the satchels and passed them out. Kai sat in the corner, observing silently, and I wished the king hadn't sent him along. I felt my every move being assessed. One misstep, and he could send our one hope at winning the war back to its own kingdom.

"I'll take first watch," I offered, changing in to my warm pants. I knew what I had to do, and I needed Kai's and the others' watchful eyes off me for it.

No one argued, curling up into spots on the ground near the newly built fire and using their satchels for pillows. I sat with my back against the wall, watching as each drifted off.

"Goodnight, my moon," Bellamy whispered beside me.

"Goodnight," I said, knowing the moment he dozed off, I would make my break.

The rest of the group slept silently as I watched over them. I let them drift into deep sleep for an hour before daring to move. Bellamy was curled next to me, the fire in front of us illuminating his face. His features looked peaceful as he slept.

I stood, careful not to make a sound. My steps were light on the stone floor as I made my way across the space, avoiding the strewn bodies on the floor.

A shadow cast on the wall stopped me before I made it through the waterfall. Without turning, I knew who it was.

"I'm going to the spring," I said quietly.

Bellamy walked closer, the sound of the waterfall drowning our voices.

"I'm coming with you," he said, and I turned to face him.

"No," I said in a hushed whisper.

"Yes," he argued. "Unless you'd like me to wake them all. If you won't tell them, or wait until sunrise, then I am coming along."

He gestured to the rest of the group asleep on the ground. I knew I couldn't wait; the moon needed to be well into the sky for everything to work. My mind knew it as a fact, even though I had heard it nowhere.

"Fine," I said, rolling my eyes. "Only because you give me no other choice."

"And here I was thinking it was my charm," he joked.

I used my abilities to part the waterfall to the side, revealing the narrow path out. We followed it down to the spring of water. Something about the way the moon reflected directly above the pool mesmerized me. I stared into it, watching the water ripple and call to me.

Everything inside me wanted to throw myself into the pool. The draw of the water was tempting, and I didn't realize my feet were moving until Bellamy pulled me back.

"Are you sure?" he said, worry filling his eyes.

"This is it. I can feel it," I said.

"I know," he said. "But are you sure this is what you want?"

I tilted my head, my lips turning down. This was what everyone needed. They needed more power to win the war, a way to force the king to give up the throne, to stop him from ever harming Abelonians or the other three kingdoms again.

How could I turn that power down? A power that could heal my sickness, that could help my mother.

"I want to make sure this is what you want," Bellamy said

gently, moving closer. "I want you to control whatever this curse is, but I only want this if it is what you choose for yourself."

I furrowed my brows.

"You could wait until after the war. The waterfall will still be here," he whispered.

"But we may not."

The realization hit me hard as the words traveled from my lips. We may not all survive, but if I could prevent that, I had to.

"I have to, for them," I said. "For us."

He nodded, but I could see the hesitation in his eyes.

"If we make it through this, we build a better world. One of peace," I went on.

"For us," he repeated.

"For us," I answered, like a mantra I would continue to repeat until each one of us clawed our way out of this battle.

"I know these kingdoms need you," he said, brushing a strand of hair from my face. I leaned into his touch. "But not as much as I do."

My cheeks warmed, and before I could change my mind, I shifted away from the prince.

I let go of Bellamy's hand and turned back to the pool of water. My hands pulled at the black shirt I wore, tugging it over my head. My pants slid off quickly, and I hugged my arms around my cold torso. I couldn't risk wet clothing.

Slowly, I walked in the pool of water directly in front of the waterfall. I sucked in a breath the moment my skin hit the water. With the water's natural warmth from the hot spring, the cold air made my naked body shiver.

I willed my body to warm, trying to escape it. I needed to be fully submerged to call out to the goddess of the moon, I could feel it. The moon's light shown down on the water, well above us.

Bellamy stood not far from the spring of water. If he called out to me, I couldn't hear, the sound of the waterfall filling my ears. It drowned out the rest of the world.

I slowly submerged myself and manipulated a pocket of air to breathe.

I let my body sink to the bottom, feeling the sand beneath me. I crossed my legs, my eyes unable to see through the darkness under the water, preventing me from seeing my surroundings.

I slowed my breathing and tried to focus.

To reach out to the goddess, I let all my power and energy be directed toward her. It came more naturally than I imagined, somehow I just knew what to do.

Oleena had explained I needed to connect my very essence with the goddess to accept the blessing of her powers.

I was moon touched.

There was no escaping, no running from it. I had to face it head on; we were running out of time.

The goddesses were preparing for war. They would rip us apart and destroy our kingdoms. They were ready to wipe us out and start over. Too many conflicts pushed them to the edge, and I was the best hope we had at preventing the fire kingdom from solidifying our fate. If the king marched his armies on the other kingdoms, he'd only aid in wiping them from existence.

I pushed all those thoughts aside. The pressure would do no good in connecting me with the goddess.

I tried to focus on something else.

My mother's image appeared in my mind, her similar white hair blowing over her shoulders. Beside her, my grandma appeared, and it continued, an endless line of women I didn't recognize before me.

I knew who they were.

The other moon touched.

All the woman who came before me who'd failed at claiming the power bestowed on us.

I slowed my breathing and squeezed my eyes shut. I knew this was what the goddess wanted, to embrace who I was., to embrace my heritage.

I would succeed. I would control it. The blessing of the moon goddess would be mine to wield.

It was never a power I wanted or needed, but I knew it was my fate to claim it. I opened my eyes again, and they were still before me. The woman smiled warmly. It could be far too late for my mother, but I knew she would be proud I'd escaped the same destiny.

"Child," a woman's voice called out.

"Who are you?" I answered. Everything around me slowly melted away. I could no longer tell if my surroundings were real or a dream. A light flowed around me, a beautiful white glow.

I was still beneath the water, but now, I could see my surroundings as the light poured in.

An orb of light hovered in the water in front of me. Its presence was warm, drawing me to reach out to touch it.

"My child," the voice carried from the glowing orb.

My eyes widened, my body filling with warmth.

"You've come to claim what the others have never found, to save those who have been cursed with the burden. Claim the companion to your own water abilities, a way to make them stronger, to control the power the moon has over the tides."

I nodded my head, afraid to speak.

I knew the goddess wouldn't hurt me, could feel it deep in my soul. I couldn't find the right words to speak. How could I plead for a power so many before me had never found?

"Don't be afraid, my child," the voice said softly. "The power is yours if you want it. It always has been."

I held my breath, listening. This was how we would win the war, how I would protect my family and make the women before me proud.

"All you have to do is reach out for it," the voice said across the water. "When the moon rises, so will the power within you. You will control the tides warring inside you."

Instantly, I could feel what I needed to do. My arm stretched out, reaching toward the orb.

The moment my fingertips touched the light, it consumed me. Energy rushed into my body, and the light from the orb dissipated across my skin. I looked down at my hands, turning them over, and saw the glow surrounding them.

It felt like I was floating to the surface. My body hadn't moved an inch, but the energy of the moon flowed through my veins. I could feel the power building inside me.

I started to feel a bit queasy, my hands shaking. The

rawer the energy that poured into my body, the more I sensed its effects.

I was afraid I wouldn't be able to handle it.

I was lightheaded, but I tried to hold on as long as I could. The light slowly disappeared, and soon, I was left in silence of darkness. I couldn't hold on any longer.

"Rest, my child," the distant voice whispered.

Slowly, I let myself slip from reality.

CHAPTER 41

BELLAMY

Koraine's body floated to the surface of the water. For a moment, I left her, afraid if I disrupted her, she wouldn't be able to complete whatever the blessing required.

She'd vanished for minutes. Only minute, yet it felt like an eternity. An eternity without air or the ability to keep going. I need her to reappear.

There was no sign of the moon goddess.

"Fuck," I muttered under my breath.

A strong gust of wind rushed by, and the hairs on my arms stood.

I abandoned the shore where I waited patiently and ran straight into the water without a second thought. I grabbed Koraine and tucked her close to me. Her body was limp, her eyes shut.

Panic took hold.

"Koraine," I said, hoping she'd wake.

She didn't move.

I pulled her out of water and watched her chest start to

rise and fall. I noticed the slight movement and let out a deep breath.

"Koraine," I tried again, but I still didn't receive a response.

I knew we couldn't stay where we were. The cold would get to her soon, unclothed and unconscious.

I kept her scooped into my arms, her head hanging back.

I carried her toward the waterfall, back toward where I knew our group awaited our return. Our disappearance may have still been unknown to them, but I wouldn't risk them waking to find us gone.

I carried Koraine up the narrow path, and it wasn't long before we were back inside the cavern tucked behind the waterfall.

Ervin was awake and pacing inside. "Where were you?" the old man scolded before noticing Koraine's limp body.

Caspian sat up and rubbed sleep from his eyes, disturbed by the noise. He stood quickly and ran toward us the moment he saw Koraine in my arms.

"What happened?" he asked, his eyes not leaving his sister.

"She's alive," I assured him.

"What happened? Where were you?" he asked, waking the others.

"I have no idea," I admitted. "One second, she was treading into the water, and the next, I couldn't see her until she floated to the surface," I explained.

My heart was racing; every second she remained uncon-scious was another I spent praying the goddess of the moon would allow her to wake.

"In the water?" Asena asked.

"What were you doing out there?" Kai questioned, his brows furrowing and anger growing on his face. We hadn't betrayed the earth king, but I knew it was where his mind immediately went.

"She thought-" I started.

"She found it?" Oleena asked, her eyes widening.

"Found what?" Kai and Asena asked.

"Did she-" Caspian started.

"I have no clue," I said. "I never saw the goddess."

Caspian head hung, and I knew it wasn't what he wanted to hear. His hope for her to escape the curse was slowly being pulled away. I could feel my own hope draining.

"This waterfall is the moon goddess' land?" Asena asked.

"She wasn't sure," I admitted.

"What do you mean?" Kai asked.

I shook my head.

"She'd been here before. When I told her the story behind the waterfall, she said it didn't make sense. The more she considered it and the pull she had to it, I think the more her mind became set that this was where she was meant to claim the blessing."

"That's ludicrous," Kai said.

Ervin's eyes remained wide on me as he stroked at his beard nervously.

I sat down on the ground, cradling Koraine's head in my lap near the fire. Asena brought over a blanket she'd pulled from her own satchel and draped it over Koraine's body.

"She needs rest. If she claimed that power, her body needs time," I whispered.

War was coming, and we were running out of time to give her.

"I'll watch her," I said.

"I'll take watch with you," Caspian offered. He sat down beside me silently, curling his knees in to his chest.

The way his eyes remained on his sister broke my heart. They'd lost every piece of family they had. Their own father betrayed them, sending Koraine away and refusing to help her. Caspian had chosen her side. I barely knew her other brother, but he'd remained loyal to his father and the King of Morwen. I knew the pain that was eating away at Caspian. If he lost his sister, he had no one.

I empathized.

If I lost Koraine, I would lose my only remaining family as well.

CHAPTER 42

KORAINE

My head ached when I finally opened my eyes. The sky was still dark, and I imagined the stars above the pool outside the waterfall. I blinked away the haze in my eyes and tried to sit up, Bellamy watching me carefully observing.

"How long?" I asked.

"Only a few hours," he said.

"Koraine," Caspian said, his voice filled with raw emotion.

I glanced around and found the entire group watching me, sitting up from where they all slept.

"Why aren't you resting?" I asked.

"We needed to know you were alright," Caspian said, and I swore, I heard relief in his voice.

"You worried them that much; did it at least work?" Asena asked.

"What?" I started.

"They know," Bellamy said gently.

"I-" I glanced down at my hands, remembering the way the power of the moon goddess had made them shine.

I still wasn't sure what being moon touched meant or what powers I held, but something had changed. There was a moment under the water where more power than ever flowed through my body.

I stood, walking toward the waterfall.

"Koraine-" Caspian started.

"Let her," Oleena said, and the group stood and followed. I could barely hear them over the call of the sea and moon.

I mindlessly walked the narrow path to the brush and followed it to the pebbled beach. My feet moved without a single thought from my mind. My eyes remained on the moon above, and I couldn't tell if this was all still part of some big dream.

Was I trapped in my own thoughts?

The ocean washed ashore, running along the pebbles. At some point, someone had dressed me in dry clothing, but I wasn't sure when.

I didn't care.

I only had one thought.

Under the light of the moon, I stepped ankle deep into the water. Deep down, I knew this new energy within me could only be called upon under the light of the moon. I'd be useless during the day.

The armies would have to hold out as long as they could when the battle began. They'd need to buy me time until the sun fell.

I raised my arms, calling on the water and the moon at the same time. Water rose before me, and a large wall formed. I pushed it even further, building the wall to impossible heights. The water glowed, a new luminance spreading across it, like the moonlight reflected on it was amplified.

I felt the eyes of the group behind me as I tested the limits of my power.

Taking a deep breath, I imagined the wall solidifying. Trickles of ice appeared at the top of the wave and slowly worked their way down. Within moments, the wall of ice held back water from the shore. I let my control drop, and the ice melted, letting a giant wave crashed down.

I let out a sigh of relief, realizing I had claimed the blessing. I hadn't imagined the goddess under the waves. I'd truly done it.

"My father has no idea what's coming for him," Bellamy said in awe.

"That handles one of our problems," Caspian chuckled weakly, but I heard the relief buried in it.

The reality was, I had terrified him.

He couldn't handle the prospect of losing someone else to the illness slowly claiming our mother. I found his eyes, and a smile grew on my face as I realized I finally had the answer for her.

"That still leaves the goddesses," Oleena noted. "The scales of balance have already been tipped, and they must be restored before it's too late. They won't stop until they eliminate all four kingdoms to start over. It's inevitable," she sighed.

"You're sure this is the start of their wrath?" Caspian asked.

"I wish I wasn't," she said. "You felt the power in Zetron the same as I. I dedicated my life to studying the goddesses, and if there's a single thing the four can agree upon, it is balance. Each goddess wants more power for her element, but she knows it is not possible. Quarrels were fought between the goddesses long ago, and the result was always the same. Their power could only exist if there was a balance. Too much of one element, and this world will crumble on itself."

I sucked in a breath, listening to the priest. I imagined what the world would be like if only one element was to exist, covering all the kingdoms. I imagined a world covered in flames, the people and towns burning to ashes. There would be nowhere left for people to exist.

"I will stop him from tipping the balance. We will restore how the kingdoms once were," I promised.

We had to find a way to stop what was coming.

"Now, we need rest," Bellamy said. "The armies will arrive soon, and we will need to join them. In the coming days, we go to war."

CHAPTER 43

KORAINE

Two days passed before we saw sails on the horizon. If we spotted them so easily, then there was no doubt in my mind the king had seen them too.

We rushed to the pebbled beach, watching as the ships approached. Every inch of me tensed with anxiety, awaiting an attack on the ships. Would the king launch the first offense of the war?

The ships stopped and anchored not far from shore, and my worry multiplied tenfold when nothing and no one met them to stop them. We had been prepared to jump into battle the moment Zetron arrived, and now, when the ships found the shores of Abelon, there was nothing but eerie silence carried across the winds.

Row boats departed from the ships, and hundreds of men and woman poured onto the beach. We pushed them further inland, toward the waterfall and the green land surrounding it. It provided shelter, water, and a base for the armies to use.

"My king," Kai said, passing by me and greeting one of

the ships making its way to shore. I watched in awe as the earth king stepped out of the boat, joining us. I'd half expected him to remain in Zetron, but here he was before me, dressed in battle armor.

"I expect you've found us a path to your father, given the unmatched arrival?" the king spoke to Bellamy.

"I've never known my father to shy from battle," Bellamy stated. "He's planned something, and I worry he will be the one to meet us first."

I knew he was right. The king of the fire kingdom was ruthless. He'd rather his men die fighting than be considered cowards. To allow these ships safe passage to the shores, he had to have something larger planned.

"I received word Luheo is not far behind us," the king stated.

Our group had spent the past two days discussing strategy and routes to the palace. The best option was to meet the king in battle there and leave as minimal damage as possible within Raden. My heart couldn't handle the burden of leaving the innocent people in the city below without homes.

I'd begged the group to consider avoiding the city, and we'd collectively agreed to try everything else first. Unfortunately, it meant taking the less direct route up through the cliffs and toward the far side of the palace.

"This way, my king," Kai said, snapping me from the memory.

He led the king off toward the waterfall, where we'd designated the cavern as a space to meet. Already, I watched soldiers pitching tents and gathering supplies as I made my way back to the space we'd created as our base.

I parted the waterfall for the group when we arrived, and already, Kai had manipulated the stone in the cavern to create a makeshift table. We stood around the central structure as Bellamy spread out a map he'd taken from the supplies.

"This is where we are," he said, pointing to the map. "These are the few routes to the palace. My assumption is that he's fortified the space, knowing the fight would come to him."

"The most direct route is this," the king declared, pointing at the one trailing straight through Raden.

"Yes, but-"

"We take that one," he said sternly.

"There are people who live there," Bellamy said. "I will not put *my* people at risk if I do not need to."

"We will not harm innocent people if they stay out of our path," the king assured him.

"It doesn't matter," I chimed in. "They inevitably will be in the path of war if we march our armies that direction."

"Then they should have left," he stated. "The king has known it would come to this."

"Do you truly believe he would evacuate his people?" Asena asked.

"If I remember correctly, you should be back in Zetron, with my nephew," the king snapped. "Do not think I have forgotten." His eyes bore into her, and she shied away from the table.

"My father will have left these people to fend for themselves. He cares nothing for them if they add nothing to his army," Bellamy said firmly. "We should take the other path up the cliff. The far side of the palace has more open land. There will be fewer unknown obstacles for us to deal with."

"We can't risk it," Kai said. "Your father could move on our army while we are still scrambling to mobilize up the cliffs. We will exert more energy than needed getting to the palace."

"Innocent lives are at risk," I said.

"You don't think I know that?" Kai argued. "This is war; people will die."

Silence rang through the cavern, and my stomach sunk.

"I know, but I won't risk innocent lives if we can help it," I countered quietly.

"It is not your choice," the king stated. "This is my army, and they march on my command. I appreciate you providing a space for us to camp, but that is the extent of your help. I have commanded this army longer than you have been alive and will continue to give the commands."

The weight of war crushed me. I could barely stomach the idea of men and women who volunteered to serve their kingdoms dying, but the innocent people we volunteered to protect? How would I look these people in the eyes one day and tell them I did all I could to save them?

I didn't.

"You don't have the final say either," I noted, and all heads turned in my direction. "When the other kingdoms arrive, you will need to make a joint decision."

Luheo or Morwen were our best chance at persuading the earth king.

"We shall see," he scoffed. "For now, I need to assist my army in preparations."

The king excused himself, leaving the cavern with Kai following.

"Well, we have his help, but I'm not sure there's anything more we can do to influence him," Caspian sighed. "Father would know what to say," he added.

My heart raced. We needed Morwen's army, but would my Father persuade the king to join? Caspian had written to him, knowing we could not receive a response. I didn't hold out much hope. He would do what he thought strategically best for Morwen, not what his own flesh and blood begged of him.

"Do you think he will come?" I worked up the courage to ask.

My brother's jaw was set, and his eyes looked to the floor.

"If I was a betting man, I wouldn't waste my money on it," he said. "I want to believe he will, but I think selfishly, he will do whatever he determines the most strategic move for Morwen."

Bellamy wrapped an arm around my shoulder, tucking me in to his chest.

"Luheo is coming," I said. "We need to pray the two are enough."

I felt the prince's chest freeze at the mention of the air kingdom.

The last time he'd encountered them was his failed offense on the kingdom at the order of his father.

"They will forgive you," I said quietly.

"And if they don't?" he asked.

"They will," I assured him. "You are going to be king.

They will have to move on and accept it. You both will need to rebuild what was lost."

He nodded, and I felt him let go of the breath he held.

"We should find our new place to sleep," Caspian suggested, breaking through the hanging tension.

We followed him from the cavern, finding spare tents mixed in with the new supplies. We worked to pitch them in a clearing beyond the spring beneath the waterfall; I had not ventured past the spring, but further into the brush, following another path, it opened into a small clearing.

Many Zetronian guards already inhabited the space. Men and women carried supplies and helped each other to set up camp. I spotted a large fire being built, logs on either side and one across to hang food for cooking.

Ervin quickly left the group, heading straight for those cooking. I held in a soft laugh; the sweet old man could not help himself.

Pantherus walked through the camp, led by soldiers and guided to the far end. My heart sped up, remembering my last encounter with one of the beasts.

"We can pitch ours over here," Bellamy said, ushering me to the left and pointing to an open space. Caspian and Asena helped us set up our tent and theirs side-by-side. The pair agreed to share a tent while Oleen and Ervin agreed to their own. The pair had already disappeared, helping with preparations and learning how they could be of use.

I didn't wish to see either on the battlefield.

"We should get rest before Luheo arrives. There will be much to discuss when they do," Bellamy said.

"And I don't trust the king will give them all of the information we shared," I added.

"Then you agree?" Bellamy asked, searching my eyes.

"On?" I asked.

"Rest," he answered, and I nodded.

Caspian and Asena said their goodnights, agreeing to turn in for an early night. During war, everyone slept when they could. Preserving energy and building strength were our priorities.

We tucked ourselves close together in the small tent. Is was barely big enough to hold the pair of us. I slid closer into Bellamy's grasp and let myself be lulled to sleep by the sound of his calming breaths.

Luheo arrived late during the night, their men making their way to shore guided by torch light. I was woken to their arrival by the prince nudging me.

"King Sloan Elrindor and his men have arrived," he whispered, and I heard the sound of boots shuffling outside the tent.

We left the tent we shared to follow the sound of the new commotion. Other men and women joined from the clearing to the shore to assist. We carried supplies from ships and led the Luheon soldiers to the base camp.

I tried not to get my hopes up; we still did not know if the King of Luheo would agree with our assessment. I had to pray that with the landscape of Luheo, the cliff path would not deter them.

"King Elrindor and King Bramden would like you

present in the general's cavern," Kai said, coming up behind Bellamy and me.

I spotted Caspian and Asena nearby and motioned for them to follow. We jogged quickly to the cavern behind the waterfall; I refused to miss the discussions. They could not make a decision without us. Asena spoke for Morwen, even if their fleet did not arrive, and Bellamy spoke on behalf of the innocent people of Abelon. That had to mean something.

We entered and found both kings already discussing around the map on the stone table. Other guards stood post inside the cavern, and I moved forward to lead our group. Kai slipped past me to stand beside his king.

"Thank you, captain," he said.

"I have faith your summoning us means you have seen the sense in taking the other path," I said, emboldened by my lack of sleep.

Bellamy and Caspian tensed on either side of me at my sharp tongue.

The kings both stared at me, watching me approach the table.

"We are taking the path through the cliffs. I will not endanger other's lives," I said sternly. "If you are willing to put innocent lives at risk, then what is the point of even fighting this war? We can let King Kaius burn the kingdoms and kill the innocent citizens for us instead."

"It is the strategic route to take," King Bramden spoke.

Kai nodded behind him, and I resisted rolling my eyes at his complete blind compliance.

As captain of his own guard, he had to see how many

people we put at risk marching through the streets of Raden. We didn't have to take the path through the capital.

King Elrindor crossed his arms, and I found my myself holding his stare. His bald head made him appear older than I imagined he was. The way his muscles tightened just at the fold of his arms, the outlines of chiseled muscles I saw through his tight clothing, told a different story.

"I agree with Bramden," he spoke, his voice deep and gruff.

"And what if Morwen disagrees?" Asena spoke, stepping next to me.

"Neither of your fathers would disagree with the logic behind this strategy, especially not yours," King Elrindor said, casting a glare in my direction.

"You do not have a say here, princess. I imagine your father will be quite displeased to know you have broken our agreement," King Bramden said. "If you wish for me to forget that small detail, then Morwen will side with this plan."

Asena held her tongue, and I did not blame her. It was not worth casting our kingdom straight into another war to disagree; it would only result in more lives lost, the exact thing we were fighting so hard to prevent.

"And if Abelon disagrees?" Bellamy asked. "These are my people, the people I will look after when my father is removed from the throne. I cannot allow you to risk their lives to accomplish that."

"Your father has put our people' lives at risk for years. You sailed to my kingdom's shores and launched an offense against my men at his will," King Elrindor spoke. "This is war, and you better than anyone should know that some-times, sacrifices are made."

I felt Bellamy go rigid. My insides felt like liquified flames, the normal cool temper of my water nonexistent, the new pull of power tugging on me, begging me to release it.

I barely registered my hands moving before I saw the guards in the cavern pull out their weapons or raise their hands. I moved faster.

Water from the waterfall flowed through the room in tendrils, lashing out and wrapping around any victim in their path. The water glowed with the same blue hue as the first time I tested the blessing of being moon touched.

The tendrils grabbed hold of the guards and pinned them against the cavern walls before they could stop me. I barely had to move, the water acting in accordance with my thoughts.

"I can't let you do this," I spoke in a fierce tone I barely recognized.

Caspian placed a hand on my shoulder, but I barely acknowledged him.

"Koraine, I think this through," he said warily.

"He has a point," Bellamy added. "This isn't the way."

I couldn't hear them over the sound of pure power rushing in my ears. The hum of the moon goddess's power was a roaring rapid I could not ignore.

More tendrils grew from the waterfall, slowly approaching the two kings. They glanced to each other before raising their hands. The earth king slammed up a wall of stone as one of the streams lashed for him. King Elrindor used his air to slice through the tendrils, forcing the water to dissipate before reaching him. I growled in frustration, all logical thoughts escaping me. I didn't care if they were two of the most powerful rulers across the four kingdoms. I couldn't allow it.

"Koraine," Asena tried, failing to snap me out of my haze of fury.

Every innocent life I thought about in Raden fueled my anger. It pushed my power to grow, springing free and lashing out at those around me.

Strong hands around my waist pulled me back, and before I could reconsider, I lashed out. My tendrils flew toward the person behind me, trying to pry them from my body. The hold tightened, and I let out a sound of frustration.

"Let me go," I yelled.

"Never, my moon," Bellamy whispered before a tendril pulled him from me and slammed him into the wall.

I turned, horrified. All the water in the room dropped to the floor, the power rescinding inside me. I rushed over to Bellamy, but before I could make it, strong hands grabbed me. Kai and Caspian held me back, keeping me from the prince.

Asena rushed over to Bellamy and helped him sit up.

"I didn't-" I started. "I couldn't stop it."

The horrific realization washed over me. I had no control over the power I had claimed. It controlled me, my emotions, and exacerbated them into raw energy I'd released.

I pulled away from the men's grasps when they realized I was back to myself and rushed to Bellamy. He held open his arms for me, and I collapsed to the floor into them.

Small sobs escaped me.

"I'm sorry. I'm so, so sorry," I choked out.

"I know, my moon," he said.

"I never meant to hurt anyone," I sobbed. " I just… I lost control."

My body shook as waves of tears streamed down my cheeks. The raw energy left me shaking, and I could barely move my hands to press them to Bellamy's chest. I felt his chest rise and fall, the familiar faint heartbeat thrumming against my touch. I could feel my nerves settling, knowing he was unharmed.

"What is she?" King Bramden said, stepping forward. "Power like this could have caused the attack on my palace."

'I didn't-" I started, but I stopped when Caspian stepped in front of me.

"Koraine did not launch the attack on your palace. You know that was the power of a goddess."

"And was that not the power of a goddess?" he inquired. "I have met many manipulators, and never in my life have I seen their power illuminate the way hers did. I have never seen water move without her lifting so much as an arm."

Bellamy held me tighter, instinct taking over. "Don't move or speak," he whispered, barely audible.

"She's moon touched," Caspian said. "She has claimed the power of the moon goddess to help us in finishing this war."

"There is no such thing," King Elrindor spoke.

"You both saw yourself. Her power is that of a goddess, and not one you have ever encountered," Asena tried.

Silence rang through the cavern. My heart pounded in my chest, and Bellamy clung to me like I could be ripped away at any moment. Would they take me away, keep me a prisoner?

Kai stared at me, and I realized he had kept my secret. The king had been unaware of my power, and Kai had ample time to warn him. He'd witnessed that night on the beach when I turned an entire wall of water to ice.

Why hadn't he said anything?

"Power like this could turn the war in our favor," King Bramden said finally.

The air king nodded, his gaze still set on me. I felt a lump forming in my throat. I'd claimed this power to save my mother, to protect my people. I never wished to be a weapon. The way their eyes shined with a new prospect made my stomach sink.

"We will use this power to our advantage," the earth king said. "Prevent King Drakon from ever recovering."

"Power like this could wipe out the enter capital if harnessed properly," King Elrindor stated.

"No," I said swiftly. "I will not harm innocent people."

"We need this power to prevent the king of Abelon from mobilizing and restore the balance of the kingdoms," the earth king stated.

An idea formed in my head. If they wished for me to be their weapon, I would. I couldn't stop that fate, but I would also use it to protect the people of Abelon.

"I will help you stop the king and lend you this power," I stated, "but only if we take the path through the cliffs."

"You would let us lose this war by withholding this power from us, all to protect those people?" the air king asked.

A world in which I allowed innocents to die unnecessarily was not one I wished to be a part of. I would sit prisoner and refuse to ever let the power of the moon goddess out if I had to. We'd find a new way to save the kingdoms, but this was not it.

"Yes," I said softly.

The kings paused, glancing to each other, the guards behind them readied. I watched as they tensed and raised their hands, ready to fight, to take me prisoner if they were forced to. The kings nodded to each other and turned back to me.

"We leave for the cliffs just past sunrise," King Elrindor stated. "War is here."

CHAPTER 44

BELLAMY

We found ourselves at the foot of the cliff at dawn.

I swallowed hard, glancing up at the route I'd taken many times before. It was steep but easily climbable. It would take hours to move all the men and women to the top, but the kings had agreed to Koraine's conditions.

Men and women appeared from the tents the moment the sun rose, carrying supplies and weapons. I found a simple sword within the assortment and strapped it to my side.

Kai hovered closer to Koraine than I liked, acting on the king's orders and keeping a close eye on her. I was surprised they allowed her to walk free from the cavern. She had directly attacked the kings of two different kingdoms. To walk away unscathed was unheard of.

I watched her white hair flow in front of me, walking toward the cliff.

The tents remained pitched back in the clearing, many staying behind to convert them into tents for healers to care for anyone injured during battle. Food and more supply rations would be prepared for when we returned from the first wave of attacks.

If we returned.

The war could be over in mere moments or stretch days.

Either way, I knew we were in for a long battle.

I caught up to Koraine and slipped my hand into hers. It could be the last chance I got. Her fingers curled around my own.

"Don't let me become that thing," she whispered.

"I won't," I assured her.

The power had consumed her, turning her into something unrecognizable when she unleashed it. She had no control over the water or her thoughts when the anger took hold. I would be the anchor she needed, the tie to this world that kept her from becoming that power. I would bring her back if she went too far.

I had to. For the sake of us all.

"Even if it means my last breath, I will keep you here," I promised.

She cast me a look of sadness and desperation. "We may not all return," she said solemnly.

"I know," I whispered. "But we will do everything we can to protect those we love."

She nodded, looking ahead to where Caspian followed Asena.

Oleena and Ervin had stayed behind in the camp to help, and before we could even exchange goodbyes, it had been time to leave. There was no time to waste. We had a long journey to the palace. If we wanted to launch our offensive today, we needed to move.

The first men and women made their way up the cliffside to the long path on the far side of the palace.

I watched guards dressed in greens and tans march side by side, air and earth moving as a single allied force. I prayed it would be enough.

The guards marched up the cliffside, and we waited for our chance to join. Too many troops crowding the path risked causing a landslide. The path was narrow and firm, but the dirt around it was filled with loose rubble and weak spots.

Already, our travel was slow paced. Barely any of our forces were on the cliffside. My nerves grew the longer I waited to climb the cliff.

A small tremor beneath my feet made me pause my shuffling pace toward the cliff. No one else stopped their march. Had I imagined the feeling? My worries were growing into full hallucinations, my anxiety about the cliffside consuming my thoughts.

"You alright?" Koraine asked, stopped in her tracks by my sudden pause.

"Did you feel that?" I asked.

"What?" She tilted her head.

People paced by us, some muttering their annoyance, avoiding us. My feet felt heavy, and for once, I stood patiently waiting. Instead of rushing onward, I listened to that gut feeling and just waited.

"What's wrong?" Koraine asked.

"I'm not sure," I answered, watching the cliff.

Caspian and Asena stood at the very foot of the cliff, the next to go up its narrow path. Another small tremor shook beneath my feet, and this time, I saw Koraine's eyes widen at the feeling.

It was so slight, but it was there.

Before I could stop myself, I ran toward the cliff.

"Get off," I shouted. Many heads turned toward me, but those on the cliff continued up. "Off the cliff!"

My shouts barely reached them. Caspian and Asena turned to see my panicked face running toward them. I waved at them to move away from the cliff.

"Get back!" I tried yelling.

The kings turned to look at me, confusion growing on their features.

"What are you doing?" King Elrindor hissed.

"They need to get off that cliff," I said, out of breath from running.

"You are the one who forced them up it, and now you want them back?" King Bramden snapped.

"Get them off, or they will die," I pleaded.

The kings studied my face, but I showed no emotion. I needed their command to call the men and women back.

Koraine caught up and stood watching with Asena and Caspian.

"What is he doing?" I heard Caspian hiss to her, but I ignored it.

Before the kings could call their armies back, a larger tremble shook the ground. It was enough to catch everyone's attention. I held my hands out for balance as the ground shook.

"It's too late," I said, my face dropping.

The ground split in a matter of seconds, tearing through the cliffside. The path broke straight in half, and men and women yelled as they were knocked down the cliffside. It was steep beside the path, with nothing to grab to. I watched helplessly as their bodies slid down the side of the earth.

"The goddesses' wraths have already begun," I stated. "We're too late."

Everyone watched in horror, unable to help. Koraine stumbled to the side, knocked by another tremor. Caspian helped stabilize his sister and Asena while I made my way back to them.

"Retreat," King Elrindor shouted. "We march through the capital."

There was no stopping them. It was the only possible path left. We had already run out of time. There would be no new strategies or planning. We had to march on Abelon, restore the balance. Otherwise, the goddesses would tear us apart. The sun was already well into the sky, and the day was rapidly passing.

Strong gusts of wind picked up, and I struggled to push forward with the others back toward the shore. We'd march along it straight to the docks of Raden.

Healers and other volunteers met us as we all stumbled back close to our camp, helping the few men and women who had made it back from the cliff with injuries. Cracks continued to form in the ground, and I heard a scream that forced me to turn.

A women cried for help as strong winds turned into a tornado heading toward her. She threw up a wall of stone, a Zetronian guard with no other protection, but the wind barreled through it. A Luheon soldier rushed to her side and tamed the winds, forcing them to change course.

"What happened?" Ervin's voice snapped my attention back to our group. We huddled together, trying to make sense of the elemental chaos.

"The goddesses," Oleena guessed, joining us.

"They're going to march through the city," I breathed out, unable to form a full thought.

"We can warn them before you father meets them," Oleena said. "We will come with you."

"No," Koraine said.

"You cannot stop us," Oleena argued. "Those people need help. Not only are armies about to tear through their homes, but now the elements."

I nodded firmly.

"I'll help them," Asena said quickly. "I can protect you while you spread the word."

Already, Luheon and Zetronian soldiers had recovered and marched toward the city, and we rushed to join the marching forces.

Rain began to pour down, adding to the nip of cold washing over me.

The moment we stepped into the streets of Raden, we were met with frightened citizens. Abelonian soldiers hadn't yet flooded the streets, but I knew it would not be long.

A horn in the distance confirmed the thought.

War had been declared.

My father bid his time and waited for the cover of chaos to make his move, and this was it. The goddesses played straight into his favor. It was a race to what would destroy the kingdoms first.

I rushed through the streets, trying to aid in warning people as Asena led Ervin and Oleena off in another direction. Bits of homes crumbled into the street with each passing tremor. I ran, hoping I could save them in time. I needed to evacuate as many citizens as I could.

Koraine and Caspian trailed behind me, slamming on the doors I missed. We shouted to anyone who would listen for what felt like hours.

I rounded a corner and froze in place.

Alaric stood before me, holding Mariam's hand, a group of small children behind them.

The look of fear in their eyes grew as a gust of wind picked up behind them. I heard the roar of the air, knowing what would follow. Another tornado formed, barreling down the road.

"Let's go," I said, motioning for them to follow. There was no time for reunions. I thanked Mavalu for finding them, but I needed to get them to safety.

"I knew you'd come back," Mariam said, her voice breaking.

"I would never leave you all," I promised.

We turned a corner, and the Earth shook again. Our group paused, unable to move much further, the shaking intensifying.

One of the children screamed as a bit of roof broke free of an overhang. I tried to push toward them, but I wasn't fast enough.

Fire flew through the air, and the chunk of stone shattered, knocked away from the children. Ervin and the other two stood opposite of us, and I watched as Ervin dropped his hands to his side.

Thank you, I managed to mouth.

"Come with us," he said to the group, waving them to follow.

Mariam stopped before me. She threw her arms around me, and Alaric grunted.

"Thank you," she said. "I'm glad to see you both back." She nodded toward Koraine.

Alaric held out a hand, and I hesitated. The man had never once acknowledged me beyond arguments and displeasure. After a moment, I took his hand and pulled him in to a hug before he could protest.

"Protect them," I ordered.

He nodded and turned without a word.

I made my way back down to the docks, weaving through as many streets as I could. Many men and women fled away from the city, heading toward where our base camp was set up.

My heart felt a little relief.

I spotted the red uniforms making their way down from the winding streets above us. In the distance, I could see the flaming gates of the palace had been lowered and knew it meant one thing.

The king had joined his army.

I whistled for Imry, needing the dragon to be ready. If my father's army mobilized, so would the other beasts of the kingdom.

I spotted a few griffins overhead, riders from Luheo directing them.

Pantheruses flooded the streets, Zetronian guards leading them in to the battle.

I heard cries in the distance and knew the war had

begun. There was no turning back. This was it, our only chance to right what my father had done.

Bile rose in my throat as my stomach sunk, knowing my father would give everything he had to battle. Every ounce of power and flames would be used to burn through these armies.

"Look," Capsian said, pointing out to the sea and snapping me from my thoughts.

Blue sails with the crest of a wave appeared on the horizon, sailing straight toward Abelon to join us.

Morwen had arrived.

CHAPTER 45

KORAINE

My father was among the first of the Morwenians to make it to shore, alongside Emmett and King Belizere.

My heart stopped at seeing my family walking the docks of Abelon.

The battle had already broken out, and Morwenians were swiftly joining, carried to shore by boats and serpents.

"Father," Caspian greeted, holding out a hand.

Emmett gave him a firm nod. The pair were complete opposites. I felt like I barely knew my eldest brother, yet here I was, forced to fight by his side to save our kingdoms.

"You came," was all I managed to say to my father.

"You needed me," he answered, his face stoic.

It was the more than I had ever expected from him. He'd traveled across the sea and marched Morwen into war again for us, for our people, to protect the kingdoms. He'd served his time and fought valiantly for Morwen before; he did not need to come. Yet, here he stood.

"Caspian's letter was very convincing," he admitted.

I glared at my brother, but he shook his head—that would be a question for a later day. There was no time. The family reunion needed to wait.

"The armies are already marching through the streets. We are trying to hold them back," Caspian reported. His tone shifted, and he instantly became the warrior my father hoped he would become.

"Lead us," my father answered.

"What?" Caspian said, shock forming on his face.

"You know the battlefield better than I do. You know the situation. Lead us where you need us," he commanded.

"I-" Caspian started as he looked to Bellamy and me.

"We'll be okay. Go," I said.

He motioned for my father and brother to follow, and they trailed behind him, hurrying to aid the other two kingdoms.

"My daughter?" King Belizere asked, pausing before me.

"She's evacuating citizens," I answered.

"She's not at the earth kingdom? She is here?" he asked, and I saw the horror on his face.

"She chose to fight for Morwen," I answered, and he nodded.

"I will find her," he said softly.

I watched as he marched after my family, warriors of Morwen following behind them.

A group of Abelonian soldiers marched down a street toward us, Morwenians rushing form the docks to meet them, instantly throwing themselves into battle.

I hurried to aid them. The sun was still in the sky, but I

could give my all to use my water manipulation to aid in battle. If we could hold out until the sun fell, I could use the full force of my power.

I fought, sending streams of water into the crowd of soldiers. Men and women fell around me, knocked aside by fire and water. Other soldiers quickly joined, air and earth joining the mix.

I didn't check to see if Bellamy followed; there was no time. We needed to hold back Abelon as long as possible.

To save the four kingdoms from complete destruction.

Minutes passed, and already, I could feel my heart racing, sweat dripping down my face, mixed with rain. The cold water and air did nothing to cool the heat of the flames surrounding us.

I pushed, hoping to keep the soldiers from forcing us to the docks, but it was no use. The streets were too narrow to hold us, and it was inevitable we would be pushed into the open space by the water.

Many of our forces were already falling back, creating a battlefield beside the sea. The kings were commanding their armies, fighting beside them as I continued to wage my own battle on the east side of the lower city.

I risked a quick glance back to search for Bellamy. I spotted the prince locked in battle with an Abelonian, who was swiftly knocked to the side. I knew the prince held back. These were his people; he didn't wish to kill them.

Neither did I.

An odd sight behind him held my attention.

I jogged closer, approaching Bellamy and looking past him to the sea.

"What?" he asked, breathing heavy.

I pointed beyond him. The sea pulled back alarmingly quick, revealing the sandy shore.

"Where is it going?" Bellamy asked.

"I think that's Odaesia, come to inflict her own destruction," I gasped.

There was no time to process the disappearing water. I had to hope if we could end the war, the looming disaster would stop.

Movement behind me caught Bellamy's attention, and I turned too late.

Nyla threw a stream of fire from only feet away, barreling in my direction. I had no time to react.

Bellamy threw himself in front of me, taking the entire hit.

The flames struck in a vibrant stream of power, the scorching red and orange of them filling my vision.

Bellamy had put himself between me and Nyla's flames.

"No!" I screamed and barely registered the rest of the world around me.

He fell to the ground, his shirt singed and chest covered with burns. He was alive, but the hit had taken a toll.

He moaned in agony and tried to sit, but he struggled, grasping at his chest.

I knelt and threw up a wall of water, blocking the fire princess out. I knew we only had seconds.

"Go," he insisted. "Bring her back."

"Bell-" I started.

"We don't have time. I'm okay. I have to find my father. You go, bring Nyla back to us," he pleaded.

I knew he was right, but I hated leaving him. He'd saved

my life, sacrificing himself for me. I couldn't just leave him. I leaned in, pressing a quick kiss to his lips.

"I will find you," I promised.

"Always," he answered, and I let the water drop around us, throwing myself in the direction of the princess.

CHAPTER 46
BELLAMY

My chest burned, a large singe mark left in my shirt as I stood.

Terror raged all around us, consuming every man and woman who stood on the battlefield. All the kingdoms were combined in one place, fighting each other and the goddesses' wrath. My eyes darted between the people I loved.

Koraine and my sister were locked in heavy battle. Rain poured all around them, and Koraine stood her ground fiercely. The power of the moon goddess illuminated her, her hair a shining white and her vibrant blue eyes glowing through the storm.

A loud explosion caught our attention, and we glanced to the mountains in the distance, now glowing a bright red.

Fire ran down the distant volcanoes, Mavalu contributing more destruction to the chaos.

It was still far off, but soon, a sea of flames would consume us all.

My heart raced, and I spotted my father commanding the guards around him.

A gust of air knocked me off my feet, and I stumbled.

My eyes glanced around wildly, searching for the source. A small tornado of wind had formed on its own with no command. I watched two of Luheo's men try to tame the winds, but they consistently failed.

My ribs ached, and I rubbed my side while I stood back up.

I raced toward where my father stood, protected by his men. I knew I needed to be the one to kill him. It'd taken everything I had to tame his flames.

Fire swerved in my path as I sprinted toward where the king stood on a nearby stone wall. He was raised enough to command his men but still protected by a mass of guards.

Dragons soared overhead, pouring flames onto innocent men and women below.

My heart sank, knowing it would take all my energy just to break through the men standing strong before him.

I launched myself into attack, flames soaring from my hands. Each attack found its mark, knocking the guards off balance and slowly chipping away at the wall they formed.

I had a sword strapped to my side in case it came to it, but I tried to keep enough distance to rely on my flames. In hand to hand combat, I knew I could take on my father, but I didn't want to lose my only weapon before then.

A wall of fire rose in front of the king, consuming and shielding him. My father raised his hands as the fire grew, and lashes and tendrils flickered out of the wall, searching for a victim to grab hold of.

Beads of sweat formed on my forehead, the temperature

rising around me. The rain coming down was not enough to douse the flames he controlled.

It helped in wearing down the other guards, but still, it was not enough.

Each man I picked off, another took his place.

My arms screamed, sore, and I could feel the power depleting inside me. The endless energy the priestess spoke of within Abelon to fuel our powers, I had yet to find.

My breathing was heavy, and I'd taken down at least twenty men. I pushed onward, surrounded by guards. They closed in on me, and I continued to lash out with my fire. I pushed them back, but not enough to break a hole in their wall.

Again and again, I tried to push forward, but it seemed the soldiers were endless.

I'd thrown myself into a hopeless situation.

Everywhere I looked through the cracks of the guards around me, the elements battled. The Earth continually shifted beneath our feet, multiple earthquakes tearing the ground apart and throwing off our balance. The water from the sea continued to withdraw from the shore, and I swallowed the lump in my throat, knowing what would be coming from that side. Tornadoes continued to form randomly throughout the battlefield, and each soldier of Luheo tried to wrangle the untamable winds.

A guard rushed forward faster than I was prepared for.

I threw my hands up and swung at him, narrowly hitting my mark. My fist connected with his face, but not without a price. Unprepared, the strike I threw was sloppy. My knuckles connected, and I could feel them swelling from the mistake.

The guard crumpled at my feet, losing consciousness.

More guards rushed forward, emboldened by the last ones attempt and realizing they could wear me out faster.

They pushed toward me, grabbing and pulling me in different directions. I thrashed and punched, taking as many out as I could. I tried to call on my flames, but they were too close now.

Any burst of fire that could push them back would burn me as well.

I knew I was doomed.

They knocked me to the ground, and I fell to my hands and knees. Flames formed above me, and I tensed, bracing myself for what I knew would come next. The fire would consume me, burning first through my clothing, then my back. It would be more painful than the burn marks on my arms.

My muscles tensed and waited, but the consuming fire never came.

Above me, men grunted and shouted. I took my chance to gain my footing and stood back up.

I threw a punch, and my target fell to the ground. He tried to stand, but water slammed into him first.

"Need help?" Caspian asked, smiling at me.

Caspian and I fought side-by-side, our water and fire complementing our every move. The pair of us moved with precision and strength. Guards surrounded us, but we pushed onward.

With each guard we took down, another replaced them, protecting my father from my wrath. It was a useless attempt; nothing would stop me from getting the revenge I sought.

I would find justice for my mother's death, for all the Abelonians who had been treated like they were nothing, for my sister who had been molded into a weapon.

Caspian had my back, keeping the guards from closing in behind me. I knew I needed to break through the wall of men, and with Caspian's help, I finally stood a chance.

"I need you to help me breakthrough their line, and then you need to return to the battle," I ordered.

"I'm not leaving you to fight him yourself," he argued.

"Caspian, I'm not asking," I answered.

"You don't give me orders," he managed to breathe out between blows of water.

"Caspian, please. If anything, help Koraine," I answered. "This is my fight."

He didn't argue, but I could feel him standing tensely behind me, resisting the urge to go against my order.

"On my command, I need you to send water straight through the center of them."

"My water won't be enough," he answered.

"I know," I called back. "Just trust me."

I heard him snort behind me and managed to smile. An Abelonian and Morwenian trusting each other—the world truly must've been ending.

We continued to push the guards back, and I waited for

the right moment. We needed enough space to build our attack and ensure it wasn't wasted.

As my flames sent one of the guards in front of me flying, I found an opening as more guards scrambled to fill in the hole.

"Now, Caspian," I ordered.

I prayed to the goddesses he was able to turn and strike in time.

A stream of water flew past my head and slammed into the guards rushing towards us. They stumbled back, and I took my chance. My flames mimicked his stream of water, barreling into the guards and forcing them to part.

A small opening formed, and I took my chance, not letting up on my flames. I ran forward, letting the stream of fire guide me and avoiding Caspian's water.

I didn't have time to even look back, but I hoped he would find his sister.

I broke through the line of guards and found myself standing directly before a wall of flame. I could feel the guards at my back, already rushing behind me to stop me.

I didn't hesitate to use my control to part the flames. Intense heat surrounded my body and threatened to burn me. I tore through the wall of fire and stepped out the other side to find my father standing there, waiting for me. He wore his armor, and for once, I stood before him with no crown or finery, ready to finally face him head on.

CHAPTER 47

KORAINE

I CONTINUED in my battle with the princess. Her tangled red hair fell into her face with each strike she sent my way, wet and straggly from the pouring rain. The water around me helped replenish my power, but it also caused a hindrance to my sight.

The black top I wore had torn, burnt from flames that came far too close to finding their mark. The material had been turned to ash in one section, exposing my rib cage, and I did everything I could to protect myself from the flames finding my skin again.

I pushed forward, trying to call on and feel the power of the moon I possessed. Night was coming, but the moon was not high enough in the sky for me to fully grasp control. I could feel bits of the power pushing me to continue.

Nyla threw streams of flames, and I drove out of the way. I stood quickly, finding my footing again. Morwenian warriors stood behind me but quickly found themselves back in their own fight against the fire kingdom.

The Abelonian army refused to surrender, remaining loyal to their king and ruler.

I sent a stream water in the princess' direction, but she threw up a shield of fire fast enough to deflect. Our attacks continued to fly back and forth across the battlefield. We pushed each other past the docks, down into the sand where the sea had begun to withdraw.

I had no time to worry about where the water that had pulled back went.

Deep down, I knew what was coming, and there was no way to stop it. Our only hope would be to evacuate before it hit land. If this battle continue to rage, the people standing along the shore would be wiped away.

My brothers and father were off within the sea of men and women fighting. I tried between attacks to find them or Bellamy within the crowd, but I failed each time.

My chest grew tighter the longer I engaged with the princess. Each attack that came closer to finding its mark and ending things brought a new wave of anxiety rushing through my body. I never wanted to see the princess dead.

Part of me knew I was holding back. With the power of a goddess, I should be able to wipe her out quickly, but with each opportunity, I found myself hesitating. Even without the entire power of the moon, I had moments where I felt it flowing through my veins.

Most of my attacks were to keep her busy and wear her down. I needed to talk to her, to make her see sense.

If not for the friendship we had formed, then for the prince I loved dearly. This was his sister.

Bile rose in my throat as the next attack I threw slammed into her chest, knocking her to the ground.

She scrambled to her feet and narrowed her eyes on me. The look on her face made her look too far gone for reason.

"Stop," I shouted. "Please."

"You brought this war on yourself," she insisted.

Her flames sprung to life in her hand and two quick balls of fire flew in my direction. I manipulated a stream of water to knock each one out of the air before they could connect with me.

We pushed further and further into the growing shore, where nothing and no one surrounded us. Our small battlefield formed around us.

My stomach twisted, and I threw a stream of water in her direction, this time stronger.

She rolled to her right and stood, sending a stream of fire back in my direction. Before I could sidestep it, it caught a bit of the pants I wore. I cursed under my breath. I tried to step forward to throw a return attack, but I winced as I felt the stinging burn on my shin. I risked a glance down and noticed the fiery red skin through the tear in my pants.

Fire had found its mark, and I was paying the price.

A wave of panic washed over me, and I knew if I didn't end this fast, I would end up with worse.

Dark eyes settled on me, and I swallowed hard, waiting for her next attack. Her arms moved in a quick motion, and a wall of fire rushed across the sand at me. I threw up my own wall of water and quickly hardened it to ice. The fire slammed into it, and shards of ice shattered around me. I covered my head with my hands, unable to think fast enough to deflect.

I quickly regained my composure and found sharp picks of ice surrounding me. I raised my hands, and as I did, the ice floated into the air. They were like small daggers hovering above the ground. I forced them forward, squeezing my eyes to see if they found their mark.

The daggers of ice flew through the air, rushing at the princess. She threw fire in front of herself, and I opened my eyes to watch as the daggers melted before they found their target.

Relief took hold of me, and I realized in that moment, all I wanted was to peacefully end this battle.

"Don't you see what he's doing?" I shouted. "Your father has manipulated you."

"You don't think I know that?" she hissed back. "You don't think I know he's turned me into this weapon, that he's using me to get my brother? The moment this all ends, he'll toss me aside. I know," she insisted.

I felt like someone stabbed me in the heart, and my composure broke. Intense sadness couldn't be kept from my face. My brows furrowed, and I fought for the words I wanted to say. I desperately wanted to tell her she had a choice. She didn't have to be this weapon her father had made her.

"You choose," I tried.

I felt like the world was slowly crushing me. Any hope I'd had for the battle bringing back the woman we'd known felt like a distant dream now. She scowled and crossed her arms.

"I already chose," she said. "I chose the minute you left me in Abelon. I chose to never be weak again. I chose to make the people who hurt me pay," she shouted.

Tears welled in my eyes, clouding my vision and slowly dripping down my cheeks. I tried to call on my water as I saw the princess forming new flames in her palms, but I felt weak. My leg shook, and I no longer felt like I could continue to fight.

She was hurt.

Not physically, but deep down, I knew her heart was bleeding. We had left a wound so large, it couldn't be closed. It continued to grow and fester, and this was the price. All her compassion, her kindness, her humanity, was slowly slipping away. Each time the wound grew, she lost a bit more of herself.

Flames flew in my direction, and the only thing I can do was dive to the ground. I covered my head as they narrowly missed, soaring above me.

Another attack quickly followed low to the ground. I rolled, but the intense heat of the flames licked against me. I knew my time was running out. If I didn't find a way to stop the princess, it would be my life in trade. I'd made Bellamy a promise, and I intended to keep it no matter what.

CHAPTER 48
NYLA

The bitch wouldn't die.

My breath was becoming labored, and I was finding it harder to hold my own against Koraine. She moved with inhuman precision, and I could feel with each attack that she was holding back. If she unleashed the full amount of her power, I would be utterly screwed.

My father sat back and watched while his guards did his bidding, leaving me alone. He couldn't spare a single one for me. I fought my own battles, and still, he barely looked at me.

I was nothing to him.

Instead, he tasked me with killing Koraine. It was my only hope at earning his respect. If I could just do that, then maybe I stood a chance at surviving in the ruthless world he'd form.

I didn't spare him another thought. My only goal was to finish off Koraine, the person who had turned me into this monster, the one who, every time I thought about all my pain and suffering, was at the end of it. I called all my energy and sent flames soaring in her direction.

My movement grew slower the longer we remained in our battle.

An orb of ice came flying at my chest, and before I could use my own fire to melt it, it slammed into me. The breast plate I wore protected my fragile body, but the force of the impact still knocked me backward.

I lost my balance and fell to the ground. I had to scramble back to my feet.

I wouldn't be weak. I would fight until I had nothing left. Strands of my dark hair stuck to my skin. The feeling made my skin crawl. I was drenched from the rain, and it did nothing to help replenish my fire.

It was becoming an annoyance.

I moved my arms quickly, forming a small flame that grew double its size, and sent it flying toward my opponent. Again, she dodged, rolling to the side. She stood up with ease, but I could tell by the way she favored her left side that the burn on her leg from my earlier attack was causing some problems.

That small ember of hope was the thing keeping me going. If I could land another attack, I would slow her down.

She had become a weapon, one that needed to be taken out of commission.

If I could stop her, I could turn the tides of the war.

"Please," she begged, and I saw the sadness in her eyes. The way she looked at me such pity made my stomach turn.

I didn't want her pity; I wanted her respect. I wanted her to realize she had turned me into something no longer human, a being who no longer felt the pain etched into my soul.

My hand fumbled to light my residual limb aflame as I sent yet another stream of fire in her direction, refusing to answer her plea. I sent two more streams following the first and took multiple steps toward her. If I could close in on her and wear her down, I could force her to yield and could finally come to terms with killing Koraine.

Even if I knew it would break my brother, I had no other option. It was my brother or me, and for once, I needed to prioritize myself. I needed to survive, make it through the war, and come out on the other side. Bellamy had made his choice.

I would prove I wasn't helpless, that my father was wrong about me. I'd earn his respect.

Water flew in my direction, and before I could parry the attack, it wrapped around me like a lasso. The water quickly dragged me to the ground and pinned me there as it turned to ice.

Rage filled every inch of me, and I let it burn unimaginably hot. The flames of my anger ate through the ice, and I was freed before Koraine could make her next attack.

If she truly possessed the power of a goddess, I needed to stop her before the moon rose above us. I wasn't willing to find out the extent of that power.

Our exchange continued, and we pushed further into the sand, away from the armies back at the docks. Out this far, no one would hear our cries for help or interfere.

This battle would end in only one way.

Only one of us would return to the war that raged behind us.

I would stop at nothing to ensure it was me.

A small dagger of ice shot through the air and grazed my leg. Blood quickly appeared, dripping down my thigh. The cut wasn't deep, but it was enough to cause me to falter. Another blade of ice flew in my direction, this time grazing my right shoulder. More blood covered my skin.

The pain was an icy sting. I gripped my shoulder with my opposite hand, and when I pulled it back, it was covered in red liquid. I moved both arms in a circular motion, forming a ring of flames, and sent it flying in Koraine's direction, wincing as I jutted my arms outward.

Again, I tried to send flames at my opponent, but she blocked them with her water, taking a step closer to me. The burn took its toll on her, but I was in no position to take advantage of the injury. We were both exhausted, slowly sending each other to our demises.

Maybe this was the way it had to be, the pair of us wearing each other down until neither was left standing. If I failed, I wanted to take her down with me. If I had to give my life to stop her, I would.

No longer would I allow her to destroy my kingdom. She'd already taken everything from me. If I did not ascend the throne, then I would keep Bellamy from it.

When this war came to an end, our people deserved peace, true peace that lasted centuries, the kind where our children's children would never know even the whisper of war.

That's what I wanted to give them. I needed it to be true.

I threw another stream of fire in her direction, this new promise fueling me and building my determination. Only feet apart, we were locked in a battle of water and fire. Red and blue filled the air and surrounded us.

I aimed my fire for Koraine's other leg, and the stream of flames narrowly connected with her skin. I watched as she faltered, missing her step and falling to one knee.

She stood back up and threw another attack of water in my direction, and I quickly blocked it.

There was no time to hold anything back. This was everything I had.

"Just give up," I said.

"I can't," she answered, sending another attack in my direction.

Before I could respond, another stream of water wrapped around my body. I was too slow to stop it. This time, it crawled along my skin and down my back, forcing my arms behind me and quickly solidifying into ice.

"I'm sorry," Koraine said, and I knew the pain behind her eyes was real.

She truly couldn't comprehend what she had caused. The pain written across her face made my chest ache. I hated her for everything she had caused. I hated that she had befriended me, that I had truly thought I found family. Bellamy had been the only thing I had since my mother died. I thought I'd gained a sister, and her betrayal left a gaping wound. I struggled against the ice, trying to call my flames to my hands, but I hesitated when I saw the orb of water floating in my direction.

There were no guards close enough to call for help.

I was truly, utterly alone.

The agonizing realization I had not been enough swept over me.

I whistled, calling for my dragon, but the water was faster.

The orb floated toward my face and covered my head. I screamed, but my lungs filled with liquid. Rage and pain filled my body, and I could feel the air fading from my lungs. There was no way for me to take another breath.

I writhed against her power, but nothing worked.

I dropped to the sand, kicking, my arms finally freeing from the ice as I clawed at my face. It was too late.

My vision was already turning black, and there was no air left. The last thing I saw before everything faded was Koraine standing above me, tears dripping down her face before black filled my world.

CHAPTER 49
BELLAMY

My father wasted no time sending flames in my direction. He dropped the wall of flames closing us in and directed them toward me instead. I blocked the fire and moved quick. I wanted to end the fight swiftly. The less energy spent, the more I could return to helping my people. To helping Koraine.

My father's time had come to an end; the reign of terror would stop.

He whistled between attacks, and I knew what was coming.

The large shadow passed over us before it made its descent. I whistled for my own beast as the large red dragon descended on the people below. It let out a breath of fire, sending soldiers scattering.

I sucked in a breath as it barreled toward me, and I waited for the last moment to duck. It grabbed my father, heading straight for the clouds with him.

Imry trailed not far behind, hurrying to grab me. I

reached a hand up and let the dragon snatch me. She held tight until we were well above the ground.

My beast let go and swiftly got beneath me, catching me from my fall. My father had already righted himself on his dragon's back.

I'd seen the beast few times as a child. It was rare my father rode it, the last time being during the prior war. It resided in the mountains instead, commanding the other dragons and sitting at the top of their hierarchy.

Imry chased close behind the dragon, gaining on it. She breathed fire, and the dragon dove to the side.

Wind slammed into my face, stronger than ever, and obscured my vision. The lower we flew, the more we felt the impact of the rain pouring down. The sun was trailing down, and I found it hard to believe the day had already passed.

I'd been locked in battle for hours.

Thunder boomed across Abelon, and my heart raced watching the men and women below. The elements clashed, and the goddesses worked at every turn to tear the battle-field apart.

My father's beast turned on us, its mouth filling with flames that spewed in our direction. I nudged Imry to roll to the right. I clung tight to her neck as we took a sharp dive, narrowly missing the flames.

She leveled out quickly, and we continued our chase.

My jaw tightened as I leaned forward, willing her to fly faster. The dragons circled the sky above the battlefield, and I dove to avoid other dragons and griffins as they too fought above Abelon.

We pushed onward, and Imry snarled as we closed the

distance again between us and my father. Her wings flapped harder, and I waited until the last second to give the command.

"Now, Imry," I commanded, and she let out a bellow of flames.

My father's beast turned, but not quick enough. The fire caught one of its wings, sending the beast roaring in agony to the side.

"Go," I directed, nudging my dragon forward toward the beast as it slowed.

It was caught off balance, and I could see its wing had major burns across the leathery skin.

Imry angled her body, swift and deliberate, and aimed for the dragon. She tucked her wings, allowing us to dive toward it at unimaginable speed. Her jaw unhinged as she attacked from the backside. She bit into the beast's tail and pulled backward.

My father raised his hands and threw a stream of fire toward my beast. I deflect the attack to protect her, but the distraction gave his beast enough time to writhe free of her grasp.

We pushed on after him, and the two dragons continued to collide in a battle of flames and claws. We bit and tore into the flesh of the beast, taking each opportunity to close in.

My frustrations grew, and I gripped tight to Imry's neck.

Imry twisted in the sky, trying to follow the other dragon's motions. We continued our pursuit for what felt like hours, a never ending chase, one that would only end when one dragon fell from the sky.

There was no other way to end the battle.

I would not allow my father to return to his men. This was it.

The others fought valiantly below us, holding their own and keeping my father's men at bay while I was tasked with ending his reign. If we took away their leader, they would have no choice but to stop the fighting.

I flew close behind him, and he aimed his beast for the mountains of flames. My stomach sunk. The area was the beast's territory, and it knew the terrain better than any other dragon. Imry had been away for weeks and rarely spent time in the mountains. She was at a clear disadvantage.

My father knew that.

I directed her to remain close, not letting my father out of my sight.

His beast dove toward one of the mountains, and I aimed my dragon down. The pure heat flowing down the side of each mountain was enough to make me forget the cold and rain.

I was sweating, and I risked reaching up to wipe the wetness from my forehead.

The liquid fire had reached the base of the mountain, and I knew we had limited time before enough poured over to flow toward the city.

It would burn through everything in its path.

My entire body burned, and I pulled Imry away from the fire, above my father and his beast. I knew they were trying to force us off, put distance between us. I couldn't allow it.

"Now, Imry," I commanded, and she bellowed, letting flames stream toward them.

Her fire matched the heat of the flames below. Although it missed its mark, it was enough to intensify the heat and force them to rise.

They flew well above the mountains before diving between a far pair again. I tried to follow but found the intensity of the heat too great again. We continued to chase after them, trying to force them up when we could.

I wanted to turn back, to fly and aid my allies, but I couldn't.

I was alone.

The clouds darkened above us, and rain poured down harder. The gusts of wind continued to challenge us at every turn. It was a battle just to push forward. I shielded my eyes from a nasty gust and directed Imry lower once more.

We aimed toward the sea, following my father. I could see the water had pulled further out, and my stomach sank at what I knew would follow.

The fire continued to run beneath me, and I recalled Oleena's words.

This was the land Mavalu intended for us, the kingdom our powers should thrive in. Instead, we'd always viewed it as a hinderance, a reason to go to war. Our lands were desolate, consumed by fire.

I tried to feel the flames that ran beneath me, beyond the heat of them and the destruction I could see. I reached out, feeling for the power it brought our land. Flames coursed beneath the very surface of the kingdom. It was the same fire pouring from the mountains, the same flames to heat the spring at the waterfall. It was connected across the land in every aspect.

I reached deep, praying to Mavalu that I could find that power, to tap into it.

Something inside me stirred. The usual heat and intensity that came with my temper was rising, but instead of anger, I felt confidence, an ember of hope I could end this war. That we would walk away from this a more unified world.

It was a dream, but one I would give my life for.

I could feel the power beneath me, and I tried to draw on it, to pour that energy into my own attacks.

We gained on my father and his beast, and I saw them turn to face us. I pulled Imry up to avoid a collision as my father sent a ball of flames after us. It clipped Imry's wing and knocked her off balance.

I pulled her to the side and circled her to face my father again. He turned and directed his dragon back toward the docks. We gave chase, not letting them escape from our grasp.

Another tremor shook the ground below us, and I heard the cries of soldiers losing their balance and avoiding the cracks forming beneath their feet. I had to put an end to it.

I let the energy build inside me until it came boiling to the top.

Fire poured from my hands, illuminating the sky red. It flew at my father, and he turned around on his beast to intercept it, but I didn't let up. I put everything I had into the fire, letting the stream fly at him.

"Is that everything?" he shouted, taunting me.

"Just stop this nonsense," I plead. "Surrender. Put an end to the chaos. The goddesses may spare us if we return to balance."

Could I genuinely do it? Could I kill my own father?

"Your sister at least knew one thing you never learned: self-preservation," he shouted as he continued to hold off my flames. "She chose the side she knew would win. She chose to be selfish. You were always a fool, always trying to sacrifice yourself and do the noble thing. You never could have handled the throne."

I pushed the flames forward and urged Imry to fly faster. She closed in on them, only feet away now.

"You will never protect this kingdom," my father shouted. "You are far too weak."

Imry threw herself forward, trying to bite the beast but narrowly missing.

"I gave these people everything. I found them land and resources when our kingdom had none. I fought wars for them," he yelled.

"You took their queen from them," I shouted back.

"That's war," he said. "And that is why you will never make a good king."

I poured everything I had into one last attack. My energy was depleting, and I could barely hold my growing anger back.

These people had suffered under his rule. This was for every single one of those wronged by my father. Forced into battles they never asked for. Forced to steal land to prosper. Forced to suffer without the queen they adored.

Imry pushed forward one last time and grabbed hold of the beast. She clenched her jaw, refusing to let go. We tumbled through the sky, and I clung to my best. We were a blur of claws, scratching to break free.

Fire soared through the sky as my father's dragon let out

a breath of flame in agony. Blood rained down on the battlefield below, and the beast continued to writhe in my dragon's mouth.

"Harder, Imry," I urged, still holding tight to her neck.

Every ounce of trust I had, I poured into her.

She clenched and let a low rumble fill her throat. I knew what was coming and managed to meet my father's gaze in the chaos of the attack. There was one emotion I found there.

Pure hatred.

He couldn't be saved. I knew it, and still, my heart ached for what would come next.

Imry let her fire go, breathing it straight into the beast she clung to. It rippled across its body and consumed it as my father let out a roar of agony.

My dragon let go, backing away as I held my hands out and poured my own flames into the assault. It consumed them, setting the sky ablaze. Fire burnt across the beast and its rider until the pair fell limp, the dragons wings stopping as they plummeted.

My father fell through the sky; I should have mourned the loss, but I barely had a moment to recover before another beast slammed into Imry, knocking us almost out of the sky. Imry barreled to the ground before I was able to level her again. We narrowly missed the stone beneath us before she took off back into the clouds.

I caught a glimpse of my father and his beast, both limp and lifeless below. My stomach turned at the sight, but I threw myself back into battle.

Cyrus rode Nondaar, sending streams of flames at any

target he could find. Griffins plummeted to their deaths as he claimed their lives.

"Enough," I bellowed after him.

"They deserve to burn," he shouted.

"They don't and you know it," I yelled.

He spun on his beast, pausing in the air and facing us. Imry and I were exhausted. I could feel the dragon's need for rest, but our battle was far from finished.

"Your father never would have wanted this," I tried.

"You killed my father. You assured he would never live to see this," Cyrus snapped.

"I know he was a brave general, one who wouldn't want you to continue this madness. He would know when the battle was over," I pushed.

"You just took the closest thing I had left of family from me," Cyrus shouted. "You and your bitch sister have ruined my life. There is no kingdom left living for. If this is how it is, then I will finish the job and make sure each and every one of you burns."

He was too far gone.

Cyrus turned and continued his indiscriminate assault on the people below. He had no regard for which soldiers he rained fire upon. Everyone in his path burned.

I directed Imry to follow.

I had to stop him.

Cyrus was projecting his blind fury into his attacks. Both his dragon and he threw flames in every direction. The beast let out a bellow that sounded pained, Cyrus' frustration and pain projected onto the dragon.

Our constant feuding and his hatred for me would soon be over. We could not both walk away, and we knew it. It has gone too far, his hatred running too deep. He would never find forgiveness for what I did to his father or the king.

Cyrus dove toward the people below, Nondaar scooping innocent soldiers off the ground and carrying them into the air. I watched as the dragon let go, letting the soldiers plummet.

I sent Imry after those falling, and she caught them just in time, lowering them to the ground. The distraction allowed Cyrus to put more space between us.

I let out a frustrated groan. My fists clenched, and I shot a stream of fire in his direction, forcing his dragon to dive to the side. It was enough time for Imry to close some of the distance between us.

"Just surrender," I called after the captain. "You will be given a fair hearing, and we will find a place for you in the Abelon we rebuild."

He scoffed. "There will be nothing left to rebuild when the goddesses are done. Do you think your father did not know the chaos he incited tipping the balance? He cast this world into chaos to destroy what the others had. He planned to rise from the ashes, a world ruled by flames."

"That's impossible," I said.

Cyrus shrugged. "Maybe, but he had a vision for our people, one where we no longer lived in desolate, useless lands. A vision where we were the ones in control. We had power over the other kingdoms and never once lived in fear."

"The other kingdoms live in fear of us," I shouted. "It shouldn't be that way."

"It should and it must. Do you think they will share their resources? What happens when that fire burns across the remaining land and we have nowhere left for our homes or crops? Will they share then? Will Morwen welcome us into their lands?"

In the past, I would have said no. My narrow-mindedness would have pushed me to believe the falsities my father spread. But then I found Koraine. I saw how we could live in harmony, how we could learn to love each other and no longer live in fear of each other.

"I have to have hope the kingdoms will come together," I said.

"Then you are a fool," Cyrus spat.

I chased after him as he commanded Nondaar to burn a trail through the lines of soldiers.

Imry shot her own flames in his direction and forced him to dive lower.

I followed him, hovering far too close to the ground. Soldiers ducked as we passed over head. I shot my flames at Cyrus, and he blocked them. I knew if I let him ascend again, we'd return to the endless cycle.

This battle needed to end.

I poured my energy into an orb of fire and let it fly towards him, following with three more. He was forced to block each, distracting him from directing Nondaar.

I tried to form another quickly, but he sent his own stream of fire toward me. I shielded myself from it, but I knew I'd missed my chance. He shifted, pointing Nondaar toward the sky.

Water shot into the air and wrapped around the body of the beast, pulling it toward the ground. Nondaar pulled, writhing against its grasp, but ice flew at the beast, piercing its wings.

The cry it let out was excruciatingly loud and filled with agony. The dragon plummeted, no longer supported by its wings. I watched as Caspian and his brother trapped the beast with ice. The fall wasn't far enough to kill the captain, but he fell from the beast's back to the ground.

He tried to stand, and I swept down, landing beside him.

Every memory came rushing back: how he put his hands on Koraine, how he'd treated my sister, how he pushed me to my limits. He couldn't be allowed to remain in power. And yet, somehow, I couldn't bring myself to end it.

My hand was on my sword at my side, but I removed it. I held it out instead to the captain.

"Please," I said. "End this with us."

He looked at my hand for a moment before outstretching his. Pride filled my chest. I could have killed him, protected us all, but I would give him a chance. I'd allow him the fair hearing he deserved and a place in Abelon.

He was hurt.

He'd lost everything.

I went to pull Cyrus up and saw the blade too late.

Metal flew toward my face from his other hand, and he stabbed toward the side of my throat. I froze, unable to do anything but watch. Death was upon me, and I'd walked myself straight into it.

A spear of ice stabbed into the side of Cyrus' neck before his dagger could reach my throat, and he dropped to his knees before me, his eyes wide. He grabbed at his neck as blood poured through his fingers. His eyes turned vacant as he gasped out his last breaths. Death was swift, taking hold of him.

He fell forward, his body lifeless.

I glanced to Caspian, who stood in silence, watching.

"Thank you," I said, the words barely making it from my mouth.

He gave me a grim nod and looked to Emmett, who watched from the side. He walked off to check the beast that laid limp on the stone ground. When he kicked at it, the body barely moved.

A large, towering wall of water shot into the sky like a beacon beyond us on the shore where the sea used to be.

I knew it had to be her.

Power like that could only come from one person. I pulled Caspian up onto Imry and took off, racing toward it and leaving Emmett behind. We landed in the sand nearby and slid off the beast.

"Go," I told Imry, allowing her to leave for safety in the clouds.

Caspian and I walked up to the wall of water and stood, waiting for it to fall, unsure of what we'd find behind it.

CHAPTER 50

KORAINE

I POURED ALL my power into the water I ran over the princess' body. She laid so still, it was hard to even spot the slight rise and fall of her chest. It grew weaker and weaker, becoming less noticeable.

I prayed to the goddesses, willing this to work. I wouldn't let Nyla die.

I just needed to stop her bombardment of attacks. It was the only way to buy time to show her reason. She'd strayed from the person she was, but that didn't mean we couldn't bring her back.

I dug deep down, pulling out as much energy as I had left. The battle had drained me, and I could feel in every moment that passed that my power was depleting. Even with the abilities bestowed on me from the moon goddess, I was still running out of energy.

The moon was rising, and I could feel the raw power rushing through my body.

I let out a cry as I pushed more power into the water, trying desperately to heal the wounds covering the princess' body. They were more extensive than she let on, and with each one I passed over, I spotted a new one.

She was caked in blood, and her lips were rapidly turning a pale shade of blue.

Water flooded around me, and I lost control of the streams. Again, I cried out, begging the goddesses to save her.

"Save her, please!" I cried aloud.

A hue of blue light surrounded me, and I felt myself reaching into the depth of my power. A stream of water grew around me, forming a circling wall. I had no control over it. Somehow, my power was manipulating the water without my own intentions behind it.

I could only focus on healing Nyla.

"Please," I cried out again.

The wall of water closed us in, blocking out the rest of the world. I could barely heard the muffled cries of war.

"I'll give anything," I pleaded.

Desperation filled me, and again, I pushed, trying to find more energy within me.

I leaned forward, letting my head fall to her chest. I listened desperately for the sound of life. I could hear her heartbeat trailing off as her breathing slowed.

"Would you give up the power gifted upon you to save her life?" a voice spoke above me, startling me.

I raised my head to find a woman staring down at me. She was ethereal, her body hovering above the ground. She shared the same blue hue I swore I saw coming from my own powers only moments before.

It was like looking in mirror, a different version of myself. Her long white hair fell over her shoulders, and it was the first time I'd ever seen someone with the same moon white hair as mine. Her blue eyes pierced into me, and as I met her gaze, it was the first time I noticed the blue moon painted on her forehead.

"Again, I ask, child of the moon, would you trade your powers to save one being?"

"Who are you?" I asked, knowing the answer.

I didn't want to believe it, but I knew exactly which goddess had answered my pleas.

"Louneer," she said. "But you already knew this."

She narrowed her eyes on me. I'd never heard the goddess' name spoken, nor did I think it was recorded within our texts. She was a being long lost to our history.

"Can you heal her?" I asked, my voice growing desperate.

Nyla had limited time, her chest suddenly seizing its movement. I knew if nothing was done in the next few moments, we would lose the princess.

"Please save her," I begged the goddess. "I'll give anything."

"You can heal her," the goddess said, tilting her head and studying me.

"I tried, but it wasn't enough."

"It will take everything you have. This gift of the moon will no longer be yours. It would live inside her. You would need to give up your connection to save her life," the goddess explained.

"How?" I asked.

"You would so willingly give up this blessing for someone who tried to take your life?" the goddess asked.

"I won't turn my back on family," I said.

It was the first time in a while that I thought of Nyla that way. Regardless of everything that happened, the fact remained true: Nyla was family.

If I could save her, I would. I would never choose to let Bellamy deal with the pain of losing his remaining family, and I would never give up a chance at making things right with the princess.

"Your power could end this war. It could put an end to all four goddesses tearing apart the kingdoms," Louneer pushed. "Do you still wish to throw that away when you've barely discovered the depth of the power?"

I took a deep breath.

"Everyone wishes to be a weapon. All my life, I have known pain and suffering, war and conflict. I don't wish for that to continue. I will not be a weapon to kill more innocent people. If the goddesses cannot accept the balance we provide, then that is a fate I must accept. I want to use this blessing for something good. Something that matters. This matters to me. She matters," I explained.

The goddess looked at me, her eyes filled with curiosity.

"Show me how," I insisted.

The goddess bent down to my level, kneeling beside me on the ground. The moment she touched the sand, her body became less of an apparition. Her skin was pale but warm, and I could see faint silver tattoos running up her arms.

She lightly touched my forehead and then, using her other hand, touched Nyla's. I watched as her body began to glow, blue light forming around her, flowing through her. I was terrified watching the ordeal, but I trusted the goddess would save her.

I felt nothing.

The power of the moon leaving my body did not hurt; all I could feel was the absence left by knowing the bargain I had made.

The goddess suddenly pulled her hands away and stood. "It is done," she said.

Before I could ask anything further, my vision began to turn black, the exhaustion finally claiming me. I knew my time had run out, and I felt my body growing weak. I had exerted too much power and energy, and when the blessing of the moon was pulled, my body gave in.

My eyes fluttered shut, and the last thing I saw before I faded was the water raining down around me, revealing both my brother and the prince, staring at me, horrified.

CHAPTER 51
BELLAMY

I RUSHED FORWARD the moment the water dropped, scooping Koraine's limp body into my arms. I could tell by the look she gave before collapsing that she had poured all her energy into Nyla.

The moon cast light onto her face, and I brushed a strand of hair away, the color dulled from its normal white.

My sister stirred as I scooped Koraine from the ground.

"Help her," I commanded to Caspian.

He didn't argue; instead, he knelt beside my sister, offering her a hand. Reluctantly, she took it, standing and glancing around at the remnants of a battlefield around us.

"Is he gone?" she asked me, her face sunken.

I nodded.

With Koraine held to my chest, I could see the rise and fall of her breathing, felt the pounding of her heart in her chest. A sigh of relief escaped me, knowing she was alive. It would take days before she fully recovered from the toll of battle.

For now, though, I would carry her home.

With my father gone and the throne left vacant, I needed to rise as the king of Abelon.

The color had drained from Koraine's face, and I spotted many of the cuts and bruises along her body.

Her eyes fluttered open, and I saw the realization on her face as she met my gaze.

"Did she make it?" she asked.

"See for yourself," I said, putting her down and letting her lean against me.

She found Nyla still standing beside Caspian. It was the first time in days I had genuinely seen my sister. My heart shattered when I noticed the spot where her hand used to be, now a residual limb. I knew it was the final punishment my father had doled out.

"You're alive," Koraine choked out.

Nyla nodded, walking toward her. I saw the confusion on my sister's face, the way she waited for Koraine to deal out her punishment or hurt her further. Her body tensed the closer Koraine stepped.

Koraine threw her arms around the princess and held her as my sister crumpled at her touch. Her body shook and heaved with each sob she let out. The pair sunk to the ground together, their adrenaline fading and the true exhaustion and stress of war wearing on them.

I approached cautiously and knelt beside my sister.

"How do I get back?" she asked.

I saw the shell of her former self, the girl who had lost herself in war and pain.

"How do I make up for all the atrocities I've committed?" she rasped, tears welling in her eyes.

"Slowly," I said, placing a hand on her shoulder. "You

start slow, and then one day, everything will fall into place again."

She held my gaze. Before I could continue, she threw her arms around me.

"I'm so sorry, Bell," she sobbed. "I'm so, so sorry."

I needed time to allow my heart to heal, but in this moment, I let myself remember the person she once was: the girl who dreamt of traveling the world, who spent hours picking out the most extravagant clothing.

In time, I knew things would fall into place, but for now, this would do.

An explosion behind me pulled our attention. The fighting had begun to cease since the king fell from the sky. Abelonians were looking for direction, and both their leaders were dead.

The mountains in the distance poured fire from their tops even faster.

"This wasn't enough for them?" Koraine asked.

"What more do they want?" Caspian growled.

Movement in the distance behind Koraine pulled my gaze. I watched as a distant, ominous wall moved toward us behind her.

I pointed the group in its direction.

"Dragon shit," Nyla muttered.

"It's going to hit land, and anyone near will be swept with it," Koraine said, her eyes wide with terror.

"There isn't enough time to evacuate?" Caspian asked.

"We're trapped in," I pointed out. The fire trapped us inland on the other side.

"There has to be a way we can stop it," Nyla said.

"You and I need to head toward the mountains," I said to my sister. 'I know you just woke, but—"

"Just tell me what to do," she said firmly. "Otherwise, we won't live to see tomorrow."

I glanced to Koraine and Caspian, hating to leave them behind.

"Go," Koraine said. "We've got this."

I trusted her. If there was anyone who could find a way to stop a tsunami, it was them. I whistled, and Nyla did the same as our dragons appeared in the sky and dove in sync. Both landed and kneeled to allow us on their backs.

"Be careful," I said to Koraine as she helped me onto Imry.

"I'll try," she said with a weak smile.

"I-" I started but paused, unable to find the right words.

"I know," she said. "Tell me when you come back."

I nodded and could see the genuine fear in her gaze. I was terrified, afraid we wouldn't live to see the next sunrise, but I had to try. I had to keep fighting.

My sister and I flew directly toward the mountains. Dragons circled above in a panic. The fire was worse than when I flew above it before. It raced toward the outskirt of the city. I dropped down to the streets with Imry, and Veros followed. My sister and I landed to find many Abelonians already lined the city border, watching in horror as the flames barreled toward us in the dark.

"We are fucked," a guard muttered under his breath.

I stood beside Nyla, preparing for the heat of the flames to slam into us.

"Can you manipulate it?" she asked.

I held my arms out and raised them quickly, watching as a portion of the lava flew into the air and splashed back down.

"That answers that," she mumbled.

"We need to slow the fire and buy ourselves time to direct it elsewhere," I shouted to the line of Abelonians. Each Abelonian instantly fell into line, listening to my command. They raised their arms, ready to control the fire.

If I hadn't claimed the throne the moment my father fell, I had now.

We held our arms firm, and the liquid fire slammed into our control. We manipulated it to stay in place, keeping it from reaching the border of Raden.

I needed a way to keep it in place or force it away from the city, back toward the mountain. I knew the men did not have the energy left to force it all the way back.

My mind raced, and I dug deep for an answers.

"Bellamy," Nyla warned beside me as the fire piled up. "Please tell me you have an idea."

"I-" I started, but no words came out.

I needed a wall, a large one, a way to protect the border and keep the fire from reaching us. It was like the wall of ice Koraine had made to hold the water back the night after the waterfall.

I remembered the way Koraine effortlessly solidified water. She'd done it on a small scale in front of me before, then with the wave when testing her blessing from the moon goddess.

It was brilliant.

If I could solidify the liquid flames, I could stop them from reaching the city.

I wasn't sure if it was possible, but I would try. If the goddess gave us these flames flowing beneath our surface, there had to be a way to control them, to claim the power and energy they provided.

I just needed them to remain still.

"Keep holding them," I shouted.

The men were exhausted, and I saw the struggle on each of their faces. The fire stayed in place, an invisible wall holding it back.

It continued to pile up, the men struggling to hold it. I reached out, trying to feel for the energy of the fire. I imagined it solidifying but felt the tug of the flames resisting.

How did Koraine do this?

I pictured the fire stilling and building into a solid mass.

The wall broke in one spot, and fire rushed toward us. I saw the guard collapsed on the ground, unconscious. I hurried to take their place and pushed the flames back to the invisible wall.

"Need help?" a voice asked behind me, and I turned my head to find Ervin standing there.

"Can you take his place?" I nodded to the man on the ground, and Ervin stepped in quickly. He raised his hands, the liquid flames stilling. He poured in the remaining energy the guards lacked. He was the last push I needed.

The hot liquid stopped, and again, I imagined it solidifying. I pictured it rock solid in my mind, the lava turning to stone and spreading across the flowing fire. It would stop the flowing river from the mountains and create a wall before us.

When I opened my eyes, I saw nothing. I let out a frustrated growl—until I saw the tiny spot where stone spread. The liquid turned to rock and spread like a contamination. It grew across the surface of the liquid and moved faster until large portions of the lava were completely halted and solidified.

I watched in awe, careful to hold my concentration and pushing more energy into the process. Nyla stepped beside me, and I watched as she took a deep breath and closed her eyes. When she opened them, the stone spread even faster.

"We've got this," she breathed.

Ervin was next, solidifying his portion of the wall of lava. Slowly, one by one, the guards figured it out. We extinguished the spreading fire, turning it to stone, leading back to the river flowing from the mountains. Soon, there was nothing left but the stone wall marking where it once was.

I dropped my arms and let out a breath.

If it wasn't for Koraine, we would've drowned in flames.

I turned toward the sea, praying Koraine was alright. I'd left her with a tsunami barreling toward shore.

"Go," Nyla said.

"We've got this," Ervin stated.

I didn't hesitate, calling for Imry. My dragon landed, and I climbed on her back, heading back to the docks.

CHAPTER 52

KORAINE

I RUSHED toward the others on shore watching the massive wave approaching. My brother's stood side-by-side, covered in cuts and bruises, but still alive. Many Morwenians gathered to stare in horror at the giant wave.

My father stepped forward, walking toward it, breaking through the line of people staring up at the approaching water.

"Father, no!" I shouted as he headed toward the towering wave directed straight for the shore.

It was gaining speed, growing in height the closer it got. Odaesia's fury knew no bounds.

"I was able to harness the power of the goddess once before; I can do it again," he said, his jaw set.

"Please, I just got my family back. I don't want to lose you again," I begged, knowing it was no use.

"Koraine, I must," he insisted.

"Don't do it! You'll die," I pleaded.

"I never should've sent you there," he said, and my heart cracked in two.

I knew there was no talking him out of this. No matter how hard I tried, his mind was set. He'd always do what was best for his kingdom, even if It left me and my brothers in pieces.

"Please," I tried again.

"You have to let me do this for you. Let me protect you like I failed to protect you before," he pleaded. "I controlled water this size during the war. I can do it again."

But I could see it in his eyes—even he knew he wouldn't walk away from this. He was trying to give me one last goodbye, but my mind couldn't wrap itself around the idea. I didn't want to believe this was it. I had just gotten my family back, and now, fate wanted to rip it from me again.

"I love you, Koraine. I love you and your brothers so much, and I would do anything to make this kingdom safe for you. I'm sorry if I wasn't always the best father, but please, let me do this one thing."

Now, I knew there was no winning the argument.

"I love you," I said, choking back tears and wrapping my arms around him. His one good arm found its way around my neck, and he held me tight for a moment. Then, he let go and turned to the approaching tsunami.

From my other side, I heard the volcano as it erupted, and I dared a look in its direction.

Hot lava ran down its sides, racing toward us. My father might stop one of our problems, but we still had no way of controlling the liquefied flames barreling toward us.

I knew Bellamy and Nyla worked tirelessly on that side of Raden. I had to put my trust in them.

I was sick of being wrapped up in the goddesses' war.

I was done with allowing them to tear us apart and push us further from each other.

If the kingdoms didn't come together now, there would be no four kingdoms left.

Abelonians prepared themselves for the crash of the tsunami as the other kingdoms battled their own elements. My father, leading the charge, raised his hands to control the large wave. I spotted the king and his daughter on the front line before it, the other soldiers prepared to give everything they had to stop the sea.

Behind me, everywhere the liquified flames touched, fire ignited, burning what was left of Abelon's land and city.

The goddess of fire would not have built the land upon flames if its people could not tame them. I held tightly to that belief.

I moved to stand at my father's side.

"What are you doing?" he said. "You are in no shape to take this on."

"If you're going to stop this, you're going to need my help," I said.

"This isn't your battle. You've done enough for these kingdoms," my father said, but in my heart, I knew that wasn't true. I couldn't stand by and watch. I had an obligation to these people, my future people.

I would gladly stand here and fight to protect them, even if it meant giving my life or the rest of my power.

"You're not convincing me to leave," I said.

He paused before giving me a soft smile. "You get that from me, you know," he said. "The stubbornness, never backing down from a fight."

"I know," I said, returning the smile. "And I'm proud of that.

I prepared my hands in front of me, waiting to meet the crash of the wave. It was still too far to feel it, but I knew any moment it would be there.

More and more Morwenians gathered beside us. We each stood in the same readied stance, prepared to meet the wall pushing toward us. I felt its power after a moment and tried to pour all my energy into imagining slowing the wall.

We needed to slow the pace, allow the sea time to shrink back to what it was, rather than the wall that would crash upon us in minutes.

I pushed and pushed, putting everything I had into holding up my power. Everyone around me remained concentrated, doing the same. I could see the determination on each warrior's face.

"Stand strong," King Belizere shouted. "We do not let this wall hit."

Asena stood beside her father, the pair putting all their strength into controlling the tsunami.

It was the goddess versus her people.

Cries of frustration and exhaustion echoed across the shore as warriors gave everything they had. I watched as some dropped to their knees, the effects of battle crashing over them. They still held their arms out, holding the wall back.

I could feel the sheer power of the water and goddess pushing back on us. The wall slowed but not enough. It still rapidly approached the coast.

My father stepped forward, and my heart raced.

"No," I called out. I knew what he planned to do. I'd seen it in his eyes when he said his goodbye before.

"I have to," he said. "Tell her I love her."

"You can tell Mother yourself," I said, knowing he meant the love of his life.

"Not this time," he said.

My heart shattered. He raised his good arm, walking toward the tsunami in front of the line of Morwenians, standing a proud general before his men.

I let out a choked sob. "Please," I begged. "Don't take him."

I didn't know who I reasoned with. I'd made a bargain with one goddess; could I with another? I prayed in my head and poured as much energy as I could spare into slowing the wall.

"General Neroe, return," King Belizere shouted. "That's an order."

"I'm sorry, Your Majesty," he said, turning back one last time. "I can't do that."

I heard the raw pain in his voice—the loyal general, protecting his men one last time.

He poured everything he had into stopping the wall, letting out a cry of pain as he gave all his energy. I watched as the pace died down more and more.

My father dropped to his knees, his body trembling.

Tears stung my eyes, and I tried to ignore them as I gave my all to aiding him. His sacrifice couldn't be for nothing.

Warriors let out war cries, pouring their energy behind their leader. Many dropped, and I watched as the king fell to his own knees. Asena almost broke from her concentration, but the king held a hand to stop her.

"Keep going," he bit out.

My father spread his arms wide, his cry echoing across the shore. The water came closer, but I watched as it slowly fell. The massive wall was shrinking.

Minutes passed, and I watched with horror as the life drained from my father. He was giving everything he had to make sure we all made it out alive.

It would take one person's entire energy force to fully stop the tsunami, and he knew that from the start. Just pouring our control into slowing it would never have been enough. It's why he said his goodbyes.

A few more minutes passed, and soon, the water lowered to a safer level. Many men dropped their arms, unable to remain conscious any longer. Others pulled them back to the safety of the cobblestone beyond the shore as the water rushed toward us. When the wave dropped, I rushed out to my father to pull him back. My brothers held firm, slowing the wave to allow me to drag him.

He collapsed before I could reach him. I tried to lift him, but his weight was too much for me. I grabbed an arm and tugged, but it was slow moving. A cry of pain escaped me, and I put every ounce of strength I had left into pulling. He barely moved an inch.

I tugged one last time, his body sliding more seamlessly.

I lifted my head to find the king of Morwen beside me, pulling my father to safety. We worked together to carry him back.

Caspian and Emmett were the last to drop their arms and rush to our father. A large wave crashed against the shore, stronger than most, but it did minimal damage. The sea sprayed against my skin, but I barely registered it.

"Please," I begged. "Please, wake up."

I dropped to my knees beside my father. "He has to wake up."

Caspian dropped beside me, pressing his head to our father's chest. He glanced up and shook his head at the king and Emmett.

"Do something," I begged. "Caspian, please."

"He's gone," he said somberly.

"He can't be gone," I begged. "Please, Caspian. He has to wake up."

Emmett placed a gentle hand on my shoulder. "Let him go, Koraine," he said softly. "It's what he would want."

They were the first words he had spoken to me since I left that day in Morwen and saved Bellamy. I knew he thought I had betrayed our kingdom, but now, it didn't matter. Nothing mattered anymore; he was gone, and I never got to tell him what I needed.

"Caspian," I choked out, pleading with my brother.

"He's gone, Koraine," he said, shaking his head again.

I collapsed but was caught by strong arms. Caspian held me to his chest, letting me cry into it. We'd stopped the tsunami, and for what? My father died saving us.

Emmett knelt beside me.

"He came for you," he said quietly. "He came because he wanted to make things right. It was tearing him apart. He knew he never should have sent you off. He came for this very moment, to make sure the world you saw possible happened. He would've chosen this fate every time, Koraine."

I choked back sobs, meeting my brother's gaze.

"I never got to tell him I forgive him," I said.

"He knew," Emmett assured me.

"How?" I demanded.

"The moment you stood beside him to face that tsunami, trust me, he knew," he answered.

Asena hurried over to us, and the moment she saw our father, she dropped to her knees. She wrapped her arms around us, holding tight.

I refused to let go.

I didn't care if the rest of the disasters still tore through the kingdom around us. I had nothing left. I could barely bring myself to face those around me.

My head was still buried in Caspian's chest when Emmett placed a firm hand once more on my shoulder and pulled me back.

"I can't—" I started.

"Look," he said, motioning around us.

I glanced up, looking around. We were surrounded by a sea of blue as warriors formed a circle around us, paying their respects to their general.

One by one, they dropped to a knee, bowing their heads. Caspian and I stood, turning in circles, watching them. Asena wrapped an arm around my shoulder and pulled me close.

"They loved him," Asena said. "Every last one of them would have fought to the end beside him."

I wiped the tears from my face and swallowed hard.

These warriors had followed him to battle and would every single time he asked. That type of respect was earned over time, by building trust. My father had always fought beside his men, and I knew he would be happy to know his sacrifice saved so many.

He'd led them in one last battle, and I knew now, he could finally rest knowing they were safe.

CHAPTER 53

KORAINE

THEY MOVED my father's body to a nearby row boat to transport back to Morwen.

Torches lit the docks and streets of Raden, people moving through the space as I stood there in awe, assessing the damage from the war. The tremors had stopped, and the tornadoes slowly disappeared.

Soldiers helped each other collect their deceased from all four nations, and the body count made my stomach turn. Many had been lost in the fighting and from the disasters caused by the goddesses.

I felt numb.

Caspian and Emmett aided the other warriors in preparations to sail home, collecting supplies and helping move the injured onto ships.

The tsunami had returned most of the ships unharmed after our efforts had kept it from crashing against land.

I tried to move my feet to help, but they remained firmly planted. My mind kept wandering back to the image of my father collapsed in the sand. I couldn't save him.

A large shadow passed overhead, and I barely registered the gust that blew against me as the beast landed behind me. Strong arms wrapped around my middle, pulling me back into a solid mass. Bellamy spun me to give me a once-over.

"Are you hurt?" he asked. His gaze stopped on my face, seemingly satisfied with his search for injury.

He wouldn't find blood or bruises; my heart was bleeding on the inside.

I collapsed into his arms, unable to hold myself up any longer, giving in to the call of exhaustion.

Bellamy caught me.

He scooped me into his arms, and I inhaled his familiar scent.

I felt safe. For the first time in days, I knew I was safe.

"He's gone," I whispered, clinging to the remaining pieces of his shirt.

"Who?" he asked, concern lacing his voice.

"My father," I murmured.

I felt selfish. I knew the prince had lost his own father, and here I was, barely able to stand on my own under the crushing weight of the loss.

"I'm so sorry," he said, holding my head against his chest, his own head falling to mine. He placed a gentle kiss on my forehead as he swept me up and carried me through the streets of Raden.

"Go rest," he commanded Imry.

The beast took off and flew toward the mountains. It was the last thing I saw before I buried my head back into Bellamy's chest. I had no energy left; everything within me, I had poured into saving Nyla and stopping the tsunami.

My eyes felt heavy.

"You can rest now, my moon," he said.

"You can't call me that anymore," I said softly. "I no longer have that power."

"You will always be my moon, because even in the darkest of times, I know you will be a guiding light."

I placed a hand on the prince's chest and let him carry me through the cobblestone streets. Soldier continued to clean around us, evacuees led back to what remained of their homes.

I knew we had a long road ahead of us to rebuild, but I was so tired.

I needed to rest.

"Where will they stay?" I asked, worried.

Bellamy thought for a moment. "The palace," he said. "Anyone whose home has been destroyed is welcome within our walls until we can rebuild. We can provide shelter and food. It's not a lot, but it's a start."

"I'd like to help," I said.

"I thought you could be in charge of it," he proposed. "There will be much I have to handle as king first, and the people need someone to look to."

"You want me to be that person?" I asked, my eyes widening.

"Yes. I want you to be their queen."

"But…" I started.

"No arguments. You need rest. You can decide after, but if you want it, the position is yours. We can even hold an official ceremony and celebration if you wish. We can invite all four kingdoms."

I thought it over for a moment. "I think I'd like that," I answered.

I didn't need the crown or title, but I knew one thing: Abelon had become my home. I'd fallen in love with the people and land. I couldn't leave them now. They needed someone to guide them through the pain and loss of war. I knew firsthand what it felt like. I was working through my own pain, but I knew if I could provide hope to these people, I had to try.

"Where are we going?" I finally asked after a few minutes.

"Home," the prince answered.

I woke after a full day of sleep.

Losing the power of the moon and pouring all my energy into the tsunami had completely exhausted me. I had shut my eyes before Bellamy even made it to the palace.

I woke the next day to Nyla in my room. I recognized the space—Bellamy's chambers.

I sat in his bed and rubbed the sleep from my eyes. My body ached, and I could barely slide myself from the bed.

All the agony and exhaustion from the day prior washed back over me.

I knew it would take time, but damn, I was already sick of the feeling.

"Where's Bellamy?" I asked.

Nyla glanced toward the washroom, and the prince

stepped out at the sound of my voice. He carried a warm, damp cloth for my face that he passed to me before sitting beside me on the bed.

"How long?" I asked.

"A full day," Nyla said.

I glanced out the window to see the sun was just barely rising. "My brothers?"

"Still here," Bellamy assured me. "Some of the soldiers left with each of the kings, but Asena, Emmett, and Caspian remained with those still recovering. Some of the injured needed time before we could send them across the sea. They volunteered to be on that ship."

"Can I see them?" I asked.

Bellamy nodded to Nyla, and she hurried from the room.

The door slammed shut behind her, and I glanced back to Bellamy.

"How is she?"

"As good as she can be," he admitted. "She's trying everything possible to make up for what she did. I keep assuring her it's not necessary, but—"

"She will never believe it," I finished.

I knew the feeling. I still felt responsible for what she had become, for leaving her behind, for being the reason Bellamy left. I knew every bit of it was necessary, but I would still spend my days making it up to the princess, rebuilding the friendship we once had.

"How are you?" Bellamy asked hesitantly.

I knew what he was asking. How was I handling the loss?

I barely had time to process it.

"It will take time for me to move on," I admitted, "but I

think that is all part of the process. The entire city needs time to heal. I am giving myself grace, allowing myself to feel."

Bellamy slid back into the bed next to me. He wrapped an arm around my middle and pulled me in to his chest.

"I spent yesterday helping clean the streets of Raden. It is almost entirely destroyed," he said.

Guilt pinched my chest for sleeping through it.

"You needed rest," he scolded, catching sight of my face. "And I needed an excuse not to dote on you all day. I visited the orphanage, and it was pure rubble."

"Where are Alaric and Mariam?" I asked.

"A floor below you," Bellamy said. "We've already moved those who need it into the palace and set up the ballroom as a dining hall. The staff has been working hard to accommodate, and the palace is fuller than my father ever allowed."

I saw the pain on his face at the mention of his father.

"You are already such a great king," I said.

"I don't know about that. There is still a lot to learn," he admitted.

"Then we learn together," I said, and his eyes lit up with delight.

I leaned in to kiss him, our lips colliding. I nipped at his bottom lip and grasped his hand, greedily wanting more of him. His tongue slipped between my lips, and I returned the favor with as much passion as I could manage through my remaining exhaustion. His hands tangled into my hair, but before I could go further, the door opened.

I tipped my head away as the prince pressed one last greedy kiss to my lips.

"That's my sister, you know," Caspian scolded.

"What?" Emmett demanded from behind him.

I rolled my eyes.

"It is our room," I noted.

"You invited us," Caspian countered.

"I suppose I did," I chuckled. The laugh hurt my sore chest and ribs, but I didn't care.

Bellamy helped me stand from the bed, and I hugged both of my brothers, thankful to see their faces.

Asena stood in the corner, her arms folded, watching.

"Get over here," I demanded, and she rolled her eyes before stalking over.

I pulled her in tight before spotting Nyla leaning against the wall and mouthing my thanks.

"When do you sail back?" I asked.

The group looked anxiously between each other.

"Tomorrow," Caspian said somberly.

My smile fell, but I tried to remain hopeful.

"We still have the day," I noted.

"A single day to do whatever in Abelon," Caspian said, and a devilish grin grew on his face. "I think I'd like to ride that dragon of yours."

"I think not," Bellamy retorted.

"You are no fun, dear prince," my brother teased, earning a smile.

"I will consider a single ride with Imry, and only because I know it will make her happy," Bellamy said, nodding to me.

"I am staying on the ground, thanks," Emmett muttered.

"I can show you the palace," I offered.

"I'll join," Nyla and Asena said at the same time, making my smile grow larger.

Already, I felt the sense of familiarity returning. Our group was back together, and I felt the pieces of my family falling back into place. After all the heartache and loss, we had only become closer.

"I heard Ervin has been cooking for everyone," Caspian added. "I vote we eat whatever he makes for dinner tonight."

"I agree," I said, nodding and missing the old man already. I was thankful to hear he had made it through.

"Where is Oleena?" I asked, realizing that left one person.

"She's getting acquainted with the priestesses here. They've already begun their own efforts to help repair Raden," Bellamy answered. "I checked on her last night; she is settling in just fine."

My heart warmed. The priestess deserved a home, one that would accept her and allow her to be the person she wanted to be after being trapped in so many cages.

My heart felt full as we left the room, knowing I had one day before we all went our separate ways. One day to ignore our problems and rest before we threw ourselves into repairing what the goddesses broke.

Bellamy hung behind to walk next to me.

"Where is your mind? I can see it racing," he said.

"I was just considering how lucky we are," I answered.

"Lucky?"

He tilted his head, his dark eyes meeting my own. I saw the fire blazing behind his gaze and reached out to grab his hand.

"To have built this family," I said. "A family worth going to war for."

He smiled, and my insides turned warm. I could feel my cheeks heating at the way he looked at me.

"Yes, my moon," he said. "I truly am lucky to have something so worth fighting for."

CHAPTER 54

KORAINE

"Everyone will be here," Nyla said, her smile bringing warmth to my very soul.

It had been months since the war ended, and I found myself in front of a mirror, staring at my reflection, glitter coating my eyelids.

"Does that include the nobles of Abelon?" I dared to ask.

"They are less bothersome with Bellamy in power now," Nyla offered as a condolence.

"I will never get used to this," I sighed.

Nyla moved behind me, her delicate hand barely hovering over my shoulder. She found my gaze in the mirror, and I nodded.

Even months later, our relationship was far from mended.

She hesitantly moved her hand and residual limb, pulling my hair behind me. She worked with it, doing her best to pull it back and away from my face. Hair pins sat on

the vanity before me, and she found ways to work the pearl-
tipped pins into my hair.

"Thank you," I said, admiring her work in the mirror.

"It's the least I can do," she said, and I heard the deeper
meaning.

Since the war, Nyla had done everything in her power to
re-build her friendships and familial ties in Abelon. It was
hard to let go of everything that had happened, but I knew
she was trying her best.

I was trying equally as hard to move on.

Only time would be able to bridge the gaps created
by war.

Her presence was constant reminder of what I had given
up, the bargain I made that kept her alive. I poured all the
power I'd been blessed with from the moon goddess into the
princess. Some days, I still felt a vague presence of power
still inside me, but I knew I would never be able to tap that
well of strength again.

It was worth it.

That power lived on inside of the princess.

I would make the sacrifice again.

When we finished with my hair, I moved on to my clothing. I found a traditional bridal set laying on the bed. It was
a vibrant blue, the color of the Vitrum Sea in the summer
months.

Spring was already making its way into Abelon, chasing
the cold of winter away. We'd held off on celebrating and
rebuilding until the coldest weeks passed and we knew no
further snow would hinder us.

I slipped on my clothing and walked over to a mirror to
admire the sight. I sucked in a breath, impressed with the

outfit and additions Nyla had made to my appearance. The pins in my hair complimented its new silver hue.

No longer was the white sheen of the moon prevalent through the strands of my hair.

Instead, it turned a shade as cool as ice.

I heard bells chime in the distance, signaling the arrival of guests, and my stomach filled with butterflies. Many had traveled far for the occasion, bringing all four kingdoms together.

Winter solstice was upon us, and the entire world was ready to celebrate, free of war and the looming threat of the goddesses.

I turned to Nyla and gave her a warm smile.

"Ready?" I asked, holding out my hand.

She nodded, holding out her left arm. My heart ached a moment when I spotted her residual limb. It had taken days before Nyla could even speak of what happened. Each time I saw it, my chest ached for her, knowing the agony her father had put her through. Guilt ate at me, knowing I was part of the reason for it.

"Stop," she whispered.

"What?" I asked, looking at her.

She frowned, studying my face. "I know that look. I know where your mind went. It was never your fault. Even if at times I blamed others, it was my fault," she said.

"Not true," I said. "I should've fought harder for you."

"You fought an entire war for me, and everyone else out there," she said as she smiled warmly.

I sighed.

"Stop living in the past," she pushed. "The war is over, and we made it out alive. I thank Mavalu daily for the second chance you gave me. That is all I need and could ask for. Even if you had fought harder, I don't think I would have been ready to hear it."

"I still wish I could have changed things," I said softly, walking beside Nyla as we made our way through the halls of the palace.

I knew the way without a second thought. This place had become my home.

"Don't; if we changed a thing, we may not all be here."

The halls were decorated in gold for the winter solstice. Snowflake-shaped decor hung from the ceiling, and other winter-themed items adorned the halls.

"When I was younger, my father forbade the palace to decorate like this for the solstice," Nyla said, admiring the decor. "He's already a great king."

Bellamy had made changes the moment he took the throne after the war, reversing his father had implemented, his first decree celebrating a long neglected holiday in the fire kingdom.

In Morwen, I'd always loved the winter solstice, playing in the snow with my brothers and returning to find tea and warm baked goods awaiting us.

Today was a chance to revive that love, to create new traditions.

My heart ached remembering the way my mother used to be the first to greet us out of the snow. I still had not seen her since the war, though I'd received letters from Caspian letting me know she was okay. The curse had ceased to exist since I claimed hold of the blessing of the moon.

The blessing that lived within the woman beside me.

We came to the doors outside the throne room and paused.

"I have to go in. Will you be alright?" she asked.

"I will," I assured her.

She slipped through the door before I could catch a glimpse inside, and I waited alone in the hall. Echoes of footsteps made my heart race; I was terrified to turn around.

"You clean up nice," my brother's teasing voice came from behind me.

I turned to find Caspian grinning, dressed in his navy blue finery. Emmett stood quiet and brooding beside him. Since our father passed, he'd quieted, his role model now gone. I knew someday, he'd find his voice again, but until then, I wouldn't push him.

I'd be there when he did.

He'd shown up for me, both in war and now. That was the most I could ever ask.

"He'd want you to have this," Emmett said quietly.

He held out his hand, a small silver pin sitting in his palm. It was shaped like a wave, and I knew it belonged to my father—the pin he wore on his warrior's uniform.

"Thank you," I said softly, tears forming.

I took the pin and threw myself into his arms. Emmett wrapped a hand around me and briefly gave me a squeeze.

"We should get you in there," Caspian chuckled. "Wouldn't want to keep him waiting. I hear he has quite the temper."

I shoved Caspian before also throwing myself into his arms in a hug.

"I love you too," I whispered.

He scoffed but returned my hug.

Emmett pulled open the door as Caspian linked his arm in mine. We took a few steps forward and stood at the top of the throne room. The dais had been turned into a platform with an arch, under which Oleena stood.

I spotted him immediately, dressed in his maroon finery. His eyes locked on mine, and my cheeks turned a deep pink.

Music started, and everyone in the room turned to look at me as my knees trembled.

It was important for the world to see. I knew it was, but my anxiety still screamed at me to run.

We were uniting two enemy kingdoms, finally coming together for the first time in decades. The world needed to witness the union.

The priestess began the ceremony as she had once before, that night we spent on her island. We faced each other under the arch, and she tied our hands together using a ribbon, connecting our souls as one.

"Through the blessings of the goddesses, I unite these two in mind, body, and soul. May their love endure an eternity, this union signifying the duty to protect, nurture, and support each other," Oleena recited to begin the ceremony as the room fell silent.

The words echoed, familiar and comforting.

"Now, Koraine, repeat after me," Oleena said with a smile. "I give myself to you."

"I give myself to you," I repeated the same words I once told Bellamy.

"And promise my love, patience, and respect," she stated.

"And promise my love, patience, and respect."

"Through every challenge, until death claims us."

The line made my heart race, remembering all we had been through, the moments I thought I lost him. Now, I would be by his side until my very last breath.

"Through every challenge, until death claims us."

"I love you today, tomorrow, and forever," Oleena finished the vows.

"I love you today, tomorrow, and forever."

Bellamy repeated the words, a smile growing across his lips.

"You will now seal your fates with a kiss," Oleena said and pulled the ribbon away.

Bellamy pulled me closer, one hand finding my waist and the other, my cheek. He brushed a strand of my silver hair away from my face and whispered, "May I, my moon?"

I didn't answer.

Instead, I leaned in, kissing him hard.

The room erupted into cheers and clapping, and my cheeks reddened, remembering the entire room of nobles and guests watching us.

I tried to pull away, but Bellamy pulled me gently back and pressed another kiss to my lips.

"Congratulations. You are, yet again, married," Oleena announced.

We turned to meet the room, and they all stood from their seats, still clapping.

"Your queen," Bellamy bellowed, and somehow, the room grew louder as he motioned to me.

I didn't know where to look, scanning the room for a familiar face. I spotted my brothers and Asena seated close to the front and gave them a warm smile.

Familiar light hair beside them caught my eye. My haw

almost dropped, and I took a mindless step forward, but Bellamy caught me before I made a fool of myself and almost stumbled off the platform.

"Mother," I whispered, and Bellamy followed my gaze.

Seated beside Caspian and Emmett, smiling larger than anyone, was the woman who had raised me. She'd fought and, goddesses be damned, she had pulled through to the other side.

"Are you going to introduce me?" Bellamy teased.

I pulled him along off the dais, and people filed out of the ballroom as Oleena and Nyla directed them toward the ballroom for the winter solstice celebrations.

I pushed through the crowd, giving quick thank yous to the congratulations I received. Still, my only focus was on the woman only feet from me.

Before I could say anything, she pulled me into a hug, and I squeezed her as tightly as I could, afraid if I let go, I would wake from this dream. It had been months since I had seen her, and now, she stood before me, healthy.

"Are you real?" I asked, tears falling down my cheeks.

"Of course," she promised, hugging me tighter.

"I'm sorry I couldn't save him," I sobbed.

I hadn't seen her since my father's death—my brothers had been the ones to return after the war and deliver the news. I knew she'd loved him with her whole heart.

"He died protecting those he loved. He would be proud to see the women you've become. You've united our people and rebuilt this kingdom," she said. "There is nothing to be sorry for. I know he would do it again and again, given the choice."

"I just wish he could've lived to see this," I said, wiping my eyes.

"Me too," she said with a sad smile. "But he remains in each of you. All of you have become everything he hoped. I see so much of his spirit in you, and I know he lives on in the new world you've built for us."

I nodded, catching glances from both my brothers.

Bellamy let out a slight cough behind me, and I almost forgot he had been standing there.

"Mother, this is Bellamy," I introduced.

"Prince." She bowed her head in respect. When she glanced back up, she smiled. "You look so much like her."

"Who?" he asked, his brows furrowing.

"Your mother," she said gently.

"You knew my mother?" he asked.

"I met her once, long ago, when we were younger. You look just like her at this age. Before I was with their father, I sailed to Zetron to see the flowers bloom in the spring. That's where I met her. She was vibrant and kind, and I knew she'd make a great queen."

Bellamy smiled, and it warmed my heart. I knew what his mother meant to him.

"She would be proud of you too," my mother added.

Bellamy pulled my mother in for a hug before she could protest. He then grabbed my arm, pulling me into the embrace.

"Shall we go find the food before it's gone?" Caspian interrupted as the room emptied. "I am not risking missing Ervin's cooking."

Bellamy and I let out genuine laughs.

"Yes, we can go find the food and others," I chuckled.

Walking from the room, I couldn't help but look back at the arch. It would forever be the space where we changed history, changed fate. Bellamy and I united enemies, thought to never be able to coexist. It seemed like a distant possibility months before, but so much had changed, and I knew I was no longer that girl who snuck down to the cliffs to watch the waves.

I had grown.

I'd become a hardened warrior. I'd found myself along the way, had met people who changed my life forever.

I wrapped my arm around Bellamy's center, and he dropped an arm over my shoulder as we left the room behind to forge a new future.

We left the room together, one united family.

CHAPTER 55
BELLAMY

MY FIRST ACT AS RULER.

The wedding was finished, and it was time to rebuild. Before we could move forward, I had one matter to attend to.

I walked through the tunnels behind the walls of the palace leading to the throne room, the same tunnels my father used to navigate the palace. I pushed that thought aside.

Even if I took his place and followed the same tunnels, I would never let myself *become* him.

A door came into view at the end of my path, and I pushed it open, natural light forcing my eyes to adjust. The first thing I saw was her.

She stood beside our thrones, waiting for me to join her.

"Koraine," I greeted, walking toward her. I took her hand and led her to take our seats beside each other.

Before us, many citizens of Abelon stood, watching eagerly, waiting for news. I swallowed, nervously awaiting the last person's arrival.

The throne room doors pushed open, the guards holding them as she stepped into the room. My sister walked through the crowd, forcing the Abelonians to part. They watched in silence as the princess held her head high, walking toward us.

Nyla stood before me in a long black gown, her golden tiara placed carefully on her head. I watched as she gave a quick curtsy.

"Rise," I said, my voice echoing.

To my side, I risked a glance at my wife. She was stunning, her silver hair like glittering stars.

My moon.

I turned my attention back to my sister. Her eyes met mine, and I saw the unspoken words, the plea for forgiveness and longing for something beyond a life trapped in the palace.

"Nyla," I began, "after committing crimes against Morwen and Abelon, you stand here to accept your punishment."

I swallowed hard as Nyla nodded her understanding. She remained silent, others whispering to fill the empty space.

"I accept whatever my punishment may be," she said softly, her eyes focused on the floor.

I glanced around the room to the Abelonians gathered. The throne room was still decorated from the wedding celebration only days prior. Morwenians had traveled across the sea for the event, including the royal family, which had given me the chance I needed.

Between the festivities and ceremonies, I had found a single moment to meet with the King of Morwen and discuss the atrocities my sister had committed under the direction of my father. I knew he was to blame, but I needed the Morwenians to understand.

"I have spoken to the King of Morwen," I began. Everyone held their breath, waiting for me to continue. I thought back to those few seconds I had to convince the King of Morwen. He had been hesitant until I mentioned his daughter. What if it had been her? Would he wish Asena punished for his actions or commands? Nyla had been ready to give her life to stop the disasters caused by the goddesses. She was an integral part in keeping Abelon from being reduced to a wasteland.

"We agree that after your aid in ending the war, you shall be offered a full pardon," I stated.

"What?" Nyla gasped, glancing between Koraine and me.

My wife wore a warm smile as she watched realization hit my sister. I could not punish her, nor would I ever. She had been through enough pain; there was no need to put her through more. Nyla needed to know her family still cared for her.

"But Bell—" she started.

"I do not wish to hear any argument," I said quickly, every Abelonian in the room watching as I pardoned my sister. "My word is final."

I wanted to set a new example for the kingdom, a rule of gentle leadership and loyal protection. Each and every Abelonian would be kept safe under my rule.

"I'm free?" Nyla asked, and I understood the words she wasn't saying.

She had been forced to reside in the palace under my

father's rule, so she'd seen little of the world until hunting me down. Our mother had filled her head with stories of the kingdoms and the beauties they held. My sister was a dreamer, never meant to stay put.

Her heart longed for freedom, the space to explore the kingdoms and live her life. Being forced into duties she never asked for was slowly draining the life from her.

"You're free," I said gently. "You can go anywhere you wish."

I knew she needed this. If I could make up for all the pain I put her through with this simple gift, then I would grant her that.

"I can see the kingdoms?" she asked, raising a brow. I could tell she still hadn't fully comprehended what my words meant.

"You can go anywhere you wish. We can handle the war recovery here," I stated.

"What will you do?" Koraine asked Nyla.

She leaned forward on her own throne. No longer did the dais hold columns of flames like when my father ruled. Instead, we sat side by side on our thrones, one fit for fire, the other for water.

We ruled Abelon together, and I never would've wanted it another way.

"I suppose I will start with finding a way to belong here once more," Nyla admitted. I could tell she was still holding back.

"You don't have to stay here," I said, her attention snapping to me. "Do something for you for once."

She remained frozen, unable to speak. I could see her grasping for words but failing to get them out.

"Where have you always dreamt of visiting?" I asked.

"The moorlands," she immediately shot back.

I smiled at my sister, knowing she already had her answer.

"You can take one of the ships and any supplies you need," I offered. "Anything you want is at your disposal, Nyla."

"That's too much," she countered.

"I want you to be happy," I said. "You've been forced to live in the shadows for far too long. Our father made you feel you didn't deserve a life beyond being an obedient daughter, but that isn't true. You deserve happiness."

She thought for a moment, a smile spreading across her lips. She stood tall before me, a new confidence taking hold of her, her red hair falling over her shoulders as she crossed her arms.

"Then I will sail for Zetron."

Nyla's story to be continued Summer 2025...

ACKNOWLEDGMENTS

I can't believe I am writing the end to Koraine and Bellamy's story. Thank you all for believing in their love as much as I have. There are few people I need to thank for making this all possible.

To my wonderful husband, thank you for standing by me every step of the way of this and for being my biggest supporter

To my sister Rory, thank you for always letting me come to you with the wildest of ideas and for never once judging me for them.

To my sister Leah, thank you for letting me text you all of the nonstop medical questions.

To Biz, this series could not happen without you. Thank you for being my alpha reader and always loving these characters.

To Kate, thank you for updating an already beautiful map. I love the additions so much. Thank you for being such a big avatar fan and always sending me Avatar content.

To my parents, thank you for the constant support. I would never be where I am without you.

To my PA Mikala, for creating the best zutara themed content out there and always somehow beating the algorithm like no one I have ever met!

To my editor Alexa, thank you for putting up with my

500 texts and constant thoughts that this manuscript might be trash. Without your edits there is a high chance it would have been trash.

To the authors of Azala Press, thank you for believing in my work and being such amazing friends to me. I am so grateful for the family we have created.

To my readers, thank you for your endless love and support of these characters!

A SPECIAL THANKS TO THE KICKSTARTER BACKERS

If you were to live within the world of the Elemental Arrangement you would belong to the following kingdoms:

Luheo

- Emily Deters
- Annabelle Joyner
- Kate Korsak
- Dragonskull817
- Mattie
- Gwendolyn Howell
- Liz Thornton
- Felicia Victoria Garcia
- Chatoni
- Alyssa Guerrero
- Tessa Nouchi
- Meredith
- Antonina Giarratana

- Elizabeth Lindloff
- Gabrielle Bouska
- KingPanderr
- The Creative Fund by BackerKit
- Vanui
- Lisa
- Dana Lattany
- Brooke Bigner
- Tina Gigioli
- Brittany
- Sydney
- Erin
- Nekia T
- Sally Vinchesi
- Brianna
- Lauren Ada
- Kawehi Kanoho
- Maggy Warner
- Baylee Engelhardt
- Alexis
- Vannesa Palomo
- Teresa Lausell
- Angie Armenta
- Malia
- Maricel
- Romy
- Jessica
- Lexi Patterson
- Kallie
- Alexusnelson
- Lex

- Cameron Sievers
- Dave
- Sami Lambrecht
- Courtney
- jazzy

Abelon

- KAT
- Taylor Heras
- Elizabeth
- Bianca Tatjana Višić Ritorto
- Lauren Kimberly Rennie
- Hannah Hein
- Qavee
- Mireiå Collado Ruiz
- Emily
- Chriistin3 P. A.
- kamalloy
- Ika
- Bailey
- Monica Chhugani
- Devon Villano
- Chanel Holm
- Rachell Rutledge
- Sarah
- Mich
- MacKenzie
- Nikki Dunn
- Meagan Armstrong
- Amanda Balter

- Dede
- Tomaya smith
- Taya Johnson
- Hannah French
- Savvy Sparks
- Ny
- Justise Briones(That/Them)
- Allison Hines
- Leonie
- Semma
- Ammie Herrington
- Jeremy Deutsch
- Lucy
- Corrine
- Vicky Salas
- Effie Joe Stock
- Jennifer Horne
- Mary Wenzel
- Chloe Jane Willis
- Carolina V
- javier
- McKenna Hubbard
- Ruby Sutton
- Jackson Fulmer
- Marissa
- Ashley
- Rochelle

Morwen

- Kate Cefai

- April
- Lily Kingsbury
- Isabel Molina
- Sherry Mock
- Savannah Mitchell
- Krista Marx
- Ashley Kendrick
- Alexandra Corrsin
- Alison Khuu
- Isabel Ramey
- Amber Cese
- Mireia Collado Ruiz
- Caroline
- Alicia Camp
- Savannah Penny
- KL Hester
- Kate Belt
- Elisabeth Johnson
- Belinda Kroll
- Brooklyn
- Mo
- Caitlin Millsaps
- Rosa
- Rebecca
- Avra Blake
- Devan
- Ashton Smith
- Gil Len
- Elena Lopez
- Headers Mire
- Chelsea Rogers

- Kimberly Sudbrink
- Cathy
- Ramiro Sandoval
- Breanna Layte
- Caitlin Murphy
- Jennifer
- Kristie Redmond
- Raleigh Daniel
- Serena Sharber
- Helena Katariina Lehtiniemi
- Jennina Delfin
- Vickie_Martinezz
- Nikia
- Humberto Mazzarro
- MonkeyMeatloaf
- Jaden Anderson
- William Raymond
- Kaneesha Roarke

Zetron

- Alexander Kusnezow
- Destiny
- Alyssa Kuzdal
- Kyra
- Christopher J. Paulbeck
- Aubrey
- Alexandra Danckaert
- Catherine Levinson
- Elisha Bryant
- Miranda perez

- Yara
- Diane Hansebout
- Jessica Beatty
- Christina
- Rhea Lynn Luis
- Jessica
- Sabrina Fonseca
- Samantha Newberry
- Sarah Huitema
- Sadie
- courtmariemd
- Celosia Starfall
- Josefine Bällsten
- Coda Joachim
- samantha
- Maegan
- Natasha Wimmer
- Lisa
- Angela
- Amanda
- Sian Griffiths
- Kyrie
- Chloe Ruggieri
- Lauren Gordon
- Charlotte Murray
- Kristina
- MissEmeraude
- Emily Blackwood
- Lata Colborn Gleich
- Lindsey McElroy
- Genna Carlin

- Ashley Belanger
- Frederyque koetsch
- Lindsey Garland
- Malia Matsuzaki
- Vannessa
- Baylee Brown
- Shayna
- Kristina
- Jojo
- Denise Becker
- Mackenzie McIntire

Promised Shadows

Crowned Light

One Hollow Love

ONE
HOLLOW
LOVE
M.K. AHEARN

www.ingramcontent.com/pod-product-compliance
Lightning Source LLC
Chambersburg PA
CBHW061103310726
48974CB00002B/373